MW00527837

THE SAFETY OF
STRANGERS

A NOVEL OF WW II

NEW YORK TIMES & *USA TODAY* BESTSELLING AUTHOR

CIJI WARE

OLIVERHEBERBOOKS

Cover design 2023 by BespokeBookCovers.com

Cover designer: Peter O'Connor

The Safety of Strangers © 2023 by Ciji Ware

Additional Library of Congress Cataloging-in-Publication Data available upon request.

Fiction, 1. Women's History--Fiction, 2. World War II—Fiction, 3. American women secret agents—Fiction, 4. Women spies in WW II—Fiction, 5. British spies—Fiction, 6. American spies—Fiction, 7. OSS, SOE, CIA, MI6 intelligence agencies—Fiction, 8. Female secret agent, 9. Spy schools and spy-craft training in WW II, 10. 20th century fiction, 11. The Comet Line 12. Women "Escape Helpers" in WW II--13. Escape and Evade operations in WW2 II 14. Barbizon in WW II 15. Double Agents in WW II 16. Harold Cole, accused double agent 17. Drue Leyton, actress 18. Virginia d'Albert-Lake, escape helper 19. MI9 operatives in occupied France.

Published by Oliver-Heber Books

For information contact: www.cijiware.com

PRAISE FOR CIJI WARE'S HISTORICAL AND CONTEMPORARY FICTION

"Ware once again proves she can weave fact and fiction to create an entertaining and harmonious whole." *Publishers Weekly*

[Ware's Spy Sisters thrillers are] a magical combination of brilliant plotting, achingly real protagonists, and an emotional roller-coaster of danger and courage, all set during a chapter of World War II that is little known...I've been haunted ever since I got to The End. CYNTHIA WRIGHT, *New York Times & USA Today bestselling author*

"Vibrant and exciting..." *Literary Times*

"A story so fascinating it should come with a warning—do not start unless you want to be up all night." *Romantic Times*

"A mesmerizing blend of sizzling romance, love, and honor...Ciji Ware has written an unforgettable tale." *The Burton Report*

"A romantic tale of intrigue...A compelling storyline and fascinating characters." *The Natchez Democrat*

"Ingenious, entertaining, and utterly romantic...A terrific read." JANE HELLER, *New York Times & USA Today* bestselling author

"Oozes magic and romance...I loved it!" BARBARA FREETHY, #1 *New York Times* bestselling author

"Fiction at its finest. Beautifully written." *Libby's Library News*

"Thoroughly engaging." *Booklist*

["*A Spy Above the Clouds*] is a rich, wonderful historical war novel and love story. As Ragtime set the gold standard for historical novels, this book includes real life characters and events co-mingled with the author's well-researched imagination to lend a verisimilitude of intrigue, romance, and history." Rick Friedberg, TV/Film Director, *Friedberg Productions/Hollywood Pictures*

"[*Landing by Moonlight*]...has excitement, betrayal, romance...what more can you ask for! I highly recommend this book." Mary Kay, verified purchase, *5-Star Amazon Review*

"From the first chapter, I was caught up in [*Landing by Moonlight*]... Not only was this novel well written with an exciting plot, the author researched, thoroughly, the time period and the actual settings in various parts of France. I recommend this novel to anyone, who is interested in [WW II] and loves spy stories." *5-star Bookbub review*

To the handful of heroic American women secret agents and escape-and-evade "helpers" in the French Resistance who joined British and French intelligence agencies—some prior to the United States entering World War II—and sheltered downed aviators who were complete strangers arriving at their door needing food, medical help, and a way to escape France.

And most especially to:

Drue Leyton Tartiére and Virginia d'Albert-Lake
Two heroines who guided the fliers on their first steps from the fields where they landed, south to the border with Spain, and over the Pyrenees, back to Britain to "fly on another day."

LIST OF FICTIONAL CHARACTERS

Brooke Bradley – Hollywood and Broadway actress; a later member of the French Resistance [b: 1908; 31 in 1939]. Marries French film star, Victor de Varney in 1940.

Victor de Varney – French film star; later Liaison Officer and translator for Charles de Gaulle; he has French and British dual citizenship [b: 1914; 25 in 1939]. His mother, Penelope Kent de Varney, died when he was 4 in 1918.

Armand de Varney – Victor's younger brother [b: 1916; in charge of the de Varney Calvados operation at their château near Rouen].

Bernard de Varney – Victor's father; an apple grower and distiller of brandy called Calvados at château de Varney, west of Rouen. [b: 1889] Married his first wife, Penelope Kent, a British cable operator in a military wireless telegraph station in WW I, in 1913, [d: 1918 in influenza epidemic]; Married second wife, American Barbara Mallory, in 1928. [Bernard is 50 in 1939]

Monique de Varney – mother of Bernard de Varney and Victor's widowed grandmother; married Victor's late grandfather, Armand de Varney in 1888. [b: 1864; 75 in 1939]

Christophe/Christopher Laurent – reporter for Radio France; later a Comet Line evade and escape leader in northern and central France. [b: 1907; 32 in 1939]

Denise Louette – French film and broadcast talent agent [b: 1900; 39 in 1939]

Arnold Warmby – Hollywood film stagehand [b: 1906; 33 in 1939]

Nicole Langlois – Alsatian refugee; housekeeper to the de Varneys [b: 1920; 19 in 1939]

Constance Vivier-Clarke, "Viv" – American ambulance driver; later British SOE agent (Special Operations Executive); she had British and American dual citizenship [b: 1913; 26 in 1939]

Jules Dumont – French poet, Free French propagandist [b: 1891; 48 in 1939]

Germaine Dumont – wife of Jules Dumont [b: 1895; 44 in 1939]

Mlle. Sabine Arquette – Brooke and Viv's French language teacher [b: 1882; 56 in 1939]

Gillian Wingate-Jones – British volunteer for the French Red Cross [b: 1901; 38 in 1939]

Lt. Olivier Renault – Victor's fellow soldier in the North Africa campaign. [b: 1911; 28 in 1939]

Luc, Felix, Antoine, Gaspard Escape and evader "helpers" in the French Resistance "Rabbit Run" branch of the Comet Line.

LIST OF HISTORICAL FIGURES

Sylvia Beach – owner of the Paris bookstore Shakespeare & Company [b: 1887; d: 1962; 52 in 1939]

Josephine Baker – African-American musical performer; later spy for the Free French [b.1906; d: 1975 in Paris; 33 in 1939]

Sir Winston Churchill – Prime Minister of Britain from 1940-1945 and again 1951-1955 [b: 1874; d: 1965]

Harold Cole – a sergeant in the British Royal Engineers; later a secret agent in the escape-and-evasion branch of British Intelligence [b. 1906; d: 1946; 33 in 1938]

Major, later Brigadier Norman Crockatt – the head of MI9 Escape-and-Evade operations during WW II [b:1894; d: 1956]

Virginia and Philippe d'Albert-Lake – Virginia [b: 1910],'s an American, and Philippe, [b: circa 1908] a French citizen, based primarily in Paris, risked their lives saving downed airmen along the Comet escape line.

Lt.-Colonel Sir Claude Edward Marjoribanks Dansey – Deputy Head of MI6, in charge of wartime espionage and counter-espionage [b: 1876; d: 1947; 63 in 1939]

Brigadier/ later **General Charles de Gaulle** – Free French leader in exile [b:1890; d: 1970; age 49 in 1939]

Albert-Marie Guérisse aka Pat O'Leary – a Belgian who became the leader of the Pat Line escape route based in Marseille [b: 1911; d: 1989]

Ernest Hemingway – American writer, foreign correspondent [b. 1899 in Illinois; d:1961; age 40 in 1939] In Europe May 1944 until March 1945; present for the Normandy Landings and the Liberation of Paris, August 24-25, 1944; In Paris, he visited Sylvia Beach and Pablo Picasso with Mary Welsh, who joined him there.

James Langley – his arm amputated early in WWII, he was recruited into MI9 in 1941 and served with Crockatt through the war's duration [b: 1916; d: 1983]

Polleen "Polly" Peabody – American ex-pat; later nonfiction author [b: 1917; d: 1996]; buried in Farmingdale, NY; Father Richard Rogers Peabody [d: 1936]; Mother Mary Phelps Jacob Peabody Crosby [d: 1970]

Dr. Sumner Jackson, M.D. – American surgeon; resident physician in Charge and Chief Administrator of the American Hospital, Neuilly-sur-Seine, a suburb of Paris, [b: 1895, aged 44 in 1939]

Toquette Barrelet De Ricou Jackson – Dr. Jackson's Swiss-born wife; a nurse in WWI; member of the French Resistance in WW II [b. 1889; d: 1968; aged 40 in 1939]

Pierre Laval – Vice Premier in Vichy French Government; Prime Minister 1942-44 [b:1883; d: 1945; age 56 in 1939]

Louise Macy – an American volunteer providing aid to refugees arriving at Gare Montparnasse.

Vincent Molet – a sound engineer at Radio Mondiale; later member of the Resistance in Paris; [in his 60s in 1939]

Ondile/Ondie – a standard French poodle [b: 1938; 1 year old in 1939]

Marshal Philippe Pétain – octogenarian Chief of State for the Vichy French government collaborating as a puppet state with Nazi Germany 1940-1944 [b: 1856; d: 1951; age 83 in 1939]

Pablo Picasso – Impressionist painter living in Paris [b.1881 in Spain; d: 1973 in France]

Woodruff Wallner – U.S. Envoy to France at the beginning of WW II; aided Resistance fighters [b. 1909; d: 1983; age 30 in 1939]

Sarah Pressley Watson – a young American running Foyer International, an organization supporting foreign students in France [In Paris 1920-1959; b:1885; d: 1959; 53 in 1939]

PROLOGUE

FRANCE, AUGUST 1943

J ust before midnight, a large, curly-haired chocolate-brown French poodle lifted her head in the direction of the cold grate of an 18th century fireplace and delivered a deep-throated growl.

Alerted by the sound, the human occupants of the La Villa du Lapin d'Or became aware of the droning hum of yet another bomber flying above their small, adopted village of Barbizon, less than an hour south of Paris by train.

Thirty-five-year-old Madame Brooke Bradley de Varney, the villa's latest chatelain, set aside her thick book describing the practical arts of cultivating grains and vegetables.

"That's at least the twelfth plane we've heard tonight," she noted, cocking her head, listening intently for a few more moments. "It's either a Lancaster or a B-17 heading for Germany, don't you think?"

"Let us pray it's one of the Allies, and not the Germans again," replied Madame de Varney's housekeeper, Nicole Langlois, 23.

During their months of shared exile from Paris, the younger woman had become a true friend to the mistress of the house. By mutual agreement, they mostly conversed in French now, thanks to Brooke's determination to master the language beyond the smattering that she had picked up since marrying Victor and arriving in France as a newcomer.

As she vowed to Nicole nearly every day, "Surely, I'm not too old to learn proper French since everyone insists that I really must do something about my atrocious American accent!"

"Ah, madame!" Nicole chastised with a smile, "you are not *that* much older than I. Each day I see an improvement."

Their conversation ceased as the sound of the aircraft's engine grew ever louder. Then, Nicole voiced the wish they both held onto tightly these days.

"Perhaps the plane is on its way to target a weapons factory or petrol storage in Germany?"

After months of Nazi superiority in the skies, the Allies were finally launching strikes deep inside the invaders' Fatherland.

In the next instant, both women were startled by the plane's steady roar abruptly shifting to what became a piercing screech. Bolting from their chairs, they arrived at the window, pulled back the heavy drapes just in time to watch the *ach-ach-ach* of German anti-aircraft tracers several miles away stitch their bursts of flame across the sky. An orange-and-yellow fireball was streaking in an arc toward a wooded area beyond the broad wheatfield that stretched behind their small housing compound on Barbizon's main street.

"Oh, Lord... the damn Krauts hit the plane!" Brooke exclaimed.

Outlined by the stone-framed window, the pair watched the aircraft's moment of impact on the ground as if seeing it on a movie screen. The nearest side of the tree-covered hill bloomed white hot for several seconds before its center turned an ominous blood red.

"Just look at that fire," murmured Nicole, staring at the sight of flames shooting above the trees. "It is spreading so quickly."

The two women nearly collided as they both raced to fling open the back door, the poodle scampering in their wake.

"Ondie, stay!" Brooke commanded, snatching two small signal flags from a nearby shelf.

With a disappointed whine, the dog obediently sat on her haunches as the two women slammed the back door shut, leaving her inside. They scurried along a path that wound through their contraband kitchen garden, charging past their secret bounty of carrots, onions, potatoes, and salad greens. Every day, they expected the occupation troops in Barbizon to discover the food and strip the rows bare for their own use.

Darting through the high, wooden gate, the two women waded into the wide expanse of a wheatfield that stretched behind their weathered sandstone house and outbuildings. A brindle-colored rabbit and several of her offspring scurried off to their right as they ran through the golden shoots ready for harvest in three days' time.

Just then, the concussive sound of another explosion rent the air. A second burst of flames like the one they'd seen through the villa's window burned even more incandescently. The crippled plane's ammunition storage bays had obviously ignited at the crash site about a mile away, causing a secondary conflagration.

Watching the intense flames, Brooke's thoughts fled immediately to Victor, her husband of less than three years, who had volunteered as a French-English translator for the Allies. How many months during this war had she wondered if he'd been shot down somewhere? Ambushed in the North African desert? Drowned at sea?

He'd promised to write and she'd regularly dispatched letters to him, but she'd heard nothing after she'd bid him farewell on the troop train leaving Paris. With the Nazis in charge now, it was wise not to let it be known that her husband had been anything other than an ordinary, defeated French soldier like so many others after Dunkirk. Her only path to sanity had been to join the Resistance against the German invaders and their French Vichy collaborators. Thus, here she was, an American ex-pat, standing in a wheatfield after midnight in central France, waving a small flag in each hand to attract the attention of two Allied fliers floating toward earth.

Brooke's thoughts were abruptly brought back to the present by the sight of an airman in a canvas flight suit dangling beneath a billowing white, silk mushroom that glistened in the moonlight a hundred meters directly above their heads.

The evening breeze ruffled Madame de Varney's blonde hair peeking out from her turban-like scarf, a 'look' Brooke had adopted to appear the typical French housewife. She suddenly shivered, realizing she'd neglected to don her jacket. She turned abruptly to face Nicole and barked an order.

"Go back to the house and get blankets, food, and water and take everything into the potting shed at the far corner of property. If these two fly boys land in decent shape, I'll meet you there with them as soon as I can." She paused for a moment to ponder. "It's the best we can do for them, that is if we're lucky enough to hand them over to the escape line quickly."

Nodding agreement, Nicole turned and dashed back toward the house while Brooke sprinted toward the parachutist nearest her who was now a couple of meters from a hard landing. Twenty seconds later, he hit the ground with a thud. His chute dragged him for several seconds, sculpting a wide swath in the thigh-high grain until he dug his booted heels into the loamy soil and came to a stop. As soon as he saw someone running toward him, he fumbled for a pistol strapped beneath his pant leg.

"Don't shoot!" she called out in a hoarse whisper in French, waving her signal flags at him. "I'm American! Are you French? A Yank... a Brit?"

Allied planes often carried a crew of several nationalities and sometimes the RAF piloted American B-17s "on loan" while they waited for new aircraft to come off assembly lines.

An astonished look transformed the downed flier's thin, pinched face. He stared up at her from shafts of wheat that she and her neighbors had been carefully tending these last months. She took a few more cautious steps toward him, wondering how many loaves of bread could have been made from the sheaves the flier had just crushed to the ground? It was hard enough to snatch these men out from under the Nazis' noses, but how in hell were she and her fellow resisters going to feed them— along with her starving neighbors —when the German invaders were stealing everything edible for their troops?

Brooke well realized that the kid cowering at her feet could have no appreciation for her fledgling efforts to cultivate this grain, along with the vegetables sprouting in her clandestine garden. It was part of a local Resistance scheme to provide desperately needed food to "safehouses" locally as well as in and around Paris where other *résistants* were protecting downed fliers like the one that had literally crash-landed at the back of her villa.

"*Tu vas bien*?" she asked, drawing nearer, again speaking in French in case this unexpected visitor had parachuted into his own native land.

Without answering if he were hurt, the airman gingerly rose to a standing position. She was relieved to see he didn't appear injured but wondered what the chances were that she could get him to safety before the squad of Gestapo based in Barbizon arrived to arrest them all.

Watching the airman divest himself of his harness and yards of silk, she began to worry about how quickly she could equip him with false travel documents and a convincing disguise. Her next step would be to sneak him into the potting shed and then onboard France's own "underground railroad," a perilous, make-shift escape route out of France and into Spain via local trains.

"Gather up your parachute," she urged in a low voice that sounded more like a croak than a command. "We'll dispose of it later. I've got to get you off this field!"

She was well aware that the flier who'd just fallen from the sky could hardly anticipate the physically arduous journey he'd soon be facing. The slow-moving night train she would put him on was jokingly referred to as Barbizon's "Rabbit Run," named in honor of the long-eared, furry creatures prevalent in the region. When this flier made it back to England—if he did—he might one day learn that his treacherous itinerary in the safety of strangers had been created by an enigmatic officer in MI9's Evade and Escape branch of British Intelligence. The French-American Captain Christopher Laurent was the same Allied officer who handed down orders to "escape helpers" like Brooke and Nicole.

Relegating all thoughts of Christopher to the back of her mind, she repeated, "Hurry up!" even more insistently, gauging how soon the other downed parachutist would land. The young man in the wheatfield continued to stare at his would-be rescuer with visible confusion and fear. "Really... are you all right?" Brooke pressed, this time in English.

The shaken flier swallowed hard as if he realized that he had no other choice but to trust her.

"I-I'm an American," he revealed reluctantly. "From Pasadena. Have you ever heard of the place?"

His welcoming committee could hardly believe her ears.

"Pasadena? *California*? You must be joking!" she marveled, feeling a smile spread across her lips. She stared at the pathetically young man with his pale, drawn features who appeared both dazed and scared. "How old are you?" she asked. "Twenty-five, maybe?"

"Nineteen, ma'am. This was only our crew's second flight over the Channel. I'm the tail gunner."

She pointed to the sky. "Look how bright the moon is tonight. You were pretty easy pickings, I'm afraid."

"Wasn't the ground anti-aircraft that got us," he said glumly. "A damn Focke-Wulf came up from behind our B-17 and we were toast."

The gunner glanced over his shoulder, spotting the other parachute floating toward the far side of the field. He swiveled his head, tilting it to one side and then the other, his worried gaze sweeping the area. He peered at her with a pained expression.

"We had ten on board the bomber... and about eleven thousand rounds of ammunition."

The sight of the plane's fire glowing brightly on the far hill made it obvious to them both that the comrades of this young American might not have enjoyed as safe a landing as he.

The gunner suddenly narrowed his eyes and fixed a stare that made his rescuer instantly uneasy.

Abruptly he exclaimed, "Wait a minute! I know you! I've *seen* you before!"

"That's ridiculous," Brooke replied quickly, her heart speeding up in alarm. She gave him a look of disparagement, but she knew from long experience what undoubtedly was coming next.

"*You're...*" He hesitated, shaking his leather-helmeted head in wonder. An enormous grin spread across his face. "You're the Hollywood *movie star*! You're that sexy, pretty girl that was in those Charlie Chan detective films before the war! Am I right? I went to the pictures every Saturday! I *love* those movies!"

A flood of fear made Brooke's breath catch. This recognition of her former self could mean her arrest and a swift, violent end to her Resistance work.

Hoping he'd buy her bluff she scoffed, "I'm very flattered you think I'm a movie star, of all things, but what would such a person be doing in a French wheatfield at midnight in the middle of a war?"

The flier shook his head. "It's *you*, all right! I'd know that breathy voice anywhere." He smiled sheepishly. "And look how beautiful you are, despite that ugly scarf you're wearing. When I was fifteen, I think I was a little in love with you, Miss Bradley."

Brooke de Varney *née* Bradley realized there wasn't time to deny she'd appeared so often in the same role of the 'hapless blonde heroine' in the potboiler detective films that it made her want to scream. Ignoring his comment, she raised her two flags over her head and waved them at the second descending airman who was now a mere two meters off the ground. It appeared the flier saw her, so she turned to her young charge once again.

"I only acted— if you can call it that —in a few of the zillions of silly Charlie Chan films they've made," she said in a rush. She forced a laugh and added dismissively, "Nobody in this part of France realizes who I am— or was, in another life —or *cares*, for that matter. So to keep us both from getting killed, *zip it,* will ya, pal? C'mon. Let's see how your friend is faring."

Brooke knew full well that it would mean utter disaster if anyone within the small confines of the village of Barbizon had any idea who she had been before moving south from Paris as Madame de Varney, the American wife married to a Frenchman who hadn't returned after French forces had been so swiftly defeated. And if Herr Schiller or his storm troopers found out who Victor really was or what *she'd* been doing in Barbizon all this time— or that, prior to the German invasion, she'd been the radio "voice" criticizing in English Hitler's aggression every chance she could— they'd execute her on the spot.

These days, the former actress looked a far cry from that glamorous young woman from Hollywood on the cusp of genuine stardom before the war. This discovery by the tail gunner from Pasadena instantly brought back her memory of boarding the

Super Chief at Union Station in Los Angeles, hatbox in hand, a
fashionable fox fur draped around her chic suit, bound for a
Broadway tryout of *Green Grow the Lilacs* in New York.

Brooke could point to that fateful decision to quit the Charlie
Chan detective franchise as the very one that had upended her
entire life and put her on a path to a whirlwind romance with
France's celebrated film star-turned-soldier.

Oh, Victor... so many things I should have told you...

Brooke's thoughts were forced back to the hazardous present by
the sight of the second crew member thumping down in the field
some twenty meters away from where she stood with the kid from
California.

"Never mind about Hollywood and all that," she said to the tail
gunner hurriedly. "Your fellow crew member also appears to have
landed safely, so gather up your chute and let's get you both off this
field, pronto."

She and the gunner watched as the downed airman pulled in
the cords of his parachute, collecting into his chest the yards of
white silk billowing in the mild evening breeze.

Observing him struggle with the unwieldy mass of fabric,
Brooke found herself wondering at the virtual evaporation of her
once-legendary ambition to be a great film star and celebrated
Broadway actress. Her single-minded pursuit of those aspirations
felt light years away from the life that had unfolded once she'd met
Victor visiting backstage at her play. They'd fallen madly in love,
and until they came to Europe in late 1939, had never spent a night
apart.

The moment the young gunner called out to his commander,
Brooke was abruptly returned to the events unfolding in her
wheatfield.

"Hey, Captain! Over here!"

Angrily, she admonished him *sotte voce*, "Shh! For God's sake,
keep your voice down! Sounds carry on the night air. A pack of
German SS are headquartered in our village. With you shouting
like that, they could arrive at any minute!"

She again waved her small flags at the newcomer. From her
vantage point, the tall figure appeared to weave unsteadily as he

trudged across the field, a mass of ballooning white silk spilling from his arms.

As the pilot approached ever closer, the gunner said in a hoarse whisper, "Captain, sir, you'll never believe it, but this woman is an *American* and she's also a famous—"

"I am Madame de Varney," Brooke interrupted, stepping forward. She shot the tail gunner a withering look that demanded he remain silent about his unlikely discovery. "And yes, I'm an American who can help you. I married a Frenchman just before the German invasion." Stuffing the little flags in a pocket of her overalls, she addressed both her men. "For the security of the three of us, that's all you need know about me." Then, she summoned what she hoped was a winning smile. "Here, do take my arm, Captain. You look a bit wobbly— and who could blame you after what you've just been through."

"I'm fine," snapped the captain, apparently offended by her offer of an assist. "For God's sake, woman! Just give me a moment to get my bearings, will you? Where the hell *are* we?"

One of *those* jerks, Brooke thought crossly, answering him tight-lipped, "This field is on the outskirts of the village of Barbizon, sixty kilometers south of Paris. That's thirty-seven miles to *you*, Captain. I can help you escape from here, but only if you follow my instructions *precisely.*"

Brooke noticed his body stiffen. Apparently, the pilot did not appreciate that a woman was the one giving orders. A siren began to wail in the far distance.

The captain said, "It sounds as if the damn Krauts have already spotted the rest of the crew."

"*If* their parachutes ever deployed," was Brooke's blunt reply. "I saw only your two. It's probably the plane's explosions that have alerted the fire brigade."

She shot a glance across the telltale trampled wheatfield. She prayed the local Nazis wouldn't scour much beyond where the B-17 crashed on the far side of their village. With any luck, the pending wheat harvest would soon erase the evidence of their presence.

Casting a sharp look at the captain whose manner and

machismo had been less than engaging, she added, "All the more reason to get you two away from this open field. C'mon!"

"But who are you, really?" demanded the pilot, his voice sharp with skepticism. "Why are you doing this? It's dangerous if the Germans catch you assisting the enemy— or are you one of those ex-pat Nazi sympathizers, thinking about collecting a reward if you turn us in and then..."

"*Why* am I willing to save your necks?" she interrupted. Swallowing a wave of annoyance over this yokel's rude and erroneous assumptions, she replied evenly, "Let's just say this is my own, private act of retribution against a certain Gestapo goon whose headquarters is just down the road from here."

She saw in her mind's eye the day the sod allowed his uniformed confederates to arrest her, sending her and other Americans living in Barbizon to a camp for enemy aliens— that was, until she tricked the authorities, yet again, and was released back to the village.

She arched an eyebrow at her new charges, warning, "Believe me, fellas, *Herr* Schiller would like nothing better than to count you airmen and myself as three new notches on his belt."

The pilot and his gunner exchanged looks of alarm.

Brooke paused and then added, "And if I help you both escape the Gestapo's clutches and you make it back to Britain to fly on another day, then maybe... just *maybe*... someone will likewise help the people *I* love— your *allies* —survive this bloody, awful war."

The bravado fueling her words rang hollow in her own ears. She paused and inhaled a deep breath, wondering how she could continue to sustain the many blatant fictions that had been central to her life for so long.

PART I

1

THREE YEARS EARLIER - FEBRUARY 1940

Dense fog began to spit rain, pelting the shoulders of Victor de Varney's dark blue cashmere topcoat. He elbowed his way past the saluting stage door sentry and headed down the long, dank corridor leading to a row of dressing rooms at the rear of one of London's most venerable West End theaters.

Without knocking on the door that displayed a large, black star and the stenciled name, "Brooke Bradley," he flung it open with a dramatic gesture. The doorknob thwacked a sharp report against the wooden paneling of the American performer's inner sanctum, startling the person Victor had come to see.

The slender, thirty-two-year-old blonde woman with amber eyes and a delicious, throaty voice that he witnessed charming that evening's audience had just come off stage in the London production of Clifford Odets' *Golden Boy*. At intermission, the producer told him that the play was ending its successful run that very week.

"Brooke! Darling!" he exclaimed to the actress's reflection in the dressing room's bulb-studded mirror. He was delighted to see her open-mouthed astonishment.

He was even more pleased when she pushed back her chair, jumped up from her dressing table, and flung herself across the room and into his arms.

"Victor! My God! What are you *doing* here?" she exclaimed in that low, breathy voice that had captured his heart the first time he'd heard her speak on a Broadway stage barely a year earlier. "I thought you and your film crew had been devoured by an avalanche somewhere in Norway. Why didn't I ever hear from you?" she demanded.

"There's a war on— or hadn't you heard, my darling?" he answered lightly, avoiding any further discussion of failing to keep up their correspondence as he'd promised her.

Instead, he began covering her flawless complexion with little kisses, relieved she hadn't castigated him as much as he deserved for his silence the last few weeks.

He was correct in saying that the war between England, France and Germany had interrupted their lives for five months since its formal declaration September 1, 1939. For those in England, it had eventually come to be known as the "Phony War" with all sides posturing and threatening each other, but with little more territory taken after Hitler invaded Czechoslovakia, along with storming into Poland when hostilities began.

Since then, rationing had commenced in the United Kingdom, but to date, that was about the only noteworthy change besides the big military buildup going on throughout the British Isles. Theaters, like Brooke's, were still Standing Room Only, and Victor's film company had managed to get his movie finished in Norway by the second week of February in this new year of 1940.

"Does your being here mean the movie has wrapped?" she queried. He'd ceased nibbling her neck and they both came up for air. "Or do you still have to go back to do some pick-up shots?"

Victor led her to the scarlet brocade divan her producer had thoughtfully installed in her dressing room. He was quick to spot a folding screen angled in one corner displaying a fine array of Brooke's silk and lace undergarments strewn over its top in the wake of one of her hurried costume changes.

Taking her hand to pull her down beside him, he answered, "All my scenes are in the can, thank the Lord." He encircled her in his arms. "Our boat from Oslo managed to dodge the offshore mines and we docked in Falmouth last night."

France's most celebrated young film star spoke English without the trace of an accent, thanks to his late mother, born in the United Kingdom. Her last wish had been to insist on schooling her two sons in her country of birth. By contrast, Victor's impeccable French came from absorbing the language during long summers with his father's family spent in Barbizon in central France, and on the Côte d'Azur. Holidays throughout the year were celebrated either in their Paris apartment or at their château in Normandy. The latter was a beautiful property surrounded by orchards whose apples Victor's father, Bernard de Varney, and his ancestors had been distilling for generations into the fine— and lucrative — brandy known as Calvados.

Sprawled on the dressing room sofa, the unusually tall French actor glanced briefly at himself reflected in the mirror across the room. He was relieved that his bankable handsome features had been blessed with a nose with a gentler arch than his father's distinctively Gallic version. Victor's dark, almost black hair was still sprinkled with the evening's mist, and his damp coat felt clammy against Brooke's peach silk dressing gown.

He kissed her again, only this time more slowly, his hand seeking to cup one of her breasts through her silk dressing gown. Its warmth and her sigh signaled that she had forgiven him his pledge to stay in close touch during the first time they'd been apart since the momentous day they had met in New York in another backstage dressing room.

"I missed you so much," she murmured. "I had begun to wonder if—"

"I'm here now, darling," he whispered against her ear, the stray wisps of her glorious blonde hair soft against his lips.

He leaned back, gently seizing her shoulders so he could look directly into those feline eyes, golden in the room's flatteringly low light.

She regarded him silently, then asked, "What is it?" One thin, pale brow arched above her steady, rather unnerving gaze. "What did you come here in such a hurry to tell me?"

As if on cue, he smoothly slipped from the sofa onto one knee and pulled from his damp coat pocket a small, square box. Its ancient black velvet covering was worn thin on two corners.

Brooke's gaze was glued on it cupped in his right hand. With his left, Victor carefully pried it open to reveal his grandmother's engagement ring, a large, oval sapphire encircled with alternating seed pearls and small diamonds.

Would Brooke agree to his plan, he worried silently, looking intently at the beautiful young woman he was determined to make his wife.

"I'm not here to tell you anything" he said softly, "but to humbly ask you to marry me. *Now*."

Brooke's eyes widened with genuine surprise.

"Marry you? Tonight?" she repeated.

"Or in the next few days, at least," he amended with a nervous laugh. "My agent has made all the arrangements for a special license so we can be wed in the small chapel at Saint Paul's... and then we'll leave directly for France."

BROOKE KEPT her gaze on the proffered ring in order to obscure her expression of complete astonishment at his dramatic gesture just made to her. It was a highly theatrical one— even for Victor — an actor whose screen presence was often praised for its intensity.

In a kaleidoscope of memories, Brooke recalled falling in love almost instantly with the charismatic young star when Victor's agent had brought him backstage in New York the night before he was to board his Pan Am Clipper enroute back to France.

The producer of Lynn Biggs' *Green Grow the Lilacs* that Brooke was performing in had wanted the internationally known film actor to see their show and to consider starring as the production's male lead when it transferred to London's West End, an offer Brooke learned later he had diplomatically declined. Victor was a movie star. Much later he admitted to her that the sight of an audience staring up at him in their seats tied his stomach in knots and he'd vowed "Never again," after his last theatre performance.

At New York's Sardi's restaurant on West 44th Street where the actors, producer, and agent met later that first night, Victor stealthily caressed her hand under their table. The soft pad of his thumb rhythmically stroking her palm signaled to Brooke that he felt the same, mysterious, almost palpable attraction that had so quickly rendered her weak-kneed with longing for him to continue his electrifying touch.

Fooling no one, the good-looking French film star offered to share a cab with Brooke and be dropped off at his hotel, leaving his agent to find her own way back to the Plaza.

What followed was Victor's postponement of his Pan Am flight from New York and a mad, passionate romance with Brooke in America. Within a few weeks he implored her to come back to Europe with him. Somehow, the lawyer she hired on short notice got her out of her Broadway contract. Once landing in Britain, Victor's agent, Denise Louette, negotiated a West End theater supporting role for Brooke, along with a starring movie role for Victor in a film to be shot both in French and English, but made in Scandinavia.

To Brooke's disbelief and dismay, after the film actor left for Norway, total silence had ensued. Her emotional distress at the abruptness of Victor's behavior was now compounded by the shock of his bursting into her dressing room only moments before offering her an engagement ring.

"*Brooke?*"

Victor's rather stern tone of voice finally penetrated her awareness that many moments had passed. He still held in his hand the open box with his grandmother's sapphire nestled inside. His pained expression indicated that his knee was most likely starting to hurt, and he'd like Brooke to answer his question: would she marry him?

There was a sharp knock on the dressing room door, followed by its opening a few inches. Victor's ever-hovering agent, Denise, peeked in.

"*Oh! Pardon! Je pensais que maintenant Victor aurait proposé et...*"

"What's she saying?" Brooke asked, both embarrassed that she understood so little French and unsettled by the interruption.

Victor waved with the hand not holding his grandmother's ring and replied sharply, "*Mais, no! Pas encore!*"

The door was hastily shut.

Brooke patted the divan, saying quietly, "Victor, come now. Off your knees and sit beside me."

He neatly choreographed his recovery, rising gracefully, and then sinking onto the upholstery, stretching out the leg that apparently had been cramping painfully. Brooke seized his free hand and searched for the right words to convey the confusion she was feeling.

"I am touched, truly, but... well... I-I must admit I'm a bit surprised and also—" She hesitated, seeking to say something that would not bruise the sensibility of a man who had just proposed marriage. "I guess I'm rather perplexed by your sudden appearance after not hearing from you for *five weeks* while you were in Norway," she declared. She gestured to the velvet box now cradled in his lap. "And now, this beautiful ring?" Seeking his glance, she added, "After such a long silence between us, surely you can understand why I'm... rather startled by your proposal."

For days, now, Brooke had been telling herself that, like several affairs in her past, theirs might merely have been a liaison between a sexually charged young actor and an actress who'd been, more times than she cared to recall, disappointed in love. The evidence seemed to indicate that she'd foolishly allowed the charms of Victor de Varney to completely upend her career as a burgeoning star on Broadway, to say nothing of abandoning her country as war loomed throughout Europe. Ignoring all sane advice from her theater friends, she'd boarded the Pan Am Clipper and flew to Europe with a man she'd known little more than a month.

And, once again, she had made the choice to forego a life she knew she ought to be making with the small son she'd left behind in Los Angeles, just as she'd left Arnold Warmby after the birth of the baby, and then divorced him, thanks to a quick trip to Reno. The mere thought of her consigning the care of her toddler to his sixty-two-year-old grandmother prompted a cascade of self-reproach. Staring at the ring nestled in the velvet box, Brooke fought to suppress the image of the little boy with wispy blond hair and his father's round face.

And the worst of it was that she had never told Victor anything about the son she'd left in California. Their love affair had been such a whirlwind, the subject of past relationships, to say nothing of children, had never come up.

Gazing into Victor's injured expression, she wondered if, for once in her life, she would act like an adult. For once could she not be that moonstruck kid who wanted this man's love and devotion so badly, she'd ignored some oh-so-familiar signs to achieve her dream. Signs like the silence from Victor's end once he left to make his movie in Norway, when before, they hadn't been apart a single night.

She held tightly to Victor's free hand, declaring quietly, "I-I can't... I mean I *shouldn't* marry you."

He stared at her, dumbfounded, as if he couldn't comprehend any possibility that she might refuse him. Brooke squeezed his hand even more firmly, imploring him to understand.

"I was..." She stopped and then amended, "I *am* terribly drawn to you. You've meant the world to me as you must know when I left everything behind to come to Europe with you, but there are things I should have told you early on, including the fact that I had a very brief marriage before I met you."

She amazed herself that the words had finally escaped her lips.

"You did?" he said, clearly taken aback. "How brief?"

"Less than six months. It was a ridiculous disaster, I realized as soon as I said 'I do'... so you can understand why I am—"

Victor waved a dismissive hand, "I've come close to nearly doing the same thing... but at least it didn't last long and it's in your past, so let's not even think of it right now."

Encouraged by this, Brooke felt her resolve growing stronger to make a clean breast of everything she'd never disclosed to him, as well voicing her serious doubts about Victor's loyalty.

"I should have told you about that long ago, but everything between us happened so fast, and besides, there are things I certainly don't know about *you*—"

"*What* things about me?" interrupted Victor, his dark eyebrows drawn together in either annoyance or distress— Brooke couldn't determine which.

"Well, to begin with, I'd like to know the reason why you didn't write me from Norway for *weeks* when I wrote you every single day!"

There! She'd said it. And she wanted an answer. One confession for another before she'd venture any further.

"You know perfectly well that the mail is censored," he said in his defense. "Half the time the ships it's on are sunk by the U-boats that the damned Jerries—"

Before he could finish speaking, she countered, "I paid extra to post mine by *air*! How is it possible that not a single one of your letters ever arrived here in London?"

Brooke felt frustrated that she wasn't expressing both her doubts about Victor's allegiance as well as her own guilt for not having been honest in any of the missives she'd sent him, letters that should have revealed certain important factors about her own life, including the existence of a two-year-old son.

"The entire world is about to fall apart," he shot back, "and you're upset about a *lack of mail!*"

It was a persuasive rejoinder that she paused to digest, yet her frustration persisted.

"Well, why be in such a rush about marriage, then?" she pressed, reflecting silently on how disastrously her previous nuptials had ended. "Why the drama of your not cabling me you were coming back to London and then bursting into my dressing room without warning?"

"Because I was busy every minute learning my lines and shooting our film on a killing schedule," he replied, a wounded expression clouding his good looks.

Brooke didn't respond.

"And because, dammit, I *love* you, Brooke!" he exclaimed. "And because— *as* the film was finishing —I learned some important military intelligence I shouldn't even *tell* you, but it's why I'm here."

"How would an actor be told military intelligence?" she demanded, and then realized how insulting her question must sound.

Victor seemed not to notice or take offense. Although no one was in the room, he lowered his voice and leaned forward.

"Our producer was given a sudden warning to finish the picture as fast as we could," he disclosed. "Someone who is high up in the government said that Hitler has secret plans to invade Denmark and Norway *soon*, despite the bastard swearing that he intended to respect Norway's neutrality. I've been told that the military bigwigs in the London War Office have no doubt that the dirty little bastard plans to invade the rest of Europe in short order."

"How does a film producer come to know all this?" Brooke scoffed, unable to disguise her skepticism.

"Some traitor in Norway named Quisling secretly met with the Führer when he visited there," Victor replied. "The damn turncoat revealed that Britain has been mining the North Sea off Norway. *Herr* Adolf was enraged to hear this, apparently, and declared what his real plans were loud enough that others beside Quisling got wind of it all. One of them told a British envoy, and he told our producer who told *me*. After all, he needed to get my cooperation to agree to our film's breakneck shooting schedule."

"So much for State secrets..." murmured Brooke. She pointed to the ring box. "But how does a possible invasion of Norway relate to... well... to your thinking that you and I should marry within a week and go to France?" she persisted.

Victor released a sigh of exasperation.

"Because we *love* each other! We need each other. There's a real war coming, not this phony one. The damn Germans are about to invade God knows how much of Scandinavia, and, most likely, the rest of Europe itself!"

Victor's tone had almost grown stentorian, as if he hoped his words would ring against the back wall of the upper balcony.

"France will need everyone on the barricades to protect her, and besides, it's my *home*... and it will be your home, too! There's lots that we can do! We can make propaganda films together, and I'll join the French Army, if they'll have me... and... and you'll meet my wonderful *grandmère* Monique at our château in Normandy where you can take refuge if you ever have to!"

Victor reached for her, pulling her close, his voice suddenly sinking to a choked whisper that she'd never heard before.

"I was only a little boy when the Great War nearly decimated France twenty years ago, laying waste to the village where I'd spent many wonderful summers." He sought her gaze. "I don't think I've ever told you... but I'd been a rather sickly child. I suffered from asthma, a chronic lung condition that still plagues me at times if there is pollen or I catch cold. After my mother had died, my father and grandmother took me to the countryside south of Paris each year in hopes the sunshine would be of bene-fit." His eyes were moist. "Another war with the beastly Huns seems inevitable and I don't think I can face it without you, Brooke."

His voice cracked with emotion and Brooke felt suddenly sympathetic. For the second time that evening, he rested a hand on each of her shoulders, squeezing them lightly for emphasis.

"It all became so clear to me when the film wrapped. I missed you! I want to be *with* you! To go through whatever is in store together. We can't wait and be 'sensible'— which is the message I'm seeing in those amber eyes of yours."

"But Victor—"

"Don't you love me?" he demanded. "Don't you want us to be together? Isn't the way we've been, the way we were since the moment we met, all the proof you need that we should marry and return to help France?"

"Except for those weeks in Norway," she reminded him, and then she wished she hadn't. She was frankly stunned by this unashamed declaration of devotion both to her and to his country and she could see that Victor's every fiber was vibrating with intensity.

"Please, Brooke," he pleaded. "Don't play the reluctant damsel, I beg you. There's a real war coming," he repeated. "Your play here is closing in five days, and I... I can't imagine life without you."

Brooke remained silent, his words ringing in her ears.

He loved her.

He'd never actually come out and said it before. Yes, he'd told her how beautiful he thought she was. She could see he considered her reasonably talented in her craft, and certainly good company, and that they got along swimmingly— but *love* her? She'd thought that his not writing all the time he'd been away had meant his passion for her had cooled. Yet, the words that had spilled from him these last minutes were precisely what she'd longed to hear the entire time they'd been together. Her entire life, probably.

Taking a deep breath, she framed his high cheekbones with a hand on each side and felt her smile stretching ear-to-ear, her heart singing with relief.

"Well... since you put it *that* way..." she teased.

"Then it's *yes*?" he demanded, his eyes alight with the boyish charm of a young man rarely denied his fondest wishes.

"Yes," she whispered. She'd told him half the secrets she'd kept inside, and wasn't that a start? She held out her left hand so he could slide the beautiful sapphire ring onto her finger. She leaned forward to meet his kiss. "My answer is *yes!*"

But should it be? whispered a voice at the back of her head as Victor enveloped her in his ardent embrace. The secret she'd yet to disclose was like the unexploded mine floating just below the surface in the North Sea. And with war threatening to come even closer to France, was she truly ready to abandon America along with everyone and everything she'd ever known?

When Victor released her, he sprang from the sofa to his feet.

"Let's go tell everyone!" he declared. "My agent and your producer knew I intended to propose to you tonight and they want to take us out for champagne to celebrate." He pulled her to her feet and kissed her again. "And my grandmother knows," he added with a laugh. "Letting her in on my plan was the only way I could persuade her to send me that ring!"

He framed her face between his hands, as Brooke had done to him, and kissed her a third time. "You're going to love Monique and she's definitely going to love *you.*"

The thought of being part of a family that would welcome her into the fold struck Brooke as a treasure far more valuable than the sapphire and diamonds he'd just put on her finger. The only child of a struggling single mother, Brooke had longed for relatives that were sane and steady and— well —*normal.* How could she turn that down when Victor had finally declared his passion for her and wanted her counted among his loved ones?

Pushing away the guilt for not having ever revealed during this tumultuous courtship on two continents and several countries that

she had a small son living in Los Angeles, she told herself that at a
better time, she'd lay that difficult truth before him— including a
bit more about her ridiculous and extremely short marriage to
stagehand and hustler Arnold Warmby.

Victor pointed to the folding screen with Brooke's lacy undergarments displayed across the top.

"As much as I adore you in that silk dressing gown, why don't
you put on something lovely to wear to the Ritz?" he suggested.
"Meanwhile, I'll arrange to have a bottle of Veuve Clicquot put on
ice."

"Oh, Victor," she hesitated, not really feeling like sharing this
moment with his agent or her producer. "Can't it be just the two
of us?"

A familiar sense of panic began to take hold. She needed time
to *think*.

*There are so many ramifications if I marry and move to France, espe-
cially if war spreads there...*

"Darling" Victor cajoled, "I've already asked them to join us,
and besides, they'll make it a jolly celebration." He pointed to her
dressing screen. "Now go on, beautiful. Put on something decent
and I'll meet you at the stage door in ten minutes."

Brooke crossed to her dressing table and stared into its mirror,
the bright bulbs surrounding it heightening the worry she saw
reflected in her features. She heard the door open and shut and
sank onto the upholstered chair, meeting her own gaze, then
closing her eyes.

It occurred to her that the serious omission about her past was
more like an unexploded bomb buried under a house than mine-
fields floating in the sea.

Would Victor still love her if he knew she'd not only left her son
behind to escape her mistakes but had to dig herself out of a serious
depression? Would he even accept her boy when he finally learned
of Errol's existence, given Arnold's sketchy background and his
insane behavior before and after the divorce? She tried not to think
of the small black-and-white Kodak snapshot of her child tucked in
a side pocket of her handbag, a photograph of a baby on his first
birthday that she'd shown no one since leaving California.

And how would Victor's grandmother respond if she learned of the secrets her new granddaughter-in-law had failed to disclose?

Brooke covered her face with her hands, certain that none of it bore thinking about.

So, she *wouldn't* think about it.

At least, not right now.

2

EARLY MARCH 1940

T he last five days of Brooke's performances in Odets' *Golden Boy* were executed amidst a flurry of preparations for the small wedding Victor's ever-efficient agent Denise Louette had arranged. Along with helping Brooke pack her trunk with her personal belongings, Denise managed to get Brooke out of her leased flat by finding another actress in the Odets play to move in and take her place.

Meanwhile, Brooke dutifully signed the manifold paperwork Denise had assembled that was required for an American woman in a country not her own to marry a man in England with dual British-French citizenship.

Then there was the matter of obtaining the documents, including her divorce decree which, fortunately, she'd brought with her passport. All were necessary for Brooke Bradley de Varney to enter France on permanent status with her new husband. Given the bustle of necessary preparations, Denise was present nearly every minute. Brooke could never seem to find the right moment to make the complete confession to Victor that she'd neglected to reveal, thus far.

"*Il y avait beaucoup de difficultés, mais je pense que tout est en ordre.*" declared Denise, placing several additional, official-looking papers on the hotel desk for both of them to sign.

"What is she saying?" Brooke asked with irritation since she knew full well that Denise's grasp of English far exceeded her own smattering of French.

In fact, it seemed to Brooke that at times, Denise spoke in the language she knew would put Victor's fiancée at a distinct disadvantage. For her part, not understanding a word they said made her feel pathetically ignorant and insecure.

As Victor commenced signing the papers, Brooke took closer stock of Madame Louette, a small, compact brunette in her late forties with feathery wings of silver hair above each ear. The theatrical agent favored trim, well-tailored suits with Hermes or Chanel scarves tied artfully around her neck, rendering her incredibly chic, day or night. Brooke had come to believe that the apparent solver of all Victor's problems and challenges had made sure that the soon-to-be groom would be lost without his bilingual Girl Friday.

With a grateful smile aimed at his agent, Victor translated for Brooke Denise's latest pronouncements.

"She's saying she had considerable trouble getting the paperwork in order, but she thinks it's legal and complete, now, and for us to sign these latest documents." He pointed to the pile resting on the desk. "Your turn."

THE NEXT DAY, the brief ceremony in one of St. Paul's small side chapels was over quickly. Brooke felt a stab of disappointment that it felt like such a hurried affair, but Victor held her glance and smiled as he slipped the wedding band onto her finger, although he had declined to wear one himself.

"Not done in Britain, much, my love," he'd explained when she asked why Denise had purchased only one gold ring instead of two. "A bit too much like a ring through the nose for us Brits, I suppose," he joked.

"What about Frenchmen?" she countered, pointing out his dual heritage.

With less than a second's pause, he replied. "Same thing, I'm afraid."

After a quick lunch at the Ritz where the famous hotel was now surrounded by sandbags and red arrows pointing to the nearest air-raid shelter, Brooke and Victor were whisked by cab onto the train heading for Portsmouth. There, they boarded a ferry to take them across the English Channel to Le Havre in Normandy. Within a few minutes, they'd settled in their stateroom with its double-decker bunks where they barely had enough room to turn around.

"Not exactly the honeymoon suite, I fear," he shrugged.

Brooke asked, "Where's Denise?"

"Just down the passageway," Victor reported. "She's a marvel at securing reservations when no one else can." He paused. "Make her your friend and you'll never be sorry."

"I don't think she's much interested in being *my* friend," Brooke replied, keeping her tone light.

"She will when you make an effort to learn French," he replied, arching a dark eyebrow. "Her only failing is that she's very chauvinistic about her language. She speaks English quite well, or she could never be both my film and my theatrical agent, but to her, French is the only civilized language in the world. Learn it— or at least attempt to —and she'll be your boon companion."

Brooke merely nodded, figuring this was just one of many things she would have to adjust to in the new life she had chosen. But even if she did improve her French, wasn't Denise's bread-and-butter *Victor's* success as an actor, not hers?

Brooke's newly minted husband stood behind her in the cabin's cramped space and folded his arms around her shoulders, pinning her back against his chest, his lips inches from her left ear.

"I shall go to sleep tonight in these rather constrained quarters," he murmured, "dreaming of all the wonderful things I plan to do with you when we sleep tomorrow night in the large, canopied bed at Château de Varney."

Brooke turned in his arms and smiled up at him, grateful for a welcome, reassuring sense that they were, at long last, launching their new life together.

She kissed him playfully on the nose and said, "What a lovely way to contemplate our arrival in Le Belle France."

"*LA Belle France*," Victor corrected, "as in la-la-la L.A. 'La' is the feminine form, which France certainly is," he teased.

"*Ah, bon*," she replied, attempting to sound light-hearted at being reproved over one of her rare attempts to speak his native tongue. The truth was, at that moment she felt like punching the pillow on her bunk.

"*La Belle France,*" she echoed obediently.

"*Ah, oui*," he said, smiling happily. "*Vive La France!*"

"*Vive la* us!'" she parried, eyeing her single bed— and began undressing for the night.

"*Rouen! Rouen en cinq minutes!*"

Hearing the conductor's five-minute warning, Victor jumped up from the upholstered bench in their private compartment on the train that had brought them from the dock in Le Havre to the city nearest his family's Château de Varney. His agent remained seated, her leather portmanteau and briefcase remaining in the overhead rack.

Victor announced happily, "Denise has kindly arranged for a car and driver to pick us up here to take us to *Grandmère's* which is only about twenty kilometers from Rouen." He turned to thank his agent warmly. "Denise, you've been an absolute brick handling all these complicated arrangements, and I can't thank you enough."

"*Ce n'est rien, mon ami.*"

"It is certainly *not* 'nothing!' It's meant everything to us, hasn't it Brooke?"

Brooke was forced to admit that what Victor said was true. It was clear that her husband's agent had moved heaven and earth with a war going on to get them to this moment.

Brooke leaned forward and offered a light kiss on each of Denise's cheeks, European fashion, murmuring with genuine sincerity, "*Merci beaucoup pour tout.*"

Denise returned her smile with surprising enthusiasm.

"*Je vous souhaite à tous les deux une belle lune de miel!*"

Brooke looked at Victor in dismay, but before he could translate,

Denise declared in English, "I said 'I wish you both a very happy honeymoon at the château... *une belle lune de miel.*'"

"Ah..." Brooke responded and then dutifully— and slowly — repeated Denise's previous words in French.

"*Bon!*" exclaimed the agent, and then said in English, "Excellent! If you like, I will find a French tutor for you to study with in Paris, and I can see already that you will be speaking properly in no time! *Au revoir, chérie!*" she trilled, cheerfully bidding them adieu as Brooke and Victor exited the compartment. "See you both in Paris in two weeks."

Brooke thought ruefully, *I speak four consecutive words in French and she's suddenly my new best friend!*

Then, it occurred to her that perhaps there was an important lesson in that.

~

"FEBRUARY CERTAINLY ISN'T the best time to see the château," Victor apologized as their chauffeured Citroën passed by vast rows of apple trees, barren of even a single leaf. "We'll come back in the spring when the trees have masses of pink and white blossoms, and the air is amazingly perfumed." He paused, and added with a rueful smile, "Although, I must say, the pollen that time of year has landed me in the hospital a time or two with a bad asthma attack."

During their half-hour drive from the train, he'd recounted the story of his English mother, a young cable operator, sent over to Normandy during the Great War.

"She'd been trained in England and, because she spoke school-girl French," he explained, "she was recruited as a dispatcher of messages, assigned to the Anglo-French relay station perched on a cliff in our region."

"And your French father? What was he doing?"

Victor smiled. "He had just assumed his first command."

"So he was her boss?"

He laughed. "Her superior *officer*," he corrected. "And just like you and me, my father says that they fell in love instantly and were married in 1914."

"So, she chose him and France," Brooke murmured.

Victor nodded. "Her name was Penelope Kent and, tragically for my father, she died in the influenza pandemic in 1918 when I was barely three and my brother, only eighteen months old."

Brooke's breath caught at hearing this.

"Why have you never told me this before? That she died when you and your brother were so *young*?" she asked.

Victor turned and stared out the passenger window. "Well, just as you've recently told me about being married briefly before we met, I've now told you how my mother died. It was so long ago and I... I just don't think about it much."

Oh, do I understand...

But to Victor she said softly, "I imagine it was pretty tragic for you children as well as your papa. Do you remember her at all?"

"I have only fragments of memories," he said in a wistful tone of voice Brooke had never heard before. He kept his gaze glued to the window. "What I think I remember probably comes from what my father and grandmother have told me over the years."

Brooke's heart had clutched hearing this. Her own little boy, whom she hadn't seen since he was thirteen months old, was approaching his third birthday, the exact same age Victor had been when his mother died.

Wouldn't telling him about Errol at this moment be terribly hurtful?

Relieved by this reprieve, she reflexively pushed away thoughts about her son and gave Victor her complete attention.

"My father didn't meet Barbara Mallory, his second wife, until a decade later at a wine and spirits conference in Paris," he related. "When I was fourteen, he decided that my grandmother should watch over me and my younger brother and keep our calvados business going while he moved to the United States to help run Barbara's family winery outside the town of St. Helena." He looked over at Brooke. "You know of St. Helena?"

She nodded. "In Napa, California? Yes? I filmed on location there once, playing my usual hapless blonde character— this time a daughter whose father's vineyard was swindled away from him." She shrugged. "Yet another good reason for leaving Hollywood."

Victor seized her hand and kissed it. "And how glad I am that you took yourself off to Broadway."

Brooke thought a moment and then asked, "Weren't you upset when your father moved to America?"

Given Victor's and his brother's childhood loss of their mother, wouldn't that circumstance make her seem even more heartless in their eyes if they knew she'd *chosen* to leave her son behind when she headed for the Great White Way?

"Like so many youngsters of our ilk," Victor explained with a slight shrug, "at eight years old, Armand and I were each sent away to school in England. Not being around my father much during my student years just seemed normal to me. We came over to France every summer or my father and Barbara came to France to see us. A couple of times, Armand and I traveled to California to visit them."

He paused and Brooke could see he was recalling a key moment in his past.

"My last year at Eton, a film director came to an amateur theatrical performance that I was in and subsequently offered me my first film role." His expression grew somber. "Armand always preferred the life of a calvados-brewing de Varney. He and his wife Lorraine pretty much run everything these days, thank God." Victor paused. "We now suppose, with the war on, Father probably won't be able to come over at all... nor any of us to travel to see him."

A few minutes earlier, Brooke had nearly blurted out an admission about her child's existence. Winning the battle over honesty was her fear of Victor's justified reaction to that shameful revelation, along with a wave of anxiety at the thought of meeting his august grandmother and Victor's brother and wife within minutes.

Instead of confessing, she took his hand and squeezed it.

"How amazing that your talent was discovered at such an early age," she said.

"The director that cast me in his film was the father of a classmate visiting his son the weekend of the play. The boy was a good mate of mine, so he brought him to see it. Being cast in the man's film was just an incredible stroke of luck."

"As these breaks usually are, don't you think?" she said.

"Complete serendipity," he agreed. "Is that how *you* got into the films?" he asked with a mischievous look. "Discovered having a soda at a drug store?"

Before she could answer, he leaned forward to peer out the front window over the chauffeur's shoulder as their car rolled past two stone stanchions holding up open, wrought-iron gates.

"Ah... look where we are. You'll have to tell me the story of fame finding you another time."

I'll also tell him about Errol, when the timing is right, and show him the photograph I have in my purse...

The tires of the black Citroën crunched across a wide graveled area fronting the two-story, sandstone-and-red-brick manor. Along the slate roof, an impressive series of Mansard windows glittered in the spring sunshine. The car drew adjacent to stone steps the color of churned butter and then rolled to a halt.

Framed in the open front door stood the figure of a surprisingly tall and erect older woman, her white hair pulled back into a sleek chignon. Brooke instantly recognized her as Victor's grandmother, Monique de Varney, from a photo he always carried with him and put in hotel rooms wherever he went to foreign cities and film locations.

Brooke took stock of the slender, elegantly dressed woman in her seventies wearing a simply cut black wool suit with an ivory silk blouse. A single strand of pearls encircled her neck with matching pearl teardrop earrings dangling from her lobes.

Victor leapt out of the car and strode to enfold his *grandmére* in his arms. This left Brooke to thank the driver and direct him around the back of the building to deposit their luggage into the care of some servant she assumed would be on alert at the rear entrance of the château.

Disengaging from Victor's clasp, Monique called out, speaking English with a lilting French accent, "Brooke, my dear, please... do come over here. Let me have a look at you!"

Before Brooke could even take a step forward, Victor's *grandmére* gracefully descended the few stone stairs and wrapped Brooke in a warm embrace. Over Monique's wool-clad shoulder, Brooke caught sight of Victor's younger brother, Armand, and his wife, Lorraine standing in the open doorway.

"Welcome, welcome!" Monique exclaimed, kissing Brooke on both cheeks. "I had truly begun to think that my grandson would never settle down and find a suitable wife like his brother has, but now I see why it took him this long." She smiled directly into Brooke's eyes with a lightness of spirit that soothed the younger woman's anxieties like a cooling sea breeze. "He was waiting to find *you,* and what a lovely, talented young lady you are."

Brooke had no idea how Monique could have formed this opinion on such quick acquaintance, but then her hostess gave her a sly wink.

"Those Charlie Chan detective films I saw you in are pure nonsense, of course, but I've loved you in every one of them! I can tell that you thought them nonsense, too, and since you never seemed to take yourself too seriously, you made it such fun for those of us in the audience to watch you on the screen!"

Monique's affectionate greeting had gone far to put Brooke more at ease about the painful subject of little Errol. Could it be that the characteristic way Europeans dealt with sending young children away to boarding school would make her own choice to abandon an infant in California to seek work three thousand miles away seem less callous and self-centered to the de Varneys than it appeared to the Americans who knew? Or to her mother?

A part of Brooke wanted desperately to believe that the de Varneys would see the situation in that light, but a slightly sick feeling persisted in her abdomen. Would Monique or Victor ever understand why she'd put a continent between herself and her child to escape from a world she felt was closing in on her from all sides? Would anyone comprehend how deep had been her gloom after her baby's birth, followed within weeks by her frantic divorce from the abusive Arnie Warmby? Were any of her new family members in France likely to sympathize with her abrupt decision to leave California in order to save her sanity?

I absolutely must tell Victor about Errol... but at the right time— and when Denise isn't around, for once.

Before she could remind herself that Denise was, at this very moment, arriving by train in Paris and she had no more excuses to delay, Monique cast her arm around Brooke's waist. Side-by-side, they entered the cool, cream-colored confines of the *petit château*, as the older woman was describing her home. Brooke absorbed the sight of de Varney ancestors clad in gilt-frames lining the walls on both sides of the high-vaulted entryway. It was as if she'd stepped out of a life in Los Angeles to which she'd always felt she'd never belonged and into a world that seemed so *right*.

To Brooke, the family portraits and Monique's immediate acceptance of her as her grandson's chosen bride had turned out to be the most marvelous welcoming committee that she could ever have imagined.

And perhaps, she thought, her new life was going to be the dream she'd always longed for with a man who loved her and wanted his family to feel the same.

For the first time, the constant worm of worry about the life she'd left behind receded to a far corner of her mind where it would be easier to ignore.

THE DAYS SPENT at Château de Varney sped by with Brooke enveloped in a cocoon of gentle acceptance the likes of which she'd never experienced. In fact, Brooke got the distinct feeling that the entire family had breathed a collective sigh of relief that the "artistic" member of the de Varneys, who had opted not to carry on the tradition of making calvados, had done more than put his chosen career on track. Brooke could also tell that everyone in the household seemed pleased that the scion of the de Varneys had— in Monique's words —"finally settled down with a woman like you, my dear, who has obviously made him an extremely happy newlywed."

On the brief occasions when they were alone— and not in bed —and Brooke had felt yet another impulse to come clean about her past, the moments they shared seemed too perfect to broach such a difficult and complicated subject.

The time and place has to be just right, Brooke told herself repeatedly, and she almost welcomed the next distraction presented to the de Varney family circle, albeit a disturbing one.

Unsettling war news began reaching the château at an increasingly alarming rate, although Brooke could tell that everyone was still doing their best to create a celebratory atmosphere for the newlyweds.

Near the end of March, Denise Louette rang Victor at the château to announce that his Paris flat on Rue Saint-Dominique near Les Invalides had been vacated. Located less than a mile from the Eiffel Tower, the tenants to whom he'd leased it while he'd been away these last months had a sudden change of plans because the man of the household had been conscripted into the army. His wife had then decided to move to the country with their two daughters to stay with her parents.

"We can move back into the flat now? That's splendid news, Denise!" he exclaimed, glancing over at Brooke sitting on the divan in the *petit salon* where the two of them often took tea in the afternoons. "That's extremely convenient, isn't it?" he enthused, "especially since you've lined up those meetings for me in town. Yes. Those dates sound fine."

Then Victor grew silent, scribbling down notations as Brooke could faintly hear Denise detailing various film and theatrical possibilities that might be of interest.

"Excellent work, Denise! I'm most appreciative."

There was another pause and Brooke could picture the talent agent going down her ever-present checklist.

Listening intently, Victor suddenly exclaimed, "What a good idea! Of course, you must have his number, yes?" He glanced over at Brooke. "She'll be thrilled!"

When he'd hung up the receiver, Brooke set aside a book printed in English that she'd found in the library and gazed at him questioningly.

Victor volunteered, "Denise just told me that a friend of mine in Paris, a radio journalist and foreign correspondent for the major American broadcasting networks, has been trying to get in touch with me. It's given Denise a brilliant idea. Perhaps she could get you some work broadcasting on the English-language service."

Brooke felt instantly buoyed by the idea and surprised that

Denise had made the suggestion. But would this fellow actually hire her only on Denise's say so?

"Who is this contact of hers?" Brooke asked.

"Like me, he's also her client. His name is Christophe Laurent. He's also a 'hybrid' as we've teased each other over the years."

"Hybrid? You mean he's French and something else?"

Victor nodded, "Half of him is your lot— American. He and I met some five years ago at a café frequented by journalists and theatrical types. In our conversation that day, I discovered that, like me, he also has dual citizenship. He got his French passport thanks to his late French father, who was also a journalist until he suddenly dropped dead from overwork due to a stroke."

"Oh, how sad," murmured Brooke.

Victor rose from his seat beside the small table where the telephone sat.

"His American mother had been studying landscape painting at L'École des Beaux Arts in Paris while *her* father was head of Ford Motors in France." Victor chuckled, relishing the tale. "Christophe's parents apparently met when his father was covering the annual Artist's Ball for his newspaper and saw Christophe's mum covered in gold paint— and little else."

"Sounds like my kind of woman!" Brooke laughed. "Is this Christophe a hard-working soul like his dad, or a wild bohemian, like his mom?"

"A little of both, I suspect. While I was spending summers here or in Barbizon or the South of France, Christophe was shipped off to his mother's parents on a lake outside Detroit, Michigan, where he had to speak English day and night. And like me, he spent the rest of the year with his father's family in their flat in Paris with avant-garde artists coming out of the woodwork round the clock."

"What an intriguing fellow," she said with a laugh, topping off Victor's teacup with the steaming brew from Monique's Limoges teapot.

Victor crossed the room to take a seat beside her and took a sip from his cup. Smiling, he proposed, "Let's plan a soiree as soon as we get back to Paris this week. I have so many interesting friends like Christophe that I'm anxious for you to meet— and for them to meet *you*."

"But they'll all be babbling away in French, and I won't have a clue what's going on," objected Brooke.

"Think of it this way, it will be a good opportunity for you to begin to gain fluency." He smiled and added, "And by the way, Denise just told me she's lined up a tutor for you as soon as you settle in. A Mademoiselle Sabine Arquette who has private, adult students come to her flat on avenue Kléber."

"Oh, God, Victor... I was terrible at languages in school."

"You'll do fine! You'll just have to decide you want to learn and you will!" he assured her. "And if we give a party, you'll be able to speak to Christophe in English. And, of course, we'll invite Sylvia Beach, the American who owns the Shakespeare and Company bookstore." He paused. "And then there's my friend, Josephine Baker."

"The Negro entertainer?" Brooke asked, her curiosity piqued by the mention of the African-American who came to France in the mid-twenties and at a mere nineteen years of age, made her bare-breasted feather dance famous— and notorious —the world over.

"The very one," he replied and swiftly looked away, appearing to concentrate on the notes he had taken during Denise's phone call.

Brooke fell silent as Victor continued to study what he'd scribbled down.

"Victor?"

He looked up. "Hmmm?"

"I'm guessing that Denise will probably have you cast in a film the first week we get to Paris, won't she?"

"If I'm lucky and my meetings go as Denise anticipates."

"Well..." she began slowly, "I must admit that I'm feeling a bit lost and trying to imagine what my day-to-day life is going to be like, especially if you go off to do a film right away and I'm alone in the apartment. I don't know anyone... and I obviously don't speak the language—"

"But you'll be busy learning it, won't you?" he interrupted, sounding pleased he'd found a solution so quickly. "And maybe there'll be doing some free-lance work at Christophe's broadcasting outfit."

"My getting an actual job so quickly is probably a longshot. Everything is so new and I don't know my way around Paris, or have a movie to do myself, or any friends or—"

"You'll *make* new friends," he insisted. "There's a large ex-pat American community in town, although you really must spend most of your time with French-speakers so... well, you know... you'll pick up the language more quickly."

Brooke turned away from him to gaze out the tall windows in the *petit salon*. She could tell Victor was mildly put out that her problems of adjustment to such new surroundings were becoming his concern as well.

But he could show me that he understood and sympathized just a little, she fretted silently.

A few moments elapsed in silence when Victor smiled as if all her problems were solved.

"I don't think working for my friend Christophe is such a long-shot, as you say. Laurent broadcasts as a foreign correspondent in *English* to the American outlets he works for, as well as in French for Radio France. Denise suggested she make an inquiry about you doing some recording for them... and I agreed with her that it's better that she be the one to contact him so he won't feel pressured by me if he can't hire a second on-air talent."

How odd, Brooke thought, that it was Denise who apparently empathized with her feeling at sea in a new country without the skill to speak French, along with no job and no friends.

Trying to tamp down her fledgling hopes, she asked, "You think Denise holds enough sway with this fellow?"

"In fact, he hired her as his agent on my recommendation when he needed professional representation in negotiations with his network bosses. He's a big fan of hers."

"My, how lucky is that?" she murmured.

"Well, he'd moved from just being a reporter to an on-air presenter broadcasting to Great Britain, Ireland, Canada, Australia — all the English-speaking countries."

"Including back to the States?" asked Brooke, feeling a flicker of optimism. Her credits as a film actress might be a plus in Laurent's eyes.

"To the States for sure," Victor confirmed. "Now with war threatening France and the avalanche of news, I'll bet the poor man could use some help."

Victor smiled, clearly pleased with himself for passing on Denise's suggestion. It wasn't an acting job, but Brooke's spirits took a definite upward swing.

"And if Denise and I do this for you, will you do what Denise wants and what *I* want? Take French conversation lessons with Mademoiselle Arquette?"

To Brooke, the idea of having to study a language whose pronunciation gave her so much heartburn filled her with instant dread. She hesitated a moment, then turned decisively and leaned into Victor's outstretched arms.

"I will. That is, if you two won't tease me all the time about my American accent," she declared, half joking and half serious.

Victor wrapped his arms tightly around her, his chin resting on the top of her head. "Oh, I can't promise that, but I think once you put your mind to it and stick with it, you'll improve a lot. Trust me, I do remember how hard it was to learn to speak decent French when I came back from my English boarding school to Paris." He gently bussed her on the ear. "But, I have utter faith in you, darling."

Then he leaned back, bent down, and kissed her firmly on the lips before pulling away.

"Oh... don't stop," she said on a long breath.

"I don't plan to," he replied. "But first let me call Denise back and have her arrange for you to meet Christophe Laurent next week and let friends know that we're hosting a soiree." He flashed her the grin that had endeared him to so many moviegoers. "Then, let's go upstairs where I plan some other tricks in French that we can practice together."

3

The train journey from Rouen to Paris took under three hours with most of the railway cars jammed with men clad in the ill-fitting uniforms of new recruits to the French military.

Brooke felt Victor's eyes on her as she gazed raptly out the train window of their private compartment at the sight of the beautiful Parisian outer boroughs coming into view. It was early April and the fruit trees and purple wisteria were just beginning to flower.

"Oh, my..." she breathed, thrilled at the sight of the two-and-three story buildings with elaborate stone scrolls and entablature over their windows and doors, their entrances shaded in summer by columns of tall, green trees on both sides of the street.

As the train began to slow in its approach to the station, she caught quick glimpses of wrought-iron-and-glass entrances to the Paris metro. Along the sidewalks, small tables and spindly chairs outside cafés awaited customers, along with the improving weather. Her breath caught at the sight of the Eiffel Tower peeking over the slate rooftops with their rows of Mansard gables.

"To take it all in for the first time is quite amazing, isn't it?" Victor said softly just as the train entered the darkened route into Saint-Lazare station.

"Glorious," she murmured.

For Brooke, it was far more than any adjective she could come up with to impress Victor. To her, the fact that she was in France at all was rather a miracle. She'd long dreamed of coming here, especially after she'd had a small part in a movie supposedly set in France. She'd been directed as a member of the revolutionary rabble to run down a lane dotted with cookie-cutter cafés on a make-believe street flanked by false-fronted faux stone buildings. From that day forward, she had vowed, somehow, to see the real City of Light for herself.

Now here she was, married to a French movie star and about to step into a world she would soon call home. She could hardly have dreamed the fortuitous path her life had taken. From the pretty little blonde raised during the Depression in the treeless flats south of Wilshire Boulevard in dry, dusty Los Angeles, her arrival in such style in Paris was truly unimaginable.

A porter, escorted by Denise Louette, suddenly appeared beside their train carriage to collect the luggage. Victor's agent bussed each of them on both cheeks, led them to a waiting cab, and directed the driver, "Number seventeen, Rue Saint-Dominique, but first, the Ministry of Information offices near Gare Montparnasse."

Once the taxi pulled away from the curb, Denise continued speaking to Victor in rapid French. In response, he smiled broadly and turned to his new bride.

"Denise says we're to drop you off for your interview at Christophe Laurent's office on our way to the flat."

"What?" protested Brooke. "Does it have to be today? I wanted us to go to our new home together, Victor, and frankly, I'd like some time to get my bearings."

The agent, who understood every word Brooke had said, commented to them in English, "Christophe is very busy, given all that's going on with France's preparations for a possible invasion. He can see you today, at this hour. Otherwise, he said he'd not be available until after he gets back from an assignment at the border with Belgium. And God only knows how many days that could be."

She's trying to help you... accept the situation gracefully...

"I see... well, thanks."

Brooke sank against the back seat and stared out the window at the large buildings looming to her right.

"Here we are," Denise announced brightly, and she opened the door.

Leaving the cab at the curb with its motor running, Victor's agent led the way into a labyrinth of corridors and offices in the Ministry of Information building. Once inside the shadowed, gloomy interior, Brooke wondered that there were no lights turned on, but soon concluded it was to save power. As they advanced down the corridor, she found the entire atmosphere totally depressing.

Over her shoulder Denise reminded Brooke briskly, "Christophe was very kind to see you on short notice."

"I appreciate your arranging this meeting," Brooke replied politely, trudging behind the woman clad in her familiar dark wool suit enhanced this day by a stunning Lanvin silk scarf.

Denise turned down another tiled hallway and paused in front of a door with a frosted glass partition that declared: *Presse Internationale.*

"I explained to Christophe that you are Victor's new wife," she announced. "He knows that you were a Hollywood actress and you've offered to help in the bureau."

"Doing what, exactly?" Brooke asked, feeling as she had, years before, going hat-in-hand to film auditions for parts she rarely got.

"I don't actually know," Denise replied, planting a quick succession of knocks on the door. "He just said things have become quite chaotic now with the threatened German invasion, and perhaps he could use someone to— in his words —'hold down the fort' when he went out on assignments."

"Well, that doesn't sound very—" began Brooke when the door opened, revealing a tall, broad-shouldered figure with tousled blond hair several shades darker than Brooke's own. The straw thatch looked as if it hadn't seen a brush in days.

Both the man's slacks and wool jacket were slightly rumpled. His cloth shirt was unbuttoned to mid-chest and looked as if it had come straight out of the wash. His face, which might or might not be handsome, had not seen a razor in a couple of days. Near the door were a canvas rucksack and a small leather suitcase apparently poised for departure.

"Oh, it's you two," he said distractedly, running a large hand through his hair with a gesture that explained its unkempt condition. "Come in, come in. This is Victor's wife, I take it?" he added as if Brooke were merely a new typewriter or a box of fresh pencils.

As with Denise's conversations with Victor, she and the man who'd opened the door began speaking rapidly in French. Brooke could only assume he was Christophe Laurent when he indicated that she should take a chair. The seat was positioned in front of a desk piled high with papers, open books, and crumpled evidence of discarded news copy strewn everywhere, including the floor.

Exasperated hearing only French, Brooke remained standing while Denise made introductions.

"Could you please speak in English," she broke in.

Christophe turned to look at her quizzically, then grinned.

"I do apologize," he said with a faint bow. "That's right. Denise told me you speak hardly a word of French and *I* hardly know *what* language I'm communicating in these days. Please, do sit down."

Denise swiftly intervened before Brooke could move a muscle.

With a nod to her she said in English, "Victor's waiting in a cab downstairs, so I'll just go get him settled in the apartment and come back to collect you when you're finished here."

And without another word, the agent turned on her heel and hurried out the door, shutting it behind her. Christophe once again indicated that Brooke should take a seat in the chair opposite his littered desktop.

As he sat down he said, "I suppose the first question to ask you is why you think appearing in a few Charlie Chan films qualifies you to be a deputy in a press office?"

Taken aback by his abruptness that cut to the chase, she managed to reply, "I can read a script with precision and appropriate emphasis, and I'm told I have a very distinctive speaking voice."

"Two points for you," he said with a nod.

"As for holding the fort in this office, you'll have to show me what else I could do to help here."

He dug under one of the paper piles on his desk and retrieved a pen that he stuffed in his thin battered briefcase. Looking up at her with a steady gaze, he added, "I need a number two in the office since I'm the sole American around here whose purpose is to try to tell the truth and let the world decide for *itself* what's going on in this war."

Deliberately modulating her voice to parrot the news broadcaster she'd once played in a thoroughly forgettable film, she declared with intended emphasis, "Another reason I might be useful is that I'm organized when I work on a project. If circumstances require, I can ad-lib quite cleverly."

Her interviewer cocked an amused eyebrow. "Well, good for you. Tell me why you want to work in a place like this?"

"Because—"

Before she could answer, he glanced at the clock on the wall and blurted, "Oh, hell! My train leaves in ten minutes. Do you type?"

Brooke was rather glad she hadn't been required to answer the question about *why* she wanted a job in a press office. The truth was, she just didn't want to sit alone in an apartment with nothing to do in a city where she was a total stranger.

"Well, do you?" he asked impatiently. "Type?"

Brooke offered a tight smile, grateful she'd taken typing in high school.

"I'm sure you'll be surprised to learn that I type a hundred words a minute— or better—when I'm not harassed by bosses screaming at me."

Brooke had sworn to herself that she would never type another *word* once she began making enough money as an actress and could abandon the secretarial pool in Warner Brothers' Story Department.

"I don't scream at women," Christophe said, the corners of his mouth twitching. "I yell. At the walls, thus far, because I have no help in this crazy outfit."

"There's only *you*, working for all the American broadcasting companies in Paris?" she asked in disbelief.

"I work for a group of broadcast news outlets in the States as well as for Radio France." He gestured over his shoulder. "A couple of other fellows down the hall are doing the same for companies like Reuters or major American newspapers. None of us can seem to find qualified help these days."

Brooke was beginning to understand the utter dishevelment of not only Christophe himself, but his entire office.

"So semi-qualified help might be acceptable?" she asked, trying to keep a straight face.

"Maybe," he said, running his hand through his hair once again and doing further damage to his blond thatch. "Since it's only me in this office, it's getting impossible to report on what's going on behind all the bullshit spewed by 'official sources' and also keep this office going."

"Which requires...?" Brooke asked expectantly.

"Oh, the usual. Answering the phone and taking accurate messages... typing up research notes, news copy, formatting scrips properly. Coming up with solid editorial ideas would be great, but mainly it's just helping me to keep my various damn projects in hand."

Christophe didn't bother to apologize for his language, and merely pointed to his desk, every inch of its surface piled high with paper.

"If you can sort out this mess and use that sexy voice of yours to deliver some of the back-of-the-book pieces on-air occasionally—"

"What's 'back-of-the-book?'" she interrupted.

"It's an old print term from magazine publications— the stuff that comes after the important news in the front. You know, fluff-and-puff. Pieces about French women now having to make their soufflés out of coffee grinds, or some such these days. Or a story of a government minister's son oh-so-bravely enlisting in the army," he said, his tone mocking. He stashed a notebook and additional pens into his briefcase. "Some of my editors in America love that sort of crap. I'll suggest stories like that, and we'll see if you can report, write, and broadcast a few each week." He gestured again to the mountain of detritus surrounding his typewriter. "But most of all, I need you to put all this into some sort of order, okay?"

Without waiting for her to answer, he rose from behind the desk and snapped shut the metal clips on his briefcase.

"I've got to get out of here this very minute to catch a train east and find my way to the goddamn Maginot Line where, rumor has it, the real battles are supposed to begin in a day or two."

"France will truly be at war?" she asked, shocked by the reality of his words after so many months of the "Phony War" non-action that followed Hitler's initial invasion of other parts of Europe.

"Looks that way."

He dug into his pants pocket and thrust out his hand.

"Here's a key to the office."

"You're giving me the job?"

He nodded in the affirmative, directing her hurriedly, "Make me a copy and have it waiting for me when I get back. Leave it with the man at the desk where we come in the building." He grabbed the case off his desk. "Get here by ten and stay until six, all right?" He bolted for the door.

"What's the salary?" she called after him.

"Salary?" He turned to face her. "Denise said you were volunteering."

Brooke pointed to the shambles on his desk.

"Look, Mr. Laurent... I'm a professional, just like you are."

"It's Christophe," he interjected, "or 'Christopher' if you like, since you're American and I'm a half-breed."

Ignoring this, Brooke declared, "If you want me to sort this mess, type your stuff, chase down and read stories of my own in English occasionally on-air, plus do all the other things you mentioned, I'll happily do it all, but for a wage. At least *something*."

The foreign correspondent paused, one hand reaching for the strap on his canvas rucksack. He flung it over his right shoulder and grabbed his small suitcase with the hand holding his briefcase. After a long moment, he nodded.

"Okay. You're right," he agreed. "You're a pro. Those films you were in were totally inane, but I thought you were definitely a 'presence' on the screen, so I imagine you can read a news script— or learn to."

He paused again and Brooke could see the wheels turning

around in his head. She tried to imagine under what circumstances this no-nonsense war correspondent would have been corralled into seeing a Charlie Chan film, but he'd apparently viewed at least one of the four she'd co-starred in— and remembered her.

"Here's the thing, Mr.— uh —Christopher," Brooke declared. "I'd love to have the job, but I don't work for free."

Christophe glanced in the direction of his disastrous desktop and proposed, "How 'bout I give you ten dollars a week out of my own salary, plus all the lousy, diluted coffee you can drink? That way I don't have to consult any of the 'suits' I work for in New York and just hire you outright. You start Monday. What do you say? Deal?"

That's about 20,000 francs. Not great, but it would pay my monthly rent if I were on my own, so it's not totally insulting.

The door to the office had nearly closed before Brooke echoed to his back, "Deal."

Oh, my God... I actually am employed as a news broadcaster!

It wasn't an acting job, but close enough to it, and maybe a lot more interesting, she thought, smiling at the door Christopher Laurent had just shut with a bang.

⁊   ∾

TRUE TO HER WORD, Denise had a taxi waiting by the curb when Brooke emerged from the Ministry of Information building. Her new boss had streaked out of the office leaving Brooke to lock the door to the press office with the key she'd been given. Within minutes she and Denise were headed in the taxi for Victor's residence at number seventeen, Rue Saint-Dominique.

As it turned out, the second-story flat wasn't quite what Brooke expected, and in some ways, was far grander than she'd ever imagined.

Only a few blocks from Les Invalides, the five-story sandstone building featured wrought iron balconies below each window. Directly across the street sat a similar, block-long apartment that had obviously been designed and built by the same architect. The two structures, therefore, filtered out most of the light in Victor's spacious front sitting room despite the ten-foot-high pane glass openings flanked by exterior shutters on each side.

"Behold the *grand salon*," Victor joked as Brooke and Denise passed the threshold.

He flicked on the wall switch illuminating a pair of electrified chandeliers hanging overhead. The room's fourteen-foot-high ceilings and the pale, sage brocade covering the interior walls were stunning examples of turn-of-the-century elegance.

Brooke's gaze swept the room, taking in the grandeur of sweeping ivory velvet drapes and thick Persian carpets blanketing the parquet floors. An intricately carved, white marble fireplace also conveyed the opulence of a previous century, as did tall, ornate mirrors with gilded wooden frames. Ennobling the flat to an even higher degree in the main living areas were Louis XIV cream-colored chairs and matching settees setting off the dark wood of several massive armoires placed against the walls.

To Brooke, the elaborately decorated chambers almost seemed like a movie set on an MGM studio sound stage.

"As soon as your tenants left," Denise explained to Victor, "I had a cleaning crew in here preparing everything for your arrival."

"You are a wonder, as usual," Victor replied.

Meanwhile, the building's concierge bustled around a mountain of luggage that their taxi driver had hauled up the stairs and into the black-and-white checkered tile foyer.

Denise pointed to a room off the entrance hall.

"Victor, the mail that arrived while you've been at the château is waiting for you on your desk in the library. Next to it I've left you a calendar marked with the meetings you have scheduled this week."

The two continued plotting Victor's re-entry to the Paris film scene, prompting Brooke to wander farther into the apartment, curious to see more of her new home.

After inspecting the kitchen with a large, enameled stove and large copper cook pots and frying pans lined with tin hanging on hooks in the ceiling, she moved down a darkened corridor toward a room that shone like a bright beacon at the end of the shadowed hall. Stepping through the doorway with its carved, wooden molding, she entered a large, sun-filled bedroom overlooking a back garden. Peering out a bank of floor-to-ceiling windows, she gazed down at tall trees and clipped hedges whose leaves were just beginning to sprout this bright, April spring day.

A bed with a luxurious beige silk coverlet was piled high with plush, pale linen pillows trimmed with lace. Attached to the wall above the bed was a gilded, semi-circular wooden coronet festooned with more beige silk cascading to either side of the tufted ivory velvet headboard.

"Well, what do you think?"

Victor stood in the doorway smiling.

"It's a chamber fit for a king," she said, guarding against the irony that could have easily slipped into her tone.

"*And* for a queen," he replied, his arms outstretched as he advanced across the room. "In all the flurry of our arrival, I forgot to carry you over the threshold, but I can certainly welcome you to our bedroom."

And with that, he gently pushed her the few feet between where she stood and the near side of the plump duvet.

As they lay on the bed and his arms enfolded her, Brooke asked, "Denise has gone?"

"Very much so," he whispered against her ear. "It's just us, now."

DUSK HAD FALLEN by the time Brooke woke up and stretched her arms above her head, luxuriating in the silk sheets caressing her bare skin. She reveled in her body's luscious, achy sensation that brought back flashes of the passion they'd shared that afternoon. She found herself relieved that being married, now, had not dulled the intense feelings and pleasure they had always evoked in each other in bed.

She looked over at Victor who was still sleeping, turned, now, onto his stomach, his head buried beneath a pile of pillows. One bronze shoulder stood out in dark contrast against the pale fabrics layering the bed.

Brooke rose carefully so as not to wake him and slipped on the linen shirt he'd so hastily discarded on the floor. Barefoot, she padded down the hallway and into the front foyer to pull her own dressing gown from one of her suitcases standing among the several left there earlier. She abandoned Victor's shirt and donned her gown.

Tying the matching silk belt around her waist, she wandered into a book-lined room she surmised was the library-office that Victor used when he was in Paris. She was surprised to see that Denise had thoughtfully ignited a blaze in the marble-fronted fireplace before she'd left, although these hours later, it was merely a modest pile of glowing embers.

On the desk, unanswered mail was standing in a neat stack, as were several Paris newspapers, all awaiting Victor's perusal.

Brooke crossed to a wall of bookshelves and scanned the rows of leather bindings, looking for something in English she might enjoy reading at some point. Disappointed in her search, she turned, her eyes landing on the mail awaiting Victor's attention. Her gaze was caught by a bold, flowery hand with an address ending in "Norway" inscribed in the corner of the missive that had been sent *Par Avion.*

For a moment, she thought it might be one of her own letters to Victor she'd posted to Norway, and now had been returned. Closer inspection revealed a last name in the sender's address that she recognized.

"Olivia Eriksen?" she murmured.

Brooke peeled back the first envelope to find a second and a third and several more penned in the same handwriting, stacked pristinely by Denise before she'd left.

Brooke couldn't stop staring at the envelopes' feminine script. Why would Victor's co-star in the movie, shot before Christmas in Scandinavia, post so many letters to Victor's home address, once filming ended?

A voice behind Brooke made her jump.

"Well, hello there, darling."

Brooke whirled in place to take in the sight of Victor, his chest nicely muscled and with the merest sprinkling of dark hair. The rest of him was clad only in his undershorts.

"Victor—"

"I see you, at least, have found something decent to put on."

Ignoring his obvious wish that she help him search his luggage for something to wear, Brooke scooped up the letters postmarked from Norway and advanced toward her husband of less than a week. She waved them in her right hand and struggled to keep her voice even as her heart pounded in her chest.

"Why would Olivia Eriksen be writing you all these letters from Norway, now that the film has wrapped?" she asked.

Victor's gaze locked on to the collection of tissue-thin airmail posts she'd extended toward him.

"What?" he said, swiftly taking them from her. "What do you have there?"

"You tell me."

He glanced down for a few seconds. When he looked up, Brooke noticed the kind of smile he often produced when he was talking to one of his fans.

"I'll have to read them later, but since Olivia lives in Norway, I expect she was asked to do some sound dubbing." He shrugged his bare shoulders. "We recorded the film in both English and French, but her Norwegian accent scrambled the dialogue more than a few times, I imagine. She's probably writing after each re-dubbing session with an apology."

To Brooke, it seemed an overly-involved explanation as she watched Victor cross to his desk, pull out a drawer, and deposit the letters inside.

He slid the drawer shut, turned the key, and said with a chuckle, "I'll deal with them later and let her know I forgive her battered English, just as I do your French."

Brooke made no reply and an awkward silence filled the space between them.

Finally Victor said, "I don't know about you, but I'm famished! What say you that I find my dressing gown and then make you a perfect cheese omelet? Denise is in the process of finding us a new housekeeper who cooks, but I'm sure she has already stocked our larder with whatever we need."

And with that, he turned and headed for the kitchen by way of the suitcases in the foyer. For several long moments, Brooke stood riveted in place, listening to him rummaging through his luggage. Then, she crossed behind the desk and reached for the drawer where Victor had sequestered the letters.

It was locked and the key was no longer in its slot.

4

The newlyweds sat on kitchen stools under a solitary shaded light bulb hung over a counter where under normal circumstances, explained Victor, someone else made meals for him. Brooke slid the last morsel of Victor's excellent omelet into her mouth, struggling not to act like a jealous fool over the matter of the letters postmarked from Norway. Try as she might, however, she couldn't let the subject go. Wiping her lips with a linen napkin, she set down her fork.

"Delicious, wasn't it?" Victor prompted. "In this country, no one can consider themselves a decent French citizen until they've learned to make a proper omelet and soufflé."

"Very impressive," Brooke replied with a faint nod.

"Poor Denise apologized that, with all this rationing, she couldn't find an ounce of decent coffee beans anywhere, but she promised she'll keep looking, even if she has to resort to the black market."

"How enterprising of her." Brooke fell silent, and then blurted, "Victor, we should talk."

He leaned back and cocked his head to one side as if her serious tone was an oddity.

"About what?"

"Did you and Olivia Eriksen know each other before you did

your latest film? I seem to remember reading something about a play you performed in together."

Victor offered a casual nod. "She had a minor part in a show we did in London that lasted less than two weeks. The project made me swear to myself I'd never act on a stage ever again. When those same producers wanted to make a film in Norway, I suppose she was an obvious choice because she did speak English and French, however imperfectly."

Brooke put a hand on his arm.

"Look, we're both not kids, and there's no need to delve too deeply into past relationships, or anything. Even so, I have to say I find it odd that you should have a pile of air mail letters from your leading lady stacked up waiting for you in Paris if there wasn't anything... well... happening between you and—"

"Really, Brooke," he protested. "You and I just got *married*! Surely you don't think..."

His voice trailed off as Brooke felt gloom settle over her like a London fog.

"Actually I don't quite know what to think. After all, you've received at least seven letters from her posted from Norway and I never received even *one* from you in London."

Victor sprang off his stool and seized her forcefully by the hand.

"Come with me," he commanded, and nearly dragged her behind him as he strode toward the library. Over his shoulder, he gritted out, "You are the woman I married! The woman I supposedly want in my life."

He let go of her hand and marched to the desk. From the pocket of his burgundy silk dressing gown he extracted a small, brass key, thrusting it into the side drawer. Yanking it open, he seized the stack of letters he had stored there less than an hour earlier. Grim-faced, he stalked over to the fireplace and threw them on the dying embers that Denise had lit before she'd left. After a few seconds of suffocating silence between them, the paper edges began to curl and turn black.

"See how much these letters— whatever they contain —mean to me?"

"But Olivia sent them to you *after* your film was finished,"

Brooke countered. "I think I deserve to know if you two were involved—"

"This kind of discussion is not a very good way to start out married life together, do you think?" he interjected, his tone curt. "If you don't trust *me*, trust *this!*" He yanked a fireplace poker from its stand and furiously stirred the remaining coals, prompting the stationery to burst into flames. "These are probably just Olivia hoping I won't refuse to work with her again sometime... but no matter." He leaned the poker against the wall and glared. "See? The letters are gone. They mean nothing and Olivia means nothing. Does that make you happy?"

Brooke searched his handsome face and saw only that he'd raised his chin with an injured air and cast her a look that challenged her to call him a liar.

Do I want to be proven right, or do I want to be happy?

Perhaps he did have a fling with Olivia Eriksen once-upon-a-time, she thought. Perhaps, what he was telling her now was true: the letters burning on the hearth were only progress reports on the voice dubbing she'd probably had to do in post-production.

But if the letters were innocent or meant nothing, then why be so quick to burn them up?

Brooke struggled to maintain her composure. She forced herself to take stock of the fact she'd certainly had a few of her own minor dalliances working on films before she'd met Victor. And even if Olivia Eriksen still had feelings for him, the actress's desire to rekindle a response in her charismatic co-star might explain why there was such a barrage of communication.

She silently reminded herself, *Victor de Varney chose you!* She summoned to mind the scene of his bursting into her theater dressing room in London with his grandmother's ring in his pocket.

Silence endured for several more seconds before she took a deep breath and searched for the oil needed to pour on the troubled waters boiling between them.

Finally, she said, "What would make me happy," echoing his words as she walked toward him, the letters now reduced to ashes, "is to know that, despite this war... despite whatever went before you and I have vowed to join our lives... we're married now.

Together, we can start a totally new life," adding gently, "'forsaking all others,' as the saying goes."

Brooke imagined that the look of relief that transformed Victor's features was the same feeling also flooding her chest.

"Come here, darling," he said, pulling her close. He smiled down at her. "I love you very much and I must tell you that I find your fit of wifely jealousy quite charming." He bent towards her, touching his forehead to hers and whispered, "I do believe we've had our first spat... and look how well we've survived it."

DESPITE BROOKE'S idea that she and Victor put all previous relationships behind them and start anew, she simply could not get past her shock at seeing Olivia Eriksen's stack of letters on his desk. The following day, she did her best to shake her growing unease and suspicion since the discovery but found herself unable to shed the doubt burrowing a hole in her gut.

And if he wasn't going to tell the truth, Brooke's guilt about not having revealed the truth about her son Errol eased. And if he suddenly confessed, Brooke realized, the truth was, she really didn't want to know the answer.

What if he'd had the affair? What do I do then? Blow up my life just as the entire world may be catching on fire?

The sound of an automobile horn startled her from her dark musings. Victor strode to one of the tall windows in the sitting room, peered down on Rue Saint-Dominique from their second-floor flat, and exclaimed with excitement, "It's here! Denise somehow did it! Come look! Your wedding present has arrived!"

Brooke slowly lifted her eyes from the pages of one of the few books she'd found in the study published in English. Whatever the gift might be, Victor had instructed his agent to obtain it and hadn't bothered to shop for it himself. The knife she felt in her midsection twisted a bit more.

He turned and reached for her hand, pulling her to her feet.

"Denise Louette should command the French Army!" he chortled. "Come. Come have a look!"

"What in the world...?" she protested, making little attempt to hide her annoyance at his interruption.

Dropping the book on the settee, she allowed him to lead her downstairs. She maintained her silence during their ride down the iron birdcage elevator and out the entrance of the building.

A man stood at attention at the curb, dressed in the livery of a chauffeur. Upon seeing them, he declared in heavily accented English, "Good day, *monsieur*." Smiling broadly at Brooke, he made a sweeping gesture that ended in a low bow and declared, as if he were reciting lines in a play he had memorized, "Madame de Varney, your wedding present from your husband has been safely delivered to your door!"

Parked next to the curb was a shiny new, jaunty two-door dark green car with chrome bumpers and black leather seats.

"It's a Simca 5," Victor said, proudly. "In British racing green, I might add." He smiled boyishly, disclosing, "I chose the color to honor my late mother."

"How sweet," murmured Brooke. "You and I will share it—"

"Certainly not!" Victor interrupted. "It's the perfect woman's car, and besides, Denise has contracted with a chauffeured driving service for all my needs." He pointed to the forest green hood. "It's compact, easy to park, yet has room for three passengers and the driver. Plus, it has a nice, spacious boot with room for whatever you might need to transport."

He threw one arm around her shoulder while extending his other hand to the delivery man to hand over the car keys. Turning, he seized her palm, and with great ceremony, placed the keys there, closing her fingers around them with his own. Brooke tried not to wince when the indented metal edges pressed sharply into her skin.

"Happy belated wedding present, Brooke, my love."

She read in his gaze an expectation of gratitude and approval for it was, indeed, a very generous gift. But was it also a rather obvious attempt to paper over flagrant disloyalty—or a genuine effort to prove how much he cared for her?

The truth was, Brooke thought as an awkward silence grew between them, the past was over and couldn't be changed. Perhaps he truly was trying to prove to her that her doubts about his fidelity were those of a skittish, once-divorced new bride.

After a long pause, she summoned a smile and said, "It's an absolutely *wonderful* present, Victor. Thank you *so* much."

He nodded, appearing both pleased and relieved to hear her words. He turned and handed a gratuity to the car delivery man, including a few additional francs for him to take the metro back to the Simca showroom.

The man, trim in his livery attire, strode off whistling, his hand in his pants pocket jiggling the money just given him. Victor turned back and offered Brooke a slight bow.

"May all your journeys in this little chariot be joyful and safe."

Brooke had the same wish. She yearned for the peace and security of a loving, trusting relationship with her new husband, and perhaps, now, they could, indeed, start anew. Her desire was especially true in the light of all the other uncertainties facing the two of them as it almost seemed inevitable, now, that war was coming to France.

Her thoughts fled to the approaching task the following Monday of finding her way via confusing Paris streets to the Ministry of Information. She could only guess what she would encounter on the other side of the door marked *Presse Internationale*, or what to expect in her new role as deputy to the peripatetic and perpetually harassed Christopher Laurent.

THE AFTERNOON FOLLOWING the arrival of the Simca 5, Denise Louette appeared at the door to their flat less than an hour after Victor had gone off to a late appointment. The agent was dressed, as usual, in her chic dark suit and white silk blouse with yet another luxurious colorful scarf draped around her neck.

Reading Brooke's surprised expression at seeing her standing at the front door, she asked, "Didn't Victor tell you? He instructed me to arrange for you to start your French lessons today at four o'clock with Mademoiselle Sabine Arquette. Mademoiselle lives on Avenue

Kléber. I thought I'd take you there myself this first time to show you the way."

Brooke inhaled deeply before replying, "No, he didn't say a word."

Denise also heaved a sigh. "Well, she'll be waiting, so I expect we should start out now. You'll be sharing your lessons with another American who is brushing up her French pronunciation. It's a Miss Constance Vivier-Clarke, although apparently, she insists on being addressed as 'Viv.'"

Resigned to her fate, Brooke retrieved her coat from the hall closet and grabbed her handbag from a table in the foyer. She hoped that en route to Mademoiselle Arquette's, Denise could point out an establishment that could copy Christopher's office key.

As Denise and Brooke climbed into a waiting car, the talent agent volunteered, "This young woman, Viv, currently spends her days rolling bandages and serving tea at the American Hospital while hoping to be trained in first aid and as an ambulance driver."

Brooke didn't have long to wait before meeting her fellow student on the street outside their teacher's flat. Viv, a tall young woman with a curtain of burgundy, shoulder-length hair, was clad in smart, gabardine slacks and a matching jacket. In her hand she held a slip of paper and was scanning the street number over the door to the building Denise identified as Mademoiselle Arquette's address.

Denise took the initiative to make swift introductions.

Brooke said to her new classmate, "I can barely speak a word of French, so I hope I don't hold you back."

Viv laughed and hooked her arm through Brooke's. "Never fear. I can speak reasonably fluently, but my mother insisted I take lessons to improve my terrible accent. Trust me, I'm approaching hopeless, so you and I should do very well together!"

"*My* accent, when I can even come up with the right word in French, has been called 'atrocious' by my husband, so perhaps we *are* a good match."

Viv laughed again. "I'm sure that we're bound to become fast friends."

Denise spoke up. "Well, then, I will leave you in each other's hands." To Brooke she added, "Give me that key and I'll have a copy made for you and bring it to the flat. I must be on my way. Victor asked that I invite a few of his good friends to the apartment this evening, so please be sure to return home in time to dress for the soiree." She glanced at Viv and added, "and please do join us, Miss Vivier-Clarke. Seven o'clock at number seventeen, Rue Saint-Dominique."

And with that, Denise walked down the street while Brooke remained rooted in place, her mouth slightly agape.

Who does that woman think she is? Brooke fumed. *The Hostess with the Most-est?*

Viv's gaze followed Denise's retreating back.

"I was told that you've just gotten married, right?" she asked. "So, what's your husband's agent doing deciding who's invited to the party at your house… and when you should show up to it?"

"I can see what you're thinking," Brooke replied tersely and with a nod in Denise's direction. "But trust me, I have no plans to be in a *menage à trois* with Denise Louette—although I wouldn't question you for wondering if I were."

Viv burst out laughing.

"*Ménage à trois.* Very good! See, Brooke? You *do* know some French! C'mon, let's face the music," Viv urged, giving the arm of her new acquaintance a friendly squeeze.

With a grimace, Brooke rang for the concierge to let them into the building. Once admitted, the two women trudged up a flight of dingy stairs and rang the bell at the entrance to their teacher's flat.

A loud dog's bark echoed within.

"Odile, *silence!*" a voice shouted.

The door opened, revealing a tiny woman of indeterminate age standing next to a large, chocolate-brown standard French poodle whose curly head reached above the woman's waist.

"*Ah, bon! Entrez, entrez!*" she greeted them while distractedly batting away the dog prancing excitedly at her side.

Brooke bent down and showed the back of her hand to the poodle's nose. She'd always loved animals and had longed for a puppy when she was a girl. Her mother had said they couldn't afford "another mouth to feed," so she'd made do by befriending nearly every canine in her Los Angeles neighborhood.

"Hello, there, Odile," she murmured, and gave a scratch under the dog's ear.

"*Non! Non!*" exclaimed the petite woman who began a fuselage of rapid speech, beckoning them to advance down a dark hallway and into a small, cell-like room with two, straight-back chairs facing a desk.

"What's she saying?" whispered Brooke.

Viv smiled grimly. "She's telling us that, once we cross her threshold, not one word of English is ever to be spoken."

"*Merde!*" groaned Brooke under her breath, uttering the one-word expletive in French that came to her without a pause for translation.

"Double shit," Viv whispered back.

BROOKE FELT MENTALLY exhausted from her time spent with the exacting Mademoiselle Arquette. She barely had time to don her midnight blue silk evening gown and matching mules before she hurried down the hallway and into the tiled foyer. Waiting for Victor to appear by her side, she grew increasingly apprehensive at the thought of confronting the gaggle of native French and American expatriates due to arrive momentarily.

Victor emerged from the study, looking every inch the handsome movie star he was, clad in perfectly fitting black evening attire.

Taking his place beside her near the front door with Denise standing ready to open it when the guests appeared, he confided proudly, "Denise also made sure to include several prominent French friends who are also in the arts. Christophe, of course, would be first on both lists if he were in Paris."

"At least he'd be *one* person I'd know here tonight," she commented, trying to keep her voice light.

"I expect you'll soon find out from the dispatches he files where the hell he decided to go to cover what the Krauts are up to these days."

Victor's agent discreetly handed Brooke the guest list she'd drawn up at Victor's request and had spent all afternoon on the telephone confirming who was coming to the flat for the impromptu soirée.

"There'll be Shakespeare & Company bookstore owner Sylvia Beach," she said hurriedly, pointing to her name, "and Victor's fellow thespian, Josephine Baker." She singled out another name on the guest list. "An avant-garde painter named Pablo Picasso told me he'd come, as did several writers, including Colette—"

Victor interrupted with a wink to Denise, pointing to another name.

"Gillian Wingate-Jones is the daughter of a rather posh family in Britain. She lives in Paris these days." He hesitated. "I imagine her parents consider her a bit of a wayward social butterfly." He glanced at Brooke, adding quickly, "Not my type at all, but she's always involved in the latest thing, so she's a lively addition to a party."

Hearing the names of these prominent-sounding figures, Brooke's stomach tightened. Even though they spoke English, Denise would no doubt offer Brooke's credentials to their guests as "the blonde Charlie Chan girl" and she silently groaned at the thought.

Victor's agent turned over the paper in her hand and pointed to yet another name. "And I do hope the French novelist, Colette, is coming." Denise paused and asked, "Surely you've heard of her?" Without waiting for a reply, she finished her recitation with, "And I was so pleased to get a hold of a wonderful poet, Jules Dumont, who is actually a very good friend of mine, more than Victor's."

Brooke glanced at her watch, her nervousness growing with each passing minute at the prospect of some famous Frenchman peppering her with questions or chit-chat about which she hadn't a clue.

Talk about being a fish out of water! How in God's name am I going to get through this...?

As the front *salon* began to fill with people and chatter, Denise introduced Brooke to a young American named Sara Watson.

"Miss Watson runs an establishment known as Foyer International, an organization supporting foreign students coming to France. She's also working with a Red Cross leader, Louise Macy, to help the refugees beginning to flood Paris from Belgium and the like."

The two nodded, but before they could start a conversation, Denise took Brooke by the arm and whispered, "See that tall man standing over there with the slender woman next to him? Dr. Sumner Jackson is now head of the American Hospital of Paris, and his wife, Toquette, was a nurse in the Great War. Victor's new film may need to shoot a couple of sequences there, so be sure to be very charming when you meet them."

Just then, Brooke spotted Viv entering the entrance hall. She nodded abruptly to Denise and strode over to greet her.

"You are so in luck!" she said to her new friend, pointing out the Jacksons just visible through the wide door framing the front sitting room. "If you haven't already, maybe it'd be helpful for you to tell them how much you want to be admitted to the ambulance driving course."

"Oh, I've met them," Viv replied. "Well, sort of. My mother's a major donor. It'd be great to get to know the Jacksons better, though... so absolutely! But pretend you don't know any of my background and praise me to the skies," she joked.

"I will if you introduce me," Brooke replied with a wan smile.

Viv nodded discreetly toward the other side of the room. "Oh, golly, there's Gillian," she whispered. "Gillian Wingate-Jones. A total snob, especially toward Americans. She volunteered at the American Hospital for five minutes," Viv disclosed with a cynical laugh. "She found the work 'too distressing' and Americans 'too gauche.' I heard she's moved on to greeting people at the entrance to the French Red Cross." Viv shook her head, teasing Brooke, "She speaks French perfectly, so don't go near her."

As the evening wore on, Brooke felt surprisingly at ease since English was spoken almost exclusively among this group of mainly ex-pats. Some were quite complimentary about her work in films, while others simply greeted her warmly as Victor's new bride.

Having Viv at her side while Victor hobnobbed with the guests whom he knew well gave Brooke the confidence to make conversation with so many strangers. In the presence of Dr. and Mrs. Jackson, she even managed to offer a hearty endorsement of Viv, emphasizing her friend's decent grasp of French and her burning desire to become an ambulance driver.

"You are such a star, Brooke!" Viv whispered as she made her goodbyes with a kiss on both cheeks, European style. "Your endorsement might just do the trick!"

THE NEXT DAY, when Brooke met Viv at the entrance to Mademoiselle Arquette's, Viv greeted her by smothering her in a big bear hug.

"Dr. Jackson called me into his office this morning," Viv declared excitedly, "and guess what? I'm now officially enrolled in the ambulance training program, and *all* because of you!"

Brooke laughed. "That's wonderful, Viv! But don't you imagine it's more likely due to your mother's donations to the hospital fund rather than anything I said?"

Viv shook her head in a vigorous no. "Actually, my mother can be... well... beyond overbearing. I don't think the good doctor holds her in very high esteem, despite her donations. Your endorsement obviously did the trick, so *merci, merci, merci!*"

Viv had confided that she and her mother had long maintained a difficult, even tumultuous relationship. Apparently, Viv had been appalled when her parent had remarried an American who sold steel ball bearings to the Third Reich's industrial war machine throughout the build-up to the recent declaration of hostilities against France and Great Britain. Viv, herself, had been sent to boarding school in Switzerland during the years her stepfather was making his deals with the autocratic German regime.

"Everyone knows that I majored in high altitude skiing and not much else," Viv joked, "so I truly believe that *your* vote of confidence in me expressed to the Jacksons, along with your marriage to the famous Victor de Varney, added weight to my application." She hesitated and then added, "There's also the fact that just today, Dr. Jackson warned the entire staff and all the volunteers like me that the hospital is soon likely to see dramatically increasing casualties coming back from the frontlines. Especially if the rumors are true that German army troops have just advanced across the border into France."

"You've heard that?" Brooke asked, aghast. "The Germans are that close to entering France?"

Viv nodded. "From what Doctor J told us, it's nothing but bad news coming from the Maginot Line."

Hearing this, Brooke felt a jolt of anxiety concerning the where-abouts of her new boss. Tomorrow was to be her first day working as his freshly-hired deputy at *Presse Internationale.* She prayed she'd learn from Christopher's colleagues down the hall where the heck he was— and if he were safe.

Having exchanged such somber news on the sidewalk in front of Mademoiselle Arquette's flat, Brooke and Viv headed upstairs to class where they were again greeted by their scowling teacher and her friendly poodle. Odile madly wagged her tail as they entered the gloomy hallway. For some strange reason, the dog then jumped up on Brooke and placed a slobbery "kiss" on her cheek.

"Odile, *non, non, non! Mauvaise chienne!*" shouted Mademoiselle Arquette, giving the animal a swat on its haunches.

Despite this reprimand, Odile pranced happily next to Brooke as she and Viv followed their grouchy teacher into the bleak study room.

Brooke whispered to Viv, "Poor Odile is *not* a 'bad dog'... she just doesn't like the *mademoiselle,* and she's glad to see our friendly faces."

Viv whispered back, "I think you have acquired a major admirer."

Brooke replied, deadpan, "Don't tell Victor."

5

Brooke was still laughing to herself the following day about the poodle's over-the-top display of affection toward her. Preparing to leave for her first day of work, she donned her coat against the blustery April chill, ready as she'd ever be to assume the role of Christopher Laurent's press deputy. She was in the process of storing various items in her handbag when she heard the elevator outside the apartment's front door clank open. Soon after, the bell to their flat rang.

Only minutes before, the car service had arrived for Victor to take him to an early morning film test with another actor, to be followed by a casting meeting for the new movie scheduled for production soon. Wondering if her husband had sent up his driver to collect a forgotten script or something else important, Brooke opened the door, only to find a nondescript young woman standing at the threshold.

In perfect English, although heavily accented by her native French, the visitor announced, "Good morning, Madame. I am Nicole Langlois."

"Hello," Brooke replied, mystified as to who she was. "How may I help you?"

The woman offered an uncertain smile. "According to *Monsieur* de Varney's agent, Denise Louette, I am here to help *you*. I am your new housekeeper, secretary, and cook."

Merde! thought Brooke. Sometimes it felt as if *Denise* were Victor's wife, free to make any decision she chose concerning Brooke's husband's needs and welfare and the running of his household.

Yet, in spite of Brooke's irritation, she had to admit that if this Nicole person were good at her job, her help would certainly make Brooke's own working life easier.

"Come in, come in," she said hurriedly, anxious to arrive at Christopher's office at the hour they'd agreed, even if he were off on assignment. "I must leave for work in a minute but do come into the sitting room and tell me a bit about yourself."

Nicole took a seat opposite Brooke, her chapped fingers gripping a worn leather handbag.

"I speak English, German--and French, of course."

"Well, thank heaven for that," Brooke said. "That you speak English, I mean. I'm just starting French lessons with a Mademoiselle Arquette, but for now, I'm afraid my French is quite hopeless."

"Not to worry, Madame," Nicole said with a rueful smile that lit up her rather plain features. "I am a refugee from Alsace. It's a section of the country to the east of Paris where the Germans are threatening to overrun our part of France once again. My Alsatian accent is certainly not popular here in Paris."

Brooke felt immediate sympathy, both for the young woman's plight as a stranger in the city and the fact that the Germans had caused her to abandon her own part of the country.

"I didn't realize that people were already fleeing from Alsace, deeper into France."

"No invasion has happened there, yet, but everyone at home says it's about to. Many members of my family were either arrested or killed in the Great War during the last German occupation, so I have no desire to experience their brutality myself. As for my work," she said, "my *vita* is on file with the employment bureau. I am twenty years old, and I held a similar position in Strasbourg for the married daughter of the mayor."

"How did you meet Denise?" Brooke asked, curious.

"I registered with an agency as soon as I arrived in Paris," Nicole replied. "Madame Louette had told them that she needed to find someone with my qualifications who could... well... work for an American who did not speak French."

Brooke smiled, pleased that, for once, Denise had taken the needs of Victor's wife into account. There was something endearing about the young woman who showed such resilience having made her way to Paris and being willing to work hard among strangers. Nicole's situation was reminiscent of her own earlier years trying to make her way in Hollywood, a place as different as the moon from the wrong-side-of-the-tracks Los Angeles neighborhood she'd grown up in.

"Well," Brooke said with a smile, "if you can keep a reasonably tidy house and you also cook, you sound perfect for the job. Especially since you and I will actually be able to communicate in the same language," she added with amusement. "I'm hoping to write and sometimes broadcast to English-speaking countries for the French radio, and if all that works out, I can certainly use your help while I type final copies of my scripts here in the flat, most likely."

"That sounds so interesting," Nicole said with a burst of enthusiasm. "And I can help you with your French conversation, that is, if you don't mind my accent."

"If you speak French— period —that's all that matters," Brooke declared with a grin, rising from her chair. "I can certainly use private tutoring both from you and my very demanding language teacher." She pointed toward the door and apologized, "I know this is terribly rude, but I must be off. An extra key is in that little dish, there, on the table beside the front door in the foyer, so take it as your own.

Brooke could see that Nicole's shoulder-length brown hair was ill-shaped and lackluster. The heels of her shoes were worn down, the leather toes scuffed beyond redemption. Her jacket and skirt were of good quality, but her blouse was wrinkled as if she'd worn it for days. Brooke quickly surmised that the poor girl probably hadn't had a decent place to stay or a solid meal since she'd arrived in Paris.

She paused for a moment, and then offered, "At the back of the kitchen there's a small bedroom which can be yours, assuming you'd like to live in."

An expression of joy and relief infused the young woman's features.

"Oh, yes, Madame!" Nicole exclaimed. "Having a room here would be wonderful!"

Brooke nodded and then pressed, "Are you happy with whatever the salary was that Denise specified?"

"Now that you'll provide my room-and-board, it is quite generous, in fact."

"Good. I've gone job-to-job my entire career, so I know how important it is to establish the terms of employment from the get-go."

"Get-go?" Nicole repeated, puzzled.

"At the beginning of a working relationship," Brooke translated. "The *commencement*," she added, giving the word her best shot at a French pronunciation.

"Ah... *oui*... I understand," murmured Nicole. "'Get-go' is what you call a 'colloquialism,' am I right?" Brooke nodded, prompting a broad smile from her newly hired assistant. "See, Madame? We both made a good try of it."

Brooke strode toward the door, and then turned to face her new employee.

"Nicole, do call me Brooke." She seized her handbag off the table in the foyer. "And when you make a list of things to be done around here, make a note: 'Teach Brooke how to make a proper French omelet and a soufflé.' *Au revoir!*"

"*Au revoir, Madame!*" Nicole answered with a smile that beamed with gratitude.

~

THE DOOR BEARING the stenciled words *Presse Internationale* on its frosted glass panel was slightly ajar. On the other side, Brooke could hear someone speaking heatedly in a one-way conversation.

"Right this moment, the God-damned Nazis are invading Denmark and Norway, Bruce! I was halfway to the Belgian border when I heard this and turned right around and came back to Paris to file the story because the lines were down. Yes! Right! I'll get the bulletin done and broadcast it as soon as possible."

Brooke hesitated to enter the office since Christopher Laurent had fallen silent, apparently listening to a stream of directions from Bruce, whoever he was— although she assumed it was her boss's boss in London or New York.

"Got it, Bruce," Christopher said, his patience sounding strained to the breaking point. "It's chaos around here... and by the way, I've hired some help. I'm drowning, man, so don't give me any shit about it, okay? Okay. You'll hear from me within the hour."

Brooke heard the sharp sound of the telephone getting slammed into its cradle. She had barely pushed the door all the way open when Christopher looked up, his hand still resting on the phone receiver. His blond hair still looked like a mop that Nicole could conceivably use on the flat's parquet floors. He was wearing the same clothing she'd seen him in when he'd left for the train two days previously that had been due to take him to France's eastern border.

"You're five minutes late," he declared, glancing at his wristwatch, "but since you didn't know I'd be here and it's also your first day, you get a pass." He rose from his desk chair. "I take it you heard my conversation just now?"

Brooke replied "yes" with a guilty nod. "I just can't believe Hitler actually ignored his pledge of neutrality and rolled into Denmark and Norway like that!" she said, suddenly recalling Victor's film producer had shared this rumored scenario with her husband when the two were shooting their movie in Norway.

Christopher pointed to his desk. "Come in here and sit at my typewriter. I'll dictate and tell you exactly how *Mein Führer* did it."

Brooke peeled off her coat and dumped it on a nearby chair, along with her hat and purse. She thanked her lucky stars she'd supported herself as a member of the all-female typing pool in Warner Brothers' Story Department in her early days looking for work as an actress. She figured she'd be a bit rusty but then reminded herself that she'd always been able to type a hundred-words-a-minute while producers screamed in her ear.

"Ready?" Christopher barked as she placed her hands on the

Royal typewriter's silver-rimmed black keys, their feel comfortingly familiar.

"Ready," she confirmed.

Christopher began to speak while pacing in front of his desk.

"Dateline: Paris, April 10ᵗʰ, 1940. Last night, April 9, despite Hitler's promise to respect the neutrality of Denmark and Norway, a blitzkrieg of German ground troops invaded these two, small Scandinavian countries. Casualties on both sides of the conflict are currently unknown."

Christopher paused, silence in the room where the clicking of the keys had filled the air. Brooke's hands were poised above the typewriter as she watched her new employer inhale a deep breath before he continued his extemporaneous dictation.

"Without warning and just after midnight, Greenwich Mean Time, German warships entered major Norwegian ports from Narvik to Oslo. Thousands of German troops disembarked and swiftly occupied key posts in Norway. At the same time, German forces moved into Copenhagen, among other Danish cities."

Christopher stalked over to the corner of his desk, dug under a pile of books and papers, and seized his reporter's notebook. He studied a page and then continued apace; his voice filled with the same underlying emotion Brooke was feeling as his words rolled out.

"With the collaboration of traitorous Norwegian confederates that coordinated both land and sea operations for the invading Nazis, Hitler's forces were able to slip through the mines Britain had laid around Norwegian ports."

"Oh, my God," Brooke murmured. "Norway and Denmark were betrayed from within?"

Brooke could only imagine the shock of the conquered Scandinavian people now wondering whom they could trust among their own neighbors.

Christopher gave her a solemn nod. "Believe me, it gets much worse," and continued dictating.

"Local garrisons were instructed to allow the Germans to land unopposed. The order came from a Norwegian commander loyal to Norway's pro-fascist former foreign minister, Vidkun Quisling. Both the British War

Office and France's High Command have, thus far, declined all comment..."

IN THE WEEKS in the spring of 1940 that followed the Nazi invasion of Norway and Denmark on April 9th, Brooke hardly saw Victor, except late at night. Each evening she arrived back at the flat utterly exhausted from researching news stories, running down leads, and typing Christopher's English-language broadcast scripts, to say nothing of the myriad of reports cabled to his bosses.

For his part, Victor had become totally preoccupied with costume fittings and learning his lines as he prepared to play the lead in a new film scheduled to shoot both in Paris and in the South of France.

"*Encore du vin?*" Brooke inquired of Victor across the small table she'd had Nicole set up in the sitting room for their late evening suppers, the silk drapes pulled closed against the spring chill in early May.

Victor looked up from the film script he'd pulled onto his lap when Nicole had cleared the plates.

"Hmmm?" He stared at her outstretched hand holding the wine bottle. "Ah... no, thank you. I have three more pages to memorize tonight," and returned to murmuring lines from his script.

Brooke sighed softly. The truth was, she had her own lines to practice before she went to bed. Fortunately, in her case she had written them herself to be read from a script in a radio sound booth the following day.

She quietly placed her linen napkin on the table, pushed back her chair, and slipped from the room and into the library to go over her radio script. Settling into her chair behind the desk, she scanned the "puff-and-fluff" piece that was typical of those Christopher had been assigning her since her second day on the job.

"I don't have the time or the patience to write or read these damn things for broadcast to Britain and the United States," Christopher had told her with annoyance, "but the suits in New

York are convinced that these so-called 'human interest stories' pump up the listenership."

Brooke had been quick to answer.

"They may be garbage to you, but these stories still take work to research and write," she insisted. "I think they'll grab America's attention in a way regular people can relate to. Maybe they'll even persuade people back home how terrible this war is getting for the average person, especially if they begin to think Hitler won't stop at conquering just Europe."

After a long pause, Brooke could see her boss was mulling over what she'd just said. He even offered a surprising nod of agreement.

"Maybe you're right," he said, finally. "I never thought about them that way." He'd handed her copy back to her. "By the way, you've done a decent job on this piece." He pointed to one paragraph, "but you've buried your lead. Put this section first."

Recalling this initial and unexpected success, Brooke leaned back in her desk chair and picked up her latest story. Line by line, Brooke carefully read the printed copy one more time.

Her lead was solid, she thought.

"*Dateline, May 1940, Paris,*" she read aloud. "*The women of France, coping with tightening rationing regulations, are finding ingenious ways to bake their daily bread and pastries by adding small amounts of finely-ground sawdust to make the precious white flour stretch...*"

ON THE TENTH OF MAY, a neighboring radio journalist from another press office three doors down burst into their room without warning. Christopher's workspace was now much tidier, thanks to Brooke's successful efforts to bring some order out of his chaos, but their excited visitor took no notice.

"Goddammit, they've done it!" announced the young Brit who worked for Reuters News service in their building situated behind Gare Montparnasse. "A cable just arrived saying that the blasted Jerries have invaded Belgium, Luxembourg, the Netherlands, and have just crossed over the Maginot Line into France!"

"*Merde!*" exclaimed Brooke and Christopher simultaneously,

and Brooke wondered with sudden consternation how long it might be before she ever saw the United States— or her family —again.

"So it's official," Christopher muttered. "The Krauts have finally invaded France."

Brooke forced her thoughts back to the present, asking her boss for an explanation. "Wasn't the Maginot Line on the eastern border of the country supposed to be a wall of concrete bunkers forming a two-hundred-mile-long impregnable fortress?"

"Bogus government PR," Christopher retorted, jumping up from his desk. "The over-hyped Maginot Line is actually a giant concrete *sieve*."

"Exactly," agreed their agitated visitor. "And anyway, the Jerries simply went around it into Belgium and advanced into France from there."

"How close are they to Paris?" Christopher demanded, grabbing his reporter's notebook off his desk.

"Oh, it'll take them a while to get here," judged his colleague, "but you and I, Chris, had better plan for a completely different way of operating... or just go to the States. Foreign correspondents will be the first told to get out— or be arrested by the invading Huns," adding only half-jokingly, "and if they really hate what we've been broadcasting lately, we could be shot."

Christopher's phone rang just as their informant spun on his heel and dashed back to his own office. Brooke quickly determined that the call was from Victor and Christopher's mutual agent.

"Really, Denise? They want me to shut down the office *now*? You can't be serious? Relocate to *London*? But how are we going to cover this war if I—" He paused, listening. "Oh, for God's sake, the boss in New York is such a total idiot! Well, what are my alternatives, then?" he demanded.

Brooke rose from her chair, moving closer to overhear as much of the conversation as possible. Christopher's expression grew darker by the second.

"I dunno, Denise," Christopher said, shaking his head with a look in Brooke's direction. "Work for the French Ministry of Information? How long do you think this government is going to exist if the Nazis are banging on the door— or shooting at it? Well, yes, it's a *job* and it allows me to remain in Paris for now. I realize that, but—"

He looked over at Brooke once more and nodded.

"Yes, I'll tell her what they've offered. Of *course,* this shaky French government'll need us to produce stories begging the U.S. to get into this war." He paused and then exploded, "But, I'm an independent *journalist,* goddamn it! I don't do propaganda, no matter how worthy the client. Yes, yes, I'll tell her. You, too? Okay. Thanks for letting me know."

Christopher slowly returned the phone to its cradle.

"Congratulations, Brooke. For the moment, at least, you as well as Denise are both invited to work in the French Information Ministry. That is, assuming you want to."

"As PR flacks for the government?" Brooke asked, her thoughts whirling as she tried to absorb the import of the tumultuous events unfolding in real time.

France was being invaded. The Ministry wants us English speakers to help with their wartime public relations?

Christopher remained next to the phone, one of his hands making a tossed salad of his hair. Her boss had been ordered by his American superior to close the Paris news bureau. Brooke felt that had to mean that the Germans would be storming into Paris soon. She could hardly catch her breath given the full force of this avalanche of sudden, dire developments.

"And you?" she said, searching his unshaven face for some idea of his next move.

"What am I going to do?" Christopher asked rhetorically, slamming his reporter's notebook on the desk. "Frankly, I haven't a clue, except..." He gazed around his office and then back at Brooke. "Except close down this place and decide if I should swallow my principles and go to work as a government hack. If we want to continue to cover this war, we certainly don't have many decent choices to remain in France once the Nazis take over."

"Maybe we can do some *good* if we work for the Ministry?" she suggested tentatively. "For as long as they let us, we can broadcast to America how our country's own welfare and way of life are threatened if Hitler takes over all of Europe." She sought his gaze. "Given the dismal situation that all of us are in, it's an honest calling, Christopher," she insisted. "Maybe even a noble one."

He stared off into space for a long moment, then met her eyes.

"Well, even if we do join the government toadies upstairs, I'm warning you, the job won't last long."

"How can you know that?" she protested. "England has a big army. France, too. They won't give up on the country so easily as you seem to think."

"Oh, I'll never give up on France," he replied somberly, "but I don't have much faith in the men currently running the show upstairs in this building. Or in the French Parliament either, for that matter."

He paused a long beat, and then declared his decision.

"I think I'll tell Denise I accept the offer— for now — *but* I'll reserve the right to quit if we— or if *I* —don't like whoever they've deputized to run it."

"Same here," she said promptly. "Just so you know, I feel exactly the same as you do, Christopher."

Her new boss paused with a melancholy look that took her by surprise. He was half-French, half-American, she reminded herself. Today's news had to be tearing him apart.

Sure enough, her sense of what he was going through was apparently 'spot on,' as Victor would say.

"Since I'm half-Yank," Christopher began slowly, "would you please continue to call me 'Christopher?' That way, we can both feel we're on the same side in this crazy world. Deal?"

Brooke felt a shiver as she held out her hand and solemnly replied, "Deal."

He offered a crooked smile, seized her hand and shook it. His palm was firm and comforting, somehow. His next words were less so. "Journalists are in for a tough time when the Germans get here."

"Yes, I'm certain they will be," Brooke replied, "but I can take it if you can."

Christopher gazed at her for a long moment.

"I believe you can, Cub."

"You mean as in a full-fledged but novice reporter?" she asked, pointing to herself. She was amazed that he had elevated her from typist and puff-piece specialist to semi-professional colleague in less than a month.

"Yes, *if* you can learn the ropes of hard-nosed reporting fast and recognize your goddamn leading *paragraph*— or I'll have to fire your ass."

Brooke offered a penitent nod and then arched an eyebrow.

"Listen, buster," she teased, projecting the voice of a gangster's moll. "Don't forget— I'm from horrible old Hollywood. Just tell me what I'm supposed to do, and I'll do my best to do it."

"That a girl!" He nodded with a grin. "Don't let anybody push you around, even the Nazis." He pointed to the door. "I want you to go out and find some Americans and ask them their reaction to the distinct possibility that the Krauts are coming our way. Where are these ex-pats going to go? What are they going to do? Do they support the Allies? The Germans? Or are they neutral, like so many Americans in the U.S.? Give me around a thousand words and have it on my desk tomorrow morning by nine. I'll book the recording booth for ten."

"Got it," Brooke replied and began to gather her things as a plan was forming in her mind. She'd head for Sylvia Beach's Shakespeare and Company bookstore to find some Americans to interview. After that, she'd go home, write the story, and give Victor the news that the German's had finally entered France and that their lives were about to change in ways neither of them could possibly imagine.

Much to her surprise, by the time she'd done her reporting, driven her little car from the bookstore back to Rue Saint-Dominique, and arrived at the flat several hours later, Victor wasn't there. Nicole, wiping her hands on a dish towel in the kitchen, reported that he'd left soon after Brooke departed for work that morning.

"And he didn't say where he was going?" Brooke asked.

"No, Madam." Nicole gave an embarrassed little laugh. "I mean,

Brooke. He had the radio on and was listening to the news when I brought him his breakfast this morning. I believe there was a phone call from Madame Louette and then he made several others from the library. After that, he left."

"Did the car service come for him?" Brooke wondered aloud, remembering he'd said he had no appointments that day.

"No," Nicole replied. "Without a word, he just bolted out of the door. I looked out the front window and saw him getting into a taxi." She pointed to the dining room. "Would you like supper now?"

"Can you bring it to the library?" Brooke requested, puzzled that Victor had left no message for her. "I have a story to write."

6

H ours later that evening, Victor arrived at the door of the library with a bulky package wrapped in brown paper held under his arm.

"The film just got cancelled," he announced. "I received a call from Denise this morning. All production has been shut down because of the German advances."

"Oh, Victor," Brooke exclaimed, rising from her chair behind the desk. "I heard the news earlier today at the bureau and came home to tell you. I am so sorry, sweetheart."

"No bother," he countered breezily, a broad smile brightening his features. "Come here and kiss your newly commissioned liaison officer. I've been assigned to some high-ranking French Army chap as his French-to-English translator with the British Expeditionary Forces in Brittany."

"*What*?" Brooke pounded the desktop with the side of her fist. "You just joined the army without even *talking* to me about it?"

In the next instant, she pushed away the thought of all the decisions *she'd* made regarding her son that she'd never found the right moment to disclose to her husband.

But this was a life-and-death choice Victor was making that could leave me a widow! she thought, her heart starting to pound. *He's just committed himself to the battlefield, for God's sake!*

Victor had made this move that had life-altering implications for both of them and he hadn't thought it only fair at least to consult her first? The irony was that before she signed the government contract currently in her handbag, she'd waited to discuss with him the pros and cons of her working for the French Ministry of Information.

"What about your asthma?" she pointed out, battling to keep her temper in check. "And what about our backup plan for you to work with Christopher and me to do the propaganda films if our regular jobs went away— as mine just has, by the way!"

Victor remained at the door, his wounded expression reflecting his apparent disappointment that she hadn't greeted him as the conquering hero.

"Acting in films during a war where the dirty Krauts are about to run roughshod over us all? That's a *coward's* way to face the threat that's coming!"

"Oh, so you think your friend Christopher Laurent is a coward, and therefore so am I?"

"No I didn't mean it that way," he said, advancing into the library while shedding his topcoat. He tossed it, along with the parcel he'd been carrying, onto a nearby chair. "It's just I'd feel that people will think me such a shirker if all I do is continue to ply my trade in the safe confines of a film studio here, or in America."

"Who said anything about fleeing to Hollywood?" she demanded, doubly shocked he'd even been considering such a move.

"Well, that was one idea I had when Norway fell."

"Oh, really? Were you planning to tell me about *that*?" Brooke countered and then had to admit she'd done something similar.

When were you planning to tell him he'd have a stepson if the two of them ended up back in the States?

Victor jutted his chin in the air, arguing, "You know as well as I do that the regular army wouldn't have me because of my weak lungs— as you so kindly reminded me." He cast her a smug look. "So, I went over their heads." He paused, and then added, "With Christophe's help, incidentally."

Brooke sank back down in her chair, stunned speechless by

everything she was hearing. After a few moments, Victor filled the awkward silence.

"Thanks to his making a few calls when I asked him to this afternoon, I presented myself as a potential translator to a bigwig he knew. That man passed me to the top officers coordinating with the British Forces that are still in Brittany."

Brooke finally found her voice, and even to her own ears, sarcasm laced every word.

"Well, considering all the bad news, lately, I didn't think many French soldiers were still *on* the battlefields and that the Brits were heading back across the Channel in droves."

"That's just *it,*" Victor said, with almost childish excitement. "I have to pack and leave tonight on the train to Rouen and from there, on to Caen where I'll join my new regiment for whatever comes next."

"You're leaving tonight?" she echoed faintly.

Brooke's thoughts were reeling at the possibility that within the space of twenty-four hours, Victor, with his delicate constitution, could be squarely in harm's way simply to avoid appearing a shirker in other people's eyes.

And he hasn't given a thought to what this means for me!

He pointed to the package he'd piled on top of his coat.

Brooke heard the defensive tone again edging his voice.

"You should know that the French top brass were *delighted* to have my services and even gave me the title of captain and a uniform to go with it."

"The 'star treatment' no doubt," she replied, the irony clearly lost on her husband. "I can't believe that you made such a gigantic decision without mentioning to me that you were even *thinking* of volunteering for duty, and on the front lines!"

Tears had begun to blur her vision as she stared at him standing in front of the library desk.

"I did this *because* of you," he retorted, his anger spilling over. "Because of what's happening to France. I did this to make you proud. To make *Grandmère* proud. I can't just stand by while every man I know is preparing for this war."

He walked around the desk and pulled her roughly into his

arms. Brooke ducked her head, her cheek pressed against the scratchy gaberdine of his suit jacket.

All she could think of was the terrifying asthma attack Victor had recently suffered when he'd caught a cold. The infection had soon burrowed deep into his bronchial system. They'd been up all night, with Brooke trying to disguise her terror that he would simply be unable to draw another breath. She'd pushed him into hot showers so the steam might help ease his wheezing. Every hour she'd brewed a cup of tea laced with lemon and honey to loosen the phlegm in his chest and throat.

The strangled sound of his every breath set off a panic she'd never experienced before, not even when Errol had his first cold as an infant. What if Victor had an asthma attack crouched in a trench full of water or taking cover in a dank, moldy concrete bunker somewhere? Her husband of less than three months could *die*! And all because his ego was at stake and his celebrity had granted him a handsome uniform and an empty title he hadn't earned.

She stepped out of his arms and met his gaze, her voice low and trembling with the emotion she was doing her best to suppress.

"But you and I could have worked together for the Information Ministry. We could have contributed to the war effort with our unique writing and performing skills. You're no more a soldier than I am!" she pronounced, her voice dull as she felt tears leaking from her eyes and down her cheeks. "You have a chronic, life-threatening condition— *asthma*! It's not your fault, Victor, but don't you think it's a disqualifier for frontline duty in a war?"

He started to turn away from her, but she grasped both his shoulders, hoping to convince him of her dismay.

"We're just starting our life together and you've told me you're leaving *tonight*?" she cried with the same sense of abandonment she used to feel as a young girl when her mother worked late and left her alone in their shabby apartment. "I just can't believe you've done this!" She squeezed her hands against the cloth of his suit jacket even harder. "To *both* of us!"

Victor stiffened under her touch and glared back.

"Well, I have, and I can't change it. I thought you'd support me in this." He pulled away from her and stomped toward the door, adding over his shoulder, "I'll ask Nicole to pack my bag and prepare something to eat that I can take with me on the train."

"I *do* support you," Brooke called after him, but her words sounded more like a sob than a sentence. "It's just that it's all so sudden. It doesn't make sense! Surely you can understand that. I love you! I-I just can't believe you're leaving..." Her choked words drifted into silence.

Victor turned to face her, his tall figure framed by the doorway's carved molding like a photograph she wanted to burn into her memory.

"Now, *that's* the loyal wife I married," he said, retracing his steps to her side, seizing her hands. "My train doesn't leave until midnight. Come with me, darling." He led her from the library and down the hallway toward their bedroom. "We still have a few more hours."

Brooke's last thoughts before they closed the door was that she was grateful that she'd used precautions to prevent any chance of becoming pregnant. There had simply been too many changes she'd had to confront in the wake of meeting and marrying Victor.

Ironic, isn't it, Brooke? You'd finally agreed with him just two days ago to stop using your diaphragm over the summer and try to conceive a baby this year. Only he won't be here...

Victor led her toward their bed with its gilt and silk-festooned coronet looming in grandiose splendor over the headboard. With a tenderness he hadn't displayed in the library, he once again drew her into his arms. His lips traced a line down her neck, his ardent embrace signaling a frantic urgency that Brooke yearned to respond to in equal measure. She longed to give way to that blinding oblivion his mere touch had always summoned in her.

And in that moment of physical closeness, she wished she'd had the courage earlier to tell him about her small son, a boy who could have a home with them, a big brother to any child she and Victor might bear together someday. But now...

Brooke took a deep breath, but the impulse to make a clean breast of it about Errol slipped by in Victor's heated embrace, in the swirling chaos of the day's events and his unexpected and imminent departure. Tonight's shockwave learning that Victor was

leaving for the battlefields of Brittany left her neither the time nor
— if she were honest —the inclination to confess the long-held
secret of the existence of her child, now nearly three-years-old.

Victor's weight pressed down on her as her mind filled with
memories of the woman she had been, a working mother with
driving ambitions and no husband anymore.

The American women she had interviewed at the bookstore
earlier this long, long day seemed like sisters to her, now. They were
faced with the same difficult task she'd had of coping with child-
rearing, day-in, day-out and earning her bread, completely alone.
As the men in their families took them to bed one last time and
then headed for the frontlines, the mothers in Europe would be
confronting the harsh reality of caring for their children on their
own during a brutal war that looked to engulf them all. She felt
both guilty and relieved that her boy was safe in California and that
she wouldn't have another.

In a strange way, Brooke felt closer to the mothers of France
than the man making love to her.

In the last moments before the warm rush of familiar pleasure
invaded her body, she was conscious once again of the deep divide
within herself for having made the choice in favor of her own
welfare and future. She was equally ashamed— as well as relieved
—that she'd continued to ensure that she and Victor would not
conceive a child this night.

BROOKE GLANCED up at the large clock embedded overhead in the
front façade of Gare Saint-Lazare. As its chimes struck midnight,
she steeled herself to face the chaotic scene she suspected would
greet them inside the cavernous rail station.

Victor seized her hand as they passed through the large brass
doors and entered the mammoth area echoing with the sound of
train whistles, milling crowds, and a cacophony of human voices. A
series of locomotives stood on parallel tracks, their cars awaiting
the hundreds of men in uniform standing in long lines, waiting to
board.

Some men attired, like Victor, in newly issued military garb were jammed side-by-side along the platforms with trains bound northwest toward Brittany.

Other groups arriving from eastern battlefields near the German border straggled off carriages with their clothing torn and threadbare. Brooke saw bloodied bandages on many heads, scores of arms in slings or bodies supported on crutches or atop canvas stretchers borne by their comrades. She could only conclude that the wounded conditions of these pathetic souls bore witness to the legions of French and British troops that had so recently suffered ignominious defeats and disorganized evacuations.

Her throat began to tighten with emotion as she noted clusters of weeping women and children dotted throughout the jostling crowd. Some appeared to be sobbing with relief that their loved ones were returning home, while others were clearly as distraught as Brooke, saying farewell to their husbands and sweethearts—perhaps forever.

"I will write as often as I can, darling," Victor assured her, as they both absorbed the disturbing scene swirling around them.

He encircled her shoulders with one arm while his other hand held on to his Louis Vuitton suitcase. She shot him a doubtful look. She knew they both were thinking of the letters she remained convinced he'd never written or sent from Norway, along with the ones from Olivia Eriksen he'd tossed in the fire.

"I *promise* to stay in touch as best I can," Victor insisted, giving her arm a gentle squeeze.

Remembering the lonely weeks in London with no word from Scandinavia, she struggled to keep her voice even.

"At least please let me know that you've made it safely to Brittany."

"I'll certainly try," he replied, leaning down to kiss her on the top of her head.

Recovering her composure somewhat, Brooke pointed to his luggage. "I packed two sweaters for you, so be sure to wear them both, along with your muffler. They should keep your chest warm."

In the end, she'd taken charge of helping him prepare to leave, insisting there was no need to summon Nicole from her room where she'd retired after dinner.

With noisy clamor reverberating on all sides, Victor made a good faith attempt to lighten their mood.

"It's fortunate, isn't it, that I can translate 'sweaters' to 'jumpers?'" he joked. From the first, he'd always teased her about her choice of the American word for his knitted garments as sounding mildly uncouth. "As Churchill says, 'America and Britain are two kindred nations separated by a common language.'"

With a smile, he raised the arm holding his suitcase and nodded in the direction of the handsome army-issue cloak he was wearing that swung from his neck to below the knees.

"Once they designated me the rank of captain, I was issued this very warm apparel with my regiment's insignia on the chest," he said with pride, glancing down at the embroidered patch on his chest. "It's rather like being clad in a woolen tent, wouldn't you say? I expect I'll stay perfectly dry."

Fighting another wave of emotion as she envisioned him sitting in a water-filled trench somewhere, Brooke managed to nod agreement. She watched him search the overhead departure board for the number of the train platform where his regiment would board.

"Ah, there it is."

He pointed to a lineup of trains on his right and led the way. Once beside the car he'd been assigned, he leaned forward and kissed her on both cheeks just as the conductor called, "All aboard" barely ten feet from where they stood. "This train leaves in five minutes!" he bellowed. "In five minutes! All aboard!"

"See?" Victor said. "We made it here in perfect time."

Men clad in similar cloaks to the one Victor wore greeted each other enthusiastically as they recognized their fellow soldiers arriving beside their allotted train carriage. Brooke observed several nudging each other's arms and whispering as they recognized the celebrity among them.

"Hello... good to see you... hello there," Victor murmured, acknowledging the ones with the boldness to salute his captain's insignia.

Brooke laid one hand on his shoulder to capture his attention.

"Please, *please* take good care of yourself," she implored as the reality of his imminent departure hit her full force. "Do you think ultimately you might be evacuated from Brittany if things become too..."

Her voice choking, she couldn't bear to express her worst fears of a German invasion pushing Allied troops into the sea.

"If the Jerries run us out like they did on the Maginot Line?" he replied, completing her sentence for her. "I expect in that case we will cross over the Channel to Britain." He stated this matter-of-factly, adding, "Much of what I'll be involved in will be hush-hush, of course, but I'll let you know everything I'm allowed to tell you."

He leaned forward to lower his voice next to her ear, his breath warm and familiar.

"I learned today that I'll be an aide-de-camp to some former tank commander named de Gaulle who's just been made a brigadier general. I suppose he needs a translator when he talks to his British counterparts."

Brooke could only nod at this disclosure, fighting off an increasing impulse to burst into tears. She almost felt as if they were filming a love scene when Victor seized her face between his hands and kissed her long and lingeringly, ignoring the crowds hemming them in on all sides.

Releasing her, he whispered, "I do love you. I hope, by now, you truly believe that. Denise and Christophe have both promised me to keep an eye on you."

Brooke found that she could barely summon a reply. Once again, a conductor's command rang out in French all too easy for even her to translate.

"*Tout à bord! Ce train part!*"

All aboard! This train is leaving!

Within seconds of this warning, the car beside them suddenly lurched forward. Her throat felt as if she were strangling.

"I love you, too!" she choked out as they began to walk beside the slow-moving train. "Please, *promise* to stay safe!"

He didn't acknowledge her plea, but urged in a rush, "Remember, darling, if the Germans overrun Paris and staying in the city gets too dicey, you can always go to the château. Monique would love that."

But Château de Varney is precisely the area the Germans are bound to want to conquer to guard the Channel from a counter-invasion...

Before Brooke could point that out or say another word in reply, Victor swung onto the moving step and was swallowed into the car packed with fellow soldiers.

She remained rooted to the spot where Victor had left her. Civilians on the platform aimlessly circulated around her as if they couldn't decide whether to stay or go now that their loved ones were leaving them.

Brooke frantically scanned the train's windows as they flashed past, but she couldn't spot Victor in any of them. Even so, she kept her hand upraised in farewell until the last railroad car became a distant, tiny speck on the tracks.

The train was heading toward a future she simply could not imagine for an asthmatic actor-turned-soldier like Victor de Varney. Nor could she envision her own life as a non-French-speaking American, alone in Paris, awaiting the despised Germans to storm the gates of her newly adopted city.

7

MAY 11, 1940

The following morning, Brooke marched through the door to Christopher's office and barely restrained herself from slamming it shut. She knew her next words could lose her a job with a boss she'd only known a month, but she couldn't remain silent.

Without preamble and making no attempt to speak in French, she asked as calmly as she could, "Did you actually wrangle an appointment for Victor with those military bigwigs and you never said a thing to me about it?"

Victor was probably in Brittany by now and each hour since he'd left, Brooke had grown both weepy and increasingly furious at her husband and her boss. Ever since the train pulled out of Gare Saint-Lazare, she'd found herself fighting a sense of utter abandonment from all quarters. Here she was, marooned in a country threatened with a foreign invasion where she knew very few people and had only just begun to learn the language.

Before Christopher could even answer her about his role in Victor's departure, she asked with glacial formality, "Did it not occur to either of you that a *wife* should be consulted on a plan for her husband— who suffers from serious asthma, by the way —to join the goddamn French *Army*?"

Christopher swept his hand through his disheveled hair and then bid her to shed her coat and take a seat in front of his desk.

"Before anymore steam pours out of your ears, let me explain," he proposed.

"I think I understand *perfectly* what happened," she replied, "The swashbuckling Captain de Varney is on a troop train headed for Brittany. I just want to know *why* that's happened."

"He called me after you'd left yesterday afternoon to do your story, and I *did* urge him to talk over his plan with you first," Christopher protested. "But you know Victor..."

"I certainly do," Brooke replied gloomily. "But you went ahead, anyway, didn't you? Set the stage for the brave young actor to go off to war." The anger edging her tone was aimed at Victor and Christopher alike.

Christopher heaved a sigh that Brooke took as a sign he hated being thrust in the middle of a marital spat.

"Well, he was pretty insistent he was going to make some rash move whether I helped him contact the powers-that-be or not," he disclosed. "I tried to point him in direction that would keep him from being behind enemy lines."

Brooke paused, taking in Christopher's last words. "Look," she said quietly, "I'm sorry you got pulled into this whole thing, especially since you and I are working together. And you're right: Victor would have managed to get what he wanted one way or the other. It's just that..."

She couldn't finish her sentence because tears were starting to clog her throat. Christopher shot her a worried glance.

"At least his bilingual language skills might actually help the war effort," Christopher pointed to a map of France pinned to a wall behind his desk. "I figured he should be relatively safe if he's attached to a brigadier general or a higher-up like that," adding with undisguised cynicism, "don't we all know that the ones planning scorched-earth strategy in war usually stay far behind the actual fighting."

Brooke battled against the expanding lump in her throat as she once again confronted the reality that Victor had left Paris.

Left *her.*

It galled her to think that Victor had roped in Christopher to orchestrate her husband's military commission as a translator without so much as a word of warning to her— and her new employer allowed him to do it! She pointed a forefinger in his direction.

"Well, please don't feel you have to obey Victor and 'look after me' like he told me he'd asked you to," she said. For emphasis, she plopped her pocketbook on top of the latest mess that had accumulated overnight next to his typewriter. "Believe me, I'm quite used to looking after myself."

"Victor didn't ask me," he countered quietly. "I volunteered to keep tabs on you. After all, you're newlyweds. I realize that this has to be... extremely difficult for you." His fingers absently began to strum the corner of a reporter's notebook that poked out from beneath her purse. "And you should know by now, I tend to keep my word."

As his dual declarations sunk in, Brooke was shocked into silence. Finally, she managed, "*You* volunteered to keep an eye out for me?" He nodded. "Victor didn't ask you?" she pressed, unsettled by the way in which Victor had portrayed his parting exchange with her boss.

Christopher avoided her glance, shifting his gaze from his notebook to a pile of papers heaped beside his typewriter. Brooke imagined that he'd probably worked all night, except for grabbing a few hours' sleep on the battered leather couch pushed against the far wall.

"Well, for God's sake," he defended himself, "what kind of heel wouldn't offer to watch out for you? Believe me, I know what it's like to struggle to master a language." He met her stony gaze. "It was hell when I was a kid and was first sent to Michigan for summers with my American grandmother. And now you're left on your own in a foreign country where the stinking Germans may soon overrun the city." He shrugged, his matter-of-fact tone an apparent attempt to minimize his efforts on her behalf. "Anyone would do the same."

"Especially, as you so kindly point out, for a wife who'd only been married three *months!*"

She hated how self-pitying that sounded but it seemed her only way to prevent crying uncontrollably— as she had far into the night. Christopher, too, appeared to be seeking a way to hold tight to an emotion Brooke couldn't quite name.

"I-I thought it would ease Victor's worries if I told him that both Denise and I promise to keep your welfare in mind, given how insane things are. God knows what the next weeks will bring."

Brooke regarded him closely. In some ways, both Christopher and Denise knew Victor far better than she did. They'd certainly known him longer. She fell silent once more as a maelstrom of confusing thoughts whirled in her brain.

Her husband loved her. That she no longer doubted, but he also loved the spotlight; he loved being a center of attention, especially when women were concerned; and he definitely loved acting the part of a soldier. Even so, Brooke knew full well that Victor did not love the thought of anyone considering him cowardly.

And impulsive? She had only to recall his decision at Sardi's restaurant in New York to reach for her hand and caress it under the table less than an hour after they'd met!

He's always recognized what he wanted... she realized with a jolt. *And nothing has ever kept him from going after it.*

With some chagrin, it dawned on Brooke that it was most likely that particular character trait that accounted for Victor's amazing success— much like her own driving ambition when she was fighting for movie roles in Hollywood. She had no doubt that his single-mindedness had elevated him so quickly to star status in the European film industry.

Thanks to Christopher's journalistic connections with important people, along with her husband's status as a celebrity, Victor had landed a 'leading role' as a translator to some war planner named de Gaulle.

Brooke exchanged glances with her boss across his desk. She had to acknowledge that it was *also* thanks to Christopher that Victor would most likely stay out of harm's way. What could be safer than to serve as an aide-de-camp to a strategist hovering over maps in an army headquarters distant from the battlefield? Surely, that was preferable to being holed up in a bunker on the front lines.

She felt her shoulders relax a bit for the first time since Victor had announced so abruptly that he'd signed up "for the duration," as he'd said proudly. She slowly shook her head.

"Christopher Laurent, I'm still pretty mad at you for helping Victor do this insane thing, but thanks for maneuvering him into someplace reasonably safe," she declared. "He has the lungs of an invalid whenever he catches a cold. He's merely played a soldier in a silly movie or two. He has absolutely no idea how to *be* one."

Christopher's expression grew troubled.

"He never disclosed to me that he suffers from asthma. He just said the army had told him his work in films was too important to conscript him."

"He hates to admit he has that damned disease," she replied. "I expect he was trying to save face when he called on you to help him get past that impediment and find a role to play in this war."

Christopher looked as if he still expected Brooke to punch him in the nose.

"God, Brooke, I am so sorry. If I'd known all this, I'd never have —" His words trailed off.

Brooke almost laughed at his look of abject contrition. She was surprised to feel the corners of her mouth turn up ever so slightly.

"Well... despite what you did," she drawled, "please know that I *do* appreciate the effort I'm sure it took on your part to connect him to your friends-in-high places." Keeping her tone light, she added "And I thank you and Denise for offering to keep track of me as we wait for the barbarians to arrive at our gate, especially since my German is even worse than my French."

Christopher's lips twitched with suppressed amusement.

"What you're telling me is you don't speak a word of *du Deutsch*?"

"*Nada.*"

"Ah, so you speak Spanish!"

"*Nada,*" she repeated. "Haven't you figured out by now that despite the efforts of Mademoiselle Arquette, I'm horrible at *all* foreign languages?" Seizing a pencil from the clutter on his desk, she wagged it menacingly. "But I'm no dumb blonde and I'll do whatever it takes to outwit the adversary."

Christopher gave her a questioning look. "Who's Mademoiselle Arquette?"

"My French teacher. She's a grim sort, but I think I told you about her friendly poodle," she reminded him. "Denise was nice enough to introduce us and *you* gave me a job here and have promised to teach me the ropes of being a reporter, so..." She offered a shrug. "Let's just agree that you, Denise, and I will look after *each other*... deal?"

Christopher nodded like a man given an eleventh-hour reprieve.

"Deal!"

Instead of shaking her hand, he picked up one of the papers on his desk. Even upside-down, she could see that it was a press release on Ministry of Information stationery.

"And here's other news," he said in a mocking version of a broadcast announcer. Brooke gripped the arms of the chair facing his desk. "We're supposed to sign our contracts with the Information Ministry asap."

"Wow... that was fast," Brooke marveled. "Where's a pen?"

"Better read it first."

"I will. Later."

He moved the paper to one corner of his desk and asked with a wry smile, "So, tell me, what brilliant ideas have you had lately to beam to the English-speaking peoples of the world?"

Brooke pointed her pencil in the direction of his typewriter, their conversation swiftly shifting from the subject of her absent husband to the business at hand.

"It's not a puff piece," she warned.

"Okay. Shoot."

"When I was coming to work this morning, I went by the train station just around the corner. You should see the poor women and children refugees pouring into Gare Montparnasse from Alsace, Belgium, and even Germany. What if you and I go over there so you can gain some idea of—"

Christopher leapt up from his chair and grabbed his reporter's notebook while he handed her purse to her.

"Great idea," he declared, striding toward the door like a horse headed back to the barn. "Grab your coat, Cub, and let's go!"

BROOKE CAUGHT wind of a foul odor less than a hundred feet from the entrance to Gare Montparnasse, a mammoth building looming near their radio studio headquarters on the Left Bank of Paris. Once inside the teeming station, she and Christopher exchanged looks, quickly surmising the smell was due to fetid air, the place now overrun with hungry, unwashed, and desperate refugees fleeing from Poland and other countries in Hitler's path.

"Oh, God, Christopher," Brooke murmured. "Look over there."

She nodded in the direction of a mother sobbing over what appeared to be her deceased infant, the babe silent, stiff, wrapped in rags, as the woman clutched it in her arms.

Brooke was suddenly reminded of the moment she was handed her baby son moments after his birth. Her labor had lasted an excruciating thirty-six hours, and he'd emerged with a flattened nose and the soft fontanel pushed to a peak on the top of his head. She remembered being shocked at how disfigured he looked, despite the nurse saying in six weeks he would be "a lovely looking child." She was young and desperately unhappy with Errol's father, not feeling the slightest surge of maternal love, but only awash in the thought of how tied down she would be just as her film career was taking off.

Would she have sobbed like this woman if *her* baby had died? Felt that depth of grief? Errol's features had returned to normal, just as the nurse had predicted. In fact, by the time of his first birthday, he'd inherited her admittedly good looks, as proven by the black-and-white snapshot she kept hidden in a side pocket of her purse. He'd been blond with her strange, amber eyes, Brooke recalled thinking how attractive the boy had become when she'd glanced back at him, crying in his grandmother's arms as her train pulled out of LA's Union Station.

Brooke repressed her disturbing vision and glanced to her right. She still wondered if she were missing the "maternal instinct" other women seemed to possess.

But how young and shallow— and selfish —I was then...

Seated on a wooden bench nearby was another woman with a jagged yellow star made of cloth sewn to her tattered coat. Unsightly welts disfigured a pretty face made worse by black-and-blue splotches blooming around her left eye.

"Holy Mother," muttered Christopher.

Brooke couldn't pull her eyes from the distraught woman rocking back and forth while holding the hand of a wild-eyed child that looked to be about six years old. The little girl's free arm hung from a makeshift sling fashioned from a torn bandana and covered in dried blood.

"This is criminal," she murmured as she felt Christopher touch her arm to steady her. "Look what somebody did to this poor woman!"

Brooke gazed about the platforms where trains were chugging in and out of the station, luggage and canvas bags strewn everywhere along the platforms. To her shock, she saw that atop the mounds of personal belongings, escapees of all ages were huddled together crying or moaning in pain.

"Why are these poor people in such terrible condition?" Brooke demanded, more to herself than to Christopher. "Hungry, yes. Frightened, yes. But *beaten* and with dead babies clutched in their arms?"

"Let's try to interview that Red Cross volunteer over there," Christopher replied, striding toward a woman kneeling beside an infant. She was focused on diapering the tiny baby for a mother who stared blankly into space. "I spoke to her one time on another story," he muttered over his shoulder.

Brooke and Christopher stood quietly nearby, waiting for the Red Cross worker to finish her task. When, at length, she rose to her feet, she gently placed the baby in its mother's arms. Turning, she apparently recognized Christopher and offered a tired smile.

"Greetings, Miss Macy," he said in English." Remember me? Christophe Laurent? I work for Paris-Radio Mondiale, now."

"Well, hello. Checking out yet one more disaster?"

"Actually, my colleague, here, Brooke Bradley, suggested we come to see for ourselves the latest result of Hitler's drive through countries that don't belong to him." He gestured toward Brooke. "Louise Macy? Meet my deputy."

"How do you do?" Brooke said, tearing her glance from the mother and child Miss Macy had been tending.

The Red Cross volunteer was staring at her oddly, providing Brooke a hint of what was coming next.

"Don't I know you?" Miss Macy asked. "I've definitely seen you somewhere... but I can't quite..."

Christopher laughed. "I'll make it easy on you, Louise. Ever seen a Charlie Chan detective film?"

"Of *course*! That's it!" she exclaimed, the fatigue in her expression brightening with a smile of recognition "You were the blonde who always needed rescuing!"

Brooke offered a rueful smile. "You must have seen 'Charlie Chan in London' where I beg him to save my brother on death row for a crime he didn't commit, but my fiancé— who's his lawyer — thinks he was guilty, so I cried in every scene."

"Yes, that was the one," Miss Macy agreed.

"Poor you," Brooke sympathized.

Louise Macy shook her head. "I thought you were delightful, and here you are, doing your bit by working for Radio Mondiale in Paris with Christophe?" she asked, using the French pronunciation of his name. "How utterly amazing."

"It sure *is*," was Brooke's wry reply and she could tell Christopher nearly laughed out loud at this exchange. "Actually, as of this week, he and I are working for the government's radio division of the Ministry of Information." She glanced around the teeming station. "The dire situation you're facing here is definitely a story that should be told."

"Good luck getting this particular story broadcast," she replied with a grimace.

Brooke shook her head in disbelief. "What do you mean? How can anyone ignore blatant human misery like this?"

"Very easily, sad to say," Louise Macy replied. "And if the Nazis storm into Paris, it'll just get a lot worse."

"But obviously you and the Red Cross need more help... more people," Brooke protested. "In America, surely they have no idea how terrible things are for refugees fleeing Hitler's advancing troops?"

Louise Macy gestured that they should walk in the direction of a more private area in which to talk.

"That's just the problem," replied the Red Cross volunteer, her voice laced with both exhaustion and anger. "As you say, these people are *refugees*. They're mostly Jews, fleeing for their lives. I doubt you'll find much sympathy with some of the blatant anti-semites in the halls of Congress or in the ministerial branches of the current French government you're working for now," she added grimly. Addressing Christopher she added, "And you can just imagine how horrendous it will be if Hitler seizes control of the entire country."

Christopher took out his reporter's notebook. "Give us some statistics to work with. How many people are you seeing come through here every day?"

"And how are you feeding them," Brooke interjected, "or finding places they can go that are safer than where they've been?"

For another thirty minutes, Louise Macy patiently answered their avalanche of questions. Back at the office, the untried partners swiftly developed a system in which Christopher dictated the bulk of the narrative based on their notes while Brooke typed their story as they went along, chiming in with her additions and corrections. Within a few hours, a full recounting of the tragedies unfolding at Gare Montparnasse was sitting on a desk at the Ministry of Information, awaiting approval for broadcast.

Christopher put the final page of their article's office copy onto the pile on his desk.

"Not bad for a Cub and a newly minted PR hack," he mused.

"It's better than 'not bad!'" Brooke protested. "And what we've written certainly can't be called 'Public Relations.' It's a solid, accurate news story."

Christopher looked up and gave a nod in the direction of the ceiling.

"That may turn out to be a problem, Cub. We'll just have to see what the suits upstairs have to say."

———

8

Brooke was quick to discover some four days later that she and Christopher had more problems to worry about than just the French government functionaries on the higher-up floors of the building.

Vincent Molet, a balding, squat radio engineer whose expertise Christopher trusted completely, came to work the following morning and delivered attention-getting bad news of his own.

"The equipment in the broadcast studio is practically inoperable!" he blurted. "The microphones are antiques, raspy, and full of feedback. The control board is falling apart, and the entire wiring system should be replaced. Every time I've made a request for repairs, the Information Ministry replies it has no funds." The engineer glared at the two journalists. "I tell you, it's impossible!"

Brooke had followed his French reasonably well since she'd specifically studied the words for the tools of her trade. She was greatly alarmed by the sight of Molet's pudgy face that had flushed scarlet during this recitation of woes. Even his body language translated into "I'm about to have a stroke."

"*Bientôt, nous ne pourron plus diffuser!*" he declared hotly.

"Diffuser... diffuser..." Brooke muttered under her breath, searching for the French vocabulary word that was floating somewhere at the back of her brain. Finally, it came to her.

"To broadcast!" she exclaimed, locking glances with Christopher. "Isn't Monsieur Molet warning us that we may not even be able to get on the air?"

"You got it," her colleague acknowledged. "Equipment repair and maintenance apparently have been a low priority with the suits upstairs."

"Oh, God... just what we need! Radio Mondiale won't be able to broadcast?"

"*C'est terrible,*" Molet exclaimed, apparently understanding more English than she thought. He declared, "*Vous devez faire quelque chose, Christophe!*"

Thanks to Brooke's latest French lesson with Mademoiselle Arquette, she understood the radio engineer was pleading with Christopher to "*do* something immediately" about the mess in his department or they'd be off the air.

Just then, Denise entered the office without knocking, waving a wire dispatch in her right hand. Before Christopher could make an urgent request to remedy Molet's production problems she announced, "The Ministry of Information just received this cable. Holland has surrendered to the Nazis."

Brooke glanced at a calendar she'd recently affixed to the wall to schedule the flow of work in their department. "Good heavens!" she exclaimed. "It's only May 15th! Barely five days since the bastards invaded Belgium, not to mention all the other countries surrounding France."

Denise nodded and inhaled a deep breath. "And here's something else to keep under your hat. The order for a full retreat of Allied forces on all fronts is expected to be given at any moment."

"Oh, shit." Christopher groaned. "'All fronts' means we're about to see a much worse defeat than we even imagined."

To Brooke, 'all fronts' also meant Brittany, where Victor had joined his regiment.

Denise added, "Orders for the first phase of retreat are expected to come down soon for evacuations from *Dunkerque.*"

"Dunkirk?" Brooke murmured, scanning the map behind Christopher's desk.

He pointed to a dot positioned beside the border between France and Belgium. "It's the French port on the Channel that's among the shortest distances across the water from Britain."

Denise's voice was absent her usual cheery, positive tone. "Troops that survived the onslaught along the Maginot Line in the east have been advised to make their way to the beaches of Dunkirk where ships from Britain are being dispatched to pick them up."

Brooke turned to Denise. "A full retreat on all fronts also must mean Brittany, too?" she asked, dismayed. She hadn't received Victor's promised message informing her that he'd arrived safely with his regiment, nor had she had any communication from her mother in America for weeks. Now, given, Denise's revelations, she could understand the reason.

Christopher's finger on the map of France moved to the left, tracing the coastline to the west, past Normandy. He addressed Denise while avoiding Brooke's gaze.

"French and British troops in the northwest will never make it to Dunkirk. Don't you imagine Caen and environs are where those regiments will scramble onto anything that floats to retreat from the continent?"

"The latest dispatch has actually confirmed they'll depart from Cherbourg and St. Malo," Denise acknowledged, pointing to the western ports facing the English Channel. "That information is extremely hush-hush, so please don't repeat it to anyone or say who told you."

Christopher offered a wry smile. "Now, Denise, you should know by now I never burn my sources, and neither will Brooke."

Denise turned and said with a kindness that soothed any resentments Brooke had felt since they'd met, "I'm sharing this highly secret information to help all of us keep the faith that Victor will make it to Britain safely."

Brooke felt her throat tighten with unshed tears.

"Thank you for that, Denise. It's so hard to believe that Victor's regiment has been in Brittany for barely a *week!* And just like that, he's going to be evacuated by boat to who knows where?"

"If anything comes through our office, I'll let you know right away," Denise promised.

Brooke looked from her to Christopher.

"So, *now* what happens?" she asked, struggling to keep her worry and concern for Victor at bay.

Christopher pointed to his typewriter.

"Now we get busy!" He looked over at Denise. "You want us on the air with the news of Holland's surrender, right?"

She nodded, but stipulated, "The Minister wants to downplay— at least for now —the plans for the total Allied retreat. So, please, no mention of that yet."

"Bad for morale, right?" Brooke said, trying to look deadpan.

Christopher quipped to Denise, "As you can plainly see, our Cub, here, has already adopted my skilled use of irony."

Everyone in the room was fully aware that news of a total troop withdrawal meant Hitler was obviously mounting a full invasion of France. If word got out now, it would panic the populace and create a mass exodus from Paris.

Christopher jabbed his forefinger in the direction of their chief engineer.

"Well, Denise, before you return upstairs, you'd better listen to what Vincent Molet, here, has to tell you about his broken-down studio. I suggest you tell the suits to get him some help in the next three hours or our operation will go radio silent."

Denise's response was simply, "I will do my best."

Turning in place he barked, "Brooke? Start typing."

Molet and Denise left the office. Brooke hadn't even sat down in Christopher's chair or put her hands on the keys before he started dictating aloud.

"*Dateline, Paris, May 15, 1940. The Ministry of Information confirms that Holland has surrendered to Hitler's forces who continue to advance westward...*"

When the news release was finished and its wording approved, Christopher headed out to try to snag an interview with the commander of the now defeated French Army.

"Vincent Molet says he thinks with some luck he'll be able to broadcast by three o'clock. Use your 'actress playing a newscaster' voice and get this out in English as soon as you can. I'll be back by four and repeat it in French. Can you do that?"

"I'll do my best but I'll probably start weeping on the air."

"Don't blame you, Cub... but just pretend you're in a film."

BROOKE WAS DEPRESSED but not surprised to learn later that day that their refugee story was set aside for more immediate projects.

"I was given a list of the kinds of pieces they want from us now," Christopher said, handing her a copy that Denise had sent down to them earlier.

"They must have liked your interview with the army guy," Brooke said, scanning the "suggested" names from whom they should get statements and build broadcasts around.

"Let's hope the French Army personnel returning to Paris in defeat don't come off like the screw-ups they are," he replied sourly.

"What about asking members of the panicked French Parliament and the Foreign Ministry what *their* next moves are?" she proposed half in jest.

"For now, we're supposed to concentrate on uncovering and repeating every rumor and theory of Hitler's atrocities in the countries he's conquered."

"What about the atrocities against the Jewish refugees we saw at Gare Montparnasse while French authorities look the other way?" she demanded. It was a reminder to both of them of the Red Cross volunteer's prediction that the French powers-that-be would consider that the despicable treatment of Jews in France—even the horrors being perpetrated on the children—was a story not worth telling.

What if I were one of them... fleeing with Errol to escape the Nazis...

"See what I meant when I told you that a job as a government hack might not be a lot of fun?" Christopher replied with his usual brand of black humor.

"No joke," she agreed, and meant it. She'd set aside some time when she got home to write her mother and hope to have news about her son whose third birthday would be soon.

"IT's AN ABSOLUTE DEBACLE," Christopher declared, stomping into the office one morning in the third week of May.

Both he and Brooke had cranked out scores of radio stories painting Hitler and his German storm troopers in the violent light they deserved. For her part, Brooke was having difficulty sleeping at night after reporting on and writing up one harrowing tale of defeat after another.

Christopher, too, looked as if he hadn't had much sleep of late. He threw his jacket on the leather couch with the force of a champion baseball pitcher.

"Oh, glory, what now?" Brooke asked.

"The French and British troops are literally running for northern coastal ports to save their necks. I just heard that more than three hundred *thousand* soldiers are streaming toward Dunkirk," he added pointing to the calendar square marked May 26th. "Flotillas of navy and civilian boats, big and small, are arriving from England in the next hours to try to get them off the beach before the Luftwaffe swoops down and kills the poor suckers from a hundred feet."

Brooke bristled. "Victor is one of those 'suckers' probably waiting to be taken off a beach in Brittany," she retorted.

Christopher looked chastened and quickly apologized.

"I just meant that the regular troops on the eastern front have truly been hung out to dry by their asinine leaders, most of whom, I'm sorry to say, are French!"

During the days that followed, Brooke was left in an agony of suspense, wondering if her husband had boarded a ship and was safely on his way to England— or was taking cover in some cliff cave in Brittany to avoid being strafed by a low-flying Messerschmitt.

Brooke could tell that Denise was worried, too, although she attempted to disguise it. "I've tried to find someone who has contact with Victor's brigadier, but thus far, no luck," she said apologetically. She touched Brooke's sleeve. "I promise, I'll keep trying."

"De Gaulle was the name, right?" Christopher asked.

"Yes," Denise confirmed. "But the only thing they'd tell me is that it's pretty chaotic up there. Same thing was true at Dunkirk, although it seems everyone who was going to be picked up there is now gone."

THAT EVENING, Nicole had Brooke's supper waiting for her when she returned from work and served it on the small table in the sitting room. The sight of the darkened dining room with its tall, silk-festooned windows and formal Louis XIV furniture had become too strong a reminder that Victor was no longer in Paris.

"Can I get you anything else?" the young housekeeper asked, and Brooke recognized the look of concern on her face.

"No, but thank you," Brooke replied, trying to summon a smile, sensing a need to express some gratitude for the kindness and care Nicole had given her since Victor had departed so abruptly. "Supper was marvelous. Thank you so much."

As Nicole quietly backed out of the room, Brooke felt as if she hardly had the energy to pick up her knife and fork. She was almost too tired from the tumult of these last days even to feel the loss of a husband who had been hers to love for such a short time.

Once in bed, she stared up at the gilded wooden coronet above her headboard, the silk hangings flowing from either side, another reminder of the emptiness permeating this most elegant of Parisian apartments. Her world was falling apart and yet it was so *quiet,* she thought, almost as if she were observing herself on this stage-set of an abandoned bedroom.

Her life now was utterly different from the plot she had envisioned, having the talented, handsome, wildly celebrated Victor de Varney as her life companion. The one soiree they'd hosted before he joined the army had given her a glimpse of what their marriage might have been without war— surrounded by brilliant artists, writers, poets, and performers. That night she'd felt intimidated, surrounded by Victor's accomplished friends, but now she realized how much she might have come to enjoy and appreciate being part of a world of real thinkers and doers, the kind of milieu that she'd longed to be a part of from the time she was that little girl living on the wrong side of Hollywood and its glamour.

But none of that dream existed for anyone in Paris now that the overwhelming power of Germany's war machine was bearing down on France.

She'd never felt so alone, despite her new profession that had thrust her into the center of the hurricane of chaotic world events. She pushed away the flashes of the terrible scenes she'd witnessed among the refugees flooding Paris and found her thoughts drifting to her daily routine with Christopher. He always seemed to know the right move to make, his judgments sound, his experience a bedrock to rely upon.

He's my one grounded stake in this maelstrom, thank God...

Eyelids growing heavy, Brooke pulled the fluffy duvet tightly under her chin, the empty space on the other side of the bed proof positive that she had absolutely no idea where her young husband was. Was he well... or ill with asthma? Would he and his regiment and the elusive commander named de Gaulle survive the coming ordeal of evacuating across the English Channel from Brittany? No doubt the troops would be making their escape under fire from the Luftwaffe commanding the skies, or attacked by U-boats cruising stealthily beneath the sea.

It occurred to Brooke that she hadn't allowed herself to truly *feel* Victor's absence. Perhaps she'd thrown herself into the frantic pace of Christopher's news operation to take her mind off the sense of total abandonment she was experiencing now.

"A woman without a country?" she asked herself in a whisper against the silken pillow beneath her head.

No.

She saw herself now as a woman without the man she had thought would always be there.

Yet *would* he have been, she wondered.

Would he ever be again?

BY THE FIRST day of June, their broadcast unit suddenly had a new Director of Information. Brooke was astonished to learn that the poet, Jules Dumont, whom she and Victor had entertained at their first soiree as a married couple, had suddenly been put in overall charge of everything that was broadcast in the name of France.

"Might as well call him the Director of Propaganda," Christopher muttered. "He certainly won't be the director of a 'news' operation or be having us crank out unbiased 'information.'"

Ignoring him, Denise, just named Dumont's deputy, gestured to Brooke.

"Come," she said, nodding toward the glass paneled door of their office. She smiled indulgently at Christopher. "Jules knows Christophe well, but he wants to get reacquainted with you."

"Really?" Brooke murmured under her breath, wondering if this poet-propogandist was going to fire her for inexperience.

As Brooke walked upstairs for the meeting, Denise mentioned that Dumont suffered from a chronically painful back.

"He was thrown from a horse in his youth and his body has never truly recovered," Denise revealed. "I tell you this so you'll understand if the pain he endures daily makes him seem a bit... preoccupied."

Oh great... what she probably means is he's a cranky so-and-so most of the time...

Denise left her at the Director's door and disappeared back down the hallway. To Brooke's surprise and relief, Jules Dumont's attitude toward her was that of welcoming a fellow artist.

"I was delighted to know you'd joined Christophe in this mad enterprise," he said as soon as she'd taken a seat.

Dumont's dark eyes bored into hers, communicating a sensitivity that seemed utterly out of place in the department dedicated to molding public opinion, irrespective of the truth or falsity of their messages. Brooke noticed that he did shift in his desk chair often as if he were continuously seeking a more comfortable sitting position to relieve pressure on his back.

"I've listened to a few of your broadcasts," he observed with an admiring smile. "You are a veteran performer, able to convince an audience of your sincerity. That is going to be key in our efforts, here."

"Given what's happening to the troops," she said pointedly, "how long do you think our jobs here will last?"

Taken aback at her directness, Dumont remained silent for a long moment. Then he replied with an intensity that startled her. "I will be in this chair as long as there is a France. A *free* France."

He handed her a sheet listing subjects on which he wanted her to research, write, and broadcast, pieces running approximately 90 seconds.

"I've given Christophe a list of his own. I'd like *you* to concentrate on the arts and ex-pat artists in Paris who are supporting the Allies in their efforts to fight the Huns." He peered at her across the desk as if he needed stronger glasses. "I'm sure by now you recognize that our job is not merely to broadcast the news-of-the-day."

"We do news, but with a certain slant, am I correct?" she posed with a touch of Christopher's irony.

Immediately, she wondered if she'd overstepped. To her amazement, however, the corner of Jules's mouth turned upwards, indicating he knew perfectly well that what they were engaged in certainly wasn't 'journalism.'

He pointed to the list now in her hand. "Your work, along with that distinctive voice of yours, will be heard in English for the expats here and throughout the world for English-speaking people," adding, "and, of course, when Christophe voices them, they'll be in French for everyone else— and you'll do the same for his scripts if he doesn't have time both to translate them from the French and then redo his broadcasts in English himself."

"But he'll do the translating, yes?" she emphasized with alarm.

Jules smiled encouragement. "Of course. Given your celebrity status in the United States, perhaps we'll get the Americans to understand a bit better that Hitler's lust for conquest might one day affect the United States as well."

"Goodness... you've given Christopher and me quite an assignment, Monsieur Dumont."

"Call me Jules, please," he urged. "For example, take the story you two did about the refugees," he said, handing her the manuscript she and Christopher had submitted. "Boil this piece down to less than two minutes. Make it clear that the cause of all the refugees' misery is due to the cruel Germans that overran their countries and brutally abused civilians in the process."

"There's no doubt," replied Brooke, "the Germans' treatment of civilians has been barbaric, but our story is also about the neglect and abuse we witnessed that they've received *since* they arrived in France," she said pointedly. "Don't you agree that the antisemitism throughout Europe, including France, is *also* at the root of the terrible treatment they've experienced once they got here?"

Jules Dumont winced. He didn't reply until he'd settled more comfortably into his desk chair.

"I do understand your view, but we can't complicate things," he replied evenly. "Always keep front-and-center that the *Germans* are the enemy and the cause of our problems."

"But the same problem of antisemitism exists in America, too," she declared, feeling she'd seen and heard Dumont's brand of deflection many times before. "Half the heads of the movie studios in Hollywood are Jews whose film productions add millions to the American economy. Yet none of them can even join a country club out there! Their children are excluded from the posh private schools and crosses sometimes are burned on their front lawns, just as bigots do to Negroes in the south! The antipathy toward Jews is a worldwide issue, isn't it?"

She leveled her gaze, wondering if she would try Dumont's patience too much. She'd always considered herself a fairly conservative type politically, focused on her own welfare and success. Nobody ever gave her a leg up on anything. Everything that ever landed in her bank account, she'd had to earn on her own. But having seen the human devastation visited on all those persecuted Jewish refugees who'd fled homelands crushed by Hitler's storm troopers, she couldn't seem to stay silent about her indignation.

"Well, we must first deal with the issue before us," Jules countered mildly, "that Hitler is about to takeover France, Jews and non-Jews alike."

"But, isn't it time we exposed this papered-over, worldwide anti-semitism as one of the root causes of why America's in no rush to help Europe and stop Hitler? The bulk of people in the States don't have any idea of the atrocities aimed at refugees fleeing persecution and war. America's antisemitism may keep people out of golf clubs, but shouldn't people everywhere learn about the horrors that are happening over here?"

Jules interrupted her, insisting once again, "I don't take issue with anything you've said, but we must solely stay focused on the Germans as perpetrators of the worst violence Europe has ever seen. The English-speaking citizens listening to you on the radio need to *despise* them, not be challenged to consider their own distrust of Jews."

"But—"

"I want you to broadcast these pieces I've assigned on Radio Mondiale's English Hour as soon as we've approved their content," he emphasized, pointing to scripts on his desk. He shifted in his chair once again as if he would stand to indicate their meeting had concluded, but chose merely to smile at her faintly, saying, "It's been... quite stimulating chatting with you, Brooke, but I'm afraid I have to get back to the tasks you see waiting here."

"Yes, of course," she murmured, rising from her chair, and making for the door.

Walking back to the office, she supposed she was grateful that she still had a job and access to whatever information there was to be had about Victor's whereabouts. Dumont clearly supported the Allied effort to stop the Nazis, but 'unpleasant' facts about the underlying causes of the support that certain French factions had for Hitler's regime apparently weren't to be discussed in public. Realizing Dumont would approve only a certain slant on what was broadcast by the State, Brooke had just confirmed for herself what Christopher had predicted: working for the Ministry of Information meant that the two of them were no longer journalists, but now full-fledged propagandists.

To think that a year ago, I wouldn't have known the difference.

Christopher wouldn't like this latest turn of events— and neither did she. But what was their alternative? Rousing Brooke from her dark thoughts, Denise intercepted her midway down the corridor.

"We just had word that Belgium is also now completely overrun by the Germans. Their government officially surrendered earlier today." She paused as if to gird herself for delivering additional bad news. "And ten minutes ago, we were notified that there's been a bombing in Paris."

"Bombing *Paris*? Oh, *merde!*" Brooke said, mixing her languages. A bolt of apprehension struck at the thought of Nicole alone in the flat. "Do we know where, exactly?"

Rue Saint-Dominique was not far from Les Invalides, the site of Napoleon's tomb. Such a place might have been a dramatic target in the heart of the city.

"At least twenty bombs have fallen on the outskirts near the northeastern suburbs," Denise disclosed. "The Germans dropped plenty more on the airfield at Le Bourget and then took off before our planes could get airborne to shoot them down."

On her own behalf, Brooke breathed a sigh of relief. The airfield where American aviator Charles Lindbergh had landed after his historic New York-Paris transatlantic flight back in 1927 was at least seven kilometers beyond the center of Paris. Even so, the site was close enough to give her pause. She wondered how bad the damage was for the areas surrounding Le Bourget.

Denise had yet more startling news to impart.

"Earlier today, the Ministry of War alerted Jules and me to be ready, if the order comes, to evacuate our agency from the city."

"What? All of us in the Information Ministry would leave Paris?"

"It won't happen right away— if it ever does —but I've just told Christophe to prepare a plan. You two must choose the broadcasting equipment you'd take with you, as well as organize transportation for the people in your bureau."

"And where would we evacuate *to*?" Brooke asked.

"That will be a last-minute decision."

"I see... and how did Christopher receive this news?"

"Not enthusiastically, but he's on the phone now putting a commercial bus on permanent standby and finding out how many people in your group own automobiles."

"I do," Brooke volunteered. "It's a very small car, but four people can squeeze in."

"Tell that to Christophe," Denise directed, hurrying toward the staircase that led to Dumont's lair.

Brooke watched her retreat, thinking that Victor would never have dreamed the Simca he gave her for her wedding present would serve as an escape vehicle, if it came to that.

Victor...

Denise and Christopher had done their best to try to persuade a few of their contacts in the War Ministry to disclose where his regiment had been bivouacked.

Christopher had told her, "Whenever I mentioned the name of that brigadier you said Victor's attached to... de Gaulle, wasn't it?... no one will tell me a thing. I went so far as to claim Victor was one of my best friends. But *nada*," he'd said, borrowing her word.

On top of that frustration, she and Christopher would now only be permitted to broadcast reports that a gaggle of government censors approved. Brooke was under no illusion that the truth of France's own internal hatreds, bungled military preparedness, and their inept battlefield strategy were not likely ever to be mentioned.

And they'll only give us ninety seconds to tell the story of the battered and abused refugees pouring into Gare Montparnasse?

Christopher would blow his top when he heard this latest edict. Echoing in her head was the memory of her boss's initial reaction to working for the Ministry of Information.

"I'm an independent *journalist*, goddamn it!" he'd declared heatedly. "I don't do propaganda, no matter how worthy the client."

Was deeply antisemitic France 'a worthy client' to begin with, she wondered?

"A *free* France," Jules Dumont had declared so emphatically just now. Perhaps she and Christopher could convince themselves *that* was what they were still working for too, even as propagandists. When the war was over, she thought with a ray of hope, she could only pray that the more liberal thinkers in Europe would be the ones to help rebuild a better world.

Brooke glanced at her watch. It was after four. If she didn't leave now, she'd be late for her French lesson. It provided the perfect excuse to avoid, until tomorrow, having to face full-on the implication of Hitler's advances forcing their unit's possible evacuation from Paris.

Climbing into her car's driver seat, a disturbing question took hold. What would be Christopher's choice if the information bureau had to leave the city? Would he leave Paris with the staff, or remain on the barricades attempting to function in that danger zone as a legitimate journalist, reporting what he saw if German tanks rolled into Paris?

9

Brooke couldn't believe the scene she encountered enroute to her French lesson at Mademoiselle Arquette's flat. Stretched in a long line down the center of the Champs-Élysées were scores of street-sweeping machines parked in a deliberate formation.

"What the hell?" she murmured, peering through the Simca's windshield.

She could only guess that after today's bombing on the outskirts of Paris, this impromptu metal barricade was erected as an emergency measure to prevent small German planes from landing on the broad avenue.

As she'd parked her car on Avenue Kléber, she heard a voice hailing her. Striding toward the curb was Viv Clarke, waving frantically.

"Did you see the smoke rising over Le Bourget today?" Viv shouted from across the street the moment Brooke stepped from the driver's seat.

"No, but I heard about it," she answered, joining Viv entering the building. "Did it rattle a few windows at the American Hospital?" she asked her new friend as they passed through the lobby and trudged up the stairs.

"A few. I figured I'd be sent to the scene to pick up the injured, but my ambulance was being serviced in the shop."

"It's not surprising," Brooke said, patting her friend on the back, "given that harrowing run you made up to Dunkirk and back."

Viv had previously related the tale of transporting a high-ranking, injured Frenchman cared for at her hospital to the port to be picked up by a British warship.

"The guy I transported was a sexy-looking but very cranky French officer the Allies wanted to get back to Britain," Viv had told her, "so off we went, driving over fields to avoid low-flying German planes along the main roads. We both almost bought the farm when our ambulance was shelled while we were sleeping in a hut by the side of the road."

"Oh, my God, Viv!" Brooke said, aghast.

"The bullet holes messed up the roof of the ambulance and the drive itself was certainly hell on the undercarriage," she'd divulged with a shrug.

Viv grinned as the two reached the top of the stairs leading to their teacher's front door. "Well, despite all today's excitement, here we are... ready to be abused by our French teacher again."

She reached out and rang the bell to Mademoiselle Arquette's flat. In the next moment, their instructor's voice, shrill to the point of hysteria, screeched at Odile to stop her exuberant barking. Once the door opened, Brooke and Viv exchanged startled looks.

Mademoiselle was clad in a rumpled housedress, her frizzy gray hair uncombed. With a wild, distracted look in her eyes, she peered into the hallway as if expecting an attack of some kind. The poodle, catching sight of the pair, danced past the threshold, wagging her tail enthusiastically and leaning heavily against Brooke's thigh as if she'd been searching for a place to hide.

Viv asked in her better French than Brooke's, "Mademoiselle, are you all right? Has something happened?"

Arquette gave an emphatic shake of her head.

"*Oui, oui, OUI!*"

This was followed by a stream of rapid, high-pitched, sentences accompanied by gestures mimicking bombs falling on all sides of the distraught woman standing in her bedroom slippers.

Breaking their teacher's hard-and-fast rule of "Only French

Spoken," Viv offered Brooke a loose translation describing the poor woman's harrowing afternoon.

"Mademoiselle was visiting her mother near Le Bourget and the house next door took a direct hit. It was a bloody mess, apparently. She says everyone died in the rubble. She and her mother are okay, but obviously this has quite unsettled the poor thing."

"No kidding," Brooke said under her breath.

Another barrage of French from Mademoiselle Arquette ended with Viv taking several steps backwards into the hall.

"*Oui, oui, Mademoiselle! Je comprends.*"

Viv grabbed Brooke's arm, explaining, "She wants us to leave. *Now.* She says she's too upset to teach. She's spouting some crazy idea that the Germans plan to hunt her down personally and kill her. She apparently wonders if you and I are now part of the plot!"

Before Brooke could say anything in response to this insane notion, the distraught woman screamed at her dog to come inside the flat and slammed the door.

Viv shook her head in disbelief. "She told us that despite her suspicions about us, we're to come back tomorrow."

"You've got to be joking," replied Brooke. "Do you think that by tomorrow she'll be more herself?"

"You mean in her right mind?" Viv retorted. "Who knows? Either way, I can't come. I have a Red Cross ambulance run delivering food to a refugee camp tomorrow afternoon."

"Oh, good grief!"

Brooke dreaded the idea of having to confront the hysterical Mademoiselle Arquette *and* Hitler's troops drawing perilously close to Paris all in the same day.

THE NEXT MORNING, Brooke handed Christopher the approved script that a messenger had brought down from upstairs.

Keeping her own displeasure under control, she explained, "No mention of the discrimination against the Jewish refugees after arriving in France is allowed in our piece, but the censors kept most of the rest of our story. Vincent Molet says he'll be ready for me to broadcast 'live' in English in ten minutes." She pointed to the script with lines blacked out, and then looked at her boss. "Vincent wants to know if you can translate our piece and be ready in an hour to do it in French? Apparently, he's managed to patch together enough equipment that's still functioning." She shrugged. "Fingers crossed it holds up."

"Jesus, Mary, and Joseph!" exploded Christopher, pointing to the first paragraphs on the page. "Jules Dumont is a very nice man in a job he's totally unsuited for. How can a poet with a seriously bad back be expected to stand up to the censors?" Christopher held up the single page of copy. "Ninety seconds, with every word *redacted* about the lack of support from the French government that arriving Jewish refugees faced?"

Brooke nodded. "That's right. All gone."

Christopher pounded his fist on the desk.

"I hate the bureaucrats upstairs! I hate this job. I pretty much hate even being in this building right now," he raged, his jaw tight beneath a chin that hadn't seen a razor in a week.

He looked at Brooke as if seeing her in a new light.

"If we have to evacuate, you should just head back to America where you won't have to deal with this shit! Surely Victor must have urged that you wave your American passport at the officials and skedaddle to safety?"

"Is that a word you learned in Michigan?"

"Skedaddle? Yes," he answered, not smiling.

"I thought so," she said, suppressing a grin.

"But I mean it, Brooke," he insisted. "Grab this chance to make a run for it while you still can."

She was amazed to realize she felt hurt that her "partner in crime" as he'd sometimes called himself, was apparently fine packing her off to the States while remaining behind to report on a vicious war on his own.

Brooke walked toward the map of France hanging on the wall and pointed.

"Victor suggested I could always seek shelter with his grand-mother in Normandy up here," she indicated, "that is, if the Germans ever reached Paris." Attempting a nonchalance she didn't feel, she added, "Given what's going on up there with Allied troop withdrawals, that's not such a great idea, do you think?" She looked Christopher straight in the eye. "So, forget it. I'm not leaving,"

"Look, I'm serious," he insisted again. "There's no reason for you to risk being here when this whole thing comes tumbling down as it's looking very likely it will. There's still time for you to get on a plane or ship out of here from Marseille. I can make some calls—"

"Well, what about *Victor*?" she flung back at him. "How would *you* feel if your wife ran for cover and never looked back to determine if you were alive or dead?"

"Victor's probably already on a ship with his high-ranking French officer, headed for Britain," he retorted. "Hasn't anyone in your family in the States urged you to come home?"

"I never actually called my life in Hollywood 'home,'" she parried, pushing away the memory of the last angry exchange she'd had with her mother. Estelle Bradley was a poor correspondent and there'd been no letters for almost a year.

"Well, what does Victor's grandmother say?" demanded Christopher. "If it isn't safe to stay with her, wouldn't she urge you to leave while you can?"

"I've met Monique de Varney exactly once," Brooke rejoined. "She's a very charming woman but she certainly has her own problems to worry about living in a château in Normandy that the Germans will probably requisition for some senior Nazi."

"That's precisely my point! She'd definitely urge you to leave."

Brooke could see that Christopher was refusing to give up.

"Victor's father lives in California, right?" he asked. "In the wine country there? Surely, he—"

"He doesn't know me from Adam!" Brooke snapped. Her hands on her hip, she challenged him, "Look, are you trying to get rid of me or something? Have I been in the way or a burden or a lousy actress failing even to learn to be a rotten propagandist? Maybe you think I'm a total pain in the ass—"

"*No*."

Startled by his emphatic answer, Brooke could only stare as Christopher slammed their script down on his desk.

"You've been none of these things. You've been great. Better than great. It's just I know how bad it's going to get now that the Germans have started to bomb Paris. The fact is..." He paused, lowering his eyes, keeping them glued to the papers littering his desk. "I'm truly worried for your safety, Brooke. If the Germans find out who you are, an American actress, and that you've been broadcasting what they'll see as anti-German propaganda— which you have and will be —very bad things could happen to you."

"I know that," Brooke answered, subdued by the seriousness of his tone.

The memory rose in her mind's eye once again of Gare Montparnasse and seeing the bruised faces of refugees that were beaten by the Germans prior to fleeing their countries of origin.

She reached out and lightly touched his hand still resting on their script. "But for heaven's sake, Christopher, you're in the same boat! They'd string you up just as fast as they would me. Your work is much better known than anybody else's in all of Paris! At least we're still able to get the word out about the tragedy of what's happening to ordinary people in this war." She moved her hand to point at the script lying flat beneath his palm. "Like the plight of these refugees!"

"But we're forbidden to mention the antisemitism that's playing a major role in this war," he countered. "Telling *half* the truth is closely allied with lying, haven't you heard?"

His observation hung in the air between them.

"I agree," she murmured. "But isn't it about all we *can* do right now? Do our best and remain on the barricades."

"If we remain on the barricades, we'll have to do more than just serve as government hacks," he countered. "We'll have to fight back and make no mistake, that's a dangerous road to travel. You can get *killed* my dear... wonderful, beautiful, talented Madame de Varney... and wouldn't that be a crying shame?"

Brooke felt a strange jolt of electricity delivered with his compliments. He held her gaze as silence bloomed between them, his last words making her feel decidedly off kilter.

Recovering, she had a question for him.

"And what about you if *you* get killed? Surely someone in your world would cry if that happened."

Christopher cast her a sardonic smile.

"Not really. Both my parents are dead. I'm not married. I don't have any kids that I know of. All I *do* know is that I'm willing to fight against what the Germans are doing to Europe... targeting the Jews and taking over countries that don't belong to them."

"But that's how *I* feel," she insisted.

"The problem with that noble sentiment, Miss Cub Reporter, is that I have a lot more experience outfoxing the bastards who want to control everything for the right *or* the wrong reasons. And in the situation you and I are in, a large segment of the French population — including a significant number of politicians in the French Parliament— find it perfectly acceptable to blame the Jews and others that don't agree with them for all their ills and grievances. Thus, they will convince themselves they can live with Nazi domination of France and the rest of Europe. My bet is they will cooperate in persecuting and even killing Jews themselves under the color of their new authority in France."

"Whoa!" Brooke slowly absorbed his words with a heavy sense of foreboding. "Do you think the Parliament will fall and the Nazi sympathizers in France will simply take over?"

"Some members of Parliament understandably dread another war after the one that decimated France twenty years ago," he said, pointing to the map as she had. "But plenty of members hate the success of Jews in banking and commerce. And just like the Germans, they hate their more liberal French colleagues. This extreme faction on the far right could very well endorse a German takeover of France, and then the current French government will surely collapse."

Brooke nodded. "Something like that may be happening in America. Even before I left the States, Henry Ford and that damned aviator Charles Lindbergh and their 'America First' crowd of Nazi sympathizers have been dividing our country right down the middle with their not-so-veiled racism and antisemitism. They never have anything nice to say about the heads of the movie studios, most of whom are Jewish."

"Now you understand why the suits upstairs don't want our story about Gare Montparnasse to broadcast for consumption either in America or France," he said. He paused for emphasis, adding, "So you see, now, that's what we're up against."

Brooke pointed to his copy of the edited script recently approved by the Ministry's censors.

"Well, at least the world should know about the plight of refugees, Jewish or not. The redacted version still does that, fortunately. Tells half the story, as you say, but it's better than keeping silent about *all* the poor wretches fleeing Hitler." She inhaled a deep breath and asked, "So, will you do it in French?"

"Well, *we* wrote it, so despite the deletions... I guess so."

He scowled, circling back to their earlier discussion.

"Now that you know that there are plans afoot to evacuate our Paris bureau, won't you please be sensible and beat feet out of here?"

"No, and I admire your grasp of American colloquialisms."

"'No,' you won't leave?"

"*No*! I won't!"

Christopher pointed a forefinger at her.

"Well, I'm warning you, Brooke. *I* might not stay in this particular job very much longer. I'm going to decide day-by-day... story-by-story... what role I'll play in this disaster drama."

Upset by the notion he might resign from Radio Mondiale, she replied, "You leave this job, I'll leave, too, but I'm not leaving France."

Christopher shook his head in frustration while she tried to coax him to smile.

"Think of it this way," she proposed. "You managed to secure that bus and park it nearby in case we have to run for our lives. I have the Simca to add to our fleet. We're a good team, so don't even *think* of bailing on me, Monsieur Laurent!"

"I'm not bailing on *you*," he protested with a defensive air, "and now that I know you have that midget vehicle parked outside, I want you to remember that you can ditch our rolling circus at any time." His expression stern, he added, "You can drive directly south to Marseilles and still board a boat heading for the Caribbean and get back to the States from there. You've got to promise me you will use your American passport to sail home if our situation seriously goes sideways. That was part of my deal with Victor when he asked me to help him get that army commission. To get you out of harm's way if it ever comes to that."

Surprised to learn Christopher might have extracted some sort of *quid pro quo* out of Victor, Brooke gazed steadily at her boss but made no promises.

Was it Christopher— not Victor —who wanted a plan established for her to flee to America if the Germans invaded France? Or was it a side-deal Christopher made with himself?

Even more likely, odds were that Victor had nothing to do with it?

LATER THAT AFTERNOON, Brooke completed an interview with the celebrated French writer, Colette, asking her to describe where she had been and what it had been like for her when the Germans bombed outer Paris.

"The war is on our doorsteps here in Paris," Colette replied, her French-accented English rendering her statement even more solemn. "And I hope America will soon see it could one day be the same in New York or Washington."

Their on-air conversation concluded, Brooke thanked her guest for being willing to conduct the interview in English.

"But of course," Colette said with a shrug of her Chanel-clad shoulders. "You are Victor's wife and a colleague of dear Christophe. How could I refuse?"

Ah... the power of the press and celebrity...

When Brooke returned to the office, Christopher was on the phone chasing down a tip he'd heard that the staff at the Louvre had started wrapping the museum's priceless works of art for safe storage in the basement.

He pressed one of the curators, "Have you been officially advised to expect that the Germans will bomb the museum?" He paused, listening to the response, and then nodded. "Ah... so you're saying this is just a precaution. Yes, I see. Well, thanks for the information."

Brooke was reaching for her coat when he hung up. He glanced at the clock.

"Off to your favorite French class?"

"Actually, I'm dreading it more than usual." She described the strange scene that had greeted Viv and her at Mademoiselle Arquette's the previous afternoon. "The woman looked on the verge of a total psychotic breakdown."

"Well, perhaps that's understandable. The casualty counts just came in. Nearly three hundred people died from the bombing near that airfield yesterday," he replied, pointing to a dispatch on his desk. "Trust me, being close to a direct hit can seriously rattle a person."

"Three hundred-plus died in the bombing?" she murmured. "I had no idea it would be that many."

Christopher nodded. "I was just a little kid in Montmartre the last time the Germans tried to conquer France. They bombed Paris too, back then. The worst was in the Marais, and believe me, it was scary as hell."

"I *do* believe you, but unlike my French teacher, I'm glad to see you still have your wits about you," she teased.

He arched an eyebrow and replied deadpan, "Barely."

Brooke let the remark pass, wondering what emotional wounds such a frightening experience might have left on a little boy who had become this outwardly self-assured journalist? No wonder he seemed so worried for her safety.

But what about his own?

Musing about this, she donned her hat and coat, and waved goodbye. "Wish me luck at Mademoiselle's. See you in the morning."

Christopher scratched something in his reporter's notebook and then looked up, catching her at the door.

"Oh, wait! First thing when you get here tomorrow, Vincent Molet is going to teach us both how to run the radio control board. Denise tells me it's a skill we might need."

"Good heavens, *us* running that cranky old thing? Why?"

"At some point, we might be minus a radio engineer or two," he explained. "Denise expects some people who work here will skip for parts unknown if the Nazis arrive. Others will be left behind if we have to transfer a skeleton broadcast crew to somewhere safer."

"Oh."

Vincent Molet was sixty-two-years-old. Brooke wondered if he'd already made it known that he'd never leave Paris.

More to the point, would Christopher take the same stance? Refuse to leave Paris? It truly didn't bear thinking about.

Brooke glanced at the clock once more.

"*Merde!* I'm going to be late to my lesson, and Mademoiselle will have my head."

"By the way," Christopher called after her just before she closed the door to the office. "The guillotine is still in use for capital executions."

10

B rooke was still musing about the fact that the guillotine remained used as an instrument of State Justice when she rang Mademoiselle Arquette's doorbell. Her teacher didn't answer right away, but its sound set Odile to barking furiously. Brooke searched for the French words to soothe the poodle whose toenails had begun to scratch frantically on the other side of the door.

"*Pauvre chienne... c'est bon! C'est moi, Brooke!*"

Odile switched to whining as if her heart were breaking.

"Poor puppy," Brooke crooned, giving up on French. "It's okay. It's just me!" She thought she heard shuffling footsteps and then silence. "Mademoiselle Arquette?" Brooke called out. "*C'est moi, Madame de Varney!*"

Suddenly the door swung open and there stood her French teacher with a very long, very sharp-looking butcher knife clutched in her hand held high over her head, as if poised to strike.

"*Good lord...*" Brooke blurted under her breath.

Sabine Arquette proceeded to unleash a torrent of French which concluded with her screaming, "*Je vous déteste, vous les Allemands! Déteste, déteste, DETESTE!*"

"I get it!" Brooke cried out, forgetting to speak French. "You hate all Germans, but I'm not one of them!"

During Mademoiselle Arquette's outburst, Odile sprinted

through the doorway and stood trembling next to Brooke, leaning into her thigh. The language teacher continued to scream epithets at her that Brooke couldn't come close to translating. She knew they were threatening her with bodily harm, however, when Arquette thrust the knife in Brooke's direction, prompting Brooke to make a dash to the edge of the stairway she'd just walked up.

A door could be heard opening on the floor below. The next thing Brooke heard were footsteps hurriedly tramping up the stairs. Near the top of the flight, the building's concierge took one look at the terrifying tableau and muttered "*Mon Dieu!*" and then shouted, and shook her fist at her tenant, "*Fini, Madame!*"

The woman swiftly retreated downstairs to safety.

You're 'done' with this mad woman, you say? Well, what about me? Brooke silently demanded, her heart beating so fast, it nearly cut off her breath.

In the next second, she made the decision to flee down the stairs as well. She'd almost reached the building's foyer before she realized that the poodle was running beside her. The concierge stood at her open door shouting to someone inside her flat, presumably for outside help. Brooke sped by, hearing the concierge scream in high-pitched French, "She is *crazy!* She's been insane for years! Call the authorities! I won't have her in this building another day!"

Brooke kept running and sped out of the building's entrance. Reaching the curb, she opened the door to the Simca and before she could get in the car, Odile leapt past her and cowered on the passenger side.

"Okay, sweet thing," Brooke said, trying to catch her breath. Slipping behind the wheel, she reached to stroke the dog's head. "You can stay with me for a while until Mademoiselle is more herself. Then, I'll bring you back," she crooned. Given Arquette's current mental state, Brooke doubted the distraught woman would even remember to *feed* her dog, let alone venture out for a needed walk. She pictured the woman brandishing her large butcher knife and shuddered. Her teacher didn't even seem to recognize her student at her door, but merely saw Brooke as a real, live threat.

Taking a deep breath to try to calm her nerves, Brooke reached under the Odile's chin and gave it a gentle scratch. "Don't worry... I'll teach you some English so we can communicate."

Odile leaned over and licked Brooke's ear. In response, Brooke placed the flat of her hand against the side of the dog's head, pressing against her cheek. They both were still trembling.

Christopher had been right, she thought. People can easily break under the terror wrought by war waged indiscriminately against civilians. With the Germans marching toward Paris, she could only imagine how much more pressure would be brought to bear on them all.

With shaking fingers, Brooke put the key into the ignition and told her new companion, "We'll just have to see what's next for that poor, unstable lady upstairs, *vous comprenez?*"

Brooke had no idea if the poodle "understood" what she was saying or not. She just knew that an unhinged woman, wielding a butcher knife and hallucinating that her least-accomplished student was an invading Nazi, was just as dangerous for a dog as it was for her.

"You want to bring him in *here*?" Christopher protested, pointing to the poodle docilely walking into the office beside Brooke.

"It's a *her* and she's very well-behaved, Christopher. See? She's already curling up in the corner, quiet as a mouse."

"A rather large one. What if we get the call to evacuate?"

"We'll take her with us. She fits in my car."

"Whose dog is she? What about the owner?"

"My French teacher's. The woman went nuts," Brooke declared and quickly filled in Christopher about events the previous day. "Apparently, she's been having various mental issues for some time and witnessing the bombing sent her right over the edge. I was told this morning that by the time the men in the white coats arrived, she was acting completely bonkers, threatening them with the butcher knife she brandished at me yesterday."

"Well that's very sweet of you to rescue the lady's poodle, but you can't just dog-nap someone's pet like this."

"I went by her place on my way to work with the dog and the concierge told me that Madame Arquette was being committed to an institution for the mentally disturbed. Even I could translate it when she said that they took her away in a straitjacket. The building superintendent *thanked* me for taking Odile off her hands."

At the sound of her name, the chocolate brown poodle raised her head inquiringly.

"See how smart she is?" Brooke said. "She knows we're talking about her."

"She's awfully big," Christopher repeated. "I thought poodles were little things that fit in a lady's purse."

Brooke laughed. "You're thinking of the miniature or tea-cup breeds. She's a *standard* poodle. They were originally working dogs. Their job was to retrieve ducks and other birds for their masters. They're also great swimmers!"

"How do you know so much about dogs?" he demanded with obvious skepticism. "And poodles, specifically?"

"I was in a film once that was supposedly set in France. A poodle that belonged to the character I played figured in the plot. The dog wrangler on set told me all about the breed. And besides, I love dogs! My mother wouldn't let me have one, but I made friends with every single canine in my neighborhood when I was a kid."

Christopher's gaze remained on Odile. Her sleek chin rested elegantly on one paw as she returned to snoozing in the corner.

"Well, we never had dogs at my parents' place in Montmartre," Christopher disclosed. "Are you sure she'll be all right alone in here while we're in the studio learning how to run the control board?"

Brooke smiled, confident she'd won.

"She'll be just fine," she reassured him. "She's very obedient and she'll guard the place while we're gone. And by the way, I've renamed her... sort of."

"What do you mean 'sort of?'"

"Her given name was Odile. It's a girl's name, it means 'prospers in battle.'"

"So?" Christopher said. "Given the Germans are bombing us now, that sounds appropriate... sort of."

He pointed to the clock indicating it was time for their lesson with Vincent Molet in the control room.

"I've renamed her 'Ondie,'" Brooke announced.

Christopher burst out laughing.

"Ondie? That's perfect! Especially since you and I are about to learn how to run the engineer's control board. *Ondie*," he chuckled, repeating the French word for 'shortwave.'

He took a step nearer the corner and reached down, scratching the dog behind her ear.

"Mademoiselle Ondie it is, and welcome to our sinking ship."

BROOKE WAS GIVEN an immediate opportunity to practice her new skill running the radio control board due to a cavalcade of interviews she conducted in the days that followed her unexpected acquisition of a dog.

Christopher looked over the list of the artists, writers, historians, and political figures that Brooke had managed to lure into their studio for interviews. His eyes resting on the bottom of the page, he breathed a low whistle.

"How did you corral all these names?" he asked admiringly.

"I just asked Denise to contact everyone I'd met at the soiree that Victor and I held at our place a while ago." At Christopher's raised eyebrow, she hastened to add, "It was the only one we gave and you didn't attend because you were on your way to the Maginot Line. When Denise called them," Brooke grinned, "she told each one of the guests that I wanted to know their views on whether France was going to need America's help defeating the Nazis now poised to invade."

Christopher nodded at the list of names.

"Obviously, they were willing to make their opinions known."

Brooke looked over his shoulder at the list of her interviewees. There was Sylvia Beach from her bookstore, Shakespeare and Company, along with the young American, Polly Peabody, who had been raising money for a field hospital in Norway. The painter, Picasso, had sat before the microphone for less than ten minutes, but made provocative and newsworthy statements about the Germans who were calling his and other western artists' work 'degenerate.'

"I see you even persuaded Toquette and Dr. Sumner Jackson to come into the studio," Christopher said, sounding amazed. "Is it true that he's preparing a basement ward to hide patients the Nazis might want to capture if they invade Paris?"

Brooke was surprised to hear this as she hadn't known about the rumor, and Dr. Jackson hadn't mentioned a word of it.

"Well, if he is, he wasn't about to tell me anything. But both the Jacksons were eloquent about how crucial the American Hospital was in saving lives in the last war— and that all the donations from the United States were most appreciated."

Christopher laughed and pointed to the last two names on the list.

"I see you even interviewed your friend, Viv Clarke, about volunteering as an ambulance driver."

"I don't just interview my personal friends," she replied defensively. "Viv Clarke had a very newsworthy story about driving to and from Dunkirk, ferrying some hush-hush Frenchman to get him back to England."

Christopher's expression altered slightly. Brooke could see he was staring at the last name on the list: Josephine Baker, the African-American exotic dancer whose feathered gyrations had taken Paris by storm.

"And yes," Brooke answered his question for him. "I interviewed Josephine Baker who had some very cogent things to say about how important it was to save French culture from being ground up by the damn Germans." She smiled at him, adding "Jealous *you* didn't get to interview her? She's quite stunning."

"Did she know...?" he asked slowly, "you are Victor's wife?"

"Well, of course," she answered. "She was one of the guests at the soirée. She was very anxious to say how much she abhorred Charles Lindbergh and his odious 'American First' campaign. In her mind, he's as much pro-racist as pro-fascist."

"Hmmm."

"What do you mean '*hmmm*?'" she demanded.

"Nothing," he replied quickly.

Just then, Denise entered the office waving a copy of an English-language newspaper printed for ex-pats living in France.

"Look at this interview with your American Ambassador to England, Joseph Kennedy!" she exclaimed. "He sounds positively *pro*-German."

Brooke took the paper from her hand, scanning the first paragraphs with rising disgust.

"And then, of course, there's the Duke and Duchess of Windsor," Christopher noted cynically. "Half their cousins are actively pro-Nazi and married to Germans."

"I didn't know that," Brooke murmured.

Christopher quickly recounted for her that the Duke had abdicated the British throne four years previously, in 1936, and had set out on a tour of Germany in the fall of 1937 where he had tea with Hitler in Berchtesgaden. Fluent in German and "proud of the German blood" flowing in his veins, he and his American Duchess took dinner on that trip with the likes of Goebbels, Göring, and Joachim von Ribbentrop.

"There were well-founded speculations that Wallis Simpson had had a sexual relationship with von Ribbentrop when he was Ambassador to Britain in the 1930s, so the trip was viewed by the Brits as dangerously cozy, even back then."

"Wow... you *do* know behind-the-scenes on just about everything," Brooke said, impressed.

Denise nodded agreement and pointed to the newspaper Brooke still held.

"Jules wants you, Christophe to write a tough editorial chronicling the verified reports we have on the behavior of the Germans storming through Poland. In it, he also wants you to chastise people like Kennedy and the Windsors and send it upstairs as soon as you're finished. Once it's approved, you're to broadcast it right away."

The next few hours flew by with Christopher pounding away on his Royal typewriter.

"Approved!" Denise declared, waving his news copy in the air after having run upstairs for the censors to read it, then downstairs with it a few minutes later.

Christopher immediately disappeared into the broadcast booth where he read his narrative and attempted to operate the control board with Vincent Molet overseeing the ancient piece of equipment.

Brooke spent the time he was gone writing thank you notes to all her interviewees, expressing gratitude for their eloquence and courage.

"I'm beat," Christopher announced, striding through the glass-paneled door and collapsing into a chair. He looked over at Brooke who was putting her last thank-you note into addressed envelopes. "What say you we head for the nearest café and get drunk?"

"You can get drunk," Brooke said, piling the letters in their mail outbox. "But I'm starving. A plate of oysters and a bowl of onion soup sounds *parfait.*"

"I know just the place," he declared. "Le Dôme Café not far from here, although I'm going to have a bottle of wine with my *foie gras* and a bowl of bouillabaisse." Christopher waved some wire copy in his hand. "Trust me, you'll need a drink, too. The latest dispatch says the Germans will likely arrive at our gates anytime between the twelfth and the fourteen of June."

"Within the *week*?" gasped Brooke. Her mind flew in a score of directions, wondering how to prepare for such an event.

He nodded. "So, my dear colleague, this may be our 'Last Supper.' Therefore, I say we order a bottle of champagne."

Feeling as if the air had just escaped from their light-hearted banter, Brooke raced over to his chair and grabbed the dispatch out of his hand.

"Oh, God... this is terrible," she murmured, reading.

"All the more reason to get ourselves to the Le Dôme this very second," he said. He stretched his hand toward her. "Help a very tired journalist-turned-propagandist out of this chair, will you?"

Brooke pulled him to his feet and turned toward Ondie, still curled up in the corner.

"I'll just run her home to Nicole to feed and meet you at the café in forty minutes.

"Take an hour," he said, pointing to the telephone on his desk. "I have a few more calls to make, but I'll wait for you there."

CHRISTOPHER ORDERED a bottle of Veuve Clicquot while Brooke glanced around the café's blood red-and-gold interior, spanking white linen tablecloths, and the gleaming brass railings that framed the velvet banquette upon which they had been seated by the snooty maître d'.

"Pretty fancy," she whispered.

"Nothing but the best at the 'Last Supper' for a dying breed," Christopher muttered under his breath as the waiter snapped open folded linen napkins and laid them on their laps.

"Doing that editorial just now really bothered you, didn't it?" she said once the waiter had retreated.

Christopher nodded, his lips in a firm line. "It wasn't so much what they wanted me to say," he explained, a weariness in his voice she'd never heard before. "Ambassador Kennedy *should* be shipped back to his boot-legging haunts in America. It's just I don't like being *told* what I should say instead of broadcasting the plain facts that *my* research and reporting prompt me to say."

Brooke well understood by now the difference between journalism and propaganda, but she longed for a break from all the doom-and-gloom she felt hanging over them.

"Really, Christopher! If this *is* our 'Last Supper,' let's at least try to enjoy it."

"I suppose," he acquiesced, "but haven't you noticed that our broadcasts are being designed solely to prop up a failing government that refuses to act, and an army that has let down the entire country?"

"It's not the army that's let us down," she replied sharply, wondering at Victor's fate as she sat in a posh restaurant about to drink champagne with his friend, she reminded herself. "The *leaders* of the army are the ones letting everyone down."

"Touché," he commented, nodding to the waiter who had returned to pour the sparkling wine.

When they were alone after placing their orders, Christopher raised his champagne flute, tilting it in Brooke's direction.

"To you, Miss Cub Reporter. I admit I had my doubts, and I definitely don't approve of poodles at the office, but you have been doing stellar work, despite everything the suits upstairs do to prevent it. You've shown what I think the Yanks call 'moxie' and I salute you."

"Oh, things aren't that bad," she said, ducking her head toward her glass to avoid his seeing the blush she could feel invading her cheeks.

Christopher's praise filled her with both pride and vague discomfort. She agreed their talents had been used shamelessly to deliver information with a definite slant to showing the current bumbling government in a better light than it deserved.

She stared into her glass, watching the bubbles fighting their way to the top, and said, "We've both gotten a few truths and some half-truths into our broadcasts, don't you think?"

She looked up, finally meeting his gaze. Something in his eyes caught her by surprise, an intensity in their dark blue depths she hadn't noticed before. His steely stare seemed to be beaming a shortwave message in a frequency she wasn't tuned to.

"Things will soon be very different, you know," he said quietly. She noticed for the first time that he had shaved at some point between her delivering Ondie to the apartment and meeting him at the restaurant.

Why, he's actually handsome, she marveled.

Not in a classic sense of Victor's perfect, good looks, but in a way that was rugged and radiated a masculinity that was probably lethal if a woman were to fall in love with him. She could see he'd combed his blond mop, and someone had carefully pressed his rumpled tweed jacket. This night he wore a nice-looking blue shirt beneath it. It suddenly dawned on her that when he took the trouble with his appearance, he looked the part of the dashing foreign correspondent he actually was!

He reached for her free hand and forced her to hold his gaze.

"I'll say it only one more time, Brooke. You are not safe staying in Paris when the Germans arrive. There will be no more Radio

Mondiale. No more job for you. The Germans will have taken note of every anti-Nazi broadcast you've put out over the air."

His stark words made it feel as if all the bubbles had just drained from her glass.

"We'll..." she countered, her heart speeding up in the wake of his dire pronouncements. "Our broadcast team'll evacuate! Head further south. We'll keep getting our messages out, even if—"

"France will fall, Brooke," he interrupted, setting down his glass for emphasis. Any celebration they might have been marking this night, forgotten. "If not this week, then this month. You have to leave. *Tomorrow* will barely be soon enough."

"Don't say that!" She hated that her voice was quavering. "I'm not a quitter and neither are you! I thought we were in this together... this business of trying to tell people what's happening in their lives? 'Partners in crime,' you said."

"As your partner in this madness, I want you to survive this war," he said with an urgency that made her heart pound even more. "I want us both to." He shook his head, a tone of defeat lacing his words. "If you don't leave Paris immediately, it will soon be too late."

Brooke fell silent within the hushed confines of Le Dôme restaurant, absorbing Christopher's ominous predictions about the coming weeks. Then, she demanded, "How are you so sure of the timetable for when the Nazis will get to Paris?"

"I know."

He did not elaborate.

Christopher Laurent never burns his sources... even with friends.

"Then, let's make a run for the Spanish border," she proposed cockily, trying to lighten their mood. "We'll wave our American passports, as you suggested for me, and—" She paused. "You *do* have dual citizenship, don't you? You have an American document tucked away somewhere?"

He nodded, "yes" so she continued formulating her impromptu plan.

"Maybe we can get ourselves to England and continue the fight from there, like that guy that Viv Clarke took to Dunkirk!"

It seemed in that moment that she'd never been a second-rate actress. That the life of a journalist and broadcaster was all she'd ever wanted to do, to *be*.

She looked down at the table and realized to her shock that, in her attempt to urge him to see they should remain a team, she had grabbed both Christopher's hands, their fingers intertwined as parting lovers' would be.

Her dinner partner remained silent for a long moment, staring down where their hands were joined. Then, he raised his eyes to stare into hers. The surroundings within Le Dôme faded from rich red to gray as he leaned across their small table, their lips only inches apart.

"You are something else, do you realize that?" he murmured.

"So are you," she whispered back.

With heart-stopping certainty she saw that he was about to kiss her and the terrible thing was, she wanted him to. But in the next instant, the honorable man sitting so close to her was just that. Honorable. He pulled back and she knew perfectly well what had prevented him from doing what they both had so unexpectedly desired.

She watched him inhale a deep breath and nod his head as if he agreed with her previous outburst that they should flee France before the Nazis crossed the border. He carefully extricated his hands from hers and said quietly, "It's likely that Victor will be heading for London by now— or is already there."

Victor...

An avalanche of conflicting emotions churned in Brooke's gut. Victor's decision to join the army had been made without even discussing it with her and she'd heard absolutely nothing from or about him since he'd left.

Her thoughts flew back to the pile of letters from his co-star in Norway he'd so swiftly consigned to the fireplace so she couldn't see what they contained. She realized in this moment that it had shattered her confidence in the relationship she'd thought Victor and she had forged. Did he truly care about her welfare with the same fervor she'd cared about his?

He's my husband. Surely, he cares and, of course, I love him. Yet here I am, actually wanting another man to kiss me!

Brooke couldn't fight the desire to have him put his arms around her and tell her they would all survive this coming Nazi nightmare.

"Christopher, I—" she began, but he interrupted her as if he already knew the two of them should pull back from the brink of doing something beyond foolhardy.

"A plan for you to head south to Biarritz and then over the Pyrenees to Spain is an excellent idea," he declared, his tone gruff. "The American embassy in Madrid can get you to Gibraltar and from there, you'll sail or fly to the U.K., or go to New York, whichever is the safer plan. Let me try to make some arrangements tomorrow."

"Not if you're not going, too," she replied, her throat suddenly tight. "We both have jobs to do in this damn war. Why are you so intent on getting rid of me and being such a sacrificial lamb yourself?"

"That is definitely not my plan," he countered.

Just then the waiter arrived with the food they'd ordered. A plate of plump oysters was placed in front of Brooke.

"*Et pour vous, monsieur, foie gras,*" their waiter said grandly, setting down the goose liver with crackers fanned along the outer rim of the porcelain plate.

Brooke raised her glass once more and tried to keep a cheerful smile on her face. Acting as if the topic they'd just discussed about fleeing France had never been broached, she fought to erase the memory of currents coursing through their clasped hands. She tipped her glass in her own direction.

"Here's to me, who is determined to maintain the course fighting this war, and to you, who will show me how to do it. Yes?"

Without replying, Christopher left his glass on the table. He picked up the small knife next to his plate and smeared the liver pâté onto one of the crackers. The sounds of clinking glasses and lively conversation of the other patrons swirled around them, filling the yawning silence at their table.

Finally, Christopher said, "In this war, it seems that each of us charts a separate course."

To Brooke's dismay, the silence between them continued

throughout the rest of their meal. Afterward, he walked her to the Simca and bid her a perfunctory good night.

Brooke glanced in the rearview mirror as she pulled away from the curb. Christopher had already turned his back on the car and was walking in the opposite direction.

11

Waiting for Brooke at her flat when she returned from Le Dôme Café that night was a short letter from her mother in Los Angeles and a cable from Victor's father in Northern California.

For Estelle Bradley's part, it was the first communication in almost a year and contained its usual misspellings and poor grammar. Quickly scanning it, Brooke saw it made no mention of Errol, but simply demanded she return home and go back to work.

Maybe that Frenchie husband of yours can help out as funds here are low.

BROOKE TOSSED the letter in a nearby wastebasket. She was upset since she'd sent plenty of funds to her mother's account and was even more disturbed that there was no news about her son who'd just had his third birthday at the end of May.

Ondie, the newly named poodle, curled herself into a ball on Victor's side of the bed. Brooke tucked the duvet under her arms and slit open the cable from Bernard de Varney. She was astounded her husband's father had contacted her and even more amazed he'd sent her a draft for five hundred dollars to his bank in Paris. Furthermore, he urged:

TAKE NEXT FLIGHT TO NEW YORK AND TRAIN TO SAN FRANCISCO STOP MONIQUE INSISTS TOO STOP

BROOKE READ and reread the words. Victor's grandmother obviously had refused all entreaties from her grown son living in California to abandon the château and come to America. Even so, Brooke reasoned, had Monique de Varney wired Victor's father about his son's marriage to her? Had she also informed Bernard that Victor's whereabouts were currently unknown? Perhaps Monique had scolded her son that he had an obligation toward his American-born daughter-in-law to get her to safety, even though he'd never met her?

Or had Christopher, ace reporter, figured out how to get in touch with the senior de Varney? she thought suddenly.

And that was the problem, Brooke mused, scratching Ondie gently under her left ear. Everyone, including Christopher, was telling her to flee when she had no idea about Victor's fate, or even if he had survived the German victories throughout northern France. They all wanted her to go... yet every instinct and desire she had was to stay. The oddest thing of all was that she couldn't even explain to herself why she was loath to leave a country facing imminent attack.

Ondie stirred from her sleep and snuggled more closely into the crook of Brooke's legs. The question for Brooke was how could she leave France at the very moment her adopted home needed every single person who believed in its sovereignty and in freedom itself to stand against the invader? As just one example, who would bear witness to the horrifying cruelty she'd seen at the Montparnasse train station?

She was starting to realize that she had fully embraced her new life as an ex-pat American journalist in Paris. Despite the looming dangers, it had become a place where she felt more alive, more *useful* than at any time she'd worked in Hollywood films. She couldn't imagine abandoning her new friends and associates at this critical hour. And how could she just leave Victor's friend Christopher to his own, reckless devices, even if she suspected he had schemed to get *her* to leave?

"Well, I won't!" she declared.

Her words caused Ondie to raise her head and look inquiringly at her new mistress. After a few moments, the poodle settled back against Brooke's knees. She, in turn, breathed a sigh and turned out the lamp perched on its Louis XIV side table.

She tried not to think about the empty pillow beside her.

THE DAYS between June 7 and 14, 1940 would be seared into Brooke's memory for the rest of her life.

The first thing to greet her the morning after the dinner at Le Dôme was Christopher waving a dispatch from his desk before she'd even closed the door to their office.

"The Norwegian royal family has fled their country and are due to arrive in England by ship sometime very soon." He scowled at her, adding grimly, "A very smart move on their part, I must say, so please take note, Brooke."

"You talking to me? Well, just forget it! As you say, we must each chart our own path in this war."

She sat down at her desk feeling almost as if their near kiss the previous night had been a figment of her imagination. Christopher was more than his usual gruff self, rendering her determined to put their exchanges at the restaurant out of her mind and close down the subject of her leaving France.

"So, the Norwegian royal family and their government have given up the fight and surrendered to the Nazis?" she commented, pulling her reporter's notebook from her handbag.

Christopher's scowled. "Surrendered, yes. Given up? No! There are already Resistance groups forming there and the royal family vows to carry on the fight from London. It's expected the wife of their crown prince will go to America to try to persuade FDR to help. The President is very aware that there are millions of Scandinavians in the American Midwest, and the next presidential election is coming up."

"With Charles Lindbergh and Henry Ford poisoning the well every chance they get!" Brooke fumed. "I wish the princess well, but good luck to her." She sighed, shaking her head. "Norway's surrendered. What next, for pity's sake?"

She didn't have long to wait. Three days later, on June 10th, someone down the hall shouted, "Italy has just officially declared war on Britain and France!"

Another country was soon to attack across the border into France? Brooke stared at Christopher in alarm.

"And where, exactly, does that leave Victor's regiment that's hung out to dry in Brittany?" she demanded, concerned more than ever about the disastrous leadership of the French army whose bumbling decisions could have— or could soon —result even in Victor getting killed.

Christopher looked up from his typewriter where he'd been pounding out the latest news for the broadcast that evening.

As if he were reading her mind he said, "If Victor hasn't already departed France, I expect he and his group are waiting for some British ships to take them off St. Malo or the beach at Cherbourg."

"What's your evidence of that?" she demanded in the exact same tone in which he always required her to name at least three sources for every single statement she made in her scripts.

"It's an educated guess," he allowed, but Brooke suspected he knew more than he was letting on. With a casual shrug he added, "Doesn't it seem logical if he's attached to a brigadier general? I managed to reach a military contact of mine to ask if there were any specifics about this de Gaulle fellow and his regiment."

"And you learned nothing," Brooke filled in gloomily.

"My source said those two spots on the coast were the most likely disembarkation points, but he couldn't— or wouldn't —

confirm anything specific about de Gaulle, which means that upstart must be climbing up in the world."

Before Christopher could continue, Denise suddenly opened the door to their office and closed it quickly, lowering her voice.

"I want you both to pack the things we've designated to bring with us and be ready with the bus and cars to leave Paris tomorrow morning at six."

"Oh, my God, *really*?" Brooke exclaimed.

"Why?" Christopher demanded. "What's the latest?"

"The Germans are expected to reach Paris in two days' time—or less."

Before either listener could press Denise further, she spun on her heel and was gone.

After a long breath, Christopher muttered, "Holy shit."

Brooke's mind began to race with concerns about how a large group of forty-three in their broadcast unit, plus dependents, could get on the road in such a short time.

"Listen, Christopher," she proposed, "I'll come in my car and collect you and your luggage at five tomorrow morning. It'll save time. Then we can be here early to help organize the others to get on the bus and line up the cars in a caravan." She summoned a cheery smile. "It'll be like my days in Hollywood when we had to corral everyone at dawn to set off to shoot on location instead of on the back lot at Fox studios."

Christopher pressed his lips shut, and his brow furrowed. Brooke waited while he appeared deep in thought. Neither of them had discussed the chill that had descended at the end of their supper at Le Dôme. With all the drama swirling around them, Brooke could only hope they'd both put aside the memory to focus on the escalating crisis at hand.

In a decisive move, Christopher dug into his pants pocket and pulled out a set of keys.

"Here, take these." He rattled off his address in Montmartre where he still owned his late parents' flat.

"Why give them to me? We're leaving town."

"If we ever get back to Paris at some point during the occupation," he said, "you'll always be able to use my place as a safehouse, even if I happen to be away."

"Where will you be?" she asked quickly. "And what do you mean 'safehouse?'"

"Who knows what's going to happen a month from now? I-I might be on assignment somewhere," he said. "And a 'safehouse' is any place where the authorities don't expect you to be. There's just no knowing what's going to happen once the Germans put themselves in charge. Like I've said, if either of us returns to Paris— and you definitely *shouldn't*, by the way —we could find ourselves in dicey situations because of having worked for the Ministry. This is just a precaution."

"Okay," she answered unconvincingly. She reached into the bottom of her handbag, retrieved the keys to her own flat, and handed them to Christopher.

She responded to his puzzled look with, "So *you* have the same option for a place to go in case the damn Jerries decide to bomb your home while we're away."

Slowly, he extended his hand and accepted her keys that he swiftly shoved in his pants pocket.

"Nicole can let you in today, I take it?" he asked.

"Yes, and I have Victor's set at home." She wagged a finger at him. "So, please be ready to go tomorrow when I swing by at the crack of dawn, will you?"

Christopher merely waved a dismissive hand in her direction and started clacking away on the keys of his typewriter.

Within minutes of Denise's announcement that morning, employees at the Ministry of Information launched into a flurry of preparations.

An hour later, Christopher looked up from his typewriter and declared, "I want you to go, right now, to the American Embassy and ask them to issue you a special seal to put on the front door of your flat on Rue Saint-Dominique."

"Why? What's that going to do?"

"It might just keep the invaders from requisitioning it as a cushy place for some Nazi swine to settle in. At least as long as the U.S. stays out of this war."

"Oh." Brooke said, amazed he knew about such details.

"Go, *now*, and do it!" he barked. Then, more politely, he said, "Then, you'd better go home and start packing."

Taken aback by the ferocity of his commands, she merely nodded, and grabbed her purse.

"See you at your place at five," she reminded him, and raced out the office door.

FOLLOWING CHRISTOPHER'S ADVICE, Brooke proceeded to the American Embassy to obtain a special seal that would be attached to the outside of her apartment's front door, perhaps warding off confiscation by the approaching invaders.

Brooke handed the embassy clerk the deed that now bore both Victor's and her names. She could only pray that by declaring the property was co-owned by a citizen of a neutral country, not a party to the war, the flat— with its official seal from the U.S. Embassy —wouldn't be taken over by some Nazi officer newly arrived in Paris.

Explaining her latest actions to Nicole when she returned home, Brooke's housekeeper responded tearfully, "Let me stay and guard it for you. I can show them the deed and—"

Brooke knew that Nicole dreaded uprooting herself once again after leaving everything she'd ever known in Alsace. Even so, Brooke couldn't imagine abandoning the young woman in a city with the Nazis due to arrive within days.

"No, Nicole," she insisted, "we are sticking together for the duration, but I promise to bring you back to Paris when it's safer."

Brooke's next two stops had also been insisted upon by Christopher.

"You know Dr. Jackson at the American Hospital pretty well, don't you?" he'd asked earlier that day.

"Yes, of course," she replied. "I recently interviewed him and his wife Toquette, remember?"

"Right. Good. Go there today and ask Jackson for a letter on his hospital stationery that says you suffer from some terminal illness."

"*What*?" Brooke protested. "That's creepy. Why would I do that?"

"Because if you're ever arrested by the Krauts, it could serve as your 'get out of jail' card."

"I don't follow you," Brooke declared with exasperation.

Christopher's voice had become grim. "You may not realize it, Brooke, but your broadcasting efforts for the current government actually make you a highly prized person to arrest if you find your-self in the wrong place at the wrong time. A letter saying you're deathly ill could keep you out of the worst prisons, or at least the Nazis might incarcerate you in an infirmary."

His words gave her a chill, but Brooke managed a small laugh. "Obviously you are very experienced in outfoxing the authorities."

Christopher was not taking up her banter.

"This is no joke! Trust me on this, will you? Go see Dr. Jackson and put that document in a safe place, like under the lining of one of your sturdiest shoes." He pointed to her handbag, urging her, "And while you're out, go to your bank and withdraw as much money in dollars as you can."

When she started to protest, he barked, "Just *do* it!"

Brooke gave him a look to let him know she thought he was overreacting, but the seriousness of his tone prompted her, when she left the Embassy with the seal in hand, to swing by both her bank and the hospital. She found Viv in the ambulance garage and asked her to show her to Dr. Jackson's office.

"Sure, kiddo," Viv replied, puzzled. "It's on the fourth floor." She regarded Brooke for a moment. "You don't *look* sick..."

"I feel fine," Brooke laughed, and explained why Christopher thought she should carry out this strange written request.

"Smart guy," Viv said, and led the way upstairs in the main building.

To Brooke's great surprise, the doctor readily complied almost as if he'd had an early warning of her bizarre petition.

"America may not ever join this war," Dr. Jackson said, signing his name at the bottom of the bogus diagnosis of uterine cancer detailed under the American Hospital of Paris' letterhead. "But if it ever does, you and I will be known as 'enemy aliens' and subject to arrest."

He stuffed the letter into an envelope and handed it to her.

"Good luck, Brooke," he said, adding kindly, "and I hope you have word from Victor very soon. I know how anxious you must be with all this happening so quickly."

Brooke nodded her thanks. She could almost picture Victor in his handsome woolen army cape, waiting impatiently on some beach in Brittany or Normandy for a skiff to take him to a ship headed for Britain.

Viv remained outside Jackson's office during Brooke's meeting with the head of the American Hospital. The fledgling ambulance driver put her arm around Brooke as they walked toward the staircase that would lead to the lobby and out the front entrance.

"So... it might be a while before we see each other again," Brooke said, the enormity of her leaving Paris accompanied by her colleagues at the Information Ministry hitting her full force.

"If it makes you feel any better, all of us in the ambulance corps were put on high alert as of yesterday," Viv acknowledged. "No more days off for the foreseeable future. We have no idea if Paris will rise up when the damn Huns beat down the gates, and we'll be fetching injured civilians from all over the city." Her change in demeanor seemed to indicate her own uncertainty about the future. "Or maybe the Parisians will just accept it all meekly and let the tanks roll past the Arc de Triomphe."

"Well... either way, good luck, Viv, and try to stay out of trouble, okay?" Brooke pleaded.

"Double ditto for you, kiddo," Viv replied, giving Brooke a quick hug. "I don't think you and I had enough French lessons to convince anyone we're natives, but we should be okay as long as America doesn't get into the war."

"Is that a good thing or a bad thing?" Brooke asked, semi-serious.

"God only knows," Viv replied.

"Christopher says I'll be a target, even with an American passport, because of those anti-German broadcasts I've done."

"Golly!" Viv said, her expression signaling worry. "I never

thought of that. He's probably right, so take good care, damn it! Now I'm *glad* you're leaving the city. After this is over, if you ever want to track me down, the hospital will know what's happened to me."

As a knot suddenly tightened in Brooke's stomach, she replied, "And Christopher will know the same about me... and hopefully, Victor, too... so let's just say we'll try to meet again on a happier day."

The two women embraced once again before Brooke hopped into the Simca and drove through the hospital's brick gates, returning to the heart of Paris, most likely for the last time as long as the world was at war.

~

"IT'S TIME," Jules Dumont declared. The grimace creasing his brow signaled that his back must be paining him. "We can't wait for Christopher any longer."

Jules's wife, Germaine, standing silently beside him, nodded her agreement.

"I can't believe it!" Brooke exclaimed, peering in both directions on the street in front of their building. "How could Christopher just leave like this without a word? I went by his flat at five this morning and no one was there!"

Denise shrugged out of her coat in the surprisingly warm early morning air.

"Actually, I think he gave us fair warning," she said. "We just didn't want to hear it. He's always considered himself a journalist. He wants to be free to write events as he sees them unfolding." She sighed. "I admire his courage but fear his recklessness."

"But where in the hell has he *gone*?" Brooke cried, hearing the frantic tone in her own voice.

Victor's whereabout are totally unknown, and now Christopher! And he didn't truly bother to warn me!

In fact, he'd clearly misled her, letting her think he'd be at his place when she came by in the Simca at dawn. A neighbor taking out the garbage had said he'd bid her farewell late the night before.

Not completely true... at Le Dôme he said very clearly 'in war, each must chart his own path.'

Brooke hated to admit to herself that there were, in fact, warnings that Christopher might refuse to prop up with propaganda a failing government he didn't believe in to begin with. She felt herself near tears and was deeply embarrassed that she seemed to have so little control over her emotions. She turned away from their little group to gaze at Jules's car parked in front of her own, along with a few other private vehicles belonging to colleagues. Meanwhile, the bus transporting most of the forty-two evacuated radio workers, their dependents, and the equipment needed to get their unit on the air was pulling ahead of the caravan to take its place as the lead.

"Really, dear," Denise said quietly, leaning in toward Brooke. "We'd best be off. The roads leading out of Paris are jammed already and it's only six-thirty."

A loud bark interrupted the conversation with Denise. Ondie had moved over to the driver's seat and was making her impatience known. A tearful Nicole was in the back seat. Beside her was Chief Engineer Vincent Molet's 'deputy,' a junior engineer named Jacques Grenier who was all of seventeen if he were a day.

Denise pointed to the dog. "See?" she urged gently. "Even your Ondie thinks we should get on the road— and we should."

"Reports are that half of Paris is fleeing," Jules volunteered.

His wife, Germaine, eyed Brooke with a sour look for holding their conversation exclusively in English.

"Yes," she said in French. "Let's be on the road. I'm worried about my father, Jules. I hope we won't be far from Paris."

"This is just a precaution, my dear," Jules reassured her. He turned to Brooke. Switching back to English, he said with regret. "I wish we'd been better prepared for everything, but it is what it is."

"Well, can you tell us, finally, where we're going?" she asked.

"The Minister of Information left Paris late yesterday," Jules reluctantly disclosed. "I'm told he was headed with other members of the government to Tours."

"You were *told*? Didn't he tell you himself?" she demanded. "He's your boss!"

Ignoring her heated inference, he replied, "We will go to Tours first and make our plans from there, once we can assess the situation." He inhaled a deep breath and then added, "The latest reports from the field are that our army is performing poorly and is in total retreat everywhere."

Before Brooke could even react to this upsetting news, Denise stepped forward.

"So we have our plan. Get in your car, Brooke. My husband and I will ride with Jules and Germaine."

In the next instant, Christopher's and Victor's erstwhile talent agent, now serving as Jules's highly capable deputy, made a signal with her raised arm. Then, she ran forward to give the bus driver the go-ahead to proceed. The mammoth vehicle packed with their colleagues and broadcasting equipment pulled forward and rolled down the street past Gare Montparnasse.

On the same block, pouring out of the train station's doors were thousands of hapless refugees loaded down with whatever possessions they were able to bring with them. They spilled into the streets, blocking the sidewalks and pavement in all directions.

"My God," Brooke murmured, standing next to her car, her gaze riveted on a little girl who couldn't have been more than two or three. The child's face was streaked with tears, crying out, "Mama! Mama!" The crowds of homeless were churning around the toddler, paying her no mind.

Brooke was just about to plunge into the melee when a young woman with a dirty scarf tied under her chin and another child in hand materialized beside the little one. Scolding the sobbing infant, but with relief etching her distraught expression, the woman grabbed the tiny, outstretched hand and all three disappeared into the seething throng.

Shaken by the scene she'd just witnessed, Brooke opened her car door and waved at her new dog. "Move over!" she ordered the poodle, and swiftly slipped behind the Simca's steering wheel.

"With crowds like this clogging the streets, it will take hours just to get out of Paris," complained young Jacques from the back seat.

"Try to sleep," Brooke ordered brusquely, attempting to push from her mind the misery swirling around on all sides. She put the car in gear. Creeping forward, she followed behind Jules's automobile, glancing in her rearview mirror to confirm the others were following along in the wake of her Simca.

"*Mon Dieu*, it's hot!" Jacques grumbled. "Can you imagine what it'll be like by noon?"

Brooke again gazed in the mirror at Nicole whose cheeks were moist, her eyes focused on the milling refugees. Brooke felt tears welling up in her own eyes again. Who would be there to guide her as a neophyte reporter covering stories of human atrocities of the kind she'd already observed? No "Cub" journalist had the skill and experience of a Christopher Laurent to chronicle the most formidable story of the century: the determination of Adolf Hitler and the Third Reich to conquer all of Europe.

Where *was* Christopher in all this chaos?

Her worst fear was he was most probably rushing toward the eastern outskirts of Paris to witness for himself the clanking tanks and goose-stepping Nazis invading the city that she now considered her home.

PART II

12

I n the hours the Radio Mondiale contingent drove along the road leading out from Paris, conditions grew worse by the kilometer. Vehicles were proceeding bumper-to-bumper, their forward progress blocked by horse-drawn carts, wheelbarrows piled high with household possessions, and even baby prams and tractors loaded with people living outside Paris— all fleeing in advance of the Germans bearing down on the region from the east.

Suddenly, the sounds of low-flying airplane engines were thundering overhead.

A hundred meters down the road, Brooke saw a swarm of them swoop down with bursts of fire exploding from their guns. With Ondie barking frantically, she abruptly turned left, leaving the pavement, and steered onto a dirt road that led into a stand of trees. Fortunately, the bus driver had done the same, and the other cars in their caravan followed Brooke's lead.

Plane engines were shrieking above the treetops, while Jacques and Nicole huddled in the back seat, arms around each other, heads ducked below the car's windows. Brooke leaned across her seat and pulled Ondie's head and hers under the dashboard.

The concussive sounds of shells exploding nearby went on for several minutes. Finally, the four occupants in the Simca heard the drone of the planes' propellers fade. Warily, they rose from their awkward crouches to peer out the front windshield as Brooke backed the car onto the main road once again.

"*Mon Dieu!*" whispered Nicole.

The vehicles and people who had not gotten far enough off the road in time were scattered in the adjacent fields, many bloody and writhing with injuries where they'd fallen. On all sides, bullet holes punctured scores of cars, disabling them where they had come to a halt.

"That was a *very* close call," breathed Brooke. She turned in her seat to peer at her passengers, murmuring, "But we're all okay, right?"

The two in the backseat confirmed they had not been wounded by any stray bullets but clearly were badly shaken. Struggling to steady her nerves, Brooke cautiously put the car in gear and fell in line behind Jules, along with the others in their group. She heard sirens, whether from ambulances dispatched from a local town, or air-raid warnings from a few villages to the north of them, she couldn't tell.

"Let's hope those are ambulances, coming to tend to the wounded," Nicole said softly from the backseat.

"I feel terrible, just driving on," Brooke replied, glancing in her rear-view mirror, "but we have to keep up with the others."

She tried her best to conceal from her passengers how stunned she was by the sheer barbarism of German planes swooping down in broad daylight to shoot at civilians like birds on a rail. She could only imagine what military forces behaving like this would do if they conquered the entire country.

BROOKE'S HANDS felt glued to her car's steering wheel during the fourteen hours she navigated through a nightmare of clogged roads. In all that time, the Simca and the rest of the Radio Mondiale vehicles had traveled barely a hundred kilometers.

"Can't we stop for a while?" called out Jacques. "I'm desperate to take a piss."

It was hours past sunset. Before Brooke could answer, the bus in the lead lumbered off the road as a summer rain began to fall in earnest.

"Your wish is my command," Brooke said, trying to make light of the grueling, long day they'd all spent together. Just like some movie stagehands she'd once known, the novice radio engineer had been nothing but a pain in the ass the entire trip. Once parked with the others, she looked over her shoulder into the back seat. "But now that we are stopped, Jacques, first please bring the food hamper from the trunk into the car for the rest of us. *Then*, have a pee."

Brooke gazed through the rain-soaked windshield with a sudden sense of gratitude for Victor's having gifted her with her own car. The other radio workers and their dependents would be forced to camp this first night beside the road outside Orleans in a summer downpour, or remain jammed side-by-jowl in the narrow confines of a bus.

Despite the rain, the June night was warm and humid. Brooke huddled in the front seat of the Simca with Ondie curled up on the car's floor. Jacques and Nicole were in near fetal positions in the rear. Yearning for sleep, two thoughts revolved in Brooke's exhausted brain:

Where was Victor at this very moment of national crisis... and what had happened to Christopher?

As June 13th dawned, the soggy group continued on to Tours, only to discover that just a fraction of the French government officials were present there, along with a handful of their Nazi-sympathizing mistresses that Christopher had told her the men kept secretly.

These women had traveled the same, snarled roads she had. They'd seen the massacre of civilians lying dead and wounded along the highway leading to Tours. Brooke wanted to slap the faces of those Frenchmen and women happily siding with the enemy. Her stomach churned thinking of the danger these Nazi sympathizers posed for soldiers like Victor and the French Army, and perhaps Christopher as well. Was there no one in the French government standing firm?

And what about Jules, she thought suddenly? If officials currently in power were going to capitulate to the invaders, what would be the fate of honest deputies like him?

The next day, on the 14th of June, at the hotel in Tours, Denise summoned Brooke to join her as she placed a call to Vincent Molet in Paris. Since Radio Mondiale's elderly chief engineer had declined to leave with their unit, he'd been instructed to "hold the fort," at their former headquarters.

Their ears pressed together, Brooke and Denise listened while Vincent, his voice betraying tears, relayed the news they'd all been dreading.

"The tanks rolled into the heart of Paris today," he reported. "They've even replaced our street signs with German ones." His voice increasingly distraught, he told them, "They've taken over Radio Mondiale's broadcasting offices. I've removed this phone to a closet. The rumor is that Marshal Pétain will be named the new, German-endorsed French Prime Minister. The old goat is reportedly going to establish a collaborationist government in Vichy."

Brooke remembered from the map that hung on Christopher's office wall that the town of Vichy was the famous spa resort located some 400 kilometers south of Paris. Vincent reported that the latest rumors were that the resort catering to the very rich would be in territory situated *below* a curving line drawn by the Nazis that would mark total German occupation of the north of the country, as well as a strip of France that bordered the Atlantic Ocean down as far as Biarritz and the border with Spain. Below that arcing line carving the country in two, the newly formed Vichy authorities would have nominal control over everything south to the Mediterranean Sea.

"Supposedly, the lower section they're calling the 'Free Zone' is to be governed by Pétain and his group of German collaborators," Vincent Molet disclosed, his voice laced with gloom, "but I'm sure it'll be just a puppet regime. Everyone here thinks the Nazis will eventually control the entire nation, headquartered in Paris."

Brooke broke in. "Have you or anyone you've talked to heard from, or seen, Christopher?"

Vincent didn't answer immediately, and for a moment, she wondered if they'd lost the connection. Finally, his voice came through the phone receiver.

"He's not with you, I take it?"

"No," Brooke and Denise responded simultaneously.

There was another pause.

"I am alone in the building, except for the lousy Krauts," Vincent Molet said in a low voice.

"But are *you* all right?" Denise asked urgently. "They haven't hurt you?"

"I was pushed around a bit when they first stormed the building, but they don't know how to work any of the French equipment, so I guess they won't kill me. Not for the moment anyway."

"Can you keep the relay equipment that forwards our signal to Britain out of their hands?" Denise urged. "It's absolutely crucial we keep contact with the London War Office."

"I can probably do that... at least for a while. Maybe I'll put a sign on it saying it's *kaput*," Vincent answered.

In the next second, he abruptly hung up.

"Some German must have come within earshot," Denise murmured.

"Let's hope that's all it was," Brooke replied.

THE FOLLOWING DAY IN TOURS, it was clear that all radio workers holding British citizenship would be better off heading for the Spanish border before the Nazis fully took over the country.

Brooke and Denise watched from the front of the hotel as their British colleagues and the few remaining officials of the erstwhile French government who were not supporters of Pétain departed in a clutch of automobiles, heading further south for Bordeaux. Most would go on to Biarritz and then over the Pyrenees to Spain and work their way back to Britain from there. Jules, because of his wife's elderly and ailing father, elected to remain with the broadcast group.

"Nobody takes poets seriously," he assured them with unfounded bravado.

Denise leaned over to Brooke saying, "You, with your American passport, are safe for now."

"You mean, I'm okay as long as the Nazis don't connect me with my previous broadcasts?" she replied.

Denise inhaled a deep breath. "Well. There is that. It would be best to only refer to yourself from here on out as Madame de Varney, and *never* mention your professional name, Brooke Bradley, that you used on air."

Nodding agreement, Brooke asked, "Any more news of what's going on in Brittany?" Both women realized that what she was really asking was about Victor.

"Nothing very specific, I'm afraid," Denise admitted. "Just that the disorganized French forces have scattered throughout Normandy and Brittany. The latest word is, ships are arriving sporadically from England to ferry whatever army units are waiting on the regions' beaches across the Channel."

Oh, God, Victor... did you manage to row out to a boat?

She could barely risk speculating where Christopher might be at this moment. All she knew was that it just felt as if he'd deserted their radio crew. Deserted her.

Then, she was forced to recall how vehemently he'd urged her to leave the country, and perhaps that's what he'd done as well... or was trying to. He'd want to be somewhere his journalistic skills and experience might still be able to do some good for the Allies.

And there was one more thing she was forced to admit silently.

Honorable as ever, he'd made no promises, damnit!

BROOKE'S WORRY about the odd couple in her life hadn't lessened by the time she and the staff of Radio Mondiale straggled into Bordeaux. The few former French officials there let it be known that the broadcasting unit should immediately requisition a studio at a local radio station.

"Prepare for someone who will be arriving here to record a supremely important announcement to the nation," one government bureaucrat advised gravely.

"*Who* will be broadcasting?" Brooke demanded of Jules and Denise, remembering Vincent Molet's tearful claim that an octogenarian from the Great War was now conferring with the enemy to decide the future of France.

Jules, his eyes closed, both hands pressed against the small of his back, sighed and said, "I have just been informed by cable that General Philippe Petain, head of the country's pro-German Vichy faction, is to record an address to the country very soon."

Brooke leaned toward Denise's ear and whispered, "The man Vincent Molet dubbed 'The old goat?'"

Denise no longer appeared the cool, collected citizen Brooke had always known.

With tears filling her eyes, she whispered back. "Yes, and God save us all."

ON JUNE 17, Brooke was surprised to discover that the broadcasting studio chosen to record General— named Marshal in 1918-- Pétain's speech to the nation turned out to be the smallest of all the soundproof rooms available at the local Bordeaux radio station.

Jules told the Mondiale team late the night before, "I have just received a cable that France's new Head of State has been officially chosen for the role." Jules offered a weary look. "He has directed there be no audience, other than the members of our crew necessary to record a broadcast for worldwide distribution."

By 9:45, Brooke and a few other colleagues had taken their positions with their backs against one wall of the soundproof booth as soon as they completed their various chores readying the room for the broadcast. They would be allowed to stay in case something went amiss that needed to be swiftly remedied. A bare minimum of radio equipment was arrayed on the floor, leaving Brooke with serious doubts whether it would even function properly.

She whispered under her breath to Denise, "Young Jacques Grenier and I did our best checking out this station's control board, but the engineer here insisted *he* be the one to run it."

Denise nodded. "Let's just pray his equipment links up properly with Vincent Molet's in Paris. With any luck, Vincent can relay the feed on to Britain right away, so they know it's official: Pétain is now the German's pawn in France."

In the middle of the room, a plain table and chair awaited the arrival of the enemy's designee. On the bare, wooden surface stood a microphone through which the nation of France would soon learn its fate. The room's temperature, normally kept cool for the benefit of the equipment, was stuffy due to the technicians scurrying in and out. The corners of the broadcast booth were cloaked in darkness, except for a small, glowing desk lamp arching over the area illuminating any notes Pétain might bring with him.

Jacques was struggling to connect the mic with a black cord that snaked across the floor where it attached to a piece of hardware brought from Paris. The Radio Mondiale crew prayed it would actually send signals to the appropriate destinations to record Pétain's speech for later broadcast.

Whispering to Denise, Brooke asked, "When do you think it will actually be aired?"

Denise gave a small shrug and whispered back, "Whenever the traitor gives the word, I suppose."

Brooke arched an eyebrow, amazed that the normally circumspect expert in public relations had made her sympathies— which matched Brooke's own —crystal clear. Then she glanced at the clock on the wall facing the desk. The hands had now reached a few minutes shy of 10 a.m. With the door open, voices and the sound of footsteps could be heard coming down the hall.

In the next instant, a very old man appeared at the threshold dressed in a black business suit, white shirt, and dark tie. Through round, *pince nez* glasses parked on his nose, he glanced into the studio. Once a hero of the Great War, retired Marshal Philippe Pétain entered the confined quarters where he was to announce the state of play between Hitler and what was left of the current French government.

He reached the chair where he was to sit, pulled it out, and gave a swift kick to the shins of Jacques Grenier who hadn't stepped back from the microphone he'd been adjusting quickly enough to suit the aging army veteran.

Brooke reached out and pulled Jacques toward her by his shirt sleeve, making room for the young man between Denise and herself and giving his shoulder a sympathetic squeeze.

Pétain sat down and pulled out a copy of his speech from his suit pocket. Nodding to Jules who gave him a signal to begin, he declared in a firm voice his "affection for our admirable army which is fighting with a heroism worthy of its long military traditions against an enemy superior in numbers and arms."

Brooke and Denise exchanged glances, with Brooke wondering what other pablum the old soldier would dispense before delivering the consequences of the humiliating defeat of the French and British forces.

"It is with a broken heart," he continued solemnly, "that I tell you today it is necessary to stop fighting. I have asked the adversary if he is ready to seek with me, as soldier to soldier, the means to putting an end to the hostilities."

Brooke sagged against the wall, thinking of the blood spilled and the carnage of battles fought and lost. In her mind's eye, she recalled the bombing of Paris, the fate of the refugees they'd seen mowed down by German warplanes on the roads. She could only imagine the horrors likely to be inflicted on France with the predicted German occupation of the country.

And her heart cried out: *What of Victor? What of Christopher? What of all those lost and those who will be?*

Brooke thought of how the Marshal had kicked poor Jacques out of the way seconds before he spoke into the microphone of his "affection" for the people already slaughtered. She could feel her heart speeding up and she clenched her fists at her sides.

Pétain droned on, "May all Frenchmen group themselves about the government which I head during these trying days and control their anguish in order to be led only by their faith in the destiny of the Fatherland."

Pétain abruptly stood up, pushed back his chair, and walked out without a glance at anyone who had made his broadcast possible.

Whose 'Fatherland?' Brooke fumed. *What corrupt deal has this old goat made with the Nazis?*

After France's new Chief of State departed, no one in the room uttered a word. Beneath the verbiage of flattery and deception, Brooke wondered what Christopher would have considered was the "lead" for Pétain's recorded broadcast? She'd bet her last *centime* he'd say that the right-wing official had decided to quit the fight to maintain France as a sovereign country and had forced the entire nation simply to accept his unilateral decision to bow to the Nazis. A free, French government was no more.

"What now?" Jacques asked miserably, still rubbing his shins.

Brooke found herself unable to reply, filled with a sense of futility and despair. She thought of the long hours their entire crew at Radio Mondiale had spent fighting for a free France these last months— and it had all come to this shameful end.

Denise finally broke the continuing silence, saying in a low, anguished voice, "It was such a surprise that Pétain asked for an armistice, and just like that, ordered all fighting to stop!"

Jules nodded. "I thought that at the least he would tell us that the government was going to North Africa to continue to fight along with the British forces. But no. Peace at any price."

"Don't you imagine that some of the remaining anti-Nazi French forces will continue to fight alongside England to protect the French colonies in North Africa?" Brooke asked, thinking of future deployments possible for Victor and his regiment if they made it across the Channel to Britain.

A frightening thought suddenly struck her which she voiced aloud. "Will the Germans command what's left of the army still in France? Will Frenchmen end up fighting fellow Frenchmen in this war?"

"The price Pétain has asked us all to pay will be France, herself," Denise said quietly.

"I imagine the price has already been paid, then," retorted

Brooke, unable to quell her dismay at what she'd just witnessed. "I think it may be that your Marshal Pétain has already made his own sweet deal with the Nazi bastards. Recording this speech is just a pacifier to prepare everyone for total capitulation to the Krauts. Perhaps the plan is for Hitler simply to annex France to German territory— and expand 'The Fatherland' that Pétain just spoke of."

The engineer working for the Bordeaux station who had insisted on running the control board had entered the room and overheard much of their conversation.

"Better be careful what you say," he warned, staring directly at Brooke, his eyes narrowed. "You're Brooke Bradley, aren't you? Those 'Nazi bastards,' as you so brazenly call them, might recognize that very recognizable voice of yours."

Startled, Brooke absorbed the hostility in his tone.

His assessing gaze swept from her blonde hair to linger on her breasts and then drifted back up to her eyes.

"I found your performances in those Chan films... amusing, I guess I would have to say. I was rather surprised to see you'd moved into this line of work," he said, gesturing toward the abandoned microphone.

"And you?" she asked, struggling to speak to him in French. "You're pleased with what you just heard is about to happen to your country?"

The man with a perpetual cigarette dangling out of the corner of his mouth shrugged. "One government is much like another, but for *you*, perhaps that's not to be the case. Don't you know that you and several presenters on Radio Mondiale have been denounced on German radio for weeks, now?" He offered a smile that held no warmth. "In fact, they've threatened five times I know about that if they caught the American actress Brooke Bradley who's been spewing vicious, anti-German propaganda, they would give her the death penalty."

So her distinctive voice— as well as her stage name — was a give-away... and could get her arrested.

The engineer took a deep drag from his cigarette. While he slowly blew out the smoke, he feigned scanning the small room. "I see that the famous Christopher Laurent did not accompany his colleagues to our fair city." He stuck the cigarette back in his mouth. "Sensible of him. I saw he's also on the latest list of German Enemies of the State."

Shaken by both this latest revelation and the man's aggressive tone, Brooke took the measure of the grizzled radio engineer. Only someone who'd seen her on the movie screen would have made the connection she was Brooke Bradley since everyone else at the station had addressed her solely as 'Madame de Varney.'

"I am married to a French soldier," she declared with all the hauteur she could muster, her heart pounding. "I live in France as his wife."

"Oh, I've read the gossip pages. I know you are married to our own Victor de Varney who so bravely joined that upstart Charles de Gaulle's regiment," he said, sarcasm coloring his tone.

"Well then, you know that my husband has risked his life to remain loyal to his country." Struggling to summon each French word, she added acidly, "Don't you think that the death penalty should be reserved for *traitors* to France?"

She shot him an accusing look before striding hastily out of the studio.

MUCH TO BROOKE'S AMAZEMENT, the management of the Bordeaux broadcasting station permitted the Radio Mondiale unit to send out a series of frantic pleas for help for France. Fortunately, Jacques Grenier, who had ultimately gained Brooke's admiration in the last days, was permitted to run the control board when Brooke did numerous broadcasts describing the wretchedness of the refugees and the machine-gunning of those fleeing Paris by low-flying Messerschmitts. Also, fortunately, the station's regular engineer whose demeanor had been so unnerving toward her, was nowhere to be seen.

In the following days of little or no sleep, Brooke filed one story after another chronicling Hitler's troops spreading tentacles across the land, physically occupying the upper half of the country. By June 22nd, her voice was hoarse and raspy as she announced to the

English-speaking world that Pétain had signed the Armistice with the Nazis that he'd foreshadowed in his address to the nation.

The following day, she could hardly choke out the words confirming that Hitler, himself, was touring Paris, having his photograph taken beneath the Eiffel Tower.

Even down south in Bordeaux, air raids had become commonplace. Brooke was about to start her nightly broadcast, relayed to Britain and on to the United States, when sirens began to wail at one-thirty in the morning. An American announcer still seated at the console leaned toward the microphone to sign off when the sounds of German warplanes roared directly over the roof of the small studio where Pétain had delivered his speech.

Pointing to the ceiling, Brooke's colleague screamed into the microphone, "Hear that, America? The goddamned German sons-of-bitches are *bombing* us now!"

Seconds later, the Bordeaux station manager burst into the studio, shaking his fist at both of them.

"You can't say such things over the air! You want to get us all arrested?" he shouted. "That's *it*! You are all to leave this building immediately!"

Denise, Jules, and a few other top officials in their group rushed into the room, having heard over the station's loudspeakers in the adjacent corridor the announcer curse the Germans to the entire world.

The station manager shouted at their group a second time, "You Radio Mondiale people, you're done! Leave. Now!"

The executive's fear was palpable despite his obvious attempt to appear in command.

Brooke's heart sank. Just like that, France's official government state broadcast agency was permanently off the air. Reeling from his rapid-fire orders, she gathered her script and other belongings in hand with the "all clear" sirens ringing in her ears. With this signal that the German warplanes had left the area and the raid was over, she followed her colleagues out of the studio.

Several Bordeaux employees stood in the corridor as the Radio Mondiale group made its sorry exit. Among them was the station's scowling engineer who'd run the control board during Pétain's address. By this time, her French was serviceable enough for her to understand his parting words.

"Our boss just received a cable listing your name as one of those the Germans are after," he disclosed with a smirk. "If you know what's good for you, Miss Bradley, I suggest you head straight back to Hollywood."

Brooke halted in place and stared over her shoulder at the man who'd just taunted her.

"Me? Go to Hollywood while traitors like you join the Nazis taking over your country?" Summoning the words of the rebuked American announcer walking directly behind her as they filed out of the building, she spat out in English, "Not on your life, you son-of-a-bitch!"

Having no idea if the man with the sneer on his face translated her insult, she turned toward the door and stalked outside.

In one regard, she thought, it felt as if she'd delivered the perfect exit line. It was pithy, it was powerful, and it expressed her rage toward every collaborator like Pétain and these local sycophants who now demanded their departure.

In the next moment, she could almost hear Christopher's assessment of her exit speech.

A stunt like that can get you killed. Keep your cool, Cub.

She tried to push away the knowledge that her name and Christopher's were on some sort of Nazi hit list. The German troops had, thus far, remained in the north of the country, so she'd have to evaluate the seriousness of that threat later when she'd had time to think.

For now, she longed for sleep.

In the cool of the night, the sirens blessedly silent, Brooke trudged toward the hotel flanked by the rest of the crew walking wordlessly beside her. She considered poor Nicole in the room they shared, keeping company with Ondie. Most likely she'd been terrified by the night's aerial raid. Brooke glanced up at moonless sky, suddenly aware that her own heart was still racing in her chest.

She repeated her now familiar litany to the heavens, *Where in God's name were Victor and Christopher this night?*

What portion of that sky arched over *them* at this very moment, she wondered. More to the point, she thought as tears began to clog her throat, were both of them even *alive* to look up at this same sky? Did Victor make it safely across the Channel to England? Had Christopher decided to do the same and ply his journalism in Great Britain, writing in English instead of in French? Or were they both dead in a ditch somewhere, mowed down by the invaders?

A rush of anxiety swept over her when she considered that the forces of Nazism had already wreaked such devastation, destruction, and dislocation for so many lives— including her own. What would the thuggish attackers do next to poor France?

And do to you, Brooke, if they ever catch you?

And to Christopher, if he still remained in the country?

Brooke mounted the steps to the hotel murmuring good night to her colleagues, her mind whirling with questions, but no answers.

The world was on fire. So, what in God's name should she *do*?

Should she stay in France and fight on with her words and a recognizable voice that might easily lead to her arrest? Or was her only sensible option to head for the Spanish border, like the escaping Brits?

How could it be that she'd heard absolutely nothing from— or about —Victor since the day he left Paris? What if she made it to England, only to find out he'd been deployed to North Africa? Or that a U-boat or Messerschmitt had got him crossing the Channel?

Her other choice was to do what that Nazi-sympathizer at the radio station had said with such venom: return to her former life in Los Angeles and the small son whom she'd left behind in her mother's dubious care so long ago.

She glanced up at the inky sky once more, studded with stars but free of marauders.

And it came to her precisely what she must do.

13

MID-JUNE 1940

"For God's sake, Christophe, why in the world did you change my transport?" Victor asked. "I had orders to board the *Lancastria*... which, by the way, at one time was a rather luxurious ship," he added reproachfully. "Now you have us crossing the Channel on *that*?"

It was a blustery June day; the two men stood on a promontory facing the churning water below. Victor pointed to a small, gray Royal Navy vessel bobbing off the pebbled shore of St. Malo on Brittany's coast.

"Trust me," Christopher replied, his bland expression masking his increasing irritation toward his current companion, "on a smaller ship you'll be less of a target for the German U-boats and the Luftwaffe dropping bombs on your deck. A requisitioned ocean liner like the *Lancastria* is a perfect target." Christopher stared at the bank of morning fog. "I spoke with de Gaulle's adjutant, and he admitted that even *he'd* declined to be onboard. The fellow managed to switch your orders before he left on some other tin bucket early this morning." He paused and then added, "By the way, de Gaulle was flown out last night to the U.K."

"And you got my transport changed, just like that?" Victor asked with grudging admiration.

"Not 'just like that.' In fact, de Gaulle's man emphasized that he didn't want questions asked about granting you this favor of departing today, so he'll not remove your name from the *Lancastria's* manifest. He simply *added* your name to board the gun boat out there," he said, nodding in the direction of the sea. "So, please don't blabber about it to anyone."

"Right-o!" Victor agreed with a jaunty salute. "I'll be glad to see London again and soak in a nice, hot tub for a change."

"The *Lancastria* will sail from Saint-Nazaire to pick up more passengers along the coast," disclosed Christopher. "Our ship leaves from right here any time, now."

"And *you* were granted passage on the smaller ship, as well?" Victor asked, with apparent amazement. "You certainly do have friends in high places."

Christopher shrugged. "A few."

He would never reveal to Victor what lengths he had to go to discover whether de Varney was alive or dead, to say nothing of locating him in the chaos of the forces' catch-as-catch-can evacuation from northwest France. Persuading the adjutant to switch ships for Victor's passage to England and beg a ride for himself was no mean feat, either. After spending twenty-four hours in the company of the film star-turned-soldier, Christopher had begun to wonder if this figure, with his stylish wool cape and self-important manner, had been worth all the trouble, even as a favor for Brooke.

Laurent, a warning voice reverberated in his head, *just do what you vowed to yourself, Denise and Jules that you would do— and get on with it.*

At least Jules Dumont had promised that Brooke would be safely out of Paris before the Nazis were due to arrive. Christopher had also secured both his boss and his agent's promise to keep their eyes on her and to not reveal why he had abandoned the Radio Mondiale unit that was heading for Tours.

"Just as I am, Brooke is now a target for arrest— and probably worse," he'd underscored to Jules and Denise that last evening at the Ministry when everyone else had scurried home to pack. "Because of our anti-Nazi broadcasts, a source of mine said that she's already on the German 'Most Wanted List.' Her movie-star voice, her good looks, and her broadcasts critical of the German advance will make her easy to apprehend."

"Well, the same goes for you," Jules had reminded him, and then smiled. "Except for the part about good looks."

"You're so right," he agreed, rubbing the stubble on his chin. He'd gazed at both of them long and hard before he said, "The government's going to fall, you know. It'll collapse without a whimper."

"But I must see it through," Jules murmured. "I can't abandon my staff or my wife and her ill father to face what's coming. And then, there's my own, pathetically poor physical state." He shook his head. "I've got to have that operation Dr. Jackson believes will relieve the blasted pain I'm in constantly." In a familiar gesture, he pressed his two hands against the curvature of his spine. "So I can't... I-I just can't—"

"Leave."

Christopher completed his sentence for him. With a wry glance in Denise's direction he asked, "I don't suppose you and your husband have any interest in making a run for England with me?"

His erstwhile agent shook her head. "I'll see it through here, too. My husband is quite a bit older than I. Like Jules, he wouldn't be up to making a dash for the Channel or the border."

Christopher nodded with understanding. "We each must chart our own course in this unholy mess."

He suddenly recalled saying something similar to Brooke the night of their difficult dinner at Le Dôme. He could well imagine how put out she would be when she'd learned of *his* decision to abandon the failing government's official information unit. Even now, he wondered if he'd done the right thing by disappearing without warning her of his plan to head for Britain to try to function as a legitimate journalist there. He'd made a decision. Had he granted her the same opportunity?

But getting across the Channel will be a dangerous business and you made a promise to keep her safe.

At least that had been his excuse for silently slipping away.

But a promise to whom, he wondered. Victor had barely asked about her in the hours they'd spent together.

And hadn't Brooke been adamant about not wanting to leave France, even if journalism wasn't an option any longer? She'd been worried that she didn't know if Victor's regiment remained in France or had made it safely to Britain. Despite these facts, Christopher realized he'd been justifying his actions these last days to ease a free-floating sense of guilt about his feelings for her, to say nothing of his failure to confide in her.

After all, they'd been partners in everything else.

She's probably beyond furious at my vanishing act...

He didn't blame her. But it was officially 'crazy times,' now. Times when people like Brooke and he and the rest of them had utterly no control over what was happening. In Jules's office that last evening before he'd left, his superior had reached for pen and paper.

"Here's where, if you're lucky, you'll still find de Gaulle's unit north of Paris," Jules revealed. "Victor is there, too, I understand."

Christopher had reached for the paper with his thanks when Jules had hesitated, pen in the air. The least Christopher could do was try to find Victor and tell him that his wife was headed toward the south before the Nazis arrived in Paris.

Jules had leaned over his desk and scribbled something else on the paper. "Look," he'd said. "If you make it to London and there's no journalist job to be had, go to this address and tell them I sent you."

Christopher took the note from Jules's hand, squinted at the last line he'd written, and reared back.

"You must be joking!" he exclaimed. He'd always hear rumors that Dumont had had some shadowy role in the Great War, which might explain how he'd have contacts at the address he'd just given him. "You're a poet, for God's sake, Jules. How do *you* know these people?"

"Never mind about that," he snapped. "This is the name of a very decent man who tells the truth, despite the lies that constantly swirl around him in the darkest corners of British Intelligence services."

Jules had looked across his desk at Christopher with a world-weary expression. The writer had been a young man in the Great War. Perhaps *he* still had a few 'friends in high places.'

"Good luck, Christophe," Jules had said, bidding him farewell, "and thank you for all the good work you tried to do here. Our superiors certainly didn't make it easy for you."

"No, they did not," Christopher replied, "But, thank you for giving me a job when my Paris bureau was shut down. I still had hope, then, that our government would stand up against the Nazis."

Denise then leaned close to him and kissed him on both cheeks, saying in a voice full of emotion, "*Do* try *not* to get killed, Christophe. Stay in touch if you possibly can."

"The same to you both. Molet says he'll do his best to keep us connected."

"Yes, he said that," Denise replied, "but we all know that will be technically difficult."

As Christopher mulled over events on his last day in Paris, the wind rose on the cliff where he and Victor stood gazing out at the Channel. His reveries vanished when Victor thumped him on the back.

"You've got to tell me, old boy, what tricks did you pull even to manage to find out where I *was*? I nearly keeled over when you walked into that tent at headquarters."

"Old journalist sources, I suppose you'd say," Christopher replied obliquely. "It was fortunate for you that I've interviewed a lot of top brass in my day."

"Well, I can see, now, that it was damned decent of you to arrange a speedier evacuation for me on a smaller vessel," Victor said, pointing to the navy ship offshore. "I don't much fancy drowning at sea just because I was on a large, moving target, that's for sure."

"And speaking of acting decently," Christopher replied, "when I first arrived in Brittany, I had a cable sent from your regimental headquarters to Brooke, by way of an engineer at Radio Mondiale. It was to let her know that you were waiting for transport to the U.K. God only knows, though, where she is by now, or if our equipment has been shut down by the Germans and she never got the communiqué."

"Even so, good of you to do that, old chap."

Christopher shrugged, offering more information about his companion's wife to gauge Victor's response to news about her.

"As of a week ago, Brooke was with our radio unit trailing along behind the failing government to Tours. She was quite concerned about you, since I understand that she'd had no word from you since you joined your regiment."

Victor had the grace to look chagrined.

"I know. I've been a rotten correspondent. Terrible of me, really, but I don't really know what to say in these situations and—"

"You mean the 'situation' telling your wife you made it safely to Brittany?" Christopher noted dryly.

"Well... it's just I've been so busy since joining the regiment and finding my footing and—"

"You've been a *translator*," Christopher replied pointedly. "Surely you had access to pen and paper?"

Ignoring Christopher's mild chastisement, Victor said with a cheer that rang false, "Well, since you've seen her more recently than I have... tell me, how is she? Getting on all right, I'm sure, with our housekeeper, Nicole, keeping her company?"

"She's been busy, just as you say you've been," Christopher replied. "Since you left Paris, she's been interviewing and broadcasting at all hours." He paused and then added, "She has a dog, now. She adopted it when her French teacher had a nervous breakdown."

"A dog?" Victor said with a horrified expression. "But my asthma..."

Christopher assured him, "It's a poodle and aren't they supposed to be non-allergenic?"

"I can't believe she took in a dog without... well... making sure that I won't wheeze around him."

"It's a *her*," Christopher corrected him, enjoying this exchange far more than he probably should. "And standard poodles are quite large, but I can report that this particular canine is impressively well behaved and adores her rescuer."

"But you said you left Paris with the radio crew. What would she do with a dog?"

"Take her in the Simca," Christopher said, chuckling.

"That nice, new car I gave her?" Victor replied, clearly upset by the idea of a dog riding in the front seat.

"That was Brooke's plan. The last I saw her, she was going home to pack and then set out with a skeleton radio crew leaving Paris before the Nazis storm in."

"Well, at least it sounds as if she has a decent chance of keeping out of harm's way," Victor replied.

But despite the former film star's hopeful words, he was frowning. Christopher conjectured that it might have been because he was worried about his wife's escape from Paris, but he rather guessed that Victor was still thinking of dog hairs on the car's upholstery.

"As for me," Victor divulged, "I've spent most of my days as an army captain not translating *anything*. All I seem to do was watch over our men digging trenches. Not pleasant, I assure you, for a man with weak lungs." To prove his point, he began to cough and pound his chest with his fist. Circling back to the subject of his wife, he volunteered, "I really didn't have a moment to sort out how the hell to get in touch with Brooke, and besides, all the chaps say it's hardly worth the effort to write anyone with the censors blacking out just about every word."

Christopher turned away from his companion to stare out over the chopping waters of the Channel.

He said almost to himself, "Let's hope to God Brooke took my advice and just kept heading south from Tours toward Spain and on to Gibraltar. From there she might get a boat or plane to England and find you in London, if you're lucky."

"I doubt I'll be there for long," Victor replied. "Rumors are the rest of us are probably headed for North Africa after de Gaulle consults face-to-face with the British War Office."

"That all sounds likely." Christopher paused, warning himself to keep his temper in check. "And just so you know... since, obviously, I won't be with the Radio Mondiale crew, I've asked Jules Dumont and our mutual agent, Denise, to keep an eye on Brooke and for both of them to urge her to leave France soon." He caught Victor's glance. "She's bound to be on some German's blacklist for her anti-Nazi broadcasts."

"Denise will see to it all, I'm sure," Victor replied with the conviction of a man whose underlings took care of trifling details.

He cast a curious glance at his companion. "If I may ask, Christopher, why are *you* going to London? Why the hell do you want to live in a city the Krauts are probably going to level before long? Why not head for America? You're half-Yank, after all."

"If I'm going to do my bit for the Allies in this war with a typewriter instead of a gun, I want to work for better bosses than the ones in Paris or New York."

"I expect the press in Britain is highly censored there, just like France," Victor warned.

Christopher looked out to sea again. "I'll figure things out once I get to the U.K., but I'm sure as hell not going to grant the Jerries the pleasure of throwing me into an internment camp."

He remembered the stern warning he'd given to Brooke about her own vulnerability when it came to the German invaders. In fact, he'd known full well that it could become crucial for her own safety that she did *not* know where he'd disappeared to. As much as it had pained him not to tell her he wouldn't depart with the radio crew, he knew it was one more thing he could do to lessen the danger to her. If ever caught and questioned, she could honestly say she had no idea what had happened to him the day he'd disappeared as the Germans invaded Paris.

But did she take his counsel seriously about getting out of France, he wondered? He was certain the government's broadcast unit would officially be dispersed very soon. And what would happen to her then? Would Brooke follow his advice? He'd tried to look out for her safety once Victor left, but now he wished he'd at least told her why he dared not keep her in his own care and make an escape together. Side-by-side, they were an even greater target for arrest. Traveling as a duo, they would have been even more likely targets of Nazi authorities at every checkpoint they would have to pass. If they'd been put on the "Enemies of the Fatherland's Most Wanted" lists, bulletins with their images would quickly advance their way across France.

And one more thing, he sternly reminded himself: if he and Brooke *had* set off together from Paris, God only knew how long his resolve to keep his distance from the compelling Miss Bradley would have lasted.

At least you're not yet in the habit of stealing another man's wife.

But the part of him that so admired her and cared for her welfare made him fairly confident that Brooke Bradley de Varney could take care of herself. Breaking into his musings that were heading in a dangerous direction, Christopher pointed to a series of flashes coming from the lead rowboat a hundred meters offshore.

"*Allons-y*," he announced to Victor. "Let's get down to the beach. Our navy patrol boat is apparently ready to haul anchor."

"Well, at least I see a few guns mounted on the bow and stern," Victor said as they made their way down the cliff.

VICTOR AND CHRISTOPHER had been in crowded, sandbagged London only a few days when Christopher found himself privy to some shocking news that even he couldn't have imagined.

Sitting in the reception area at *The Daily Telegraph* on Fleet Street, he heard shouting through a half-opened door of the War News editor's office occupied by a man whom Christopher hoped to meet about a position as a print reporter.

A young journalist faced the middle-aged editor across the desk, his shirtsleeves rolled up to his elbows. Christopher watched as he threw down a mock-up of the newspaper's front page with apparent disgust.

"Churchill's imposed a complete blackout on this?" the young man protested loudly. "Blimey, Nigel! My sources are telling me the *Lancastria* went down off Saint-Nazaire barely twenty minutes after the damn Jerries bombed her from the air! How can that be kept a *secret*?"

Christopher leaned to his right and could just make out the two-inch high headline blaring on the *Telegraph's* front page. From what Christopher was overhearing, it apparently was an edition that was destined never to land in the news kiosks of London— or anywhere else.

LANCASTRIA BOMBED! *4000*

WOMEN, CHILDREN & MILITARY
FEARED DROWNED!!

"Well, we'd *better* keep it a secret that there's been four thousand dead or the Government will close down this newspaper!" barked his boss. "I hear that our diplomatic editor, Gordon Lennox, is already under surveillance by MI5 for the things already published in our paper."

"But this has to be more people killed than the sinking of the *Titanic* and *Lusitania*, combined!" exclaimed the reporter.

"The Prime Minister fears that if this disaster was made public right now would be beyond devastating to the morale of the nation," responded the War News editor, his voice harried and sounding as if he were about to lose his temper with his dissenting employee. "I can't say I blame Churchill, actually. Everyone is digging bomb shelters in their back gardens, expecting the damned Krauts to invade our island any day now. This news would crush our will to keep fighting."

The newsman who had written the *Lancastria* story pounded his fist on the front-page mock-up.

"But you can't keep a story like this under wraps! It's for damn sure that some other paper or foreign correspondent working in the U.K. will violate the government's embargo. Just think of it! Four thousand people *died!* Won't their families start asking 'Where *are* they?'"

The reporter's boss pointed at the paper draped over his desktop and ordered angrily, "I am ordering you to burn this and any other copies in the office, and keep your mouth shut, Roger, or you'll be out of a job, do you understand me?"

Hearing the finality of the editor's decision, Christopher rose from his seat and walked toward the receptionist who had shown him where to wait for his interview. The editor who had just told "Roger" that the largest maritime loss in British history would be withheld from the public was not the sort of man for whom Christopher wished to work. He didn't really blame the agitated newspaperman. Even so, his observations that afternoon made it crystal clear that being a member of the print journalists' fraternity in Britain during wartime would be just as frustrating as serving as a propaganda flack for the radio division of the French Ministry of Information.

Of course, what he'd learned by sheer chance sitting in the waiting room at *The Daily Telegraph* meant that his Royal typewriter was probably going to gather dust for the duration.

"So be it," he mumbled, heading downstairs. He supposed he could always volunteer for what was left of the French Army...

Be a ground-pounder, taking orders from a bunch of idiots? Not for this garçon...

Emerging onto Fleet Street, he pulled out the scrap of paper on which Jules had scribbled:

Room 425 Metropole Hotel
Northumberland Avenue
(Major Norman Crockatt-MI9)

CHRISTOPHER FIGURED he had one more card to play.

LIKE MOST PEOPLE, Christopher knew MI5 was the British government intelligence agency in charge of domestic security. The more informed, like he was, knew something about MI6 that oversaw situations affecting national security in Great Britain and abroad.

But what the hell was MI9?

From the tidbits Jules had been able to tell him of the MI9 unit, formed barely six months earlier, the aim of this fledgling intelligence bureau involved debriefing men and women fleeing Continental Europe. Jules had hinted the agency might also take part in other clandestine activities, but didn't elaborate.

Christopher fingered the edge of Jules's note. If he couldn't beat the suits controlling print or radio journalism, maybe he should see what Major Crockatt at MI9 had planned for this war?

His throat was parched, and he considered nipping into a nearby pub, recalling the BBC broadcast he had listened to at the cheap London hotel where he and Victor had finally managed to find a room. Pétain's speech announcing France's total and complete capitulation to the Nazis had been pathetic, he thought. A sudden stab of worry struck him as he realized that Brooke was probably in the thick of it in Bordeaux where Pétain had recorded his tacit surrender to the invaders.

What would she do next? Where did she go after that day of the speech?

I was a fool not to just declare aloud that night at Le Dôme that I've never felt more drawn to a woman than the way I was to her... that perhaps I should have given her the choice to leave with me?

Christopher was shocked to realize that every day since he'd left Paris he had come to dread the thought of anything happening to her.

Yet, *he'd* been the one to pull away after their meal in the restaurant, hadn't he? He'd convinced himself he should ignore his mad impulse that night to kiss Brooke in the middle of their meal and take her to bed afterwards— and to hell with playing the role of noble friend. Instead, he did what he always had done: kept his feelings to himself and left town to chase the next story.

And so, he admitted to himself, he'd departed from Paris without a goodbye, entrusting the safety of the woman he couldn't seem to banish from constant thought to Jules Dumont, a man with a bad back and a wife clearly jealous of Brooke's beauty and brains. Christopher could only pray that Brooke would figure out a way to stay alive in a world where a ship with four thousand men, women, and children could be sunk by a supposedly civilized European nation— and that war crime be kept secret by the victims' government leaders.

Christopher pulled the collar of his trench coat closer to his neck and headed for the nearest tube station. He wasn't particularly looking forward to bunking with his self-absorbed "roommate" even one more night. In the past week, he'd seen enough of the French film star to wonder what married life had really been like for Brooke.

Pushing away such unsettling thoughts, he steeled himself to be civil yet another evening, given it was Victor's last few hours in London before deploying for North Africa. Christopher supposed he could endure sharing the bottle of malt whiskey he had managed to snag through a contact-of-a-contact on the Black Market earlier that day.

Yes, he thought, descending the steps to the tube station, getting thoroughly drunk was probably the best way to navigate through the next few hours in Victor de Varney's company. In the morning, he'd head to the Metropole Hotel on Northumberland Street to meet the mysterious Major Crockatt.

14

Thinking back, Christopher remembered that Victor's last evening in London had started off amicably enough. The actor professed his undying gratitude and relief upon hearing Christopher's news that he'd not been aboard the ill-fated *Lancastria*.

"Rather sobering, that," Victor had murmured. "Good thing you got us passage on that smaller gunboat."

"Well, keep what I've just told you about the sinking to yourself, will you? Just today, Churchill's ordered a news blackout on the disaster, so I'd prefer not to be charged with treason."

Nodding, the actor-soldier immediately grabbed a piece of hotel stationery and the room fell silent for several minutes as Victor appeared to be composing a letter.

"What are you doing?" demanded Christopher. "I just told you, you can't write about the sinking to anyone."

Victor didn't respond for several minutes. Finally, he looked up.

"I haven't mentioned the *Lancastria* in all this, but cheating death this week has given me pause. If I don't come back from North Africa," he said in a sepulchral voice that struck a strange note with Christopher as if they might be playing a dramatic scene together in Victor's latest film, "I want you to give this letter to Brooke, will you, old boy? I want her to have something to remember me by."

"Why don't you give it to someone at the War Office? There's a division that handles these next-of-kin matters, and besides," Christopher added pointedly, "there's no guarantee that *any* of us will make it through this carnage."

"I won't have time to leave this message with them now," Victor grumbled as if somehow that were Christopher's duty to do as he'd been asked. "Once I'm off to the docks in the morning, it's on to North Africa, God help us all." He'd shifted his gaze to the bottle of whiskey Christopher had earlier set on a small table placed in front of the fireplace and flanked by two battered leather club chairs. He handed him the envelope he'd addressed to "Brooke de Varney," instructing, "Put this somewhere safe, will you, and see that she gets it if I'm killed."

"What if *I* get killed?" Christopher replied.

"You're a humble scribe. You should stay safe enough," he retorted with a disgruntled air.

"And if you *do* make it back?"

"Tear it up when we meet at the Ritz for a glass of champagne," Victor said, his good humor returning. "And speaking of drinking." He pointed to the whiskey. "At least tonight we *do* have time to make a good show of consuming that lovely bottle you managed to nick."

By the wee hours of the morning, however, Christopher had had more than his fill of both whiskey and the famous Victor de Varney. As the hours passed and Victor became increasingly inebriated, Christopher was forced to listen to longwinded accounts of the actor's self-acknowledged brilliance in various roles he'd played, to say nothing of recounting the many sexual liaisons he boasted he'd enjoyed along the way.

"I'd say I had every female from the actress in my very first film, to my latest co-star, Olivia Eriksen, a delectable little package, by the way," he confided, chuckling. "Apparently she quite fancied me during the last movie I made in Norway."

"Didn't you make that film just before you got married in London?" Christopher asked, mildly appalled that the man would confide such intimate activities to someone who had been his wife's former colleague.

Victor smiled as if he enjoyed revealing what a naughty boy

he'd been. "I figured it was too good a situation to pass up before the old shackles would be clamped around my ankles."

By the end of this recitation, Christopher had downed his third glass of whiskey. The next thing he was subjected to was Victor describing his on-again, off-again affair with the befeathered entertainer, Josephine Baker, a relationship that Christopher and everyone else in Paris had been aware of for years.

The drunker Victor became, the more intimate and detailed were his descriptions of his female conquests, including someone he recently encountered whom he'd known as a youth.

"I ran into her totally by accident when briefly on leave visiting my grandmother at Château de Varney."

Victor paused, taking another swig of spirits as the clock on their wall showed it was just past four in the morning. By this point, Christopher had all he could do not to toss the contents of his own glass in Victor's face. The only thing he could think about was how loyal Brooke had been to this cad to whom she'd been married less than a year!

In an attempt to keep control of his fraying temper, he simply stared into the amber liquid coating the bottom of his glass. When he heard Victor chuckling, he looked up.

"Don't you find it amazing," the actor asked, "how women just *crave* being fucked by good-looking cocksmen like us?"

Victor raised his glass as if in a salute to a co-conspirator. Christopher sank more deeply into the leather club chair facing the low burning fire and took another gulp of his drink.

"Speak for yourself, de Varney, and do spare me any more gory particulars of your illicit love life, will you please? You might remember that I worked with your wife and admire her immensely, so I am definitely not on a 'need-to-know' basis for how cheerfully you've cuckolded your new bride."

"Only *men* get cuckold-ed!" Victor hiccupped.

In that moment, Christopher wished like hell he'd been the one to cuckold the famous Victor de Varney. He wondered, now, why had he been so self-sacrificing the night he and Brooke had dinner together at Le Dôme. He'd wanted to tell her how he felt. That it had taken every bit of self-control he possessed to walk away in that moment when they bid farewell next to her Simca. That the damned war might mean they'd never see each other again if one of them ended up in the wrong place at the wrong time.

But he had done the honorable thing, and for what? *This* rotten excuse for a husband? It seemed curious to Christopher, though, that instead of merely bedding Brooke like all of the other actresses he'd known, Victor had married her. Christopher could easily answer his own question.

Because she's a spectacular woman, that's why. Even that bum knows he'd never find a better partner in life!

Christopher wondered if Brooke had any suspicions that Victor had betrayed her trust only weeks prior to their wedding. She had once told him that Victor had left her in London performing in Clifford Odets' *Golden Boy* while he went to Norway to be in the film shot there just before the Nazis invaded that country. They'd gotten married in St. Paul's, she'd said, the week after his film wrapped in Scandinavia. It was hard to imagine how devastated she would be to know he'd grabbed a piece of casual ass when he took leave at his family château rather than coming into Paris to see her.

Christopher had a sudden memory of his own mother, sobbing in his parents' bedroom when she'd discovered his father had consorted with any number of women in the course of his own journalistic career. Christopher had sworn then he would never inflict that kind of pain on his wife, that is, if he ever were to have one.

It was all he could do not to grab the actor by the throat and smash him against the hotel wall. His disgust began to seriously corrode his ability to maintain his outward composure. He leaned toward the matching leather chair where Victor sprawled, his long legs like two parallel lengths of lumber stretching toward the fire. Christopher reached for the bottle.

"You do the honors finishing this up," he said tersely. He tipped the last contents into Victor's glass. "I'm going to bed, although I know I'll regret it when I wake up."

And regret it he certainly did when he reluctantly swam to consciousness a few hours later.

As if down a long tunnel, he heard someone moving about the

hotel room. It was Victor, of course, opening and slamming shut drawers packing his gear.

"Good God..." Christopher heard himself groan, his head throbbing at every abrupt sound. The instant he became fully awake, the pain registered with full force and he felt like bloody hell. Opening one eye, he barked at de Varney, "Shut the damn curtains, will you?"

Only gray, foggy London skies penetrated through the dirty hotel window, but it was enough light to make him squint in agony.

"I have to *see* to be able to pack my bloody luggage!" retorted the irritated but modulated voice that could only belong to the equally hungover film star. "I wager I feel a lot worse than you do," complained Victor. "Are you sure what we drank wasn't denatured alcohol, tinted with tea?"

"Could well have been," Christopher replied barely above a whisper, his own head spinning.

"Well, no matter. I'm due on a train in less than an hour to get to my ship." Victor's tone turning petulant, he added, "Those of us who don't have the luxury of sleeping through this war must meet their fellow soldiers dockside to set sail for North Africa tonight, old boy."

"Oh, sod off!" mumbled Christopher, burying his head beneath his pillow. "You're a *translator* for top brass, not some frontline hero. Cut the posh bullshit!"

"Where's the bloody bellhop?" Victor yelled in response.

"Probably dead in a trench somewhere, so shut the fuck up, will you?" Christopher grunted, burrowing more deeply into the covers.

A few minutes later, Victor furiously kicked shut the door to their room, his arms apparently laden with luggage and his army traveling kit.

Christopher didn't bid him goodbye or even lift a hand in farewell. He felt no sympathy toward Brooke's husband even though he was heading for a blooming battlefront somewhere in North Africa. The letter de Varney had written to his wife, undoubtedly professing his undying love, lay on the table next to the empty whiskey bottle.

Christopher hoisted himself onto one elbow pressed against the lumpy mattress and stared at the envelope, wanting nothing so much as to toss it into the fireplace.

But the ashes on the hearth were cold.

"MR. LAURENT?

Christopher looked up at the uniformed subaltern who'd called his name.

Seated on the hard wooden chair he'd been directed to take on the second floor of the Metropole Hotel, he answered, "Yes, I'm Christopher Laurent."

As he said the words, a shooting pain knifed up his neck, the latest reminder of his mother-of-all-hangovers.

The hotel waitress at breakfast had kindly given him a packet of Aspro for his raging headache as well as pouring him several cups of an egregious brew the English called coffee. Unfortunately, it hadn't done much to soothe his wickedly throbbing temples, nor erase the memory of the disgusting recitation from Brooke's husband that he'd listened to for hours.

"Please follow me, sir," directed the young man.

Christopher trailed behind him down a corridor and into Room 424, with its sign over the door indicating the inner office of the head of MI9, the shadowy British Intelligence agency curiously housed in a hotel bedroom suite.

Major Norman Crockatt rose from behind his desk to extend a hand to his visitor. Christopher was startled to see he was dressed in full military uniform with three rows of combat ribbons and decorations. This was combined with a resplendent, knee-length kilt denoting the major as a member of the Royal Scots Guards with whom Crockatt had served in the Great War.

"Ah... the journalist," he greeted Christopher with a genuine smile of welcome on a face blessed with handsome features, a trim mustache, and a gently receding hairline. The major, who appeared to be in his mid-forties, said, "Please, do take a seat."

"Thank you, sir," Christopher replied, noting the easy, friendly manner of a man who ran one of the most enigmatic services within the British Intelligence establishment.

"So, I understand from my friend, Jules Dumont, your bilingual language ability and deep knowledge of France might offer our war effort— and MI9, specifically —some much-needed skills. You've been a radio journalist, I understand. Used to making keen observations and judgments in your line of work, aren't you?"

"If that means I try to hunt for the truth in the stories I'm covering, I'd say, yes. That's how I saw my job."

"And when I last communicated with my friend, Jules, I gather those kinds of efforts to seek the truth became impossible as the German territorial gains increased, and the French collaborators ruled the airwaves."

Christopher tried to disguise his amazement that a self-effacing poet like Jules Dumont would ever have encountered such a decorated military figure like Crockatt, let alone had any contact with the "dark arts" associated with Britain's intelligence services.

"How do you know Jules?" Christopher ventured to ask, wanting to conduct an interview of the major as much as Crockatt was quizzing him.

"I served in France in the Great War," Crockatt revealed, "and afterward, I was a stockbroker before being recalled to service in thirty-nine. Over the years, before and between the wars, I often went to Paris, with the thought of improving my French. I spent considerable time at the Shakespeare and Company bookstore. Do you know it?"

"Doesn't everybody in Paris?"

Christopher was struck by what seemed to him a possible "cover story" for a military man like Crockatt now running MI9, a newly created branch of the all-powerful MI6 that appeared focused on some initiative that few outsiders knew anything about.

Crockatt continued with an easygoing smile, "Believe it or not, I first met Jules at a poetry reading there before I'd even gone to Sandhurst, our country's military college. We met again during the war itself and coordinated some informational operations back then. We've always stayed in touch, he in his world, I in mine."

A Scots Guardsman was long-term pals with a poet? Jules must have been assigned fairly high-up in French spy craft trade in the last war, Christopher surmised, or perhaps, he'd never truly left it?

"It would seem your two worlds overlap to some degree," suggested Christopher.

He noticed a faint smile playing across Crockatt's lips.

"You might say that." He leaned back in his chair and cast a steady gaze at his latest applicant. "So tell me, would you be interested in attempting to ferret out whether an arriving refugee is truly fleeing the chaos on the Continent or, rather, entering Britain as a spy for the Germans?"

Christopher paused. "May I ask exactly what is MI9's *method* of 'ferreting' out information from a refugee?" he asked pointedly. "Because if the intelligence services in Britain use anything like German techniques, I don't think I'm your man." He cast a jaundiced eye in Crockatt's direction, adding, "I do admit, however, we journalists sometimes feel as if we'd like to grind a lighted cigarette butt into our subjects' arms to get them to talk. Even so, we lowly scribes generally shy away from that sort of thing."

"You're asking does MI9 torture information out of the people we must assess?"

Christopher nodded and noted how Crockatt's expression darkened.

"Certainly not!"

"Well, that's reassuring to hear," Christopher replied.

"We do, however, conduct thorough, exacting, and extensive interviews with our subjects," the Major affirmed, immediately recovering his calm demeanor. "After that, another team double checks the information extracted in the interviews to the extent that we are able. Once we have a file on a subject with enough solid facts, we then determine whether they may stay in England if they're non-citizens or be sent back if we deem them undesirables."

"And if they are British nationals?"

"We still thoroughly debrief. Many are soldiers that didn't make it in time to be transported from Dunkirk. These chaps are just now finding their way back to Britain as you have recently done. Some of the men we're interviewing these days are British and French former prisoners-of-war, escaped from German hospitals and detention camps."

"I suppose you need to determine if they've been 'turned' by the Germans and become enemy agents?"

Crockatt offered an admiring nod.

"Exactly. Some have even gained information that can be very useful to our side. And now," he added, "we are beginning to see a portion of our downed airmen arriving back in Britain. They're aviators that we very much want to repatriate so they may fly for us on another day." Crockatt gave a small chuckle. "A more effective program to help get them out of France and Belgium is under consideration when our bombing of Germany ramps up."

"You mean an active effort, in country and run by MI9, to get the surviving crews that bail out to evade capture once they hit the ground, and then help them escape from France?"

"Exactly!" Crockatt replied with a pleased look that Christopher had grasped MI9's new mandate so swiftly. "We're still on the drawing boards with all that, but the War Office is constantly reminding us that every pilot brought back in one piece saves them some fifteen thousand pounds that need not be spent on training a new recruit."

"But as regards MI9's mission at hand," Christopher said, bringing the conversation back to the job Crockatt had been describing, "what I believe I hear you saying is that you need a few more nosy, inquisitive types that speak French as well as English for this interviewing assignment of incoming refugees?"

"Precisely." Crockatt paused a moment, then asked, "You probably are aware that the Nazis have now taken over complete control of Paris and the entire north of the country. Right now, our intelligence regarding what's really going on with our forces that didn't make it to Dunkirk or the departure points like Brittany is practically nil. And except for what we glean from the debriefs this office conducts, we have little early warning of Nazi troop movements or the locations of future assaults, so our work here is crucial for the war planners."

"I can certainly see it would be," Christopher agreed, happy to contemplate that what he might do for MI9 would actually be useful to beating back the Nazis.

The Major regarded his visitor steadily. "Would you ever consider going back to France at some point?"

Taken aback, Christopher sat back in his chair. "As a secret agent for MI9?"

"Something like that, but in a slightly different capacity than you probably assume— and that I'm not at liberty to describe."

"Well, when you are able to describe the role, I'd certainly entertain going back," Christopher replied.

He'd never even imagined that returning to France might be a possibility before the war was over. He immediately envisioned the look on Brooke's face if he should suddenly appear— and then he quickly shut down such idle speculation.

"Do you speak the German language by any chance?" asked Crockatt hopefully.

"Some," Christopher replied, "but I can't say I'm fluent."

Crockatt nodded, as if making a mental note of a deficiency in this current candidate for MI9.

"Well," he said, his expression faintly droll, pointing to his right ear, "I can hear that you speak 'American' English and was told you have an impeccable French accent. I can only hope both will come in handy if we can just persuade your FDR to join us in keeping the Huns from taking over the world."

"That was a theme of ours at Radio Mondiale," Christopher volunteered, "propagandizing America to enter the war." He met the Major's glance. "But I must warn you, I'm only interested in this work if I can simply chronicle what I learn from these people arriving in Britain. No slanting. No puffery. Just pursue the facts as best as I can and report them honestly to MI9." He paused, and then added, "And I have your word that the information I extract will not be twisted into some narrative the War Office finds more to their liking."

Crockatt nodded, clearly pleased by the tenor of Christopher's reply. "That's the very approach we have insisted upon in this office — take note of the good, the bad, the ugly, and the *suspicious*, and back our judgments with the best evidence available in each category."

The Major pushed a sheet of paper across his desk in Christopher's direction.

"This is the Official Secret Act. If you sign it, you have sworn never to reveal anything of our work here except to those who have also joined our ranks. Even then, we will tell you how you are to keep certain knowledge compartmentalized."

"And if I sign, what happens next?"

"We run a check on you, which has already begun. If that comes back clean, you'll immediately come to work in a room down the hall from here."

Crockatt then laid out the pay and the offer of temporary quarters on a higher floor of the Metropole Hotel until Christopher could secure lodgings of his own.

"If you come on board with us, we will grant you the rank of captain in the British Army."

"Me? A captain?" Christopher replied skeptically. "I've never been a part of any military organization in France or the United States."

"Advancement is swift when there's a war on," the Major replied with an ironic laugh. "But we won't be pinning on the insignia until the review of your status is completed. You will be notified shortly if you are invited to join us here."

"Or be tossed out of the country?" Christopher asked, also with a laugh.

"I see you have a perfect understanding of our work here." Crockatt's expression grew serious. "Does all this make sense?"

"It does, but may I quickly look over what I'm signing?" Christopher asked, pointing to the Secrets Act on the desk.

"By all means do," answered Crockatt approvingly.

Christopher skimmed the text, thinking that Major Norman Crockatt had proven to be an impressive figure as government bureaucrats went. The job he was offering was probably the best a French-English speaker with dual French and American passports stored in his typewriter case could be expected to land. After all,

Christopher was considered a refugee, just like all the others flooding Great Britain.

"May I have a pen, sir?" he asked, and the Major handed him one.

He swiftly signed his name and in the next instant, Crockatt rose to indicate their interview was over.

"As soon as we have an answer for you, we will be in touch," he said, holding out his hand to shake Christopher's. "Leave word with my subaltern how best to contact you."

Departing from the Metropole through its slightly down-at-the-heels front lobby, Christopher wondered what in God's name he would do next if MI9 turned him down.

15

EARLY JULY 1940

During the days Christopher waited for official word from the powers-that-be at MI9, he wrestled with the idea of attempting to contact Brooke. What if he sent a cable to Radio Mondiale's engineer, Vincent Molet? Surely Vincent would know where she'd gone after Pétain's speech delivered at the Bordeaux radio station? As much as it pained him, she had a right to know that Victor had made it to England and was now on his way with de Gaulle's Free French fighters to North Africa. Surely, she would reply and let him know she was well.

Then, he remembered that signing the Official Secrets Act made it treasonous to tell anyone *anything* pertaining to troops and deployments. He wouldn't even be able to tell her how or why *he* had crossed the Channel on a British Navy vessel.

"So much for that notion..." he mumbled to himself as he cleaned the keys of his Royal typewriter while sitting on his bed in the gritty hotel room he and Victor had managed to rent. Even being in touch with Molet at the former radio headquarters was probably out from now on, unless authorized by Crockatt— *if* he was hired.

Grateful that he now had the room to himself, he did his best to put the memory of Victor de Varney and everything he'd learned about the blighter in the farthest corner of his mind.

Each day following his employment interview at MI9, he waited on tenterhooks for a message from Norman Crockatt's office. It arrived less than a week later with an invitation to return at "0900 hours to the Metropole Hotel."

The major greeted him with a hearty handshake and a pat on the back when he entered his new boss's inner office.

"Congratulations! You, my dear Captain Christopher Laurent, are hereby deemed a full-fledged member of an intelligence agency very few people even know exists." He added, "Mind that you keep it that way, yes?"

"Of course, sir," answered Christopher, wondering what, besides interviewing refugees, his duties as a British Army captain would eventually entail.

That very day, Christopher found himself billeted in a spare hotel bedroom on a higher floor above his new office at the other end of the corridor from Crockatt's.

A sign announced **Interview Room 4** above the door to Christopher's allotted space which consisted of a wooden desk, two chairs, and a loo leading from the former small hotel bedroom.

Less than two hours after he was commissioned and issued a new uniform with captain's insignia, Christopher began to give the third-degree to a succession of new arrivals to Great Britain. He found quizzing them thoroughly to be very much like being on deadline for a lead news broadcast for his old job as Paris Bureau chief for the American radio network that had employed him.

Within the first week, a colleague named Stephen Barrager asked him to join him for a pub lunch at a place just around the corner from the hotel.

Barrager, slight of stature and with a self-deprecating air, had exchanged his accountant's green eyeshade for the two lieutenant's double bars on his uniform.

"Damned if I didn't manage to pass some bloody 'aptitude test' showing I had an ability to detect errors and misstatements," he told Christopher when he'd explained how he'd landed at MI9. "Who knew it would mean interviewing refugees? And what about you? How'd you end up on the second floor of this fleabag of a hotel?"

"Crockatt decided that my former journalism trade on radio wasn't too different from the job he wants us to do."

Barrager curled his lips in a knowing smile. "Actually, old chap, don't you find the experience of grilling these people more akin to writing exposés for the *Tatler?*"

Both men laughed as they stepped up to the ancient wooden bar and ordered their pints of Guinness.

All in all, Christopher found his new job and a certain camaraderie among the other MI9 interviewers were vastly more enjoyable than the role of propagandist that Jules had bestowed upon him at the French Ministry of Information. When his news bureau had closed, he'd merely been glad he could remain in Paris and continue to work with Brooke. Before long, however, he'd felt he was betraying himself every day he'd worked as a government flack. The only plus had been partnering with her, but even that became disconcerting, considering he had to ignore the attraction he could feel was bubbling between them.

No, Christopher reflected as he accepted a second pint from the personable Barrager, he'd probably found himself in the best situation possible, considering the unpleasant alternatives.

Following their noon break, the last interviewee of the day turned out to be a very blond, very muscular young man who claimed he was an Alsatian fleeing from oppression in the wake of Hitler's takeover of his area in France. Both his faltering knowledge of the Alsace region and his sometimes hesitant answers on a few other subjects didn't hold up under Christopher's barrage of questions. By day's end, Christopher had been able to expose him as a suspected German agent sent to infiltrate Great Britain.

"Good show, old boy!" Stephen Barrager complimented Christopher when he'd heard the news. "You must teach me a bit more of that 'who, what, why, where, when, and how' technique you former scribes know so well."

"It's called *curiosity,*" Christopher confessed with a shrug. "Every person on this planet simply loves to talk about themselves if you ply them with the right questions... *unless,* of course, they have something to hide. This character grew surly when I asked about what wines were associated with Alsace. He couldn't name the most famous one in the region."

At Barrager's puzzled expression, Christopher disclosed with a laugh, "Gewurztraminer!"

"He must have been a devoted German beer drinker," Barrager joked.

∼

TOWARD THE END OF AUGUST, Major Crockatt appeared unexpectedly at Christopher's office door. He made an imposing figure leaning against the threshold, resplendent in his combat medals and pleated kilt.

"Sorry to intrude, Laurent, but I thought I'd stop by and ask you how you're getting on?"

Christopher rose swiftly to his feet and saluted as best he knew how.

"Very well, I hope, sir— that is, if my work meets your standards."

"So far, it does, and quite well, too. I take it you were able to detect the presence of another German spy without resorting to any lighted cigarettes in their eyeballs?" he asked, a ghost of a smile playing at his lips.

"No commissions of war crimes on my part that I'm aware of, sir." Christopher laughed and added, "Actually, I find the work very intriguing and much more akin to what I was used to as a working journalist."

Crockatt nodded approvingly. "I had a bit of a hump to get over convincing the MI6 boys that a radio journalist was just what was needed in this job, but you've proven me right."

"So MI6 has the last word over MI9?" Christopher asked.

Crockatt scowled, clearly not warming to the question. Surprisingly, Christopher thought, the major's grimace was soon followed by a full-blown smile that lighted his face.

"In the end, *I* had the last word, thanks to your nabbing those two Kraut agents trying to sneak by us. It's made certain quarters in this game we're in sit up and take notice. That neat accomplishment of yours didn't do any harm to my credibility, so I thank you."

Astounded by the praise and aware, now, of MI6's claim of jurisdiction over Crockatt's fledgling intelligence agency, Christopher could only nod. He saluted again when the major spun on his heels and headed back down the hallway to his own inner sanctum.

During the rest of the summer and despite the war raging on the Continent, Christopher almost felt as if he were merely plying his old news-gathering trade again, except for the fact he donned a uniform every morning.

And then, in the first week of September, his world and the rest of London turned upside down.

SUMMER LINGERED in London into September with unseasonably warm weather a fact instead of autumn chill.

"You've got to admit that even warm beer outranks a hot cup of tea on a day like this," Christopher declared to Stephen Barrager as the two sat in a stuffy pub near the Metropole.

"Do call it a pint, not a beer, old boy," teased his colleague as the two clinked glasses and downed their first gulp.

On this typical Saturday workday, they had, between them, knocked out seven refugee interviews with Christopher ending his long work week debriefing a returning British soldier.

"The guy had managed to escape from a poorly-run German prison camp not far from France's border with Spain. It was remarkable to hear how complete strangers volunteered to ferry him to safety as he made his way to Biarritz and over the Pyrenees."

"Lucky fellow," Barrager nodded, and the two raised their glasses to drink to the man's health, touching their rims with a resounding clink.

As if they had set off a signal, the sudden roar of approaching airplane engines was soon followed by the whistle of incendiaries falling nearby. A few seconds later, a series of concussive explosions shook the pub's foundation and shattered its windows on the far side of the room. The detonations growing even louder, Christopher glanced at his watch and noted out of the habit of a veteran journalist that it was a few minutes after four o'clock.

"The Jerries? Bombing London in broad daylight?" yelled Christopher's drinking mate.

"The Luftwaffe bombed Paris," Christopher yelled back. "Why not London? They've threatened it often enough."

As the sounds grew even more deafening, both men dove beneath the heavy wooden table where they'd been sitting, managing to take their pints with them.

"Bugger all!" shouted Barrager and inhaled a large slug of his Guinness.

Christopher followed suit, the malty brew cool against his throat. Draining his glass, he wondered if this would be the last alcohol he'd ever consume.

A WEEK later on September 13th, more bombs dropped in a night raid, shaking Christopher awake. He jumped out of bed in the wake of the bone-rattling sound of an explosion striking the Metropole Hotel.

"Fire! Fire!" someone shouted from the hallway. "A corner of the building's been hit!"

Christopher scrambled into his clothes. Avoiding the elevator, he dashed down the stairs, his thoughts filled with memories of that first weekend of London bombings that had lasted from four in the afternoon until 4:40 in the morning. Four hundred thirty Londoners had been killed in less than twelve hours that day and some sixteen hundred were badly injured.

"Damnation!" shouted one man in the crowded lobby as they all ran for the nearest tube station currently serving as an air raid shelter. "I wonder if tonight will be as bad as Black Saturday?"

It was.

The all clear didn't sound until daybreak. Christopher trudged up to the second floor since a sign on the elevator noted it was "Under Repair." Walking past Major Crockatt's office he paused at the half open door, hearing voices raised. Christopher quickly surmised his commanding officer was speaking on the telephone with Claude Dansey, the number two man at MI6. Word was Dansey's iron fist kept tight control over all activities at MI9 as well as MI6.

"I'm telling you, Dansey," Christopher heard Crockatt say, "the entire staff of this agency might *die* in the rubble next time we have a strike like last night! A corner of the damn building was blown away and it set part of the hotel on fire." There was silence before Crockatt's voice boomed even louder. "Yes, they put it out," he retorted, sounding exasperated, "but I want to move MI9 *out* of London, and the sooner the better. I'm from Buckinghamshire and I think I have a line on an estate out there we could requisition without too much disruption. Yes!" he said emphatically, asking in the next breath, "so do I have your agreement I can begin the process of relocating MI9 and start *today*?"

Christopher went up to his room to shower and shave. By the end of the day, he walked into Crockatt's office to leave his debriefing reports with the subaltern.

"Ah, Laurent. Come in, will you?" called the major from the inner office. When Christopher took a seat, Crockatt said. "I see you survived in one piece through our little visit from the Jerries last night."

"Not a pleasant way to wake up, but yes, sir. Fortunately, the bomb hit on the other side of the building from my room."

"I'm happy to report we've had no loss of life among MI9 staff," disclosed Major Crockatt, "but two of the hotel kitchen staff were killed. I've been telling Dansey and the rest of the chaps over at MI6, that one well-placed incendiary could snuff out our entire special branch in a single shot."

Christopher nodded. "I hope they're listening. We've had bombings every single night since last Saturday."

"Fortunately, they *have* listened," Crockatt replied, sounding both pleased and relieved. "I've just been given the go-ahead to move MI9's headquarters into the countryside and I think I already have found a suitable site."

Within hours, Christopher learned how quickly Crockatt was able to initiate the agency's change of location.

A day later, Barrager appeared at the door to his colleague's office with some additional welcome scuttlebutt.

"I heard the major had a wealthy old army comrade living near him who was more than happy to have the War Office take his stone pile off his hands," Barrager reported.

"Did you hear where we'll be?" asked Christopher.

"The word is Beaconsfield," Barrager replied. "That's a town in Buckinghamshire."

Christopher smiled inwardly. Buckinghamshire was Crockatt's home county, so the rumors floating along the second floor appeared to be true.

By October, an estate known as Wilton Park was officially requisitioned by the government.

"It's a large Palladian manse only twenty-eight kilometers and less than an hour by train to London," Major Crockatt announced cheerfully to the staff. "My home just happens to be in Ashley Green a few miles away," he added with a wink.

Christopher could only speculate that the commencement of the London bombing that everyone had taken to calling "The Blitz" gave the major a welcome opportunity not only to move everyone to a safer location, but to get his secret organization away from interference by the likes of Claude Dansey and the other jealous operatives in Whitehall.

As for himself, Christopher was thankful the move meant he'd be billeted at Wilton Hall, eliminating the need to find a place to live in London where rentals were being bombed into oblivion on nearly a daily basis.

At a later meeting with Christopher and the rest of the "Debrief Squad" as they were known, Crockatt leaned over his desk and said in a low, conspiratorial voice, "I'm going to start a school on the Beaconsfield property I'm calling Camp 20. I plan to develop techniques to groom soldiers on the art of escape and evasion before they are sent abroad."

His gaze swept over the puzzled expressions on the faces of some of his listeners.

"The more men we can rescue from the battlefields and the more downed pilots we bring back, the more we can gather intelligence and launch warplanes with repatriated Allied pilots at the controls. MI9 will be preserving lives as well as recycling manpower." He laughed and lightly struck his fist on his desk. "How can any bureaucrat be against our saving millions of pounds for His Majesty's government?"

BY THE TIME Christopher had moved out of the Metropole and into Wilton Hall in Buckinghamshire late in 1940, he figured he'd done nearly three hundred interviews. Among them were at least a dozen suspected characters, several who turned out to be wanted by Scotland Yard and five confirmed to be German secret agents.

One night, lounging in the paneled library of Wilton Hall, Crockatt invited Christopher to join him for a whiskey.

Approaching one of the leather club chairs, Christopher took note of the new insignia on his commander's uniform.

"I see congratulations are in order, colonel."

Crockatt rose from his leather chair and went over to a mahogany sideboard where a large silver tray corralled a cut crystal decanter and a cluster of matching glasses.

Deflecting the compliment he replied, "As I said to you at the outset, advancement can be swift when there's a war on." He handed Christopher his whiskey. "By the way, I've been meaning to ask you: how are your accommodations here? I trust slightly more comfortable than at the Metropole, especially without nightly bombing runs?"

Given that Londoners had been coping with non-stop air raids the previous four months, he decided not to mention that some underling of the camp commandant had a grudge against "Yank bastards," as the martinet was often heard to declare. "Overpaid, oversexed and over here" was his occasional refrain. Upon Christopher's arrival at the Palladian mansion, the twit had assigned him a former maid's room at the top of the house where the heat seldom seemed to rise.

"I'm very comfortable," Christopher lied, "and obviously quite a bit safer. I got a full eight hours' sleep last night."

As Christopher settled into his chair before the roaring fire-place, it gave him no end of amusement to see the same nasty fellow who'd banished him to the servants' quarters walk by the library's open door, and peer inside. He did a double take when he realized that the "Yank bastard" had been invited to share a whiskey this wintery night with the newly elevated Colonel Crockatt, the overall leader of MI9.

~

IN LATE MARCH of the new year, 1941, Crockatt again invited Christopher into the library for a drink after dinner.

"Your debriefs are the best ones that land on my desk," Crockatt began, keeping his voice low while regarding Christopher over the rim of his glass. "I've been thinking... there might be a role you could play back in France, but before I describe what it is, I must ask you something important."

His curiosity piqued, Christopher put down his glass with a thud on the side table next to his chair.

"What is that, sir?"

"Are you willing to go through our escape-and-evade course we give here to departing soldiers?"

Christopher hesitated a moment, calculating that Crockatt might have plans for him to be an instructor at Camp 20, the new facility being constructed on the property that was close to completion.

"Yes, of course, I would," Christopher agreed. "However, I don't know how well suited I am to teach silent killing or forging documents—"

"Oh, your taking the course is not for the purpose of teaching it to others," Crockatt assured him.

"Then why—?"

Without explaining, he interrupted, "Here's another question for you." The newly minted colonel took a long sip of his drink. "How willing are you to be sent to Parachute School up in Manchester?"

"So that I could be inserted into France?" Christopher asked, his heart beginning to race. "Absolutely willing, sir."

"That would be one option for your re-entry."

"And if I land safely, to serve as what?" pressed Christopher.

"Ah... that is the very thing I want to speak to you about more in depth."

The Colonel topped off Christopher's glass and then rose to yank on a velvet pull hanging to the right of the elaborate fireplace mantel.

"I want you to meet a recently repatriated chap named James Langley. He lost an arm in the recent fighting in France and was imprisoned by the Jerries after Dunkirk. He managed to escape there and got himself over the Pyrenees and back to England via Gibraltar."

"Quite a story," Christopher said admiringly.

"It is. Exemplary, in fact."

Just then, there was a knock on the frame of the library door.

"Ah... here he is now. Welcome, James!" he said, as a young man entered, the sleeve of his missing left arm pinned neatly to the waist of his uniform. "I want you to meet Christopher Laurent."

Christopher nodded and extended an arm to shake Langley's right hand.

Crockatt bid them both take seats in front of the fire and poured Langley a whiskey.

"What I have to tell you both is all rather hush-hush, as I expect you have the wit to assume, but..." He paused for dramatic effect. "Now, I want you both to tell me what you think of the plan I have in mind for the two of you."

PART III

16

MARCH 1941

Brooke walked down the hallway from the bedroom she had shared with Victor during the short time they'd lived together in Paris before he'd joined the failed French Army. She intended to check on her houseguest who'd been in residence these six months before she left the flat with Nicole to try their luck at locating some bread, vegetables, and perhaps even a half a pound of coffee to purchase.

She peeked into Victor's library. Jules Dumont, Christopher and her former boss, sat as usual propped up by pillows on the daybed she had installed following his back surgery in September that had been performed by Dr. Jackson at the American Hospital in the Paris suburb of Neuilly-sur-Seine.

After Marshal Pétain's infamous broadcast in June, the previous year, the Radio Mondiale staff dispersed back to Paris and elsewhere. Meanwhile, Denise had taken charge of the seriously ailing Jules, shepherding him, his wife Germaine, Brooke, and Nicole briefly to Vichy and quickly assessing how little resistance to the German takeover of France there was. The group immediately repaired to the home of a friend of Denise's near Bordeaux for some weeks and then, finally, back to Paris when it became clear that Jules could not delay surgery any longer.

It had been quite the harrowing journey north at the end of that momentous summer. In early September, getting past the German checkpoints leading into the city had been due to nothing but sheer luck. Jules miraculously pulled a pass out of his pocket, a document that specified Jules was in the throes of a "medical emergency." The paper, with its official-looking seal, somehow satisfied the officer cursorily checking the documents of everyone traveling in the car with the patient. Most likely a result of the chaotic scene at the final "Occupied Zone" crossing point, they were waved through the last checkpoint into Paris without incident. Brooke, however, had pinned her blonde hair on top of her head and squished a broad-brimmed felt hat down to her eyebrows.

She whispered to Denise, "How did you pull that off?" as their car sped toward Neuilly, heading for the American Hospital.

"Don't ask," Denise had advised, acknowledging Brooke's puzzled glance.

"A friend in Vichy waved a magic pen?" Brooke surmised aloud.

Denise nodded, adding, "And that's probably the last favor the fellow ever does for me. He's vying for a job in Pétain's inner circle."

The day before they'd crossed the border into northern France, Jules's wife Germaine had left their group and rushed to her ailing father's side in the Loire Valley. She had reluctantly agreed to Jules staying with Brooke on Rue Saint-Dominique as the best solution for the poet's long period of recuperation after the operation.

I do wish the woman would realize that I see Jules as only a friend and colleague and not give me that 'look' as if she'd like to scratch my eyes out, Brooke complained silently.

On this chilly March day, she noted from the library doorway that Jules still looked pale and despite his surgery, still suffered from pain. He was staring with a grim expression at a cabled telegram that he held in his hand. Startled, he looked up and with a smile that appeared forced said, "Ah, Brooke. Come, sit down a moment."

She couldn't help but notice how his brow furrowed— whether from the information he was about to impart, or from the lingering discomfort of a procedure that had not completely resolved the injury he had suffered when thrown from a horse years before.

Her breath catching, Brooke's only thought was that a cable rarely brought good news these days.

"So, what is it?" she asked, pointing at his hand.

"Come," he repeated.

He gestured toward the vacant chair beside the desk where he sat parts of the day to compose *La Libération,* the newly inaugurated Resistance newsletter he wrote each week.

Obediently, Brooke sank into the chair, glancing at the latest edition she'd recently typed and soon would be taking to the printer. Somehow, she knew that whatever Jules was about to reveal had nothing to do with the clandestine work they now did together in their underground efforts to fight the Nazis.

Pointing to the cable, she stated flatly, "It's about Victor, isn't it?" For nearly a year, she'd faced absolute silence since the day she bid him farewell at the train station. She'd continued writing him, of course, and sending the letters to the headquarters address he'd given her, but she'd never received a reply. Her feelings had alternated all this time between worry for his physical safety, frustration with the postal bureaucracy, and hurt— followed by anger —at Victor's prolonged silence.

"He's been killed, hasn't he?" she said, staring at the small, paper rectangle Jules held.

Jules replied, his voice gentle. "This is a cable sent months ago by some French ship-assignment officer in Brittany, charged with notifying military families saying Victor was to board the *Lancastria* scheduled to transport him to England."

Relieved to hear this reprieve from her darkest assumptions, she asked, "Why was the cable so delayed?"

"It was sent to me via our engineer, Molet, who hid it from the Nazis occupying the Radio Mondiale offices last June. He only recently learned where I had ended up after my surgery and had someone he trusted bring it by."

"Well, at least we know Victor survived the defeat of the French Army and was sent to England," she said, letting out a breath she hadn't realized she'd been holding. She met Jules's gaze, adding with a tartness she couldn't repress, "And that's a great deal more than what we know about what's happened to Christopher. Too bad no one is sending us a cable disclosing *his* whereabouts."

Jules lifted both eyebrows but made no comment. Brooke started to rise from her chair, but he signaled for her to remain.

With a heavy sigh, he reached for a newspaper resting on a side table near his daybed. It was a German publication designed to convince readers that Hitler's forces were unstoppable.

"Molet's friend also brought this, along with the cable," Jules disclosed and pointed to the headline. "The Germans claim their warplanes sank a British ocean liner that had been converted to a troop ship. It happened back in mid-June as soon as the ship pulled out of the harbor at Saint-Nazaire."

He handed her the paper, its front page displaying a picture of a large, ocean liner half submerged a few miles into the English Channel, the name *Lancastria* barely visible on the partially exposed prow.

Brooke could only stare at the image, stunned by this unexpected blow.

"How could we only be hearing about this *now,* nearly a year later?" she cried, her heart turning over on itself.

"Apparently, Churchill called for a news blackout about the disaster— which the media in the U.K. honored for a long time. Almost everyone on board... is feared drowned."

"Oh, my God," whispered Brooke, wilting against the back of her chair.

"The Kraut bastards kept waiting for the news to hit Britain, hoping it would crush the country's morale. When there was never a word about the ship's fate in British media, the Nazis decided now was time to claim proudly they'd killed some four thousand aboard, including hundreds of women and children, as well as military." He winced as he leaned toward Brooke to touch her hand. "Once the Germans claimed responsibility, Britain was finally forced to release the ship's manifest naming who was on board." Jules pointed again to the German newspaper, now in Brooke's hands. "On page four, the Germans have gleefully republished here in France the list of passengers, for all to see."

Brooke could feel her heart pounding, and her hands trembled as she thumbed the pages, looking for page four.

Her eyes scanned for names starting with 'de' as Jules said

quietly, "Victor's name is there, Brooke. The Germans just list it as 'Varney.'"

The sight of the tiny, printed words "Victor Varney' sandwiched among the thousands of others reported lost in the *Lancastria* sinking made Brooke feel as if she was suddenly living in the first reel of a horror film. That *couldn't* be Victor! Not *him*. The shock that the charismatic actor who had been her husband for such a short time had gone down with some four thousand others was unfathomable.

"A-All those months— we didn't know where he was," she choked, recalling how they risked arrest listening to the radio they kept hidden when not in use.

Jules said, "I'm sure it was pure chaos in Brittany from the time Victor joined his regiment and was then evacuated from the beaches there. The post was probably nonexistent during those weeks and highly censored as well."

"Well, no wonder I didn't hear from him! He was *dead* on the bottom of the Channel!" Slamming the newspaper on the desk, her voice rising, she declared, "And the BBC and all the British newspapers were just *silent* about this disaster? Not a word about the drowning of all those people? How did Churchill and the papers get away with this?" she demanded, her cheeks flushed with anger.

"They didn't," Jules said. "An American news service broke the story some months later, but still there was very little written or broadcast, especially here in France, because the details were so murky and the casualty numbers nor identities couldn't be confirmed." Jules paused, then added, "Until recently. You don't read German, so I didn't say anything until we knew the details for sure."

"The 'details,'" she noted acidly, "were probably kept secret by the British government toadies so that's why we haven't at least heard *hints* about this on the BBC!"

"I imagine many news outfits besides the BBC suspected that the Germans crowing about four thousand dead was merely the Nazis making false claims for propaganda purposes. Sadly, it all appears to be true. Thousands went down with the ship."

Brooke kept staring at the long list of passengers that spilled onto the newspaper's page five.

"Does Denise know?" she asked, her voice low.

"I told Molet's messenger today to give her the news."

And indeed less than an hour later, Denise appeared at their door.

Standing in the foyer, the two women embraced for a long moment, then Denise said, "I came in person since we all should assume our phones in Paris are now monitored by the occupiers." She sought Brooke's gaze and said with urgency, "It's best if no one realizes you were married to a soldier who was attached to de Gaulle's unit fighting against the Vichy."

Brooke nodded her agreement. As it was, she rarely left the flat, except with a scarf tightly wrapped around her head to cloak her distinctive blonde hair.

"Come" she offered Denise, attempting to hold her tears at bay. "I'll have Nicole bring us something to drink in the library. I think we still have a decent bottle of wine somewhere."

"Or something stronger?" replied Denise, wiping the tears from her cheeks.

After greeting Jules who was still leaning against pillows on the daybed, Brooke offered Denise the desk chair and wandered to the window, staring down at the street where the little Simca was parked. Suddenly, her own tears began to flow.

"I- I just can't erase the picture in my mind of his body somewhere at the bottom of the English Channel!" she said, her voice breaking.

"Has there still been no official confirmation of his death?" asked Denise.

Jules shook his head. "We only had the proforma government cable saying he was about to leave on the *Lancastria* with the troops for England and the German newspaper that published the ship's manifest where Victor's name is listed among those on board."

"But has his body has been recovered?" Denise asked gently.

"No, and probably never will be," Jules said, glancing worriedly in Brooke's direction.

For her part, Brooke found she could not bring herself to voice the other horror she feared— that perhaps one day Victor's corpse would wash up, unrecognizable, on some rocky shore. No one to mourn the discovery or bury him properly.

She wondered how she would ever get word to Victor's grandmother if their telephones were being monitored now and their mail opened. Victor's entire family could suffer Nazi reprisals if any authorities figured out the famous film star had been a soldier for the Free French forces opposing Hitler.

Brooke was well aware that her own history working for the defeated French Information Ministry also put her in Nazi crosshairs. Once she'd returned to Paris, she'd kept a low profile these long months, especially given she was sheltering Jules Dumont, a man who had proven to be well connected to factions in France that continued to strongly oppose fascism.

Interrupting her thoughts, Nicole appeared with a tray of glasses, each filled with less than an inch of Château de Varney Calvados. They raised their apple brandy in unison, but Brooke could only manage to whisper, "To Victor..."

"To Victor... God rest his soul," the others murmured back.

IN THE WAKE of the shocking news of the *Lancastria* disaster, Brooke was only able to block the horrifying thoughts of Victor's fate by throwing herself into work as Jules's literary assistant. Each day she typed his articles and then donned her disguise. In addition to her scarf and dark glasses, her masquerade included a wardrobe of dowdy, shapeless clothes that camouflaged her trim figure.

"Rather like dressing for a part," she told Nicole.

As a further precaution, she never pedaled her bicycle along the same route twice to the sympathetic printer's shop where Jules's typed copy was turned into broadsheets. She had instituted this practice of varying her routine after once spotting a headshot of herself taken from a production still of an old Charlie Chan film. Her dewy-eyed, blonde image was plastered on one of the many "Wanted by the German Authorities" posters that were constantly being put up in Paris.

In April, a month after she'd learned of the sinking of the *Lancastria,* Brooke begged Jules for more tasks. She'd missed the busy routine of working at Radio Mondiale along with the interactions she'd enjoyed not only with Christopher, but with her colleagues up and down the hall at the Information Ministry.

"I'm sure there's something more I can do than just typing for you!" she implored him.

Jules regarded her with a troubled expression.

"You're risking enough as it is," he replied. "I made a promise to keep you safe and—"

"A promised to whom?" she demanded.

Jules clamped his lips shut. Then he said, "To myself." He shook his head. "I have to confess, though, I could use your help. The person who used to distribute the printed broadsheets to the drop boxes for pick up by other *résistants* has either quit or been arrested by the Gestapo."

"I can take over that chore," she quickly volunteered. "Write down the places where I'll find the drop boxes—"

Interrupting her, his voice adamant, Jules snapped, "Nothing of that sort is *ever* written down, do you understand me?"

Brooke was taken aback by Jules's usual mild-mannered tone becoming so harsh. She could see that he realized how out of character he sounded, for he added more mildly, "If you're sure you want to do this, you'll have to memorize what I'm about to tell you."

Within the week, Brooke added to her normal routine the job of taking Jules's broadsheets from the printer's basement lair and then traveling on her bike from there to various drop boxes throughout the city.

On the next delivery day, Jules called to her from the library as she was about to leave on another of her missions for him.

"Wait, Brooke! Let me have a look at you," he said.

Brooke went to the door to the room and showed off her latest disguise.

"Dark hair?" he observed as she tied a scarf around her head.

"A wig left over from one of the few films I didn't play as a blonde," she shrugged. Now, whenever she left the house, she always wore her brunette wig with a scarf covering her head to keep it secure, and dark glasses shading her recognizable face. If Nicole went along, Brooke let her do all the talking.

Jules nodded his approval, but added with a troubled frown, "We can only pray that the broadsheets will be picked up by those for whom they were intended so that these trips pedaling all over Paris are worth the risks you're taking."

Waving *adieu*, Brooke announced, "Nicole will be bringing you your lunch in a minute. I'm just going to pop into the kitchen for a quick bite myself before I leave."

"You're going alone?"

"Yes. Nicole finally secured some flour and is baking bread today."

"Well, promise me: home before dark," Jules ordered.

"Promise," she replied and retreated down the hall, her thoughts drifting, as they so often did, to the horror at learning what had happened to everyone on board the *Lancastria*. What shocked her even more was to realize that receiving the news about Victor did not result in an overwhelming sense of grief.

"I feel a deep sadness that such a talented young man died in the prime of his career and that he perished in such an awful way," she had confessed to Nicole who was now far more a friend than a hired housekeeper. "I have such guilt and a sense of terrible shame for *not* feeling utterly broken by... his loss. I supposed that truly makes me a totally heartless bitch."

"No, not at all," Nicole had assured her. "I think perhaps you and Monsieur de Varney had not enough time together to forge those deep bonds that long-married couples can have."

Wise lady...

Brooke nodded. "For certain, I know that I'll never forget those first weeks when we met in New York," she murmured, silently recalling days and nights of intense emotion and delight in discovering their mutual obsession with the acting profession and their extraordinary sexual compatibility.

But after their Atlantic crossing to Britain, Brooke's main memory of the time that followed was one of anxiety and uncertainty. She had constantly wondered if Victor was as committed to their relationship as she felt she was.

Was he... well... faithful to the vows we shared at St. Paul's?

Brooke entered the kitchen, inhaling the rare and wonderful aroma of bread rising in a large, ceramic bowl on the counter. Thinking back on the paltry number of days she and Victor had actually spent in each other's company since arriving in Europe, Brooke was forced to acknowledge that they had been together only sporadically both in London and later in France.

Nicole studied Brooke's pensive expression, reaching for the teapot she kept on a corner of the stove top.

"The bread hasn't gone in the oven yet, but here's a cup of tea. Why so glum, although I can guess. Thinking about—?"

Brooke nodded, not wanting her to say it.

"You know what's even stranger about what's happened?" she asked Nicole as the younger woman filled her cup with tea before she was due to leave for the printers with Jules's latest manifesto. "My life here, in this apartment, has barely changed even after Jules showed me Victor's name on the passenger list of the doomed ship. The truth is, I'd been living pretty much on my own here, with Victor off filming screen tests and scouting locations all over France before he'd left with the army. How can it be that now it doesn't feel much different? It's just this eerie sense of detachment from the fact I am now a 'war widow.'"

Nicole pulled the bowl closer to the edge of the kitchen counter and began to knead the raised bread dough.

"Well, why not concentrate on the present?" she suggested carefully. "The most important thing, now, is to be very careful not to draw attention to yourself," she urged. "You've recovered somewhat from the shock of hearing about Victor, and you may find yourself feeling almost normal again." Nicole shook her head, sinking her fist into the bottom of the bowl. "We must both remember that the world beyond the front door of this flat is *anything* but normal." She grimaced, and Brooke could tell she was thinking about what had happened in the part of France where her family lived. "Once the Nazis took over in Alsace," she said, "nothing was ever going to be the same again, and now the same is true in Paris."

Brooke rose from her chair with Ondie standing in response.

"You are so right. The Nazi restrictions and inconveniences here grow worse by the day." Then Brooke laughed, prompting a look of surprise from Nicole. "No, really, think what their takeover of Paris has wrought in just our own household. Under one roof we have a poet-anti-Nazi agitator, a former actress-turned-journalist-turned-Resistance courier, a refugee from Alsace who's become my best friend and a wonderful baker of bread!" She gave Ondie another scratch under her ear. "To say nothing of an outrageously large French poodle that consumes more than her share of our ration points!"

For a brief moment, she allowed herself to wonder if there'd been any major changes in the lives of her little boy, Errol, and her mother. Did life on the West Coast seem a million miles removed from any war?

17

DECEMBER 1941

The household on Rue Saint-Dominique continued on as before through the rest of 1941, as reports of the war going badly for the Allies continued to pile up.

Then, three weeks before Christmas, 1941, no one was prepared for the shocking December 7th Japanese attack on Pearl Harbor—and America's declaration of war on Germany as well as Japan.

A few days later, Brooke was startled by the shrill sound of the front doorbell. Having just dressed for the day, she hurried down the hallway from her bedroom to answer the ring's summon in case it was one of Jules's couriers coordinating information from his other Resistance colleagues scattered around Paris.

When she opened the door, standing at the threshold was a woman of about her own age who looked vaguely familiar. Next to her was a slender young man in a khaki trench coat and a black fedora who appeared distinctly British with his thin, military mustache and a silk cravat wrapped around his throat.

Puzzled and mildly alarmed to see two unexpected visitors arrive without invitation, she forced a smile and said, "Hello. May I help you?"

"Hall-oo, Brooke," chirped the woman dressed in a smartly tailored Harris tweed suit, her auburn hair perfectly coiffed. "Or should I say Madame de Varney?"

Brooke wracked her brain for a clue as to who these people might be.

"I can see you don't remember me, but I am Gillian Wingate-Jones. You had me to your soirée... or at least Victor did... oh, quite some time ago."

Suddenly popping into Brooke's memory was her friend Viv's cynical opinion of the young woman standing on her doorstep. Gillian Wingate-Jones had been a volunteer rolling bandages and serving tea to patients at the American Hospital. She'd apparently found the work "too distressing and quit," Viv had snidely whispered to Brooke when the woman had arrived at the first— and only —party that Victor and she had ever hosted.

Gillian waved a manicured hand and declared, "My family in Britain were jolly good friends of Victor's mother's family in London."

Brooke seemed to remember that Victor told her once that his mother came from a quite ordinary background in Britain, a fact that seemed at odds with elegantly-clad Gillian's posh claims of a close association between the families. In the next moment, the young woman's voice grew mournful in a tenor Brooke didn't quite find convincing.

"I was so gutted to see Victor's name listed in the newspaper account of that dreadful disaster at sea that I thought that I must stop by to convey my deepest condolences. Such a talent," she said, wiping an invisible tear from her cheek. "Taken from us all too soon."

Her slim companion whom she hadn't bothered to introduce nodded his agreement, but remained silent.

Merely hearing Victor's name spoken aloud sent shards of sadness through Brooke as she recalled the harrowing descriptions of the *Lancastria's* passengers drowning in the Channel.

"W-Well... thank you for your concern," she managed to reply.

A knot tightened in her stomach, for Jules had sternly warned her not to acknowledge Victor's reported loss or discuss it with anyone she didn't know and trust.

Of course, people like Gillian Wingate-Jones would recognize the famous film star's name, even without the 'de' in front of 'Var-

The Safety of Strangers 233

ney,' but why was she a subscriber to a paper published by the Germans in France that was nothing but Nazi propaganda?

Christopher, too, had warned her that the wrong people linking her to her professional name, Brooke Bradley, the former 'voice' on Radio Mondiale and the American broadcaster, put her in danger. Surely Gillian had seen one of the "Wanted for Crimes against the Fatherland" posters with an image of her from the Charlie Chan films displayed all over Paris.

Which brought her back to wondering why these particular British ex-pats had knocked on her door today at such an early hour.

Gillian Wingate-Jones gestured toward her companion.

"I'd like to introduce you to Harold Cole." She smiled at him warmly and added, "He's... well... he's been a great supporter of the French Red Cross and is also involved in... well..." She turned toward him. "I guess you'd call it a rather hush-hush, business wouldn't you say, Harold?"

The thin, dapper young man shrugged slightly, removing his black fedora, but made no comment.

Gillian set Brooke's teeth on edge when she gushed, "I did so enjoy that smashing get-together when you first arrived in Paris as Victor's bride." The unwanted guest peered around Brooke's shoulder, obviously expecting the pair of them to be invited in. "It was such a mah-velous party," she enthused. "We so miss hosting those, don't we? Even the French Red Cross, where I volunteer, no longer holds those charming gatherings for their donors." She gazed at Harold Cole and then looked back at Brooke. "I supposed it's all due to the bloody rationing, thanks to this awful war."

Brooke inclined her head but merely nodded.

Would these two not take the hint and leave?

No such luck, Brooke realized.

Gillian stroked her companion's sleeve and said, "I was just telling Harold on our way here that he'd so enjoy meeting a celebrity like you. I always thought Victor's place was quite stunning and was sure it was something he'd love seeing."

So you've been here more often than just the soirée... Brooke mused.

She was thankful that the door to the library was closed. Jules was at work writing his latest broadsheet for *La Libération*, one she was due to take to the printers later that day.

Unable to think of an excuse to deny entry to a "friend of Victor's family," she led the way into the sitting room just as Nicole appeared in the hallway that led back to the kitchen.

"Ah, Nicole. Good," Brooke said with relief. "We've had some unexpected visitors," she added with veiled meaning, her back to the company. Turning, she apologized, "I'm afraid we can only offer you a glass of water or possibly some very weak tea, and then I'm afraid I have an appointment in an hour."

"Oh, tea would be divine!" Gillian cooed in her posh British accent. She marched into the sitting room saying over her shoulder. "So kind of you." Gazing about the room she said, "Look, Harold. Was I right to describe Victor's place as a jolly fine example of French good taste?"

As soon as the two were settled on the silk settee, Gillian quickly began to chat about life since the Vichy regime had assumed alleged leadership of France.

"*You* were in Vichy for a time, weren't you?" she said. "How did you find things there?"

Brooke's antennae were instantly on alert. How in the world could Gillian have learned that? No one but Brooke and Nicole knew that Jules and Denise had wanted to assess if there was any chance of mounting a propaganda effort against the conquerors. Directly after Pétain broadcast in Bordeaux, Brooke drove their small group there in the Simca. Once there, the pro-fascist sentiment among many upper-class American and British ex-patriots in the spa town of Vichy— as well as among France's far-right government sympathizers currently in power —was overwhelming. Jules had insisted their group leave and drive to the home of Denise's friend where they laid low until the emergency with Jules's back problems prompted them to return to Paris.

Although her pulse was pounding, Brooke folded her hands in her lap and inquired conversationally, "So, if you're asking me about the atmosphere in Vichy after Pétain's faction took over, I'm afraid I can't tell you much. We were only there less than two days."

"Given the chaos of those days, what prompted you to go there?" pressed Harold Cole.

"To pick up a friend due for surgery soon in Paris," Brooke lied. "It just so happened he'd been there taking the waters, which had done him little good."

Each question posed by these oddly inquisitive visitors made her increasingly reluctant to disclose even the most minor detail of what they'd observed while in Vichy.

Gillian cast a brief look at her companion. "Then you had no time to judge if there was any resistance building against the German takeover?"

"No time at all, I'm afraid. Why do you ask?" Her gaze neutral, her mind was spinning in response to Gillian's latest question. On impulse, she inquired mischievously, "Are you a Free French partisan, by chance?"

"Pity your time there was so short," said Gillian, ignoring her question. "It would have been useful if you had been able to evaluate whether any serious pushback was developing against the Vichy officials."

Useful for whom? she wanted to ask.

But instead she replied with a shrug, "In the brief time I was in Vichy, all I was concerned with was getting my friend to the hospital. He was in excruciating pain."

To be charitable, it was always possible that perhaps Gillian and her friend Mr. Cole were merely anxious to know what rumored moves against British civilians marooned in France might be in the offing. Perhaps Gillian thought that someone famous like Victor and his wife could have better connections or more information on the status of ex-pats than she or this Mr. Cole.

In her gut, though, she doubted this visit was so innocent.

Again, Harold Cole spoke up, his British accent so beyond 'old school boy,' it almost sounded as if he were playing in a West End farce.

"Gillian has said I can trust you not to repeat this," he began and then paused, as if bent on making sure Brooke realized how privileged she was to be included in revealing his genuine reason for their coming to her door. "I've been... ah... recruited, I suppose one would phrase it, to report if there are groups in France encouraging anti-German sentiment."

"Report to *whom*?" Brooke asked, gazing at him steadily.

"The Allies, of course," he replied, his tone indicating she'd offended him.

"What branch, specifically? Army? Intelligence services?"

Harold Cole's eyes narrowed. "Naturally, I'm not authorized to say *specifically*," he replied with a nasty edge.

Brooke felt as if she were in a strange game of cat-and-mouse, with the alarming possibility that she and the others in her household might be considered mice. The two unwanted visitors asking these questions out of the blue before she'd even had breakfast only served to make Brooke want to be rid of them as quickly as possible. She forced a warm smile as Nicole entered the sitting room carrying a tray of tea things.

"Ah. Here we are," Brooke said with as much hostess charm as she could muster. "Thank you so much, Nicole." She allowed a glance in the direction of the library where she could picture their only telephone resting on Jules's desk. "Nicole, can you please answer any calls that might come so we won't be disturbed while our guests are having tea?"

Nicole nodded signaling to Brooke that she had the clear understanding she should warn Jules to remain silent and in the library.

"Yes, of course, Madame," Nicole replied in her most convincing housekeeper tone. She swiftly backed out of the room, shutting the sitting room door.

Pouring two cups of the anemic-looking brew, Brooke suggested, "I would imagine the two of you are forced to be rather careful here in Paris, being Brits, and all." She handed each a cup, apologizing for not having milk, sugar, or lemon to offer as accompaniments. "Aren't the Nazis starting to send civilians whom they deem 'enemy aliens' to internment camps?"

Gillian sat up straighter. "Not those of us who volunteer for the French Red Cross," she replied crisply.

"Ah, so Mr. Cole also volunteers there?" Brooke asked, shifting her glance to gaze at Cole expectantly.

Harold Cole made no reply to her query but seemed to be

studying a portrait of Victor's father framed in gold leaf on a nearby wall. After taking a sip from his cup, he looked back at Brooke.

"I'm surprised you're not serving de Varney Calvados instead of tea," he said. "I understand it's considered first rate."

Brooke cocked her head. "Well, after all," she pointed out tartly, "it *is* before lunch. And besides, I have no doubt that, by now, the Nazis have requisitioned whatever was in the family cellars. We certainly have no stores here, I'm sad to report," she fibbed.

So this stranger knew of Victor's family and the source of their wealth. Had the Wingate-Jones woman given Cole the entire de Varney family background? Or had he some *other* source of information?

And what was the real reason the two paid this call to Victor's home in the first place, clearly operating as a team? She could see that the two were British, all right, but which side of the war did they support?

She could almost hear Christopher's warning to suspect "everything anyone tells you until you verify they're legit."

Her friend Viv's tone had dripped with sarcasm when she'd mentioned that Gillian Wingate-Jones was a "bitchy Brit who despises us Americans."

So, why was the woman being so ingratiating toward an American widow of a French film star who'd supported the defeated Free French government?

Brooke took a deep draught of her tea and then rose from her seat.

"I am terribly sorry to be so rude, but I have an appointment with a car mechanic about my Simca you might have seen parked outside. It's making a strange noise, and the only the time he has to see to it is mid-morning today."

Her guests had no other option but to stand and prepare to depart.

Brooke crossed the sitting room, held open the door, and ushered them into the foyer, relieved to see the entrance to the library had remained shut. Meanwhile, she caught Harold Cole sidling up to the small table near the front door where Brooke tossed her keys and the incoming and outgoing mail was laid.

"Mr. Cole," she said, startling him so that he turned back to face her. "In the future, I'm afraid I must ask you both not to come by again or call me on the telephone. I'm sure you're aware by now that the German authorities have ordered British and American nationals to be watched, their phones and mail monitored. Surely, none of us want to be thrown into an internment camp for enemy aliens, do we?"

The two made no comment.

Brooke summoned a smile to soften her next words.

"So *please*. It is probably safer for British and American citizens living in France to have few contacts with each other these days to avoid complications and suspicion. Let's do each other all a favor. Please do not seek me out again and I will give you the same courtesy."

She noticed Gillian pursed her lips with unmistakable irritation while Harold Cole stared stonily into the distance.

Brooke opened the front door.

"Let us hope to meet again when this war is over, and the Allies have won."

Cole took a step forward and then paused to stare at Brooke.

"It's a wonder you didn't return to America when you had the chance," he said, eyeing her steadily.

"It occurred to me to ask you the same question," Brooke parried pleasantly. "Why haven't either of you gone back to Britain? It's a much swifter journey across the Channel than my attempting to sail the Atlantic with German U-boats and the Luftwaffe shooting at everything that moves."

Cole announced flatly, "As of now, it's virtually impossible for foreign nationals to obtain the travel documents necessary to leave the country." His words indicated to Brooke that Harold Cole must be very familiar with the German travel embargoes.

Brooke plastered an expression of admiration on her face and said to Gillian, "You are such an example of doing good works in these trying times. Perhaps you would recommend that I volunteer for the French Red Cross? It would also be nice if it provided some protection to keep us all from being sent somewhere quite disagreeable?"

Gillian made no offer of introductions to anyone at the French Red Cross. Instead, she took steps to stand beside her companion.

"Well, we'd best be off," Gillian said with a stiff smile. "Thank you for the tea. Cheerio!"

"And again, our condolences, Miss Bradley," said Harold Cole, tipping his black fedora.

He's calling me by my professional name... and it sounds like a warning— or a threat.

Brooke cast him a hard-eyed stare.

"I prefer to be addressed as Madame de Varney. In honor of my late husband."

"I'm sure you do," he replied, and walked through the open front door with Gillian in his wake.

As soon as Brooke closed the door, she turned and braced her back against its carved wood surface. She could feel her heart pounding in her chest and her mouth was dry despite sipping half a cup of the dreadful tea she'd served.

At that moment, Nicole emerged from the shadowy hallway that led to the kitchen.

"Who *were* those people?" she demanded.

"I'm not quite sure," Brooke replied, giving silent thanks that the door to the library had remained closed and Jules's presence not exposed. "But let us hope that they got the message not to show their faces here ever again."

ALL THROUGH DECEMBER and into the New Year of 1942, everyone in Brooke's household remained on edge after the "visitation"— as they deemed the appearance of Gillian Wingate-Jones and the mysterious Harold Cole. Every trip Brooke made on her bicycle dressed in her various disguises set her nerves on edge.

Brooke's main concern was that her unwanted tea guests would inform the German authorities that the rather reclusive woman living on Rue Saint-Dominique was the "blonde movie star" on their list to arrest.

Despite their ever-present anxiety, nothing further happened following the pair's strange appearance at their front door. Even so, from that day forward, she and Nicole had kept their forays outside the apartment to the bare minimum. Each time they were required by necessity to leave the flat, both agreed they felt as if they might have been followed. Every time Brooke sensed this, the vision of the rather sinister Mr. Cole came to mind.

Confiding these ongoing fears to Nicole after Brooke's latest delivery of Jules's broadsheets to drop-off spots in the Marais, she complained, "Don't say anything to Jules, but I feel as if I'm being pulled between being sensibly cautious and wildly paranoid."

Three days after the non-joyous celebration of New Year's Eve, Brooke discovered that her bicycle chain kept slipping off the sprocket.

"I'm really going to have to take it to the bike shop for repairs," she announced to Nicole. "We just can't afford the petrol for me to take the Simca on my rounds, and besides, I hear the Nazis are starting to requisition people's cars right off the street."

Nicole promptly volunteered, "I'll go with you so at least we can see if there's anything decent to be had at the open-air market. I can have my bike tuned as well while we're there."

Even though the last dusting of snow in the city had melted, the pair dressed warmly in layers to shield themselves from the bitter cold and threatening skies as they rode through the streets on this wintery day. Brooke had pedaled three blocks from the flat before she realized she hadn't donned her black wig.

"Your scarf practically covers your whole head," Nicole assured her, shivering as she stood by her bike where they'd stopped at the corner.

"It's too cold to go back," Brooke acquiesced. "Let's just get this over with."

After leaving their bicycles at the repair shop and finding no loose flour, but at least one loaf of bread to buy, they walked to a nearby café for a cup of acorn-laced coffee to try to warm up while waiting for their bikes to be fixed and tuned.

As they entered through the café's front door, Brooke's heart lurched with alarm. Out of the corner of her eye, she caught sight of two men, both in overcoats and wearing black fedoras, standing across the street.

"Oh, my God!" she hissed to Nicole. "Don't turn around, but I think one of those two men over there is that Harold Cole creature."

Finding them a seat near the bar, Nicole peered through the window.

"Yes," she agreed, fear lacing her words. "I-I think you're right! He's the one with the mustache, no?"

"Odious little creep," Brooke said, nodding.

Just then, the waiter approached to take their order. Once he retreated to the kitchen Brooke whispered, "The other one next to Cole is clearly German, blond hair and all." She could hear her own swift intake of breath. "Oh, goodness! It looks like he's going into that call box, see?"

"If Cole was going to inform on you to the Germans, why didn't they just come to the flat and arrest you?"

"I think he and that thug have probably been following me lately to confirm I deliver Jules's broadsides all around Paris. Today, they happen to spot us on market day when they hang out looking to nab people for whatever infraction they choose."

"And Cole collects his fee," Nicole said angrily.

"That's his game, apparently. Despite my disguise, Cole is able to identify me and so, maybe they're about to—"

Brooke stopped talking while they both stared as the muscular-looking German entered the telephone booth and shut the door. Mere seconds later, a phone near them began to ring. Their waiter, carrying two cups of coffee on his tray paused, set the tray on the bar, and picked up the receiver. Listening, he glanced over to where they were seated and then shifted his gaze out the window at the street.

Nodding, he grunted a short, unhappy, "*Oui.*"

He hung up the phone and hurriedly set their coffees on the table, their contents sloshing into the saucers. Without a word, he raced back to the kitchen as if the two of them had leprosy.

Brooke watched as the German in his fedora emerged from the call box and conferred briefly with his slender companion.

"That's *definitely* Cole," hissed Brooke, "and he's just confirmed to his thug-buddy who we are. C'mon!" she croaked, throwing down a few coins. "Out the back door!"

Speeding through the café to the rear exit, they dashed into an alleyway. Brooke pointed toward the street that would lead back to the repair shop. They arrived there just as the mechanic was setting Brooke's bike back on the shop's wooden floor. She dug into her purse, pulled out a bank note, and handed it to him, exclaiming her thanks. He stared at the sum and then at her.

Ignoring him, she said, "Look, Nicole. Your bike's over there!"

"But wait!" the shop owner exclaimed, "We haven't even looked at it."

"Go!" Brooke cried to Nicole. "But first, let's exchange coats and ride home separately. With my hair covered and wearing your coat they might not spot me." She gestured to Nicole's dark hair. "And even with *my* coat on, you won't fit my description!"

"But—" Nicole began to protest.

"Go! Go *now*!"

Brooke pointed to the back of the shop, asking the bike mechanic, "Is that way the rear way out?"

He nodded, peering at her curiously. Nicole immediately wheeled her bike in the direction he'd indicated.

Brooke said hurriedly, praying that her French was perfectly understood. "The extra money is for never admitting we were ever in here, agreed?"

"*D'accord,*" the mechanic replied, and she could only hope the generous tip would persuade him to keep his word. She bolted toward the back door, following Nicole. "And thanks for fixing my chain so quickly," she added over her shoulder.

The streets were now slick with water as gray skies overhead had begun to unleash a deluge of rain. She could barely make out Nicole pedaling swiftly down a street and turning left around the corner. Brooke hunched over her handlebars and sped as fast as she dared, beseeching the fates that she could make it through the crowded square where vendors were scrambling to put away their market goods and escape the worsening downpour.

Luckily, the area was teeming with everyone scurrying toward dryer destinations. Brooke's silk scarf had become plastered to her head but at least it still completely covered her blonde hair. Nicole's coat was a bit small for her, but she barreled her bicycle around pedestrians and down a different street than the one Nicole had chosen.

As buildings flew by, she could only hope that Harold Cole and his henchman would discover they had missed their prey and seek shelter from the rain in a bar somewhere.

Paris, Brooke realized with a jolt, was no longer a "safehouse" for anyone living at the flat on Rue Saint-Dominique. Harold Cole knew where she lived.

But where can we go? Not the Château de Varney and put Victor's grandmother in jeopardy.

Wherever their next destination would be, she thought, glancing anxiously over her shoulder, they should leave the city as soon as she could help Jules Dumont downstairs.

18

"How in the world did you know to find this place?" Jules asked Brooke, wedged next to Nicole and surrounded by piles of their belongings stashed in the back seat of the Simca.

Ondie had climbed into the front passenger seat when they were departing from Paris less than an hour after Nicole and she had pedaled home— and she wouldn't budge. At the end of their hurried escape these hours later, the poodle remained curled up, asleep, on the seat beside Brooke as she drove slowly down the main street in the town of Barbizon.

With a laugh, she said over her shoulder, "In my panic last night to get us all out of Paris before the goons came knocking at our door, I remembered Victor speaking about the wonderful, sunny summers an hour outside the city where he and his father and grandmother leased a villa named after rabbits."

"Rabbits?" echoed Jules and Nicole simultaneously.

"Yes, rabbits! He said that his asthma symptoms disappeared from the moment they arrived in Barbizon at a house called La Villa du Lapin d'Or."

"The House of the Golden Rabbit? How quaint," commented Jules dryly.

Brooke suddenly wondered if Jules's wife, Germaine, would eventually join them once he was able to get word to her that they'd so precipitously decamped from Paris. But rather than raise the subject, Brooke continued to explain why she had determined that this little town had been their best— and only —practical choice to evade Harold Cole and his henchman.

"Besides Victor always feeling healthier here, he told me how he loved the legacy of the little backwater as a gathering place for many impecunious French Pre-Impressionist painters and other creative people in the mid-nineteenth century."

"Ah, yes," Jules replied, smiling faintly. "The famous Barbizon School that put this tiny place on the map with its more naturalistic approach to landscape painting."

"And led the way to the Impressionist painters who came afterward," Brooke added, slowing the car as she scanned the surrounding houses, looking for the villa in question.

There certainly was no warming summer sun in Barbizon this frigid January day, but Brooke was thankful she'd recalled Victor telling her that it had been an American who owned the vacant property the de Varneys had rented for many summers.

Brooke also counted her blessings that a local policeman she'd hailed had pointed to a small abode on the main street in town where a Madame Alice St. Claire was now living in a two-bedroom flat with her nurse-housekeeper. It proved only a few doors down from the larger property Madame still owned and the woman herself had answered the door when Brooke had knocked an hour previously.

"My dear, of *course* I'd be willing to have a de Varney lease the villa once again," their new landlady had informed Brooke as soon as she'd proposed renting it and asked about transportation to and from Paris.

"Barbizon is only a bicycle ride from Fontainebleau where there is decent train service to Paris via Gare de Lyon."

With Madame's husband, Gabriel St. Claire, long in his grave, his widow proved only too delighted at this fortunate opportunity to rent out her former home in the dead of winter to a fellow American. Brooke and she quickly agreed on a price and terms and Madame St. Claire handed over a large metal key.

"There's just one thing," the old lady said from her chair by the fireplace, raising a forefinger to get Brooke's attention. "The care-taker, Felix Gervais, lives on the back of the property and comes with the lease." She smiled faintly. "I'm sure your Victor would remember him from his youth. Felix worked for the St. Claires long before I married Gabriel."

The news that there would be someone Brooke didn't know living amongst them gave her pause, but she knew she had no real option but to sign the simple agreement that Madame St. Claire quickly composed on her personal stationery.

"It's the last dwelling on the town's principal street, *Grand Rue*," Madame St. Claire explained. "The property backs up to hectares of wheatfields for which this region in central France is quite well known. France's 'Breadbasket' I suppose you'd call it." She rang a small brass bell beside her chair. "I'll just have my housekeeper nip down there to alert Felix we have new tenants," she said with a pleasant smile.

Then she frowned. "One thing, however. You and your friends will have to register with Mayor Porchard. He's a complete toady to the local commandant, I'm afraid."

"There are Germans stationed here?" Brooke asked, attempting to disguise her alarm.

"A small contingent commanded by a pudgy little fellow named Edgar Schiller," Madame disclosed, nodding. She gave a derisive snort. "I'm told by my housekeeper that in a previous life, the man managed a feedlot in Germany somewhere. Apparently, he prances about town as a bit of a peacock, all brass buttons and 'Heil Hitler' salutes." She shook her head and sighed. "Now that the U.S. has entered the war, you won't be surprised to learn the Nazis aren't particularly friendly toward us American ex-pats."

"Have any Americans living in Barbizon been interned as 'enemy aliens' like the Brits?" Brooke asked.

"None that I've heard about— yet."

Brooke groaned inwardly, wondering if her picture on a "Wanted" list was tacked up on the wall in Commandant Schiller's nearby headquarters.

She hastened to inform Madame St. Claire, "We intend to keep a low profile," suddenly wondering if the move had been so wise after all. "I hope you will keep our arrival to yourself?"

"Of course," Madame St. Claire assured her and Brooke could only cross her fingers the woman would keep her word.

Brooke realized that she would immediately have to concoct a convincing cover story for why the disparate group of Jules, Nicole, and she had come to Barbizon— but at the moment, could not conceive of what that was.

Meanwhile, Madame St. Claire had summoned a cheery smile while she tucked in more firmly a blanket that wrapped around her legs. "Shall you leave your first month's rent on that table over there?" she suggested.

Brooke could only surmise the woman would more than welcome the money she was being paid and prayed the group from Paris staying indefinitely in Barbizon would serve as added incentive for Madame St. Claire not to blow their cover. Brooke swiftly dug into her handbag for some of the cash she'd kept hidden at home. On the advice Denise had dispensed the week following the Pearl Harbor attack, Brooke had withdrawn substantial funds from the bank and hid the large denomination notes between the pages of a shelf-full of Victor's old film scripts which she'd quickly stowed in the Simca just before leaving Paris.

With the impromptu lease in hand, she'd returned to her car, relating to her passengers the amazing luck she'd had securing them a new roof over their heads away from Paris.

Now, as the Simca slowly passed down the Grand Rue that cut through the center of the village, she soon spotted a wrought iron sign twisted into the shape of a large rabbit and bolted to a high stone wall announcing the location of La Villa du Lapin d'Or. Madame St. Claire had described the nearly 300 year old villa as consisting of a modest, three-bedroom main house with several outbuildings.

Gazing, now, through the car's windshield, Brooke took in the welcome sight of high stone walls surrounding the residence that would afford protection from prying eyes. She was startled when the tall, wooden front gates began to open with the screech of rusty hinges. An elderly man in blue coveralls appeared and offered a friendly wave.

Before her passengers could ask questions, Brooke announced, "That must be Felix Gervais, the caretaker. He comes with the lease and lives at the back. Hopefully, he can help us with things like heat and hot water."

Brooke waved through the driver's side window and called out, in her best French, "*Bonjour,* Monsieur Gervais! I see that Madame St. Claire warned you we were coming."

Felix slowly made his way to the driver's side of the car. Brooke figured he must be eighty years old if he were a day but he seemed spry and fit enough to handle the heavy gate, at least.

"Ah, she did indeed just alert me about your taking a lease, here," he said. "Welcome to the 'rabbit hutch' as your husband used to call his summer home."

Brooke's breath caught. Apparently, Felix had known Victor as a little boy. She fought back a sudden surge of emotion as the reality of his being missing and presumed drowned rushed back, full force.

"W-Well, it's lovely to meet you," she managed to say, suppressing her tears. "I hope we won't be too much trouble for you," Nodding at her passengers, she told Felix, "We're a quiet bunch, seeking some solitude after the German takeover in Paris." She gestured toward Jules and Nicole in the back seat. "This is my house-keeper, Nicole Langlois, and Monsieur Dumont is a dear friend of Victor's and a marvelous poet who is recovering from back surgery."

To nip in the bud any speculations Felix might have she added, "His wife, Germaine, will be joining us when she has settled her ailing father with someone to look after him."

"And Monsieur Victor? He is well?" Felix asked.

Brooke steeled herself to give the answer Jules had insisted upon from the day they'd seen the German newspaper listing Victor as one of the *Lancastria* casualties.

"Sadly, Victor has not been heard from since... well... since our forces were overcome by the Germans entering France."

Felix's expression grew pensive. "I am so very sorry to hear that, especially for you... such a young bride, as Madame St. Claire's housekeeper told me. But, as they say, 'no news may be good news,' yes? He could be a prisoner-of-war somewhere, like my poor nephew who was captured when the Krauts overran the Maginot Line."

Relieved that her French had improved enough to have understood what Felix had been saying, Brooke promptly replied, "Yes. That may well have been Victor's fate. We shall all have to be patient, won't we?"

But all she could think about was the sight of the name 'Varney' on that list of thousands who were thought to have perished on the *Lancastria*. But could a miracle have happened? Could Victor somehow have been among the known survivors?

Felix appeared to inhale a deep breath and summoned a smile.

"Patience is what's is called for these days, indeed, Madame." He gestured toward the gate. "So, welcome to you all. It will be good to have some company on the property." He paused and then added, "But I assure you, you'll have complete privacy, as is my custom with all guests who have rented the place in the years since Monsieur Gabriel passed away. Come, let me show you where you will be living."

The caretaker of Brooke's new abode, turned away from the car and opened the two high, wooden gates fronting the Grand Rue. He then motioned for Brooke to drive through to the inner courtyard.

Vines devoid of foliage spread like spider legs up the walls of both the main house and three smaller stone structures enclosed by the circle of walls that protected all the leased residences from the surrounding streets. In the center of the paved courtyard stood a fountain empty of water, and toward the back, a kitchen garden consisting of six large, raised beds lay fallow of any plantings.

Brooke pointed to her right.

"Jules, Madame St. Claire said that the little building over there is a small guest cottage that reportedly served as a studio for the painter Jean-Françoise Millet. She told me that he was one of the founders of the Barbizon School and was known for painting local farm workers harvesting the wheat."

"How wonderful!" Jules enthused. "Millet is one of the most celebrated artists of that era."

Brooke gestured toward the caretaker who was walking toward the back of the main house to open the door. "Felix lives in the one-room stone cottage over there in the back, left corner," she said, pointing toward the rear of the enclosure. "Madame told me that she used the other building you see over there on the right as a potting shed. Apparently, she'd been a keen gardener during the years she lived here."

"You mean, you've never before seen this place yourself?" Jules asked with alarm. "How do you know it even has heat?"

Brooke laughed. "Can you imagine our Victor living in a place without the luxury of heat or running water?"

Jules raised an eyebrow and shook his head "no."

Brooke parked the car at the far side of the courtyard next to one of the eight-foot-high stone walls. Once they'd all emerged from the Simca, Jules turned in place, nodding his approval.

"It's rather like being protected by a small, stone fortress."

Brooke smiled, saying, "We are incredibly lucky I could even remember the name of this place! Madame said that she'd told her husband on the day of their wedding, 'You married an American. If we buy this villa, Gabriel, we will install central heating in the house, an Aga cooker in the kitchen, hot water, and indoor bath-rooms." Brooke gave a small laugh, adding, "She admitted that a few things may need some repairs, but she claimed that the basic electric works and plumbing are probably the best in town, except for the hotel down the street."

"And a hotel is bound to have a bar, if all else fails," Jules chortled.

Brooke's smile faded. "But, our situation isn't perfect, I'm afraid."

By this time, Felix had disappeared into the house as Jules and Nicole both cast worried looks in her direction, hearing her last remark. Brooke motioned for them to step closer to the car.

Lowering her voice she told them, "Barbizon also has a small detachment of German authorities next door to the hotel at the other end of the street. Madame St. Claire told me that we three must register with the mayor later today. That probably means that the commandant will be informed of our arrival in town."

"*Mon Dieu!*" Jules exclaimed. "Wouldn't you say living in a town with a bunch of uniformed Germans is just asking for trouble?"

Brooke motioned for Jules to keep his voice down.

"No less than in Paris, and at least here," she countered, "you and I are far less known. We'll be living behind high, stone walls and will keep to ourselves, letting Nicole be the one that people in Barbizon recognize." She smiled reassuringly. "Madame St. Claire assured me that Americans married to French husbands will not be harassed."

"As long as they don't know that *your* French husband was attached as an aide to de Gaulle against the Vichy French," Jules retorted in a harsh whisper. "And Lord help us all if they figure out that Madame Brooke de Varney is also Brooke Bradley who broadcast anti-Nazi propaganda! And we're really done for if the Gestapo ever realize that I was the head of the Information Bureau before the takeover— to say nothing of the work I'm engaged in now!"

"The name de Varney is common enough," Brooke soothed with far more reassurance than she actually felt. "If anyone around here asks if we're part of the de Varney family making calvados, we'll just say 'We think we might be distant cousins.' As for being Brooke Bradley," she added, feeling a shiver ripple down her spine, "I think I'll register as 'Madame B. de Varney' and tell everyone here my first name is 'Brianna'— and we will not use my real first name, Brooke, in front of others, agreed? And the same goes for your former life with the old government, Jules. It's a subject we never discuss."

Both Jules and Nicole nodded. Then Jules spoke up once again.

"But how will I get my work into the right hands in Paris?" he demanded.

"Madame told me that there's a train station from Fontainebleau, only a few kilometers up the road from here. Nicole will be able to deliver your broadsheets to the printer and then distribute to the usual drop boxes once a week."

Brooke gestured for them to proceed toward the courtyard

entrance of the main house that Felix had unlocked and through which he'd disappeared inside to get the heat started.

Nicole nodded and reassured Jules, "I miss Paris already, so I'll be glad to have an excuse to go to the city."

"Come," Brooke urged with forced cheerfulness, stepping over the threshold and into the main house. "Aren't you both anxious to see where we'll spend most of our time?"

Brooke would rather forget the harrowing trip out of Paris in the dead of the previous night. From the minute she and Nicole had shaken off Harold Cole and his thuggish companion the previous day, the two of them had swung instantly into action. They scrambled to assemble the household items they'd need if they were to be gone from the city for an extended length of time. Included were the disguises Brooke and Nicole had begun using in the early days of distributing Jules's broadsheets to the printer in Paris.

Once they left their neighborhood, Brooke had fast-talked her way through several check points along the road, her blonde hair covered by her dark wig and a Hermes scarf, and her face encased in the darkest of her theatrical makeup to make her appear years older.

Now, glancing over her shoulder across the villa's empty courtyard, Brooke was also grateful that she and Nicole had managed to strap their two bicycles with rope onto the roof of the Simca itself. Nicole and she could ride them to the market and to Fontainebleau if they wanted to catch a train.

"I'm freezing," Jules announced as he stepped inside the main house.

"Then, let's see how Felix is getting along," Brooke urged.

They found their inherited major domo kneeling in front of the hearth. He looked around at the new arrivals and announced, "It won't take long to get this entire place warmed up." Pointing at the fire beginning to ignite, he added, "I'll stack more wood just outside."

Brooke surveyed a large window in the sitting room facing the street, and beyond it, the wheatfields that Madame St. Claire had described. She made a mental note to hang a thick curtain to block passersby from seeing inside their new abode. Any trusted visitor would be instructed to tap on the window before knocking at their front door or at the gate leading to the walled courtyard.

"*Voilà!*" Felix exclaimed under his breath. "Now, I will be getting the boiler lit, and make sure the water is turned on here in the main house and in the studio."

To Brooke's relief, Felix Gervais seemed surprisingly cheerful about having work to do and new tenants to look after.

But then, another thought struck her.

She and the others would have to watch what they said within Felix's earshot until they knew if he had a habit of reporting— for money —the activities of newcomers to the German authorities just down the street.

Nothing is ever simple in this world of war...

The thought of their having to appear before the mayor to register as new residents made her increasingly anxious. She would definitely have to disguise her looks when they appeared at the Barbizon city hall. Glad for the scarf that continued to cover her blonde head, she asked Nicole to bring in the "Costume Department" suitcase from the car, even before they dug out the linens to make up the beds.

"Jules?" she queried, turning to the erstwhile poet-propogandist, "If you'd prefer, you are most welcome to claim the studio where Millet did his painting as your own little sanctuary."

"If Felix, here, can guarantee I won't freeze out there, it sounds like the perfect place for a writer," he replied.

Felix rose from his knees, gesturing toward the fire he'd started that was currently burning brightly.

"*Monsieur,* I am at your service." He cast a glance at Brooke. "The fireplace and its flue in the artist studio are sound, but we will need to secure more wood if *monsieur* is to sleep out there."

Brooke mentally calculated the cash she'd brought and nodded.

"I think we can manage— that is, if spring comes a bit early this year."

Felix nodded solemnly and headed out the door.

Brooke mentally began to tote up other looming expenses: food, petrol, and money for Nicole to take the train into Paris each week.

With a start, she suddenly realized that she had been delegated the head of a very strange household, indeed.

Their unorthodox ménage certainly was one that they must take care not to attract the attention of German authorities— or any local Nazi collaborators.

~

THE FOLLOWING DAY BROOKE— dressed in her dowdiest outfit, her dark brown wig covering her blonde hair, and her face devoid of any makeup —led Jules and Nicole into the outer office of Mayor Porchard. The three quietly filled out the paperwork now required by the Germans for any new resident coming to the town. A photograph was taken of each of the newcomers, so Brooke now had an image of herself as a brunette on an official document.

As she'd determined earlier, she'd merely signed the document as "Madame B. de Varney, a widow," and stepped aside for French citizens Nicole and Jules to scratch their signatures on their identity forms noting they had taken up residence at La Villa du Lapin d'Or.

The trio slipped out the side entrance before Mayor Porchard had returned from the protracted lunch his deputy revealed that Porchard took each day at his home with his comely young wife.

Jules insisted they enter Les Pleiades Hotel at 21 Le Grand Rue to survey the bar there before returning to the villa. Before they could reach the door, out walked a stocky, middle-aged man wearing the dreaded gray-green uniform of a Nazi officer.

Hailing their little group, he halted their progress, declaring in guttural French, "I had been told three people have taken up residence at the Saint Claire property."

His pronunciation was as grating on Brooke's ear as she imagined hers was to many French speakers. She couldn't help but wonder who among the villagers was the Nazi's snitch.

"I am Commandant here," he announced, his eyes narrowing, "I hope you have registered with the mayor's office as required by all newcomers."

Jules spoke up, replying pleasantly, "We have, sir. Edgar Schiller, isn't it?"

Schiller looked surprised and then apparently pleased that they knew his name and had followed orders to register.

"Yes," he confirmed clicking his heels. Looking at the two women he said, "And you are?"

"Madame de Varney," Brooke answered in the best French accent she could muster, with Nicole quickly stating her name.

"You are American," he declared to Brooke. "And I must say I am rather curious. Why have you three come to Barbizon?"

Jules spoke up, amazing Brooke with his *sangfroid* in the way he calmly offered explanations to the inquisitive Nazi.

"I have recently had a serious back operation and my doctors in Paris urged me to seek the peace and quiet of the countryside to recover. My wife, who is tending to her sick father, will be here soon, and meanwhile, our dear friend," he continued with a nod toward Brooke, "was kind enough to urge us to come stay with her. It's so lovely to share the villa that her husband's family has leased on and off for many years." He offered Schiller a grave look. "Sadly, Madame is also recovering from recent news her husband, a French citizen, is... like so many during these difficult times... currently unaccounted for." Schiller merely raised an eyebrow. Jules continued dolefully, "She was drawn to come to Barbizon as her husband often spent summers here as a child."

Oh, Jules... don't give away any more information about us...

She could only hope that Mayor Porchard wouldn't brag over a glass of schnapps with Schiller that the wife of the French movie star whose family frequented Barbizon in years past had become a new resident.

Brooke kept her eyes averted as Jules gestured toward Nicole.

"And Mademoiselle Nicole Langlois, here, was good enough to come with us to cook and keep house."

"And you have a lease to verify what you have just told me?" Schiller demanded.

Brooke hastened to retrieve from her handbag the handwritten agreement provided by Madame St. Claire, along with a note she'd obtained that morning from the old woman declaring the lessee's family was known to her and had rented her villa in previous years.

"I am so pleased," Brooke added with a nod in Jules's direction, "that I can offer one of France's foremost poets and his wife a place of quiet refuge to aid in his recovery."

"A poet, eh?" Schiller repeated. He compressed his lips in thought and then declared, "I write a bit of poetry myself. Perhaps you would be willing to read some of my work and offer your opinion, *monsieur*?"

A former feedlot manager who writes poetry? What next... Brooke wondered silently.

Jules coolly nodded agreement, placing his two hands on his back as if it were paining him, which it probably was, Brooke speculated.

Jules offered a faint wince while assuring Schiller, "As soon as I'm a bit more on my feet, it would be my honor to read your work, sir."

To Brooke's astonishment, Herr Schiller briefly scanned the lease papers she'd handed him, flashed a warm smile at Barbizon's latest newcomers, and offered them a hearty welcome.

"It's delightful to know painting and literature can be found even in the French countryside as it certainly can in my *own* country," he said proudly, returning the lease papers to Brooke.

Clicking his heels smartly and raising his right hand in the "Heil Hitler" salute, he then bowed, swiveled on the balls of his feet, and strode down the street in the opposite direction.

Brooke grabbed an arm of both Jules and Nicole.

"Hold on to me, please," she whispered. "I think I might faint."

19

On an evening in late January, Brooke hurried to the back studio to deliver Jules's dinner tray, announcing excitedly, "The BBC just confirmed that American forces have begun arriving in England!"

"Well, I hope you kept that radio you brought from Paris tuned low," Jules warned, "and don't keep it on too long. The word I get from the intelligence Nicole heard on her last trip to Paris is that the damn Krauts now have what they call 'locator vans' that can trace the radio waves beaming into French homes from across the Channel. If they catch us listening, they'll take the radio and might even arrest us."

Brooke placed the tray with Jules's supper beside his typewriter with an annoyed thump.

"I'm well aware of all that," she replied, trying to mask how irritable she felt, cooped up within their stone walls for so many days on end. "I listen for the top of the news and then switch it off and hide the radio in a barrel in the pantry with piles of stored potatoes on top."

"Good," Jules replied shortly. He didn't look up but kept typing on his latest essay.

With a sigh, Brooke tiptoed out of the studio and across the shared courtyard, heading back to the main house to finish packing up the root vegetables that Nicole had bought at the local market and was due to ferry to a few Paris safehouses the next day, along with Jules's latest literary effort.

"Our friends in the city are nearly starving to death during these cold months," Nicole had told her. "Even red beets and carrots are greeted like heroes from the garden."

The weather continued to be dank and cold for the rest of January and most of the next month. Even so, Brooke was relieved to discover that the home improvements made to the structures that Madame St. Claire had demanded of her French husband so many years ago rendered their interior living spaces warm and dry within their stone walls. The high barriers surrounding the property and heavy drapes installed in the front sitting room window shielded the Paris refugees from any curious passersby ambling along Le Grand Rue.

"And isn't this coal-fired Aga cooker the greatest invention ever?" Brooke exclaimed to Nicole.

"It's wonderful," the housekeeper agreed, "as long as we can keep securing coal," she added worriedly. "Perhaps the Aga people will make one that runs on oil one day."

Brooke watched as Nicole placed her latest batch of cooked squash and potatoes on the hob to keep warm. Soon they would have produce of their own that they were beginning to plant outside their kitchen door, dedicating any surplus to the safehouses in Paris that Jules designated.

Brooke had learned from Felix that their new abode had originally been a farmhouse on the edge of town, but in the last hundred years, small houses, shops and other villas had extended the village to include the home. Fortunately, for their privacy's sake, the land just beyond their street melded into vast wheatfields that would sprout as spring came on.

"Our local baker's family raises wheat and also has a millstone," said Felix, pointing in the direction of the nearby fields, "so if the Nazi scum don't steal all his grain, Barbizon shouldn't run out of bread."

And perhaps we can buy extra grain and bake some of our own, Brooke mused, convinced, by this time, that Felix was 'one of them,' a man who resisted the invaders in every way at his disposal.

If only they could obtain the needed supplies, Brooke thought, hoping one day to spirit loaves where needed to people with hardly a crumb of starch to eat, hiding from the Nazis in Paris as the food rationing there became ever more severe.

"Supplying food may not be considered genuinely part of the Resistance," Nicole had said on day, packing carrots purchased at the local market for transport to the city, "but without it, our side might starve."

As the weeks went by, Nicole and Brooke were kept busy cultivating the seedlings that had begun to sprout in all the raised vegetable beds. As the tender shoots appeared in the soil, they could only pray Commandant Schiller and his confederates wouldn't confiscate their produce as they often did from hapless farmers at the village market each week.

Meanwhile, Jules devoted his days to writing a series of essays on the fall of France: what he deemed caused it, and what loyal French citizens should do about restoring their freedoms.

"I also have begun to plan efforts to organize groups of *résistants* among writers, doctors, dentists, booksellers, poets, and painters I know that are still residing in Paris."

Brooke, thinking of Victor's friend, Pablo Picasso, asked, "And how will you do that from Barbizon?" She was highly skeptical that such an ambitious proposition would have success if done from such a distance.

He pointed to Nicole who had just propped her bicycle against the wall beside the studio and was coming up the path to his door to report on her recent foray into Paris with Jules's latest literary effort.

"Nicole has been invaluable to that end, haven't you Nicole?" Jules said as she appeared at the door.

"To what end?" she asked wearily, sinking into a nearby chair.

Jules had not only asked that Nicole take his work to the printer every week, but he was now having her deliver copies to all the 'drop boxes' around the city where fledgling partisans then passed along his call-to-action messages to others whom he hoped to recruit into the Resistance. It was a dangerous activity, given that

any one of her contacts could betray her actions to the local
Gestapo.

"Promise me you'll keep an eye out for that duplicitous snake,
Harold Cole," Brooke pleaded, uneasy every time Nicole set off for
Paris.

"Oh, believe me, I will and I do," their housekeeper said with a
shudder.

After a long day of anxiety, Brooke now felt the knot in her
stomach begin to relax at the sight of the young woman resting in
the chair, the poodle Ondie stretched out on the floor beside their
little group.

Jules reached for a bottle of calvados and poured a small glass
for all three gathered in a circle. They sat near the floor-to-ceiling
wall of paned windows of the former art studio that looked out at
the courtyard and the back of the main house on the other side of
the central fountain. The peace and quiet of the place sometimes
tricked Brooke into forgetting that a war was raging all over Europe.

"I was just telling Brooke that on your trips to Paris, Nicole,"
Jules said, "you are also spending some time reaching out to
contacts in the arts and sciences that may be willing to join our
underground. We must all prepare to mount a fight against the
Nazis when the time is right."

"I was able to speak with Mademoiselle Colette this trip," Nicole
reported. "I also saw Josephine Baker briefly backstage at her club
and she was happy to receive a copy of your latest essay."

"Good God, Jules!" Brooke exclaimed, amazed to hear her
housekeeper was now associating with people who'd been on the
guest list of the one soirée that Victor and she had hosted before
their world had utterly changed. "You might have told me about all
this before you cast poor Nicole in such a treacherous role! She is
my employee— and friend," she added fervently. "I have a right to
know—"

"I volunteered," Nicole interrupted. "I hate the Nazi bastards for
what they have done to Alsace." She turned to Jules, her expression
grim. "But I have bad news for you, I'm afraid. Today I heard from
one of our contacts in Paris that some arrests of people you know,
Jules, have already been made and a renewed warrant for *your*

arrest was just posted all over Paris." She paused, and added, "Your chief contact says you mustn't stay here in town any longer, given the proximity to the German contingent headquartered in Barbizon. The fear is that local authorities will be given your name to watch for."

Jules shot a startled glance at Brooke that conveyed his undisguised dismay. They all had worried about the day the commandant would undoubtedly arrive with sheaves of his poetry for Jules to critique.

"And where did this contact suggest I go next?" he demanded, looking from one to the other. His gaze around the studio clearly conveyed how upset he was having to leave such appealing living quarters.

Nicole took a sip of her drink and carefully set it down on the small table beside her leather chair.

"He suggested that Brooke and I seek an abandoned farmhouse for you between here and Fontainebleau. Something out-of-the-way, but not too far from us in Barbizon."

Equally unnerved to hear this news, Brooke chimed in, "Who *is* this person ordering Jules to live in some hovel that probably doesn't have heat or indoor plumbing?"

Nicole looked questioningly at Jules, but before she could elaborate, he declared, "In this work, we share the fewest names or identification of our fellow resisters as possible to protect the group, should one of us be arrested." Jules hesitated a moment, and then declared grimly, "What you don't know cannot be tortured out of you."

Unaccountably, Brooke felt a rush of resentment settling over her.

"So you two have created your own private cell of resistance, but don't deem me a worthy member?"

"You certainly are 'worthy,'" Jules said with an ironic arch of his eyebrow, "but higher ups believe you are too recognizable to risk getting you more deeply involved than you already are."

"And exactly *who* is meant by 'higher ups?'" she demanded. "And would you deign to tell me where these orders are coming from?"

She looked at both of them, in turn, for an answer. Nicole gave a Gallic lift to her shoulders and remained silent.

Jules said mildly, "Not allowing you to know such names is for your safety, Brooke. Please be assured that you have been hugely useful to the cause merely by whisking me, Nicole, and yourself to safety as you have and finding this perfect outpost."

"And now you must find another 'safehouse?'" she retorted, feeling a surprising sense of having been abandoned once again. Christopher had left without so much as a by-your-leave. Victor was presumed dead, and now Jules had to go away. No doubt Nicole might be recruited to go somewhere by whomever was ordering them about from Paris. Before long, Brooke could find herself alone in a village overseen by the pompous Edgar Schiller.

She felt Jules's glance searching her face and sensed that he was about to make some sort of proposal.

"If you'd like to be useful to the cause," he said carefully, "then you might ask Madame St. Clair if she knows of any abandoned farmhouses, or even a barn tucked away across the wheatfields somewhere. Apparently, I'm a risk to you both if I remain in the villa. And I refuse to do that."

"But what about Germaine?" Brooke protested. "I doubt your wife is up to living in the sort of rusticity as you're likely to find around here."

"If it's agreeable to you, she can have my bed in the studio here, and come see me on days you deem safe."

Nicole spoke up.

"Knowing you'd been urged to move to a safer locale, Jules, I spoke on my way back here today to one of the wheat farmers whose bread I buy at the weekly market. His name is Antoine Boucher and he was at his stall selling his wares when I stopped to buy our baguettes."

"Ah, the man Felix knows whose family has its own millstone, yes?"

Nicole nodded. "That's right. He and his wife are the town bakers and from his attitude toward Schiller and his underlings when they stroll by, Antoine clearly hates having the Krauts in Barbizon. When I asked him about possible places further out in the countryside, he told me he knows of a spot about two kilometers from the end of our road." She gave a soft laugh. "As Brooke predicted, Jules, the farmstead Antoine has in mind is definitely rustic, but it could provide somewhere that any other *résistants* you recruit can meet with you without the curious eyes of our local townspeople. He'll let me know what he finds out from the owner."

Jules raised his glass in a salute.

"Nicole, you are a wonder! A tucked-away farmhouse, also surrounded by wheatfields not too far from Barbizon, sounds like a good spot where we could receive arms and munitions air drops when the Allies finally begin to mount such efforts." Nodding at Brooke, he said, jovially, "Perhaps you both can help me gather my things, load the Simca, and take me to my hideaway amidst the flat land I hope will one day serve as landing strips!"

"And what will you do for food?" Brooke asked pointedly, worried that she and Nicole would garner unwanted attention if they were seen coming and going from their villa.

Nicole took a last sip of her calvados and rose to her feet.

"I can ride my bicycle to and from there, and if I'm ever stopped, I'll just say I go to a farm up the valley to secure carrots for the rabbits. And you, Brooke, could wear your usual dark-haired wig and farm clothes disguise and only deliver food to Jules after the sun goes down."

Brooke couldn't help but look at Nicole with amazement. The shy young woman fleeing devastation in Alsace who had turned up at her door seeking work as a humble housekeeper had blossomed into a full-fledge *résistant*! Not only had the two of them planted vegetable seeds in the six raised beds out back, but they'd also managed to hammer together a make-shift rabbit hutch with the intention of capturing some of the ubiquitous hares that abounded in and around Barbizon.

Soon after the hutch was finished, Nicole met a woodcutter named Raymond Pouillet who procured them a ferret, the one rodent especially adept at cornering the local rabbits in their underground lairs.

"This clever little creature drives them into traps like these, see?" Raymond explained proudly when he delivered the contraptions to their gate. He'd held up one of the metal devices to show Brooke and Nicole. "It will capture our furry friends, but not kill them when it snaps shut."

Both to Nicole and Brooke's relief, Raymond agreed to become their 'executioner,' in exchange for needed vegetables for his family's table.

"We raise the rabbits for protein, and the rabbits need carrots," Nicole said with a smile. "It's the perfect cover story when Jules moves to the farm."

"Cover story?" Brooke repeated. "Have you officially been recruited as a spy?"

Nicole flushed and murmured, "Not a spy."

"I think the correct term we're to call you is 'helper,' right Nicole?" Jules said with a smile. "And if your rabbit scheme is a success," he continued with an unusual burst of enthusiasm, "Nicole can take tasty *tartes du lapin* to our future safehouses in Paris, along within supplies of the produce you're growing under the Nazis' noses." He cast an amused look in Brooke's direction. "Nicole, I trust, is willing to teach you how to bake?"

"Rabbit *pie*?" Brooke repeated, incredulous. "I don't know how to boil *water,* let alone how to skin a rabbit and turn it into something edible. What's wrong with having our farmer friend Antoine sell our rabbits at the weekly market?"

Jules raised his glass again in a final toast.

"We can do both," he said cheerfully. "Or rather you will when you master the art of making rabbit pie."

"Pies will be too difficult for Nicole to transport," Brooke countered, quietly refusing to become a pie-maker to the Resistance. "We can package the meat and let it be cooked by whomever receives it in Paris."

The issue of the rabbits decided, Jules set down his glass with a clink.

"So let's get me packed up and ready to move."

As Brooke rose to her feet, she wondered who was actually the head of their household now. She fought against the hollow feeling in the pit of her stomach. After all, making rabbit pies, or even growing rows of vegetables, was not exactly what she pictured being part of the Resistance movement would be like. Everyone else but she seemed to be moving on to more important roles, leaving her to live alone in Barbizon with only carrots and rabbits for company.

She suddenly thought of her little son Errol whom she'd left in Los Angeles and wondered if the unwanted circumstances evolving in her new life these days were some sort of cosmic payback for abandoning *him* to her mother's unreliable care. With no one in the room as a witness, she fished out of the side pocket of her purse the small Kodak snap taken of him on his first birthday. His paper hat was tilted and he had cake frosting on his chin. He wouldn't know her, now, she mused.

A mantle of gloom settled over her and she could only wonder what would happen if no one else was left in her world and the war went on for years?

THE NEXT DAY, Nicole returned from the open-air marketplace with good news for Jules, but it only served to underscore for Brooke how fast things seemed to be shifting in her world.

Nicole clapped her hands excitedly, reporting, "The wheat farmer, Antoine Boucher, confirmed there *is* a lease for a nearby farmhouse that's available on reasonable terms because, just as Brooke predicted, it's rather rustic."

"The sooner I can remove myself there, the better," Jules declared, his brow furrowed as he turned to Brooke. "Perhaps you could copy most of the terms in the ad hoc lease Madame St. Claire composed when you rented our villa, and we could strike a quick bargain?"

Within the hour, Nicole took Brooke's handiwork to the farm's owner and had the lease put in Nicole's sole name in case there was ever a need to show legal papers to Herr Schiller.

"If Schiller ever comes around for you to read his poetry, I can say you had to move to the South of France for your health."

"Good thinking," Jules agreed, adding "and it is better that a full

French citizen be the lessee, so fewer questions," he explained to Brooke.

The farmhouse was positioned at the far end of a small valley that branched off the large wheatfields at the edge of town. The previous tenant was among those men who'd been recruited into the French Army and never returned. His wife and small children had melted into another part of France to take up residence with distant relatives, leaving the owner only too happy to lease it out for an equitable sum.

Jules settled into his newest safehouse just as the weather began to improve. As spring approached and the succeeding weeks rolled by, the Resistance writer appeared healthier and happier than he had been since the shutdown of Radio Mondiale.

Once a day, Nicole or Brooke broke away from duties tending to their vegetable garden and the small beasts that were beginning to crowd the rabbit hutch they'd pieced together. They brought Jules his dinner and supplies soon after the sun had set. On these forays, they would return with his current essay hidden beneath the dirty dishes in their bicycle basket.

Thanks to the routine of these exchanges, Brooke began to have less concern about being recognized beyond the villa's high walls. She would don her brunette wig before she left her bedroom, along with a pair of blue bib overalls of the style that French farm girls favored. Felix, by this time, was a trusted compatriot, so Brooke felt safe displaying her own blonde hair within the villa's wall.

When it was her turn to deliver Jules's daily meals, she pedaled her bicycle along the road that cut across the baren wheatfields nearest the villa. Less than two kilometers from their gate, a dirt lane, crusted with frost, led to Jules's ramshackle farmhouse at the end of a curved track.

Meanwhile, Nicole continued to transport Jules's written attacks against the occupying forces to the underground printer's shop in Paris, along with delivering produce to various safehouses there. Worried for her housekeeper's safety, Brooke had created a disguise for Nicole as well.

"You will pose as a pregnant woman," Brooke told her, feeling as if she were a costume designer on a new film. She held up a canvas pouch of vegetables she then strapped around Nicole's waist to demonstrate. "You can carry the shopping bag with produce in it on your arm to our local train station, then slip immediately into the carriage's restroom. After attaching this to your waist, under your loose housedress, you'll emerge as a woman the Nazi guards at the checkpoints in Paris are not likely to harass as you make your way through Gare de Lyon."

"But what if some Nazi official sees me in the morning and notices I'm no longer bulging in my middle when I'm on my way back to Barbizon?" Nicole asked with a worried frown.

"Hmmm..." Brooke murmured, groping for an answer.

Nicole suddenly laughed.

"I know! We can add a pillow to stuff in my waist along with the vegetables. Once I deliver the food, I'll wear the pillow, puffed up, under my clothes for the return trip. I can shed it in the train's restroom right before I get off in Fontainebleau. Then I'll carry it home in the vegetable bag I sling over my arm until I can put it in my bicycle basket for the ride back to Barbizon! On my next trip to Paris, I'll wrap it around the vegetables we put in the sack under my baggy dress, and off I'll go again!"

"You'll probably look as if you're ten months pregnant at times, but it's the best we can do," Brooke agreed.

She could only marvel at the changes in Nicole and fervently wished that she, too, could play a bigger role in the work being done to fight the occupying Nazis.

When she lived in Paris, it had been infuriating to be recognized constantly for playing the dumb blonde in a bunch of second rate-movies. And *because* of this, *she* was consigned to a role behind the scenes.

Brooke could only wonder what Viv, her friend from her French classes, had been doing for the Allied cause these days— that is, if she'd survived her new calling as an ambulance driver.

And then there was Christopher Laurent. Heaven only knew what he'd been up to since he slipped away just before the Krauts marched into Paris, damn him!

And Victor...

She fought the haunting vision at the back of her mind of her husband's body buried in sand at the bottom of the English Channel.

"Stop it!" she whispered aloud and marched into her bedroom. She was an *actress,* for God's sake, which meant she could assume any part she chose and play it to the hilt!

Brooke grabbed her wig off its canvas headstand on the dresser and shoved it onto her head. She was due to deliver Jules's daily ration of food to the farmhouse. While she was there, she was now determined that she would have a serious talk about more concrete ways she could help the Resistance efforts.

If Jules Dumont had become the de facto leader of a genuine underground cell headed by some mysterious boss he reported to in Paris, *she* would demand a role to play as well and would refuse to take "no" for an answer!

It was the least she could do to honor Victor's death and fight against Hitler's plan to take over the western world.

~

IN THE DUSK of early evening, Brooke pedaled around the last curve on the dirt path that led to the decrepit wooden farmhouse. A single candle glowed in the front window, a nightly sign it was safe to approach.

Years before, the surrounding wooded area had been cut back at the rear of the structure to provide room for a kitchen garden that had long been neglected. The land on the front of the house soon gave way to the farm's fields that lay fallow of wheat, or any other crop. Land cultivated by more successful farmers could just be glimpsed at the turnoff to this sad excuse of an agricultural holding.

Leaning her bike against a weathered fence post, Brooke found herself wondering if Nicole's farmer friend, Antoine Boucher, could advise them on raising some wheat of their own on this deserted property? He could harvest and mill it for an in-kind fee and Nicole could teach her to make bread which was sorely in short supply. The loaves would certainly be a welcome addition to the foodstuffs they delivered to the gaggle of safehouses assigned them in Paris.

Interrupting her musings, the door to Jules's latest abode suddenly swung wide open.

A tall man stood in the shadowy doorway, his trim businessman's suit severely out of character with his surroundings. Behind him she could just discern the figures of two other strangers.

Good God! Had Harold Cole's henchmen found Jules's hideout already?

Her heart speeding up, Brooke drew closer, peering through the gloom at the man's face distinguished by high cheekbones and a slightly curved, Gallic nose. He was a handsome specimen of manhood, she judged, despite the narrow mustache so favored by Europeans—especially by Nazi officers —but it was a look she intensely disliked.

"Brooke?" the man called out in a low voice.

She felt her breath catch, froze in place ten feet from the farmhouse front porch, and could only stare.

She'd immediately recognized the voice, if not the man, who had transformed himself into someone she would never have thought could be the radio reporter who'd pulled a disappearing act on her.

"We've been expecting you, Cub. Thank God Jules warned me about your wig or I'd have shot you just now. I hope your beautiful blonde hair still lies beneath that monstrosity you've got on your head."

"Hello, Christopher," she forced herself to reply coolly, although she felt like punching him in his magnificent French nose.

Without another word, she walked right past him into the farmhouse carrying Jules's basket of food.

20

C hristopher remained silent in the aftermath of Brooke angrily stalking past him with her dismissive greeting. He turned and watched her standing inside the farmhouse, hands on her hips, staring steadily at Jules who sat at a small table beside a typewriter and his latest manuscript.

If the atmosphere hadn't been so charged at that moment, Christopher would have smiled at the sight of her. Brooke's dark, shoulder-length wig cast her as some mysterious Mata Hari, while her blue farmer's overalls served to disguise what he knew to be her distinctly feminine figure.

This view of his former "partner-in-crime" could not stem the lustful thoughts that seeing her again had instantly conjured. It seemed like another lifetime since they'd shared that sumptuous dinner at Le Dôme. It hit him like a boulder how much he'd missed having her part of his life... and how much he wanted her now, a desire that had been pointless then and was probably pointless now.

"So who's the boss of all this?" she demanded of Jules while brandishing her forefinger in Christopher's direction. "Him or you? And who the hell do you *both* work for?"

Jules reached for a bottle of calvados Brooke had packed with his things when she'd moved him to the farmstead. Christopher watched him pour an inch into a glass and hand it to her, but she refused to accept it. With a shrug, Jules took a sip himself and indicated she should sit down in a nearby chair.

She remained standing.

"You knew where he was from the very beginning, didn't you?" she accused Jules, gesturing a second time at Christopher. "You knew he hadn't been killed or drowned, like Victor. You knew he was in France *all this time,* didn't you?"

During her tirade, Christopher walked from the front door and stood behind her. He told himself that it shouldn't give him such a goddamned thrill that she was so furious with him. People didn't get this angry over a mere friend or an acquaintance losing touch.

His mind flew back again to their last meal at Le Dôme and the moment when their lips were inches apart. How close he'd been to deepening their relationship that night. Seeing her again, he felt an almost physical pain imagining what she'd been through in the two years since he'd left for England. He had been privy to it all, thanks to his contacts with Jules. She'd had to flee Paris with their radio group and then return to face the brutal occupation. He could only imagine the shock of her seeing Victor's name on the passenger list of the *Lancastria.*

And then, of course, thanks to that bastard, Harold Cole and his Nazi henchman who'd threatened her with arrest at a café in Paris, she'd had to flee the city a second time and set up a safehouse for Jules, Nicole, and herself at the villa in Barbizon.

All Christopher wanted this night was to claim that kiss he'd refrained from at Le Dôme, and more— if she'd have him.

But Victor de Varney had been the reason he'd pulled back then, and he was the blasted reason he had to do that now.

He stepped in front of her to address her directly.

"I haven't been in France until I returned in January of this year," he declared as calmly as he could, wondering how much he could explain things to her without violating the Secrets Act he'd signed.

Brooke poked his chest with her forefinger. "Well then, where the hell have you been? Why didn't either of you tell me why you left without a word and never got in touch?"

"For one thing, the war..." Christopher replied mildly, wishing he could simply lay it all out for her. "I knew the Germans would want to arrest me— just like they do you —for our anti-Nazi broadcasts," he pointed out. "Only I was the bigger fish and they'd be after me the minute they invaded Paris. I left the country before they got to the Information Ministry building, and you," he added wryly, "clearly were smart enough to leave the city, too. At least I knew that you were immediately heading out with Jules who was supposed to persuade you to keep going south to escape to Spain and go back to the States" he added, with a scowl in Jules's direction.

Jules shrugged. "She couldn't be convinced."

Christopher sighed. "Clearly not."

After a pause he continued. "Once I got to London, there were myriad British government news embargoes and telephone and telegraph blackouts, so nothing could get to you that way," he explained. "And after I settled in with the job I have now, a few other matters kept me from contacting you."

Like joining MI9... he reflected silently. *And then there was spy school in Scotland. Parachute training in Manchester. And now the other reason why I'm here...*

Almost all of which he could not reveal to her. At least not yet.

It truly boggled his mind how much his life had changed since the day he'd walked into Crockatt's office at MI9. Gazing at Brooke in her farmer's overalls, the ridiculous wig covering her gorgeous crown of blonde hair, she'd come a long way from the Chanel suits and classic silk scarves she'd worn when they first met.

But the fire in her eyes hadn't faded. To him, it was an emotional glare that signaled she considered their relationship had been more meaningful than merely having been colleagues at the Ministry of Information.

He'd only just told Jules today how he and Victor dodged death by taking a different ship than the *Lancastria* when evacuating with the British and French troops from northern France. Christopher realized that news of such a lucky survival would be stunning for anyone to hear, especially to a woman who had been convinced her husband had drowned after she and Jules saw Victor's name in print on the ship's casualty list.

What kind of man doesn't do his damnedest to get word to his wife, somehow, that he made it to England, at least?

And, as Jules had confirmed to Christopher today, what bastard doesn't write before he leaves for the fighting in South Africa? Christopher was certain that if *he* had been her husband, he would have found a way to let her know he had made it safely to England, at least. With a rush of sympathy, he reached out and put a hand lightly on Brooke's shoulder which she immediately shrugged off.

"Don't!" she muttered, twisting away.

He pictured Victor's letter to Brooke tucked in the rucksack sitting on the floor mere feet from where she stood ignoring him while continuing to berate Jules for keeping so many secrets. Christopher had been sanctioned to hand Victor's missive to her only on the occasion of de Varney's confirmed death. He had no doubt that Victor had probably penned words declaring his undying love. Would Brooke ever realize what a total cheat her husband had been?

Christopher's recollection of the night the actor had left the hastily scribbled letter on the table next to the bottle of whiskey they'd consumed was seared in his memory. He'd been a captive of Victor's shameful, tawdry, preening recitation of infidelity— and now it was up to him to tell Brooke that her husband had *not* gone down with the ship.

"We have to talk," he murmured, conscious of the others in the room.

He turned to address Jules. "I will be back for some final words before I have to leave tomorrow. I can save Nicole a trip by taking your latest essay to the printers in Paris."

His two companions had remained in the shadows of the small room. They were among his trusted local contacts in the human escape line he was setting up aimed at transporting prominent civilians and downed pilots out of France.

To one of these deputies he ordered, "Luc, tonight you are to connect with those people near here we've discussed and be ready to meet me with your progress report in Fontainebleau at the usual place by noon, tomorrow." He nodded at the other man. "Your friend can help you with this, but only you are to meet at the designated spot."

The two men merely nodded and shuffled out of the room. Christopher again put his hand on Brooke's shoulder, only this time she didn't flinch.

"I would like to accompany you back to Barbizon."

"I rode my bike," she said curtly.

"So, I will walk."

"You don't know the way."

"Yes, I do."

"Well, you don't know the *house!*"

"The Villa du Lapin d'Or, isn't it? At the very end of the Grand Rue."

Her startled look told him she now realized he'd been in the area before today. The angry flush invading her cheeks was yet another sign that it mattered to her, even if it stoked her ire.

"Very well," she acquiesced grudgingly. "Knock on the window, first, so I'll know it's not the local Gestapo."

He sensed a fatigue and vulnerability in Brooke that made his chest hurt. God only knew the terrible toll these two years of war had taken on her, to say nothing of the very real dangers she still confronted every time she showed her celebrated face in public.

She barely nodded farewell to Jules and retreated to the front porch and down the farmhouse steps. Stomping a path to her bicycle leaning against the nearby fence post, she pedaled off in a cloud of dust.

"*Adieu,*" Christopher murmured to Jules and then followed in her wake.

He might very well be violating the Secrets Act, but Brooke deserved to know some heart-wrenching truths, and he could not avoid being the one to disclose them to her.

∾

KNOCKING GENTLY on a solitary window facing the street, Christopher waited impatiently for Brooke to open the villa's front door. Instead, he heard one of the tall, wooden gates off to his right creak on its hinges and Brooke's breathy voice whisper harshly, "Over here! Quickly!"

A low growl floated through the tall, wooden barrier's one-foot opening, followed by Brooke's hushed command, "Ondie! Quiet! You know this man! *Sit!*"

Once inside the courtyard, she pointed to a small, stone structure whose front wall consisted of numerous square glass panes.

"Nicole's asleep in the main house, so we can talk in Jules's old studio. Follow me."

Christopher remained rooted to the spot, allowing the poodle to have a satisfactory sniff of his legs and crotch. Then, with the dog trotting happily by his side, he followed Brooke across the courtyard and into the chilly quarters where Jules apparently had lived until Christopher urged Nicole to warn Jules to vacate immediately. It wouldn't do for their unit's chief lieutenant in their newly formed escape-and-evade enterprise to be arrested before their plans could even be put into operation.

As for Brooke's safety, he had prayed from the day he'd left Radio Mondiale that she would immediately depart for the States. He had been worried about her for the last two years since his sources had confirmed she had remained in France following Hitler's invasion.

They entered the one-room studio and Brooke handed him a blanket to wrap around his shoulders in the frigid space she'd chosen for this rendezvous that Christopher had hoped for since the day he'd headed for Brittany.

Brooke seized a coverlet off the daybed and swathed her own shoulders to keep warm. Watching her, Christopher once again resisted the memory of almost kissing her the night of their last dinner in Paris.

You don't seduce other men's wives, he warned himself.

A voice in his head answered that de Varney was the last bastard on earth who deserved her loyalty— or his. How ironic that it had fallen to him to inform Brooke that Victor wasn't dead, nor was she the widow she might have assumed. Jules had told him how she'd refused to accept her husband's death without proof of a body washed up on the shore.

I taught her that much, I suppose— of demanding the facts.

Earlier, Brooke had certainly made it clear how upset she was with Christopher for leaving Paris without telling her. What would be her reaction to the news Victor had never set foot aboard the doomed *Lancastria*? How would that stunning truth affect Christopher's own relationship with Brooke from here on out?

His thoughts colliding, he pushed them to one side and demanded, "Can you please take off that damn wig? I want to be sure I'm talking to the real Brooke Bradley."

She whipped it off her head and shook out her golden curls.

"There!" she shot back. "Make no mistake, it's me, and I can't believe I'd ever speak to you again after what you did. You *ditched* us!"

Us? She means I ditched her...

From the heat of her words, Christopher instinctively knew *she* was the one who had felt abandoned, not her radio colleagues... and she still did.

"I didn't want to endanger any of you by telling you I wasn't going to continue working for the Vichy," he began.

"You know perfectly well that I wouldn't have revealed that to anyone!" she protested.

Christopher bid her sit on Jules's daybed while he took a chair beside it.

"I know you wouldn't have meant to betray anyone, but the German goons who put cigarettes out on bare flesh and hang people by their heels for hours at a time have a way of loosening lips. The less you knew about me and where I'd gone, the better for everyone concerned."

"Nonsense! The Germans hadn't even taken over Paris back then. You just left because it was what you wanted to do."

Christopher could see Brooke was definitely in a take-no-prisoners frame of mind.

Ignoring her latest jibe, he replied, "But the Germans, as I predicted, occupied Paris and northern France soon after, didn't they? And later," he countered, "you were scared enough about Harold Cole stalking you in Paris to flee to the countryside. Correct? You had choices you had to make, and so did I. We made the best ones we could, at the moment, under the circumstances."

"How did you find out that I was stalked by Harold Cole?" Brooke demanded, clearly astounded he already knew how she had come to live in Barbizon.

Christopher saw no danger in disclosing the obvious.

"I've been in touch with Jules for quite a while through mutual contacts in Paris and London."

"Ah! So you went to London!"

He shrugged his shoulders but remained silent. He'd been aware when he agreed to work for the French Ministry of Information that Jules had been an old hand in military intelligence matters since the days of the Great War. Why else would the former French government make a little-known poet the head of the government's propaganda unit? Brooke, he realized, had never been aware of their former boss's background and still wasn't buying his explanation.

Lips pursed, she scoffed, "*What* contacts did Jules have in London? He's been stuck in this backwater as long as I have." Suddenly she paused, cocked her head as if coming to her own conclusions, and declared, "Ah... I see now. Jules sent Nicole with his anti-Nazi essays to the printer— who's a partisan —in Paris. *You* now have underground connections to that printer and the printer's in touch with Jules via Nicole going back and forth, am I right?"

Christopher offered up a sigh.

"See? You already know too many of the links in this clandestine operation, which merely puts you in more danger."

"Face it, Christopher. We *all* are in danger. We have been from the moment the damn Nazis crossed into France. Especially those of us who broadcasted against our enemies."

"That was yet another reason you and I couldn't make a safe escape from France together. I'd heard we were already on some 'Enemies of the State' list for our work."

Worriedly, he ran his hand through his well-combed hair.

Brooke's softening stare made him realize that now he probably looked more like himself in his reporter days.

Abruptly she announced, "I hate that mustache on you, by the way."

"I wasn't too crazy about that wig on you, either!" he retorted, gesturing toward the pile of dark hair she'd plopped down on a nearby table. "The mustache is supposed to help convince the enemy I'm just a French businessman who sells ink and paper supplies to several printing shops in and around Paris." He shrugged, pointing to his face. "So far it's worked, but possibly because the shops I service also print Nazi posters for the local German authorities who 'ask' the poor owners to do it for free."

Her eyes narrowing, she declared, "You've given me a few facts I didn't know before, but there is so much *more* you owe it to me to tell." She shot him a defiant stare, adding, "And I have a few things to tell *you*."

"Like tell me off, you mean?" he replied, testing her sense of humor.

Brooke clearly was trying not to smile at his last remark. She crossed to a wooden cabinet, brought out a bottle of wine and two glasses, and set them next to her abandoned wig on the small table.

Ondie had curled up contentedly at Christopher's feet, and if the two humans weren't both shivering from the cold, Christopher might have thought they were in for a lovely, possibly romantic evening.

Brooke poured wine into both glasses. "I forgive you, I guess, for leaving the radio team without warning me," she allowed, "but only because now I know a few things I didn't before. You, Jules, and Nicole were the ones organizing getting food to safehouses in Paris to protect innocent people attempting to evade the Gestapo there, am I right?"

"So, you can understand why everything had to be completely off-the-record?"

"I guess so," was her reluctant reply, adding, "I suppose that Nicole and Jules didn't tell me you were involved in the scheme we were part of since *I* wasn't the one traveling from Barbizon to-and-from the city."

"Exactly," he confirmed, relieved Brooke appeared to be gaining an understanding of all that had transpired during the tumultuous time the Germans were overrunning France. "Jules's decision to use Nicole as a courier and keep you out of the operation once you'd all left Paris was solely because that rotten traitor, Harold Cole, has you in his sights," Christopher revealed. "He still does."

"But what about Nicole? He's seen her two times."

Christopher gave a shrug. "Men like Cole rarely take note of servants. He was concentrating on *you* each time you met."

He felt a familiar rush of anger that Colonel Crockatt at MI9 could not seem to convince his superiors at MI6 that Cole was playing both sides against the middle. Christopher, himself, had only lately learned the British con man, who'd emerged from a British prison to join the army, had been posing as an Allied intelligence officer. It wasn't long before the lout began ratting on his British *and* American colleagues for German money. Christopher's sources confirmed that the turncoat soldier had more than a taste for gambling, seducing women, and high living.

Brooke shot Christopher a startled look.

"Tell me what *you* know about Harold Cole."

"I wish I could give you more details about the son-of-a-bitch," he replied evasively. "As soon as Jules and I first made contact with each other after the Germans invaded, he told me about how Cole tried to entrap you and Nicole at the café. He knew the SS had a bounty on your head. It took him a while to gain their confidence and convince the local Gestapo he could led them to you— for money, of course." He took a sip of his wine and gazed at her over the rim of his glass. "Only your fast thinking avoided complete disaster, Brooke, so brava you."

"Lucky I had a car and could decamp quickly."

Nodding, Christopher set his drink on the table and reached for her hand. "The way you whisked Jules out of harm's way that same day— as well as yourself and Nicole —literally saved lives in Paris you don't even know about."

She gave him a puzzled look.

"Whose lives did I save except the three of us who fled?"

He offered her a faint smile. "If they'd captured Jules, and tortured him, many other Resistance contacts would have been compromised."

"Ah. I see," she murmured. "One link leads to another."

"You should know that what you did has been duly noted by the good guys."

"And just who, exactly, *are* the 'good guys?'" she inquired, withdrawing her hand.

"I can't tell you that, but just know I am working for them now."

"You were in London, so it must be the British government. No more journalism?" she asked, and he felt in her searching glance a genuine sympathy that he could no longer ply his writing craft in a way he could stomach.

"I've found I can use those reporting skills in a new way."

"A way that fights the Nazis," she replied softly.

He was bowled over when she motioned for him to sit next to her on the daybed.

Her expression suddenly deadly serious, she declared quietly, "And in your clandestine exchanges with Jules all this time, did he tell you that Victor went down on the *Lancastria* along with thousands of retreating Allied troops and civilians that were on board?"

Christopher had only learned from Jules this very day that both the erstwhile poet and Brooke had good reason to assume that France's most celebrated film actor had been drowned in that disaster. He remained silent, watching her stare into her lap for a long moment, and then look up to meet his gaze.

"Can you believe it?" she said, "to this day, there's been no body returned and we've never received any official word from any government that Victor died. All we know is that his name was on the ship's manifest in a German-published French newspaper Jules saw months later."

Christopher's, hearing her speak of Victor, thought ruefully, *Trust Brooke to make it easier on me by bringing up the subject on her own.*

He placed a careful arm around her shoulders. "Hearing about the ship going down in the Channel in that way and then seeing Victor's name on the casualty list must have been a terrible shock."

Brooke nodded, staring blindly across the studio at the panel of glass squares, black as the night sky outside.

With a sidewise glance she confessed, "I hadn't heard a word from him in so long that I felt strangely detached, somehow." She set her wine glass aside while he let his arm slide from her shoulder to his side. "When the news finally penetrated that we'd probably never get his body back or proof he'd drowned," she continued, "I felt terrible for the way he'd died, of course, and horribly sad for his family." She turned slightly to face him. "But to be honest, mainly I just felt guilt for *not* being overwhelmed with grief. We'd lived together such a short time and then we were apart for two years. Plus..." Brooke's words trailed off. "Plus, there'd been a few things that happened between us before he left that... well... impacted how I've reacted when I was told the news of the ship's disaster."

She didn't elaborate, but Christopher wondered if Victor's bride had had her own suspicions about her husband's loyalty during their brief courtship and marriage.

Brooke briefly closed her eyes and murmured, "I'm constantly plagued, though, with the awful vision of him and all those others buried in sand at the bottom of the Channel. It's what makes me want to fight the Nazis with everything I've got— which probably isn't much, since I can't show my face most places!"

Christopher longed to gather her in his arms and declare, finally, how sorry he was for everything she must have gone through since he'd seen her last. He wanted to tell her how much he admired all the courageous things he'd learned she'd done from Jules after he'd split for England. How, from the very early days of their working together, he'd appreciated what a quick study she was and that he'd come to care passionately about her welfare.

Loved her— if he'd just face it squarely.

Instead of telling her any of this, he merely seized both her hands and squeezed them gently to convey his sympathy for what she'd experienced the last two years— and in anticipation of what he dreaded telling her now.

"Brooke, I..." he began. "I came to Barbizon with... news."

Christopher found completing his next revelation more difficult than he could have imagined. He absorbed the sight of her clad in bright blue farmer's overalls, her beautiful blonde hair hanging loosely about her shoulders. If he'd commanded a film studio instead of a clandestine unit of MI9, he'd have installed her as his number one movie star despite her being clad in a very unorthodox outfit as did not befit a former heroine of the Charlie Chan detective series.

She rose from the daybed where she'd been sitting next to him and moved to stand in front of the bank of shadowed windows that formed an entire wall in the old artist's studio. Her slender figure and near perfect facial features served as a further reminder to Christopher of the international celebrity she'd been before coming to France.

She turned to fully face him, asking with irony tingeing her tone, "What news, at this late date, could have brought you all the way to my door?"

Her back was to the bank of windows and the questioning look in her eyes heralded the sentence he'd dreaded saying.

Christopher inhaled a deep breath.

"There's no other way to say it except just to tell you."

"Tell me what?" she said impatiently.

Here goes...

Christopher wished she wasn't standing so far away from him.

"Victor did *not* die on the *Lancastria*. At the last minute, he boarded a different vessel off the coast of Brittany."

Brooke stared at him without responding, her expression reflecting shock and utter disbelief.

At length, she said on a low breath, "*What*? B-But his name was on the *passenger* list and—"

Christopher interrupted her.

"I understand that. But here's what happened. The day after I left Paris I found him bivouacked with his regiment in northern Brittany. I called in a favor owed me by a military functionary I'd once interviewed and managed to get us both on a smaller British patrol gunship taking select groups of troops back to England."

Brooke merely shook her head as if rejecting his every word while Christopher soldiered on.

"It just seemed to me that a big ocean liner like the *Lancastria* evacuating Allied combatants was too inviting a target for the Germans." Not wanting to play the hero he added, "I got myself assigned to that smaller ship to save my *own* neck. Since Victor was with me at that point, I secured a place onboard for him as well."

"But Victor's *name* was on the *Lancastria's* manifest and we've had absolutely no word about him ever since!" she repeated.

Christopher could tell she'd entered a state of shock learning she wasn't the widow she'd finally come to believe she was.

"Stupid paperwork!" he declared. "The guy who did me the favor didn't want to cause waves with his superiors when he secured us passage on the other ship. It seems he never notified the purser on the *Lancastria* about the change, so Victor's name remained on the passenger list."

"But it's been almost *two years*!" Brooke protested, starting to pace in front of the tall windows. "Even if what you say is true and he crossed the Channel on another ship with you, I would have *heard* something from Victor in all that time— or from you," she accused, "and there's been nothing but silence!"

Because the jerk was too lazy to figure out a way to get word to you before he left for North Africa...

If only he, Christopher, could just tell her the truth. He shifted his gaze from her and stared at the floor.

Finally, looking up he said, "I signed the Secrets Act in London, so I was forbidden to put anything in writing to civilians about troop movements."

From her forsaken expression he wondered if the news Victor wasn't dead— and that she hadn't known it —underscored a deeper distrust he imagined she'd held about her husband for some time. Her hands on her hips, she glared across the room at him.

"So what you're telling me is that my husband made it safely to Britain and never found a way to let me know? He let *me* drown in worry and anxiety and fear for his safety and he never bothered to send a single letter or cable or *anything*!"

She was nearly screaming now. She pointed a trembling finger at him.

"Well," she cried, "if *you* knew he hadn't been on that ship,

Secrets Act or not, you and I supposedly were *friends* We trusted each other, I thought. Why didn't you get word to me?"

Christopher shook his head in defeat.

"It was Victor's place, not mine, to let you know he'd made it safely out of France." He looked at her steadily. "I stupidly assumed that he would."

Christopher could see that Brooke was trembling with conflicting emotions, some directed at him. He hastened to defend himself, if only in hopes that once she knew the few facts he'd finally been given permission to disclose, she'd better comprehend the bizarre sequence of events.

"Brooke," he appealed, "what you need to understand is that as soon as I'd learned the *Lancastria* had gone down, that very same day Churchill imposed a news blackout and I'd just— that same day, believe it or not —*signed* the Secrets Act! I only recently got permission from my higher-ups to tell you that I knew Victor wasn't on that ship and that I'd crossed the Channel on the same vessel he'd transferred to."

"I think I'm beginning to understand, now," she murmured.

He paused, aware that his next revelation might make her hate him, but what he was about to tell her was an ugly truth.

"Victor, himself could have told you he'd made it to Brittany in good form and asked his superiors in Brigadier de Gaulle's elite unit to send you word he'd evacuated to England," he said gently. "For whatever reason, he didn't. That's the reality you have to live with."

It squeezed his gut to see her nod dully, as if she were absorbing the devasting truth that Victor didn't take the time to tell her he was safe before boarding another ship sailing to his next post.

Christopher rose from his seat and attempted to get her to look at him, saying, "Once I'd signed the Secrets Act, I have sworn an oath to keep my mouth shut on pain of being hanged. So, yes, I didn't get word to you, either, until my boss said it was safe to do so." He gently touched her arm. "I'm truly sorry, but I'm not allowed to tell you much more."

"But Victor never wrote or got word to me about *anything*," she repeated softly as she continued wandering up and down in front of the windows. Suddenly she froze mid-step and turned to face him.

"Maybe I've never heard from him because by now, he's been killed fighting somewhere else?"

Christopher saw tears welling in her eyes and attempted to sound reassuring without belittling her legitimate fears. It was a convincing way for her to explain Victor's long silence and allow her to think he hadn't chosen of his own volition not to communicate with her.

"Given his job as a translator, it's unlikely he got mixed up in the actual fighting, but in war it's always a possible explanation."

He refrained from pointing out the fact that Victor, wherever he ended up after leaving London, was probably ensconced in a reasonably safe area, given the top military echelon to which he'd been assigned in North Africa.

Brooke brushed away the moisture from her eyes and looked at him with renewed suspicion.

"You swear you don't know where he is now? How can I trust anything you say anymore?"

"Well, trust this," he said, "Victor and I were only briefly together in London and he never told me specifically where he was being sent."

That part was true beyond Victor's mentioning that he'd guessed he was bound for North Africa. By now, he could be in Libya, Egypt, Syria, or wherever battles were being planned by his military superiors in that region. Christopher simply didn't know for certain and was relieved he hadn't bothered to ask Victor where in Africa he was expecting to be deployed.

And even with Victor on his way with the Free French troops to North Africa, the military 'upstart' de Gaulle, as the brigadier was known derogatorily around Whitehall, could still be in London fighting with fellow Allied bigwigs to gain status as France-in-exile's titular head of state.

"Well, where do you *think* Victor might have been sent?" Brooke demanded. "Italy? North Africa? I heard on a BBC broadcast this week that British forces have arrived in Greece."

"All those are good guesses," he responded obliquely, hating the world he now inhabited where he tried never to spin falsehoods but often was forced by the Secrets Act to withhold salient information.

As he'd often said to Brooke in their journalism days, the intentional omission of important, known facts is the same thing as lying.

Even so, to regain her trust, he yearned to be able to convince her that he truly knew no more about Victor's current fate or where he'd specifically been sent than she did. Meanwhile, he wrestled with the question of whether he should tell her another truth: That her husband had shown a complete disregard for Brooke's feelings both as her spouse and lover.

It was the latter that had him wishing he could read her mind right now. Did the knowledge that Victor hadn't died rekindle her feelings for the man she'd obviously loved when they first married? If so, he should take it as a sign to keep his mouth shut about revealing Victor's disgraceful behavior as well as keeping mum about his own strong feelings for her.

Brooke had remained standing by the artist's window staring into space as if she had gone somewhere she couldn't be reached.

Christopher resumed his seat on the daybed, patted a spot next to him once more, and said softly, "If you'll come back and sit beside me, I will tell you something I shouldn't, but only to convince you that I will never intentionally lie to you, even if there may be times I can't tell you some things I *do* know, okay?"

The silence lingered between them. Finally, Brooke murmured, "Okay," and resumed her place beside him.

With a welcome sense of relief that he may have regained her confidence to some degree, he said, "What I can positively confirm is that after Victor left England, I didn't have any contact with him, nor heard any news *about* him from anyone else since the summer of nineteen-forty."

Another long silence lingered before Brooke acknowledged the bitter truth.

"Just the same as you, I've never had communication from him of any sort, including not one letter."

It almost felt to Christopher like physical pain to see the stricken look in her eyes and sense the deep hurt Victor's carelessness obviously had caused her. To spare her feelings further, he offered excuses as convincingly as he could— although it gave him heartburn to do it.

"You realize, of course, that mail of every sort is strictly censored," he suggested, nearly choking on the words. "And you've heard, I'm sure, that letters are often lost in transit."

Remaining silent about all this and leaving Victor 'dead' would have increased the odds Christopher might have a chance with her, but that wasn't the way he wanted her to come to him, was it?

He'd journeyed to Barbizon to give her the news she deserved as Victor's wife: the man hadn't died on the *Lancastria*. Was it also his duty to grant her a tiny shred of hope that maybe Victor had tried to get in touch— because he might have?

"Look, Brooke, it may well be—"

Before he could finish she countered, "It may well *be* that Victor didn't bother writing. Period." A cynicism colored her voice in a way he'd never heard before. "Believe me, it wouldn't have been the first time."

Christopher knew he was offering pablum, but said, "The fact is, in situations like these, we just don't know anything for sure."

She cast him a look that said she knew he was throwing her a sliver of hope.

"There is a lot we don't know about what goes on in a war like this," she said. "But all I *do* know is that I would have moved heaven and earth to let someone I was married to know I had escaped harm's way."

Christopher rested his forefinger lightly under her chin.

"So would I," he told her.

She met his glance.

"I believe you would, Christopher Laurent. *If* you loved someone."

He took a deep breath, knowing he was about to show cards he should probably keep close to his flak jacket.

"That's why I told Jules I wanted to see you this trip," he replied. "I was given permission to tell you as much as I knew about Victor not being on the *Lancastria*— and now I have."

"Permission from whom? Surely you don't report to Jules anymore?" she scoffed.

"No," he said with a laugh. "You've probably guessed by now it's rather the other way 'round these days. Which means that I can't answer your question about who's my main boss. But since I'm now back in France, I wanted someone you knew to give you the official confirmation that Victor wasn't on that ship and..." He hesitated, and then continued, "And I wanted you to know that you and I are still fighting on the same side. We're with the good guys."

21

C hristopher was intensely aware of Brooke's gaze and her long silence. Then she leaned forward and kissed him gently on both cheeks, European style.

"Thank you for coming here. I'm actually relieved to confirm that you and I *are* on the same side," she murmured, casting him a look that he couldn't quite interpret. "And you should know that I never stopped hoping that was true all the time you were doing whatever the hell you were doing after you left Paris without saying goodbye."

"I can see that still sticks in your craw, but I'm glad you kept the faith, Cub."

"Cub. Schlub," she scoffed, grabbing her glass of wine off of the side table and taking a large gulp. "We're both way beyond tutor and acolyte at this point, don't you think? Nicole and I have been raising food right under the nose of our local Nazi Commandant. So far, Herr Schiller has no idea that Nicole takes parcels of vegetables, rabbit meat, and sometimes bread to the Paris safehouses." She laughed outright. "And now I know *you* were the one to designate which houses they were! Nicole also miraculously manages to get Jules's work to the printer's and delivers copies all over Paris each week without getting caught."

"Oh, I'm well aware of all you are doing at the villa to see Nicole has the supplies she needs," he said. "That's what's got me worried."

"Well then, we're even!" she retorted. "I've been in a state of worry and anxiety about you and Victor and all my friends still in France *for two years*! We might as well face it, Christopher. This is the way it's going to be for the duration. High anxiety all around. You and I and the others will just do our best to try to end this horror. I, for one, wish I could be doing more."

"You're doing too much as it is," he said firmly. "'Wanted' posters with your gorgeous mug on them are still plastered all over Paris."

Ignoring him, Brooke complained, "I'm actually jealous of Nicole and the part she's been playing. I hate that my stupid celebrity holds me back. There's no escaping danger anywhere. We're *all* in a life-or-death struggle, so who cares if I get caught because I'm recognized for a dumb movie I was in, or you're picked up because some Brit turncoat betrayed you? It's all the same. Good guys against the bad and who knows how it will end? To my way of thinking, one is all in, or one is the enemy. What other choice is there?"

"That's quite a manifesto," he said, disguising as best he could how moved he was to hear her brave words.

Brooke set her wineglass aside, rose from the daybed, pointing at the mattress.

"Look. It's late. Keep the blanket and here's mine to lay on top of it," she said, whipping the coverlet off her shoulders. "I'll see you on the morning." She scooped up her wig from the side table. "And don't you dare just disappear before dawn."

"I have to be somewhere by noon, but I won't leave without saying goodbye," he promised.

He saw her breathe a small sigh of resignation. "Finish off the wine if you want," she suggested.

He watched wordlessly as she strode to the door of the studio, the wig dangling from her hand. Ondie instantly awoke, scrambling onto her paws and padding out of the room by Brooke's side. Poodle and mistress walked across the courtyard, barely discernible in the light from the studio spilling through the tall window. She briefly turned back and gazed in his direction before disappearing through the rear door of the main house.

The distance between the two stone structures was mere meters and Christopher yearned to have the right to follow in her footsteps and take her straight to bed.

But for all he knew, Brooke's husband remained alive and might very well make it back if this war ever ended.

Those were the *facts*, and especially in war, Christopher did his best to pay attention to them— and try to stick to his principles. But after seeing Brooke again, he wondered how long he could abide by his own rules, let alone obey the severe constraints demanded by his oath to the Crown, to say nothing of MI9.

A wave of physical and emotional exhaustion finally hit him. He drained his wine glass and poured himself another hoping it would help him sleep. Downing it in less than two minutes, he stripped down to his skivvies, lay prone on the mattress, and pulled up the covers, inhaling the faintest scent of Brooke's perfume lingering on the blanket she'd handed him.

His mind began to review all the events of this day. Just as he'd expected, in the time they'd been apart, the woman he now knew that he loved had become as fervent a partisan as he was. But should he involve her in the perilous scheme being put into action by MI9, a plan that Crockatt had judged Brooke Bradley de Varney was perfect for? Or should he reject her bid to play a key role in order to protect her?

Was it *his* choice to make, Christopher wondered, or was it hers?

Love and war, he mused, praying sleep would come. *It's a recipe that can kill— or get someone killed.*

NICOLE SAID little as she placed a precious poached egg in front of the villa's visitor along with a few slices of bread, but no butter. She then poured cups of coffee heavily laced with ground acorns and announced to the two sitting at the kitchen table that she was going out to the studio to tidy up.

Brooke reached for a piece of bread off Christopher's plate. "Will we see you again any time soon?" she asked, taking a bite.

"It's always foolish for me to speculate about that," Christopher replied, avoiding her gaze. In the next split second after a sleepless night wrestling with a decision, he suddenly made up his mind.

He trusted Brooke to decide things for herself.

Just before he'd parachuted back into France, his boss Crockatt at MI9 had reviewed the file Jules Dumont had created about Brooke Bradley de Varney. To Christopher's surprise when he heard about this, Crockatt had given his approval to include the former American actress in their plans targeted specifically for the rural region around Barbizon and its neighboring town, Fontainebleau. He calculated that the few, lowly German functionaries posted there weren't likely to recognize the former film star, thanks to her unorthodox efforts to disguise herself that Jules had described in his report.

"She's passing for an ordinary American married to a French soldier who continues to be missing in action," Crockatt declared with a pleased look as he gazed at the Dumont file on Brooke. "I can't see the Nazis there recognizing her now, or harassing her if she keeps a low profile, which Jules says she does."

Crockatt had given Christopher a penetrating look.

"Jules also says here you worked with her at Radio Mondiale for a short while. Is she as smart and clever as he maintains?"

Christopher had responded with a casual shrug and replied, "Given her good looks, one might think she's just a dumb blonde, but yes, I found her clever, very resourceful, and willing to work hard at whatever she was assigned."

With a pleased look, Crockatt had put her file in his top drawer and moved on to other subjects.

Thinking back on the conversation, Christopher picked up another piece of toast and offered it to Brooke and casually proposed, "I was given permission to lay out for you a bit about some future plans regarding the coming months of the war."

"To *me*?" she said, looking surprised.

Christopher nodded. "Expectations are that Allied air forces will soon begin bombing raids into Germany."

Brooke sat up straighter, her eyes alight with interest.

"Well, that's certainly good news. And?"

"Well, first of all," he began, "I want you to know that certain people in London think you are doing far more than just making it possible to ferry food to various safehouses in Paris."

"But apparently you, Nicole, and Jules are in some exclusive club doing far more— and I'm not a member," was her tart reply.

Christopher covered her hand with his and marveled at how roughened it had become, no doubt due to her cultivation of the vegetable beds and raising wild rabbits outside the kitchen door.

"I'd like you to consider heading up a club of your own," he proposed and could see that he'd definitely garnered her attention.

"This 'club' you're talking about is designed to do *what*, exactly?" she asked, her chin up as if she expected him to offer her something insignificant to quell her complaints.

"After I describe for you the mission to be based in this region, I want you to think long and hard before you decide if you *do* or *don't* want to take part. And if you do decide to participate in what is being proposed, you must continue to convey to the others you encounter in this work that you *still* don't know if Victor did or did not go down with the *Lancastria*."

Brooke jumped up from the kitchen chair in response to Christopher's cryptic remarks and the warnings regarding her safety he quickly issued in the next breath.

"Hold on!" she exclaimed. "Before you go on and on about how *you* think that I probably shouldn't be part of some mysterious operation you all are planning, at least tell me what it is."

"It is going to be a high-risk endeavor regardless of whatever you decide, Brooke," he emphasized in the hope that she would realize he was being deadly serious. "And if you decline taking part, it won't change anyone's admiration for what you've already done to help the Resistance."

"Fine! I get what you're saying," she exclaimed with impatience. "Just tell me what you're proposing that could be so important out here in the countryside."

Christopher paused, carefully considering his next words.

"It would involve making arrangements to hide escaping prisoners-of-war, along with prominent Jews trying to leave France, and any airmen shot down around here by the Germans."

"Goodness!" she exclaimed, clearly surprised. "You're right.

POWs, fleeing Jews, and shot-down fliers? Hiding people like that from Nazi arrest would be quite an undertaking, for sure." She paused in thought, then asked, "When do you imagine we're going to see *our* planes heading for German targets? So far, it's the Germans raining down hell and havoc everywhere."

"Well, if rumors are correct, in the coming months the RAF and the US Air Force will be giving the Luftwaffe a run for its money."

As soon as the words had passed his lips, he immediately wondered if he'd just flagrantly violated the Secrets Act.

"So, you think that the Allies are preparing to counterattack Germany from the air—finally?" she asked.

He nodded without further comment. "So," Brooke said, eyes alight, "the bigwigs in London want resisters in France to hide the fly boys who get shot out of the skies *here*?" she asked incredulously. "Hide them a few blocks from our local Gestapo run by Commandant Schiller who, by the way, would like nothing better than to catch townspeople who are enemy aliens like us betraying the Fatherland?"

"As I've just told you," he said, keeping his voice even, "it's a scheme fraught with danger, but you would be part of a nationwide team of civilians we're calling 'escape helpers' to assist in the escape-and-evade efforts we're already running in other parts of France and Belgium."

"But where do these poor people escape *to?*" Brooke asked, doubt written on her face. "Here in central France we're quite a ways from any border, you know."

Christopher was pleased she wasn't the sort to merely accept orders or opinions without ferreting out the facts for herself.

"Mostly, they'd be escorted to neutral Spain by a series of helpers who put them aboard sections of southbound night trains as quickly as possible."

"Spain! That's almost eight hundred kilometers south of here!"

Christopher used the point of his table knife to illustrate.

"I see you know your geography," he deadpanned. "You, however, would only be responsible for a small portion of an underground railroad of sorts. Your assignment would include hiding arriving escapees until it was safe to get them from the

Fontainebleau-Avon railway station and on to our Paris collection center. Once you arrive at Gare de Lyon, you'd escort them over to Gare Montparnasse where you would meet a fellow helper there who would accompany them on a night train headed back south toward Bayonne on the Atlantic coast. That same evening, you would then return, alone, from Paris to Fontainebleau-Avon on the next train out of Gare de Lyon."

"And I would ride my bicycle wearing whatever disguise I was using from Fontainebleau back to Barbizon, yes?"

"Exactly."

"What happens to the escapees after they board the train from Paris?" she pressed.

"Well, from there, the designated helper you met at Gare Montparnasse would take them some sixty kilometers by train. Another team meets that train and escorts the 'packages,' as we call them, to the next depot— another sixty kilometers or so down the line — ultimately the team would have ferried them to Bayonne or Biarritz."

"The resort? But how do they get from there to Spain?"

"Very stealthily," said Christopher. "From the Bayonne-Biarritz region they'll be guided by helpers expert in climbing mountains and fording rivers to the border town of Saint-Jean-de-Luz. At that point, they must get over— or swim —the La Nivelle river across the border into Spain."

"That's still a long way from Gibraltar," she replied, speaking of the British territory at the very bottom of the map of Spain.

"That it is, but from there, British consular officers who are still allowed in Spain will meet them, taking them by car on back roads across the country to British outposts where they'll be transported by ship or air back to Britain."

"And if they're airmen, they'll fly on another day," Brooke murmured, her response laced with admiration. "That's blinking brilliant! But will it work, Christopher? That's a very long, scary trip they'd be making."

"It's *been* working," Christopher replied. "We've already gotten a couple of hundred people over the mountains into neutral Spain or Switzerland. The powers-that-be estimate that increasingly the need for the Resistance to help with all this means we have to enlist many more civilian recruits on the ground."

"And many more recruits also mean many more chances to be betrayed by the Nazis or the others who support them," Brooke pointed out.

"Very true. I can tell that we're both thinking of the infamous Harold Cole."

She nodded but remained silent. Christopher wondered if his frank description of the dangers might dampen Brooke's previous enthusiasm at being a part of something bigger than growing vegetables and feeding caged rabbits. He certainly wouldn't blame her if it did, and rather hoped it would.

Brooke asked, "Were those two local men I saw you with at the farmstead last night already enlisted in this... project? Are they the first 'helpers' you've recruited for this crazy enterprise?"

Christopher avoided the question by replying, "There are various escape-and-evade lines already in operation, although we suspect people like Harold Cole are assisting the Germans in brutally stamping them out as quickly as we can organize them."

He seized her hand that rested beside her cup half-full of undrinkable coffee.

Forcing her to meet his gaze he said, "What I've just described to you is an operation that's beyond perilous, Brooke. Many resistors in this work are bound to be apprehended, perhaps tortured, and probably executed."

"But it's bound to help win the war, especially if downed fliers can be rescued and returned to Britain to climb back into our American B-17 bombers."

Christopher couldn't help but be impressed, as always, by Brooke's quick grasp of any new subject presented to her.

"It certainly might help us win. Now that America's in the war, those flying fortresses coming online should make a big difference. Every flier costs the Allies some fifteen thousand pounds to train and equip— to say nothing of the price of the aircraft. If we can recover even ten or twenty percent of those who survive their planes being shot down, it's hoped that we can make a real difference in the air battle that has been so brutal since the German Blitz began."

"Maybe now our side can begin to mount a blitz against *Berlin!*" Brooke said with fire in her eyes.

"I'm only asking you to *consider* becoming an escape helper," Christopher warned. "Take time to think it over carefully." He paused, adding, "Now that you know Victor did not drown on the *Lancastria,* it certainly may alter your thinking about all the risks you've been taking."

She gazed at him during a long moment of silence. Then she said, "Since the moment the Jerries invaded France, I have only thought about what I could do to help drive the damn Krauts out of the country."

"But you might feel differently, now that Victor is—"

She cut him off.

"I felt the way I do about resisting the German thugs when I thought Victor was alive and felt the same when I thought he was dead," she said flatly. "Even now— though I don't know for absolute sure he hasn't already been killed wherever his unit was sent —it doesn't make a bit of difference either way." She pointed in the direction of the courtyard. "We have a potting shed back there that could be converted into sleeping quarters, and the artist studio too, of course." She gave a small laugh. "And, besides, I'm an *actress!* I can play the role of any part you assign me, including that of helping to hide downed fliers and speeding them on their way back to Britain!"

Christopher had to smile at Brooke's dramatic outburst, "I'm an *actress!*" She'd never seemed particularly proud of her previous profession, but now she seemed excited to make use of it.

He pointed out, "You'll need some convincing disguises for the men in your charge, to say nothing of yourself. Don't forget about your very own personal 'Wanted' posters."

She looked at him with a mischievous glint in her eye.

"On Nicole's next trip to Paris, how about I ask her to beg a nurse's uniform and couple of strait jackets off Dr. Jackson's psych ward at the American Hospital? Then I could escort these fellows by train as if they were on their way to an insane asylum!" Laughing, she pointed to her head. "Or I'll give them berets and tell the guards at the checkpoints they're a bunch of farmers exempt from military service, headed to Provence for the grape harvest. There are any number of scenarios I can think of!"

Christopher couldn't help but be impressed by her creativity, to say nothing of her bravery.

"Crazy stunts like those just might work," he reflected, "but if any one of them fails…"

Brooke brushed aside his concern, declaring excitedly, "As you can see, I can be a mistress of *many* disguises! Here at the villa, we're blessed with surroundings where I can easily hide the costumes of an erstwhile nurse or a farmer's wife." Pointing out of the kitchen window to the yard surrounded by its eight-foot-high stone walls, she assured him, "This villa is our very own version of a B-17 'Fortress.'"

"What you've just said about being a convincing actress is why Jules and our leader in London considered you as a candidate for this project." He looked down at his empty breakfast plate and then said, "You should know, however, that I told them both that I felt the scheme is way too risky for you."

"I'm glad you were outvoted because this is *my* choice to make," Brooke shot back, looking him straight in the eye.

With a faint nod he reluctantly replied, "I figured as much."

Brooke suddenly raised her right hand as if to halt all conversation.

"But wait! What about Felix?" she posed. "The caretaker here. I've grown to trust him, but I've never had a frank discussion of where his true sympathies lie."

"I have."

Brooke stared at Christopher, her mouth slightly ajar.

"*You?*"

Her beautiful amber eyes were blinking rapidly in a reaction of surprise that almost made him laugh out loud.

"Yes, me. I am violating every rule in the book telling you this, but Felix Gervais is one of us. He has been since war was first declared. His brother Gaspard is a railroad worker, based in Fontainebleau, and is part of our Comet Escape Line, with Felix reporting to him from Barbizon. Your caretaker, here, was the final piece that fell into place when Jules contacted us about this region being part of the larger escape-and-evade plan in France."

Brooke shook her head with amazement.

"So that's what you call this insane operation? 'The Comet Line,' using the *slowest* night trains in the country? I love it!"

"Well, never repeat this to anyone, but the line has been known to transport people out of France in less than a few weeks."

"Then, maybe we should call our local branch of the Comet Line 'Rabbit Run,'" she joked, "after our local hares and the slowest-of-the-slow trains in all of France."

"I like the irony, given all those furry creatures I've seen around here," he replied. "'Rabbit Run' it shall be."

"Nicole is recruited for this scheme, too, I take it?"

Nodding, Christopher pushed back from the table and prepared to depart.

"You have to leave now?" Brooke asked, also rising from her chair. "I thought you didn't have to be anywhere until noon." She glanced at her watch. "It's only quarter past nine."

"You pay too close attention to everything," he groused.

"I'd *better* pay attention if I'm going to be any good as an escape line helper."

He gazed at her smartly tailored pair of gabardine slacks and the cream-colored silk blouse she'd donned that morning that molded to her breasts and slim waistline. He reached for her hands one last time and felt his stomach clench when she clasped his fingers firmly and took a step closer.

"Will you be the one to tutor me how to be an effective rescuer of men shot out of the sky?" she asked, her lips stretched in a smile only inches away.

"Brooke, listen," he urged. "Don't you think you should give all this more thought?"

"I don't need to give it more thought!" she said impatiently. "Count me in and just tell me what I have to do."

Hearing the conviction in her voice, Christopher couldn't bring himself to let go of her hands. He leaned forward and mirrored the kiss on both cheeks she'd given him the night before, only he lingered beneath her left ear longer than was customary.

"The Comet Line thanks you..." he murmured.

When he pulled away, Brooke's widening smile and the small dimple winking on her left cheek nearly undid him.

"Brooke..." he began, hearing the huskiness in his voice.

"My, my," she teased, her eyes alight. "Kissing a married lady? Frankly, I'm shocked."

"Frankly, so am I." His voice still sounding rough in his own ears, he gazed at her a moment longer before he said, "I've got to go. A *bientôt,* Madame de Varney."

"Yes, until next time, *Monsieur Mystérieux.*"

She laughed up at him, her eyes golden in the shaft of morning sun slanting through the kitchen window.

The next instant, Christopher found himself kissing her again, only this time on the lips. Their softness was as he'd long imagined and her eagerness to kiss him back shook him down to his flight boots. Inhaling the scent of the distinctive perfume she'd bothered to dab behind her ears before breakfast was also proving danger-ously intoxicating. At any other time or place, he knew they would have fallen into bed and remained there until noon.

When he finally forced himself to release her, he searched for something lighthearted to say by way of farewell.

"Thank God your French pronunciation has improved," he managed finally.

Brooke swiftly took a step away from him.

"You must be kidding? That's *it?* That's how you're going to say goodbye after kissing me like that?"

"Kissing like that was probably a serious mistake."

"You louse!" she said laughing. "Why a mistake? This is a damn war! Who knows if we'll ever kiss again?" She offered a provocative wink. "Do feel free to ravish me any time you happen to stop by."

"*Not* a good idea," he replied, trying not to grin while absorbing the evidence that all might not have been well between Victor and Brooke even before the actor-turned-translator left for the front.

"Not a good idea we kissed?" she said softly, "I truly believe it could be a very good idea. A very *lovely* idea."

Considering Brooke's frankness and his own feelings churning in his gut and elsewhere, he knew, now, they both wanted far more than an embrace. Even with the news that Victor had not been on the doomed ship, for her, the honeymoon clearly had long been over. Shaking his head, Christopher took another step back, the kitchen chair he'd been sitting on grazing his thigh.

"War is complicated, Brooke. What the Resistance is trying to *do* is complicated. If you and I are to perform our jobs properly, we can't let personal ties confuse things even more."

After a long pause she nodded in agreement. "I understand. Knowing you, at least I think I do." She gave a small, unladylike snort of laughter, adding "Doesn't the saying go 'don't dip your pen in office ink?'"

"More like— don't start an affair with another soldier's wife."

"A soldier that never contacts his wife, you mean?" she retorted. "And let us not forget what we almost did that night we dined at Le Dôme?"

So she felt the same magnetic pull even back then?

"What a smart cookie you are," he said, gangster style.

"Admit it, Christopher," she replied, with a faint smile. "This cookie tastes damn delicious, doesn't it?"

He steeled himself to ignore her comment but in the end had to agree.

"Yes it does. All the more reason to put the top back on the cookie jar. I'd better be on my way."

He turned and walked toward the kitchen's back door, leaning down to pick up the rucksack that he'd left there when he'd come in from the studio. In his mind's eye, he pictured Victor's "In Case of My Death" letter to Brooke that lined the bottom of the canvas bag. He, like Brooke, had no idea if the time had come to hand it to her, so until he knew, he wouldn't. Before he exited, he offered a brief wave.

"To avoid the main street, I'll leave through the gate on the back side of the rabbit hutch and head through the wheatfields."

"Don't tramp your big feet through them!" she admonished. "Go around them on the farmer's road. We need every single grain for the bread we'll make this year."

Seconds later, he shut the kitchen door behind him and strode across the courtyard. Thinking of all that lay ahead, he reviewed the heightened dangers he and Brooke would face each and every day of this war. He tried not to calculate the probabilities that he might never see her again, let alone that they might never make love.

22

MAY 30, 1942

Brooke did her best to forget the moment she and Christopher kissed in her kitchen. The simple fact was he'd brought the news that Victor was alive. She was still the wife of another man. She and Nicole immediately flew into making preparations for harboring anyone sent to them to be helped by the Comet Line to escape capture and find a way out of France. However, two months passed before anyone landed on their doorstep.

Brooke's introduction to the world of 'escape helpers' was the sound of urgent pounding on the kitchen door in the wee hours of a warm spring night.

Waking from a deep sleep, her heart beating wildly, her first thought was that it might be Commandant Schiller's men arresting her in the dead of night for the household's sub rosa activities of growing and distributing contraband vegetables. She wrapped her bed's blanket around her shoulders and stumbled toward the racket.

She opened the back door a crack, only to find two harried-looking men who appeared vaguely familiar to her. The pair flanked a pale-faced figure in a flight suit who seemed ready to drop on his feet. Behind them in the shadowed courtyard, Brooke could just make out the outlines of the rabbit hutch at the back of the property. There was the faint rustle of the animals awakened by the visitors as they passed through the back gate.

Brooke soon recognized that the two men who'd pounded on her back door were those she'd seen at Jules's farmhouse the night Christopher suddenly appeared.

"You're the local 'escape helpers' that were at the farmstead, yes?" she whispered hoarsely. Both men nodded, looking relieved she didn't slam the door in their faces.

Motioning to them she urged, "Quickly! All of you, come inside," and ushered them into the kitchen.

She remembered one of the escorts' names.

"You're Luc, yes?" she asked.

The wiry young man nodded. "And this is Louis," he disclosed, pointing to the person standing beside him who was about his same age and build. "We were directed to bring any escapees to you."

"And he is?" Brooke asked with a nod in the direction of the shivering third figure standing in her kitchen.

"Shot down this evening. We saw him land and brought him here."

"I'll take it from here. Be sure you bury his parachute nice and deep in a field and then go home. We'll give this man some food and drink and put him to bed. Tomorrow, we'll see him on his way to the collection point." Gesturing in the direction of the rear of the property, she urged, "Slip out the back gate again." She paused and then added, "And thanks, but next time, do knock a little less loudly. We don't want the neighbors to hear."

"Sorry. This was our first mission," Luc confessed.

Brooke completely empathized as this was her first "mission" as well, one in which they all could be executed for what they were doing.

Up to this moment, she realized, she and Nicole had only been putting themselves and Felix at risk. From now on, the villa's "helpers" group was responsible for strangers they'd never met who had to trust them with their lives.

Louis, Christopher's other designated local deputy, ducked his head sheepishly.

"We were scared no one would hear us and didn't know what to do next. Schiller's men are combing the other fields for parachutes or any flier they missed shooting down."

"I understand. You've done a good job... now go!" she said, glad to see the pair slip off into the gloom of the shadowed courtyard.

Nicole, roused by the commotion, appeared in the kitchen and immediately began to boil water on the Aga and heat up some vegetable soup she'd kept on the hob.

The rescued man limped toward the kitchen table and sank gratefully onto one of the chairs.

"Ah, you've sprained an ankle?" Brooke asked, continuing to speak in French.

The flier shot her a look that clearly conveyed he didn't speak the language, so she repeated the question in English.

"Good heavens, you're American!" came the clipped British response. "Whatever in the world are *you* doing here?"

"It's too long a story for this late hour," Brooke answered, setting a spoon in front of him and asking, "Are there no others who bailed out safely?"

"I heard shots ring out as I floated down into the wheatfield outside your place," he answered grimly. "The wind took me south, but I think the rest of the crew was picked off, one by one, by German sharpshooters on the other side of your village."

"Good Lord, how terrible," Brooke said. "I'm so sorry."

"I had barely put two feet on the ground, twisting this one," he said, pointing to his left leg, "when those two... whoever they were ...tramped through the wheat and brought me here." He looked around. "I'm glad it wasn't a Gestapo headquarters."

Nicole placed the hot soup in front of their visitor, saying to Brooke, "I'll just go out to the potting shed and ready his bed."

Nodding agreement, Brooke was pleased that the preparations they had made the day Christopher left were finally going to be put into use.

"My name is Lieutenant Nigel Thompson," declared the airman. "I'm a navigator. Or was. And you are?" he asked. His appreciative glance signaled he'd given Brooke the once over and liked what he saw.

"I'm surprised you gave me your name," Brooke said with disapproval. "The less we know about each other, the better."

"Well, can you at least tell me where I am, if you don't mind my asking?"

"Actually, it's safer if you don't know the answers to either of your questions. Just be assured you are one of the fortunate ones. We're going to get you out of France, but from here on out, you must follow my instructions and do exactly as I say."

"Really?" he replied in a mocking tone Brooke had heard often from men who didn't appreciate being told what to do by a woman.

"Yes, really. That is if you value your life."

No more Miss Genial Hostess with this guy... Brooke thought.

She pointed to the bowl of soup. "Eat your fill" she advised briskly, "and here's a glass of rather inferior wine, but it's all we have. Then, I want you to get a good night's sleep— or what's left of it. There are plenty of blankets out there and an old privy outside, behind the potting shed. Don't make any noise, and don't, under *any* circumstances, leave the compound or you'll get us *all* killed. The other woman you just saw will bring you your meals until it'll be time to go."

"Go where?" he demanded, his demeanor less friendly than before.

"If you want to see Britain again, you'll learn soon enough," Brooke replied crisply. "Now eat up and thank your lucky stars you landed where you did— and not upwind, like your crew."

THE NEXT DAY, the late spring sun set after eight p.m. Brooke knocked on the potting shed door and then opened it without waiting for a response.

"How's the ankle?" she asked the British navigator.

"Better." Then he stared at her in amazement. "What happened to your hair?"

"It's a wig," she replied without further explanation. She handed him a threadbare shirt and a pair of worn overalls. "Get dressed in these and then put this beret on your head."

She handed him a handmade cardboard sign with twine attached like a necklace on each end.

"Sling this around your neck, please."

The flier looked at the French words, attempting to read them aloud. "*Je suis sourd et muet,*" and then asked, "What's *that* mean?"

"Your sign says 'I am deaf and dumb.' You're to wear this all the way to the Spanish border. Try not to react to sudden sounds, and if anyone speaks to you, act confused, as if you don't understand anything— which you probably won't anyway. And *never* open your mouth, do you understand? Never!"

"But—"

Brooke ignored him, continuing, "I will escort you to our escape line collection center in Paris. From there, someone else will accompany you on the next leg of your journey south to Spain."

The flier looked at her, dumbfounded as if the sign spoke truth, which brought a smile to her lips.

"Just pretend you're in a play at the posh boarding school I'm sure you attended. Assume the role with conviction and it just may save your life." She pointed at her watch. "Be ready in a half hour, and I'll meet you right here."

She was halfway out the door before she turned and winked at him.

"By the way, when we travel together, I'm your dutiful sister-in-law, so be nice to me— got it?"

BROOKE HAD SUMMONED every acting skill she possessed as she'd made her way with her 'package' from the small station at Fontainebleau-Avon to Gare de Lyon, and then across Paris by the metro to Gare Montparnasse. Dressed in the nondescript clothing of a French housewife and holding the airman by his arm, she guided her charge with an anxious expression, as if the sign he wore around his neck was a burden for her, too.

At the first check point, perspiration had begun to drip down her sides with the effort to maintain this fiction, but the masquerade got them past a host of German guards posted at the entrances and exits of the various rail and metro stations.

When one did accost her, she dug out her identification papers and pointed to the "I am deaf and dumb" sign hanging around her companion's neck.

"He's my husband's brother. I am taking him to a care home where I'm hoping they'll teach him sign language and maybe he can work in a factory."

"He has no documents?" the guard inquired harshly.

Thanks to Brooke's nerves feeling as taut as on a first night in the theater, she easily managed to conjure tears in her eyes. "I simply can't cope anymore! He's such a big boy, as you can see, and I can't make him understand how to behave. He caused a terrible scene when we took him to get his identification papers and the officials made us leave." She brought a handkerchief to her eyes and emitted a small sob. "Please, sir, he needs to be taken to the *care home*! It's the only way I can possibly cope anymore."

"Yah, yah, you can go!" interrupted the guard, embarrassed by her wailing which had attracted attention from passersby.

Without waiting an instant longer, Brooke pushed her charge through the door and into the large, echoing waiting area. She swept her gaze around the cavernous space, made to seem even bigger because of the late hour and only a handful of travelers waiting for their next train. Jules had advised her to look for a woman with hair "as dark as your wig. She'll be standing near the kiosk when you first come into the station."

At first, Brooke could spot no one that fit that description until a woman with jet black hair lowered the newspaper she had been perusing. Relieved to see someone who matched Jules's sketch at the designated rendezvous spot, Brooke led her charge to her contact's side, praying she was the right person.

"Clever you," the woman murmured, raising an eyebrow in the direction of the deaf-and-dumb sign around the airman's neck. "Should be a nice, quiet journey for us."

She took hold of the flier's arm and said to Brooke by way of farewell, "I'll see him to his next stop. *Merci et bonsoir*."

Brooke nodded, bidding her counterpart, "Good night. Thank

you," Nodding in the direction of Nigel Thompson she whispered in English, "And good luck to you."

"Quite a performance you gave back there," he whispered back.

Ignoring his obvious sarcasm, Brooke turned and made her way out of the railway station with a huge sigh of relief. She'd gotten the first flier in her charge safely to the collection point and he was no longer her responsibility. Outside, she stood on the curb inhaling the warm spring air of early June, feeling her shoulders relax and her stomach unclench. She should be heading back to Barbizon, but first, there was one more thing she wanted to do while in Paris — and Christopher wouldn't like it.

IN THE SHADOWS across from her old flat on Rue Saint-Dominique, Brooke gazed up at the darkened windows on the second floor. She knew full well that she should have immediately retraced her steps to Gare de Lyon and returned directly to Barbizon. Christopher would have her hide if he knew she'd dared to come near this street in case the Germans had requisitioned the de Varney place for their own use in her lengthy absence from Paris. Gazing up at the elegant building that had been her home as Victor's wife, the temptation had been too great to forego retrieving a few treasured possessions she'd neglected to pack on the night Jules, Nicole, Ondie, and she made their hasty retreat.

By the time she'd crossed the city again, it was a few minutes after the evening curfew. The airman's late-night train had long since departed for its first stop on his trek to the Spanish border. Fortunately, not a soul was on the street, nor was there a light in any window of her former residence.

Removing her shoes and slipping her key into the front door lock, Brooke crept noiselessly through the marble lobby, past the concierge's apartment door. She tiptoed up the staircase to the landing above, ignoring the birdcage elevator that had always seemed to her the epitome of a classic Beaux Arts building in Paris.

As she cautiously approached the front door to her flat, she spotted the US Embassy Seal still affixed to the center of the right panel, a reliable sign that no German had taken over the place. Looking in both directions down the corridor and seeing no sign of life, she inserted the second key on her ring and gingerly turned it in the lock. The click reverberated like thunder in her ears. She swiftly stepped inside the black and white tiled foyer and closed the door, leaning on it for support while waiting for her rapid heartbeat to return to its normal rhythm.

Still she listened, her ears cocked to hear the slightest sound.

Nothing but silence greeted her.

She was suddenly aware that her stockinged foot was standing squarely on an envelope someone must have slipped under the door after she'd departed for Barbizon.

Brooke set her keys on the nearby table and retrieved the letter off the floor. Walking through the entrance hall and into the library, she angled the envelope's front panel toward the window and the beams shining from the streetlight below. Peering down at the address, her breath caught at the sight of the familiar handwriting spelling out her name on the front.

She swiftly pulled the curtains shut and turned the switch on the desk lamp. She sank down on one of the leather chairs near the desk where she had typed so many news briefs for Christopher's broadcasts at Radio Mondiale. Running her shaky forefinger under the stiff paper seal to open the envelope, she withdrew a lined piece of paper that an elementary school student might have ripped from a notebook. Unfolding it, she stared at the date, written in November 1941, and absorbed the familiar, childish printing written with a pencil in her mother's uneven hand, every fourth or fifth word misspelled.

Hello, Beverly—

It was the name given her at birth before she "got real fancy" as her mother had said snidely when Brooke had announced she'd chosen a professional name.

In language that was as unemotional and as matter of fact as a shopping list, Estelle Bradley's stated reason for writing her daughter hit Brooke like a German incendiary bomb.

> *Your son Errol died last week.*
> *He caught my cold real bad and cud not breath.*
> *Doc said it was flu.*

Brooke's hand clutching her mother's letter began to shake so fiercely that she had to steady it by encircling her wrist with her other thumb and forefinger. In an ill-formed, scrawl Estelle wrote:

> *Don't blame me for the boy's death, tho I know you will. I did my best for him. At my age, takin care of a baby just startin to walk and with the war on, and all, was too hard on me and made me miss my AA meetings.*

Her mother bailing out of the Alcoholic Anonymous program meant only one thing to Brooke. Estelle had fallen off the wagon—again.

She reread that sentence. If her mother had quit AA and started drinking again, God only knew what that had meant for Errol's safety and well-being. Taking a deep breath, Brooke forced herself to read on.

> *It was a terrible time for me. The landlord was going to evik me if I didn't give him back rent by Thanksgivin, so I got a job workin nites at a laundry where I guess the low lifes there gave me germs and I got real sic.*

The landlord was going to evict her for back rent?

"But that's impossible!" Brooke whispered. She'd lost count of the many times she'd wired her mother funds to pay for household needs as well as toys and gifts for Errol. Just before the Germans crossed into France, Brooke had directed her bank in Paris to dispatch an even larger amount, in case it was eventually impossible to transfer money if the Nazis took over the country.

Estelle missing rent payments confirmed Brooke's worst assumption that her mother had had another 'slip' last year, like the dozens during Brooke's own chaotic childhood.

Estelle always had an excuse for why she drank, thought Brooke bitterly. A *reason*. The rest of her letter was a totally predictable and familiar litany of why nothing bad that happened was ever her mother's fault.

> Bev, I toll you to come home after the play closed but you didn't. I've had him three years, now and a boy needs his mom, but you just dumped Errol on me and then ran to Europe with some Frenchie actor you'd just met. Maybe what happened to your son is your punishment by God.
>
> I'm real sad my young grandson passed away, but takin care of him was your job, not mine!

Brooke's gaze froze on "...taking care of him was your job" with the "your" underlined three times. Three years in a child's life was an eternity, she thought, guilt slicing through her defenses. Tears filled her eyes and slid down her cheeks, blurring the letter so that she could barely make out its closing lines.

> I've gone back to my meetings. My AA sponsor says I only have control over myself, not over you. She also said I should write to admit I did bad to

miss meetings and drink again and tell you I'm sorry your son died.

"*Sorry?*" Brooke exclaimed aloud. "Sorry he *died?* Sorry you drank when you were responsible for a four-and-a-half-year-old child now? Sorry for exactly *what*, Mother?"

The final paragraph topped off the rage and grief— and remorse —that had begun to seep into Brooke's bones.

I suppose with the war and all, you won't come back any time soon so tell your LA bank to let me cash your last checks that arrived here from Charlie Chan. They won't let me and when I tried at the studio, they throwed me off the lot.

Your Mother

P.S. Errol is buried in the Warmby plot in Tarzana. Arnie says you have to pay for a headstone.

Brooke stared at the ragged one-page missive, her mind spinning.

Errol's father wouldn't pay for a headstone and her mother could only think about how to cash the last of the Charlie Chan residual checks?

Brooke's boiling emotions nearly cut off her breath. She'd long realized that her mother was one of those 'Jekyll and Hyde' drinkers. She could be perfectly sane when sober and then completely nuts when she went on a bender.

So, was *that* how all this happened? she thought, shaking the letter back and forth like a fan. Had 'Mrs. Hyde' been too soused to tend to a desperately sick child in her care and now little Errol was gone?

No. Not gone, she thought. He was *dead.*

For God's sake, she raged silently, she had entrusted the care of her toddler to a woman who'd been sober for *a year-and-a-half* before Brooke had left for New York! How could Estelle let this happen?

A voice in the back of Brooke's head brutally reminded her that she'd known before she departed for the Broadway tryout that it was a risky decision to leave Errol with her mother, but she was determined to head for her Broadway tryout and it was all she could afford at the time. Even so, it would hardly have been surprising to anyone who knew the 62 year old failed actress if Errol's grandmother hit the bottle again, especially if life became even moderately stressful.

Brooke's gaze returned to the letter's first sentence: *Your son Errol died last November...*

Had Estelle been at the 2 AM Club down the street from their place when Errol had been so sick?

That notion had barely surfaced in Brooke's mind before another swiftly took its place.

Whoa! Wait a minute, dearie!

Brooke realized instantly that she was doing what her mother always did: *blame someone else.*

It wasn't what Estelle had done. It was what *she*, Errol's mother, had done that mattered here.

As the letter so accurately pointed out, in the deepest cells of her soul, Brooke knew it *had* been her job to make sure her son was in safe hands, just as it was her job to have been a loving and attentive parent— and she had completely failed on both accounts.

Brooke always felt that somehow she had been missing that maternal 'piece,' that supposedly natural, feminine inclination to want to nurture young offspring.

What she'd always wanted to do was nurture *herself.* Nurture her career so she'd never have to rely on her mother again.

With sudden and savage self-awareness, she saw that her deficiencies in the Motherhood Department had turned her into the "it's-all-about-me" movie starlet solely focused on getting cast in her next role. She'd become so self-absorbed that she'd left her toddler with a woman who'd been in and out of sobriety all Brooke's life. A woman of advancing years that her little boy, barely out of diapers when she'd left Los Angles, depended upon for his well-being.

For his very life, as it had turned out.

The demands of Brooke's blossoming fame as the husky-voiced blonde in the Charlie Chan films meant she had shrugged off the responsibilities of her unwanted pregnancy. After she'd divorced Arnie, she had chosen her independence, her freedom to advance her career, and the embrace of a handsome, young French actor who convinced her to come to Europe with him. She had *chosen* to fly across the Atlantic when anyone with brains knew Europe was on the brink of war.

Brooke could no longer ignore that she had known the funds she'd left to take care of her son would never be enough. From the time she was thirteen, most of the money she earned as a teenage model or in films went to pay for Estelle's Old Crow bourbon and Lucky Strike cigarettes. Brooke had a sudden vision of herself as a 7 year old scouring the pantry for something decent to eat in those days.

After all, wasn't *she*— little Beverly Bradley —the one who had long needed nurturing?

Immediately, the stern voice in her head spoke loudly again: *Don't keep trying to palm off Errol's death on Estelle!*

Despite everything Brooke always knew what happened when her mother drank, she'd left Errol with his unstable grandparent.

But what about Errol Warmby's *father,* she thought in her own defense. Where was Arnie when their child got sick the previous autumn?

No doubt the jerk was in a bar, just like Estelle...

Arnie's sinkhole of choice was out in the wilds of the San Fernando Valley where all the film crews and stunt men lived. Her former husband drank, too, so who knew better than Brooke that he could never be relied upon either? What an insane *fantasy* it was to think Victor was any more dependable!

It was so clear to Brooke, now, that like her mother's weakness for a series of deadbeat lovers, she'd inherited her terrible taste in men. Arnie, the stagehand, had been a three-night-stand on location at a picturesque winery in Napa. Victor was an *actor,* for God's sake. Like most of their breed, he was a grown child, always putting his wants and needs first and foremost.

"Our tribe is so pathetic!" she exclaimed to the letter she held in her hand.

Wasn't it time to admit that a deadly cavalcade of her *own* selfish decisions had led to fatal consequences for her little boy?

Brooke buried her face in her hands, convinced by the reality and finality of her child's death that Errol Flynn Bradley Warmby had deserved far better than two lousy birth parents and a hopeless drunk for a grandmother. No wonder back then she hadn't wanted to have a baby. With a lousy inheritance like hers, the odds were overwhelming she'd be the worst possible parent... which had turned out to be the case.

Struggling to suppress a keening cry that welled in her throat, Brooke could only conclude that any child born to the Hollywood branch of the Bradley clan should have been given up for adoption at birth. Why hadn't she had the guts to place Errol with a family who would have loved and cherished him?

Waves of self-loathing swept over her. What an egocentric, willful young actress she had been in those years, she thought, harshly reminding herself that *she* was the one who left her child in California, not Estelle. Not even Arnie!

Irony of ironies. Her little boy was dead because of the role she'd refused to accept as a mother.

Brooke crumpled the paper in her fist and slid off the chair's leather upholstery onto the library floor, another surge of wracking sobs convulsing her into a fetal ball.

Not a soul in France was aware she'd even given birth to a child. No one knew that she had knowingly consigned her baby son to the care of a woman who'd been the worst mother in the world to Brooke herself.

The lessons of this damn war had come far too late, Brooke concluded brokenly. Too late to realize what truly mattered in life was loyalty, constancy, getting the job done, caring about someone else as much as she cared about herself.

Only after she'd seen the devastation among the refugees fleeing the cruelty of the Third Reich had she begun to gain a sense of empathy and compassion for the innocent and defenseless suffering in Hitler's wake. When she'd been thrust into working at Radio Mondiale and observed Christopher's determination to tell the unvarnished truth in his news dispatches, she had finally witnessed what it was like to be a truly principled human being.

It was a message coming through to her loud and clear now, but it couldn't bring back her son. If Estelle Bradley had been a dreadful parent, hadn't she taught Brooke to match her in spades?

That's just yet another of your excuses, my girl.

All she'd ever done as Errol's mother was *make* excuses, she rebuked herself. It didn't matter about the tenth-rate parents she'd been dealt. Wasn't it still her duty to have done better by her own flesh and blood?

Brooke stared, unseeing, at the stern portrait of Victor's grandfather hanging on the wall above the library desk. Yes, indeed, the real Beverly Bradley was certainly being "punished by God."

And the hell of it was, she thoroughly deserved it.

It suddenly occurred to Brooke that taking the risks she had today, escorting the British flier safely to his next destination, was the very *least* she could do as the penance she owed Errol.

How many downed airmen and Jews and POWs must she save to make amends to that dead little boy? How many before she'd earned her own forgiveness, to say nothing of anyone having an ounce of compassion for her if they knew her wretched story?

It didn't matter how many chances she took today or tomorrow or as long as the war lasted, she thought, dragging herself to her feet in the shadowed library. She vowed on Errol's unmarked grave that she would repay that debt, even if her Resistance work got her killed.

The only thing that counted now was doing what she must to help the "good guys" while not *ever* putting herself in their category.

One thing Brooke now knew for certain: no decent man— and certainly not a good man like Christopher Laurent —would love or even accept her in his company if he knew the truth of what had happened to Errol, a little boy who hadn't asked to be born to someone like her.

Brooke turned off the desk lamp, dragged herself onto the

upholstered chaise, and curled into a ball as the midnight darkness enveloped her in its gloom.

Perhaps risking all for the French Resistance *was* her only answer, Brooke thought, emotional exhaustion keeping her from doing anything more than closing her eyes.

Even for the good of the cause she had joined, Christopher wouldn't like it if she took too many chances. But then, she thought, Christopher would never know the real reason why she did.

23

B rooke had fallen asleep on the chaise fully dressed without a pillow for her head or a blanket to cover her body. She awoke feeling disoriented, her muscles painful and stiff. As dawn broke, the first truly hot day of early June seeped under the sills. Already the flat, with its pulled drapes and shuttered windows, was becoming insufferably stuffy.

On the floor next to her were her mother's letter and its envelope that she'd crumpled in two small balls. Struggling to sit upright, she put both in an ashtray on the library desk, set the paper aflame, and then dumped the ashes onto the cold hearth.

Zombie-like, she padded through the rooms putting a few valuables and some needed household items into a knapsack that Nicole had often taken to a local, open-air market. Stowing a potato peeler and a roll of kitchen twine as the last objects that would fit inside, she began to calculate the odds she could get past the German checkpoints on her way from Gare de Lyon to the Fontainebleau train station without having anything confiscated.

She caught sight of herself in the mirror that hung in the front foyer above the table where she'd left her house keys the night before. Her dark wig was slightly askew and she looked like death warmed over.

She settled the hair piece properly on her head and smoothed both its sides with her hands to make herself slightly more presentable as an ordinary French housewife.

Play the part, Brooke, baby. It's just one more role you'll assume to stay alive and keep your secrets...

She glanced down the hallway that led to the bedroom she'd once shared with Victor. She realized in the cold light of day that serving as an escape helper was the sole reason not to gulp down the bottle of her husband's sleeping tablets that she knew was in the medicine cabinet only steps away.

She turned and faced the front door, wondering if she'd ever return to this flat again. Her life had narrowed down to Nicole, Jules, Felix, Ondie, and her own survival, along with the survival of any downed flier who fell from the sky and made it to her door.

Brooke quietly departed from the second floor, tiptoed down the stairs, and let herself out the building's front door, grateful no one was up and about at this early hour. Turning the corner, she headed in the direction of the nearest metro to make her way to the train station. Coming alongside a fence, she abruptly halted to stare at her own photograph looking back at her from a tattered "Wanted" poster that had obviously been plastered there for months. The blonde publicity shot from a film she'd been in was so jolting and foreign that Brooke squeezed her eyes shut and leaned against a nearby light pole to keep her balance.

Coming face-to-face with herself in a former life, she thought, *Behold the Brooke that was... and the mother that wasn't...*

She inhaled a deep breath to steady her nerves, then resolutely kept walking at a normal pace, her one goal not to attract anyone's attention. Gare de Lyon was crowded with morning travelers heading out to various destinations. To her relief, the German guards and French gendarmes didn't give her a glance when she boarded the coach for Fontainebleau.

Her luck changed, however, the moment she plodded down Barbizon's main street and approached her own gate.

"Ah, Madame de Varney! Just the person I was coming to see."

Brooke turned and met the cool gaze of Commandant Edgar Schiller, his buttons straining at the bulging front of his gray-green officer's uniform.

With a glance at her plump carry bag, he observed with a curious expression, "I see you've done a little shopping."

"Yes, I've walked to the market at Fontainebleau and back, and I must say, I'm quite fatigued in this warm weather today."

"Tell me, did you hear about all the excitement of a British plane we shot down near the village?"

Brooke's hand on the gate's metal latch trembled slightly, her thoughts spinning. She could only wonder if the Gestapo had found the navigator's parachute the two helpers were instructed to bury out back. The mere notion of such evidence being found so close to the villa gave her a stab of fear.

"We retire early here," she replied, attempting to keep her gaze steady, "and being at the end of the street as we are, we hear little beyond these walls. A plane crashed near here?"

"Yah," Schiller said, his eyes narrowing. "My men believe they saw a parachute blowing away from the group of enemy airmen they had... ah... apprehended."

Shot down like ducks on the wing, you bastard! she thought.

Schiller's lips formed a crocodile smile. "It won't take long to answer the few questions I have for you."

Brooke looked over her shoulder and asked, "Would it be possible for us to talk after I've had a bath and a little rest?"

"It's important I speak to you immediately," he answered, and pointed at the high, wooden gate. "Allow me to come in."

With a studied shrug and racing heart, Brooke opened the gate to allow Edgar Schiller to enter the courtyard. Once inside, she shot a warning look to Nicole who was just coming out of the kitchen's back door. Ondie had bounded out, too, and raced to greet Brooke with an ecstatic wiggling of her tail and entire body.

Commandant Schiller, a rotund man of short stature, cast an apprehensive glance at the poodle whose back came to his midthigh.

"Ondie, sit!" Brooke commanded as she handed her canvas carry bag to Nicole, who took it with thanks.

"I'll just put these in the larder," the younger woman said smoothly. "I hope you found a few tomatoes at the Fontainebleau market?"

"I'm afraid not," Brooke replied, in case Schiller should demand to see the contents. "Just some old twine, a rusty potato peeler, and a few other items you asked me to look for."

She turned to face Schiller, grateful that his back was to the raised vegetable beds and the rabbit hutch at the rear of the property.

"Please forgive me these domestic matters, Commandant. What did you wish to speak to me about?"

He pointed to the dog.

"Does it bite?"

"Not nice people," Brooke retorted more pointedly than she should have.

The previous twenty-four hours had pushed her to the breaking point and she struggled to smile to soften her last words.

"Ondie is a strange name," he said. "I wouldn't know what that means in German."

Brooke felt sudden alarm. Ondie's name, "Short Wave," weren't words she'd want Schiller to associate with a woman who used to be a radio broadcaster railing against Hitler. Thus far, no German official outside of Paris had linked Brooke Bradley to the Madame de Varney living in Barbizon, nor associated the name of de Varney with the well-known French film star.

"Ondie is just a silly nickname. Meaningless, really," she said.

Schiller looked at her as if he were waiting for her to invite him inside the villa.

"Do you mind if we speak in the kitchen?" she asked. "It's the coolest part of the house and I can offer you drink."

The commandant brightened somewhat at Brooke's mentioning a libation, even if it were before lunchtime. Even so, he cast her a calculating look as they went through the back door of her home. She gestured for him to take a seat at the kitchen table.

Nicole swiftly turned to a sideboard and poured Schiller a small glass of cognac while Brooke sank down on another kitchen chair across from her unwelcome visitor.

Seizing the glass, he jutted his chin in the air and asked, skeptically, "Did no one in this household see or hear about a flier who bailed out of the plane our anti-aircraft shot down two nights ago?"

Nicole, who was unpacking Brooke's knapsack in the nearby pantry called out, "I heard in the village shots rang out in the wee hours as the men bailed out of the plane."

"Yes, indeed," Schiller acknowledge in a pleased tone of voice "but that plane carries a crew of ten and only nine men have been accounted for."

"Have you searched the wooded hills on the other side of the wheatfields?" Brooke asked, steeling herself to appear calm and only mildly interested in their discussion.

"Yes, of course we have," was Schiller's clipped response. "We think the wind might have blown his chute toward this end of the village."

"We were asleep in our beds shortly after sundown," Brooke said. "Just waiting in line to buy bread each day is exhausting," she noted, pointedly, "to say nothing of walking to Fontainebleau to see if we can find anything else decent to eat."

Nicole swiftly seized the bottle of cognac. "May I top off your glass, Commandant?"

Clearly annoyed by Brooke's critical inferences, Schiller shook his head and waved Nicole off, flinging a second question at Brooke as if he already knew the answer.

"Well, if you didn't hear the plane that was shot down, did you by chance see that the name 'Varney' was on the list of casualties after our planes sunk the *Lancastria* recently?"

It was obvious to Brooke that Schiller's words were meant to be cruel. His button eyes glued to hers, she could tell he was closely judging her reaction to his provocative query. Her heart lurched with alarm, but like the actress she once was, she concentrated on thoughts of Errol's death to prompt genuine tears to her eyes.

"Yes, I've heard about that," she replied, her voice low. She brought one hand to her face to swipe the moisture from her cheeks. "Someone in the village who read a German newspaper that printed the passenger list asked me if I knew the name 'Varney' was on the manifest." Real tears escaping the corner of her eyes, she bit her lip. "I absolutely refuse to believe it's my husband, though!" she cried. "Our name has a 'de' in front of it. To this day, I have received *no* official word from the Allied army or Vichy officials that he was even *on* that ship or is known to have died!"

"Typical of the French," Schiller snapped, his cheeks puffing out with disdain. "Terrible record-keepers! Your husband drowned, most likely," he added in his guttural French that grated like the squeaking wheels on a braking locomotive.

Brooke countered, "But the newspaper also said there *were* known survivors! Surely, I would have been notified if he had died on that ship!"

"Varney was listed by *name* among the casualties," Schiller insisted, his voice shrill in Brooke's ears.

"As I just said, our name has a 'de' in front of it," she repeated. "Perhaps you don't know, but 'de Varney' is not a rare name in France." She shook her head, exclaiming, "As I told you, I've had no official confirmation from anyone. Nothing!"

Schiller's glance narrowed again. "You are an American, yah? I must tell you that there have been enquiries about you in Melun," he volunteered, naming a larger town not far away from Barbizon. "This means, of course, that if your husband is, indeed, dead, your status is bound to come under investigation by authorities of higher rank than I."

Brooke adopted a puzzled expression, though her stomach roiled and her hands grew damp.

"My status?"

Schiller warned, "As I am sure you're aware, Americans residing in France are now Germany's declared enemies. You should be prepared that, if your husband is dead, you may no longer have the protection of being married to a French citizen. You will be declared an enemy alien in territory controlled by us."

"Which means what?" she asked, her breath catching.

Schiller gave her another of his smug smiles, and a shrug. "It is always difficult to predict the 'what' in times of war, yes?"

"But I *was* married to a French citizen and as far as I'm concerned, I still *am*! No one has proved that he's been killed!"

She recalled her shock when Christopher told her Victor had *not* been on the *Lancastria,* but she dared not say that to Schiller or she'd have to explain how she acquired such accurate knowledge.

"As long as there is no proof he has died," she insisted hotly, "the authorities in this region should not harass me about this or say I'm now some 'enemy alien!' It's been an agony, not knowing what is true or false. What if *your* wife was mistakenly told you had died, but you hadn't? How would *you* feel if she was stripped of her status in Germany?"

Schiller looked discomforted but merely asked, "May I see your marriage license, then? To confirm you're wedded to this particular de Varney?"

Brooke felt a wave of panic threaten to overwhelm her. Her marriage license was issued in England where they were wed in St. Paul's chapel. The last thing she wanted was for the truth of who she and Victor really were to be known to Schiller or to anyone else in Barbizon. Squeezing another tear from her eye, she also manufactured a little sob.

"I-I left our marriage license in our Paris a-apartment," she said, her voice faltering. She glanced down at her hand, bare of her wedding ring. "And I'm not wearing my gold band because of the housework, and all. It's in my room. I can bring it to you so you can see the initials on the inscription inside."

"Fine. I'll wait," he said, his lips in a straight line.

She wondered how readily she could put her hands on the ring that she'd tossed in a drawer after Christopher left.

"If you'll just excuse me," she said softly and left the kitchen.

After long minutes searching in her dresser's top two drawers, she finally felt the band's cold metal against her fingers. Racing back into the kitchen, Brooke extended her arm, the ring clutched in her hand.

"See?" she said, her fingers trembling as she held it up for Schiller to squint at the inscription inside. "*'V de V loves B B forever...'*" she announced. "Do you need spectacles to read this?" she asked, hoping he did as the engraving was in English.

"The sentiment is very touching," he said sourly without examining the ring closely.

Brooke had no doubt that Victor's agent, Denise Louette, in the race for Victor and her to get married and leave for France, had arranged to purchase the ring and ordered the inscription.

"And what was your maiden name?" Schiller demanded, peering at the ring but not reaching for the glasses Brooke could see peeking out of his breast pocket.

She dared not say 'Bradley' and sent up a silent prayer he wouldn't demand to see her birth certificate.

"It was... Breuer," she pronounced.

Schiller's stern gaze soften slightly. "Ah... Breuer... a good German name."

"German-American," she lied. "My people settled in Minnesota."

Another lie. Her maid who dressed her in the play Brooke had co-starred on Broadway had been Miss Anna Breuer. She'd once mentioned that her German parents had gone from Ellis Island to farmlands in the Midwest.

Pushing back his chair from the kitchen table, Schiller took a last sip of the remaining cognac and set down the glass.

"Where is your friend, the poet?" he asked, glancing around the kitchen. "I had hoped to show him a bit of my work, but..."

Schiller looked at her expectantly.

"Oh... Monsieur Dumont?" Brooke's heart sped up. "He had to seek a warmer climate for his health. He departed with his wife for somewhere near Nice, I believe."

Schiller frowned, handing back her wedding ring. "How disappointing. He should have informed the mayor's office he was leaving."

Brooke nodded. "I think he simply must have forgotten. I'm so sorry."

Schiller clicked his heels.

"Well then, I will leave you now, *Frau* de Varney. You must report to me immediately should you receive the official word your husband is dead. I understand the Vichy authorities are attempting to notify all of the *Lancastria's* next-of-kin."

"And if he is? Dead, I mean?" she dared to ask.

"Ah... the future is not up to me. Authorities in Melun or Paris decide the fate of our enemy aliens... and..."

He allowed his sentence to dangle, along with what might pass for a sympathetic shrug of his shoulders.

Authorities in Paris?

Brooke pictured the image on the "Wanted" poster she'd seen on the fence earlier that morning. The head shot from her starlet days now seemed to be of a woman who was almost a stranger to her. Her only hope was that the Paris officials wouldn't make the connection between Brooke Bradley— the blonde actress-broadcaster hailing from glamorous Hollywood —and a dark-haired American and supposed widow living in Barbizon and married to a French soldier, possibly deceased.

God help her if the Vichy turncoats produced an accurate list of who actually boarded the ship, let alone if the London War Office would send official word that Victor had *not* gone down with the *Lancastria*— but that the renowned actor-soldier was deployed with his battle unit to some undisclosed location. Fortunately, there was little chance either functionary would know where to reach her.

Encouraged by the notion of bureaucratic inefficiency, Brooke promised Schiller in as sincere a tone as she could muster, "If I hear anything official, I'll be sure to let you know."

Nicole quickly chimed in, offering, "Sir, I'll let you out our front door that is much closer to the street."

Rather than allow Schiller to spot the raised vegetable beds or rabbit hutches, Nicole ushered the pudgy Nazi through the villa's front sitting room and through the door they rarely used.

Drained of her last ounce of strength, Brooke sank her head onto her arms, listening as the pair disappeared into the next room. She considered the irony of her situation and Schiller's latest inquiries.

I'm damned if Victor is still alive... and damned if he's been killed wherever they sent him later with his regiment!

Either way, the one person Brooke knew was truly dead was her four-and-a-half-year-old son.

The sight of her mother's letter with its childish scrawl rose up in her imagination, the reality of the news about Errol coming back in a rush. Before Nicole returned from escorting Schiller out their front door, Brooke dragged herself from the kitchen and went to her bedroom to avoid having to speak with another soul this terrible day.

It wasn't even the noon hour yet, but she undressed with the drapes drawn and slipped between the bedclothes, a headache beginning to throb. Laying on her back, the snapshot of Errol on his first birthday floated through her mind. Like some sadist poking at an open wound, she turned on the bedside light and pulled out her only memento of ever having been his mother. For several minutes, she stared at the frayed photograph that lived in a side pocket of her leather purse.

She remembered Errol crying as a newborn when she hadn't a clue what to do to make him stop. Now, she couldn't seem to take her eyes off Errol's image, her sense of her own inadequacy as a parent rushing back, along with feelings she'd stuffed down the moment she'd boarded that train for New York.

The reality of her failures and the way it had all come to an end slammed into the deepest recesses of her heart. Turning out the light with one hand, while clutching the photograph in the other, deep sobs welled up in her chest, threatening to burst into uncontrollable wails.

I did this. This was my fault. A child is dead because of me.

Brooke swiftly rolled over onto her stomach, her pillow muffling the wrenching sounds of her cries.

As June rolled into July, Brooke felt as if her emotions were imprisoned behind a stone wall higher than those of the Villa du Lapin d'Or. It was an airless, dark space where she could hardly breathe. Still numb from the news her son was dead and the avalanche of guilt that accompanied that truth, she went about her daily chores like a sleepwalker. The bottled-up grief and regret that filled her thoughts were subjects that she refused to burden anyone with, including Nicole. She forced herself to join in their evening meal, but could hardly bring herself to say anything much more than, "Pass the carrots, please."

During the ensuing two months, such an abrupt emotional withdrawal on the part of the villa's *chatelaine,* did not go.

"Something has happened to you," Nicole declared bluntly one morning.

Brooke knew that if she opened her mouth on the subject of what had happened to Errol, she would lose total control of her emotions. Nicole handed her a solitary piece of toast and a cup of hot water with a slice of lemon from a spindly citrus tree they'd discovered just outside their back gate. Her housemate made it plain that she was not to be deterred from discovering Brooke's abrupt change of behavior.

"You are not yourself and haven't been since you returned from taking that first airman, Lieutenant Thompson, to Paris."

Her throat tight, Brooke could only stare at her mug and the slice of lemon floating on its surface.

After a long moment, Nicole said in a gentle voice, "Please tell me what it is. What has happened?"

Brooke grabbed at the first excuse she could think of, but could hear the emotion in her voice. Flashing through her mind was the memory of stepping on the envelope in the dim light of her flat's foyer and opening it, seeing the first line, *Your son Errol died...*

Battling tears pushing at the corners of her eyes, she managed to reply, "I'm just tired from all the farm work, aren't you?"

Nicole had been fighting a nasty summer cold. Her nose was red and her eyes constantly watering. Brooke pointed to her.

"Just look at you, Nicole! You should be in bed!"

"I'm tired, yes," Nicole responded, "and not feeling very well, but it's not the same as you. You hardly have a thing to say anymore. What's wrong?" she insisted.

"Nothing's wrong!" Brooke snapped, rising abruptly from the kitchen chair.

How could she tell Nicole— or anyone for that matter —about the death of a son no one in France even knew she'd had? A son she'd deserted for a second husband who, in all practical ways, deserted *her*. There was simply no way she could begin to explain it all.

She grabbed a battered straw hat from a nail she'd pounded in at the side of the kitchen's back door and stomped outside. She could feel Nicole watching her from the threshold. Ignoring her friend, Brooke crossed the courtyard and strode in the direction of the rabbit hutches to perform her day's chores.

THE NEXT MORNING, Nicole didn't appear in the kitchen at her usual time, her cold having turned into croup overnight.

Brooke approached the bedside of her housekeeper-turned-friend with a mug of hot water and lemon and a plate with a precious egg scrambled on toast.

"I'll take Jules's work to the printer's today," she declared firmly, "and deliver the copies to the Paris drop boxes."

"But it's so dangerous for you every time you set foot in Paris," Nicole replied, her hoarse voice barely above a whisper. "Christopher said you were only to make the trip in one of your disguises if there was an escaper to take to the collection point."

"Christopher isn't here and you're sick," Brooke pointed out impatiently. "I'm going. Give me the address of the printer, please."

"It's a new one and he won't know who you are. He'll feel worried that you're a snitch or something."

"I'll convince him otherwise. What's the address?"

"Jules is the only one authorized to say," Nicole answered with a stubborn look in her eye that took Brooke by surprise. She reached for Brooke's arm and bid her sit beside the bed.

"You just aren't yourself, Brooke, so don't try to fool me." She peered up from her pillow, her face flushed. "Did the news that Victor went down on the ship *finally* hit you? Is that what's made you so sad? Any idiot can see that you've become more depressed than any of the rest of us. Admit it."

Christopher had urged her not to tell anyone that Victor was still alive— at least as far as anyone knew —because it could, indeed, link her to the French film star who was attached to a high-ranking Free French brigadier. That, in turn, would connect her as his actress-wife, the notorious anti-German broadcaster.

"It's safer for you if the question of Victor's life or death is in limbo," he'd advised.

On the other hand, if Victor's death were officially proven true, it might well alter her status to that of a dreaded "enemy alien," liable to be sent to an internment camp. Brooke figured it was better to maintain the ambiguity she was in and keep even Nicole in the dark.

Brooke trusted Nicole with her life, but she simply could not bring herself to explain the murky tunnel she'd entered since learning of her son's death. Gazing at her ill, bedridden fellow *résistant*, she sought other excuses to explain why she had hit rock bottom.

"We're all depressed and weary of the war," Brooke replied, rising from Nicole's bedside to leave for Jules's farmstead. "I'll try to cheer up, I promise."

24

Once Brooke arrived at the farmstead, Jules, too, became upset at the idea of her taking his manuscript to the brave man now printing the underground publication.

"I'll get in touch with Luc," Jules declared, "although I haven't seen him at all this week. He can take the typescript to the printer."

"Either I take it, or you miss your deadline," Brooke said, her irritation growing. "In Paris, you have a warrant out for your arrest, Jules! I merely have a poster tacked up here and there," she said in an attempt at humor to placate the writer. "Just tell me where I have to go."

Reluctantly Jules answered, "It's in an abandoned newspaper building. LeBlanc Publishing. In the Second Arrondissement, the same district as *Le Figaro* which the Nazis have shut down, of course."

Brooke nodded, fairly sure she could find it without too much trouble. She put out her hand.

"And give me the list of the drop boxes where I'm to leave copies of *La Libération*."

Jules, clearly unsettled by this change of routine, barked, "You know better than to ask for that! No lists. It could be disastrous for all concerned if you were caught carrying it. Nicole has memorized the addresses and if I tell you where they are, you must do the same." He shot her a piercing look. "And you must swear to return to Barbizon straightaway, do you understand? No side trips while you're in Paris!"

For some reason, she wondered if any of Christopher's minions in Paris had shadowed her on her first mission as an 'escape helper' when she took Lieutenant Thompson wearing his 'Deaf-and-Dumb' placard to meet his escort at Gare Montparnasse. Did someone also follow her to Rue Saint-Dominique and report back to Christopher?

She gazed speculatively at Jules sitting behind his desk in the bare front room of the farmhouse. He was Christopher's eyes and ears in Barbizon. Did they *both* now know she'd made an unauthorized stop at her former flat during her first venture into Paris as an escape escort? Christopher could have gotten word to Jules through their shared local deputy, Luc. Given Nicole's voicing her concern about Brooke's behavior lately, Jules, too, seemed to agree that Brooke had not seemed herself of late and—

Stop speculating and just get on with the things that must be done!

The proverbial caution among *résistants*, "Trust No One," floated through Brooke's head. She determined that those would become her watchwords from here on out.

She addressed Jules in a businesslike tone. "Okay. Tell me where the drop boxes are so I can file them right here," she proposed, pointing to her forehead.

Fifteen minutes later, Brooke bid Jules a peremptory farewell. She set out on her bicycle down the narrow path that led to Fontainebleau. With Jules's latest essay wrapped in a teacloth and stowed beneath a dead rabbit in her wicker basket, she could only hope that the disgusting odor of the creature would dissuade any German authority from inspecting things too closely.

As she pedaled her bike, Brooke had time to reflect that her personal battle against the Nazis and her need to keep secret her shame surrounding the life— and now death of her son —had narrowed her world even farther down to just herself. She silently vowed to offer safety to the strangers brought to her door and would depend upon no one else to help her do the jobs she felt compelled to perform as atonement for past sins.

The fact she'd been mother to a little boy who had died because of her neglect and abandonment was merely one more undisclosed secret that Brooke would guard with her life— even if most of the secrets she kept could get her killed.

BY SUMMER'S END, with their vegetables ripening daily, Brooke insisted on shouldering Nicole's erstwhile tasks of depositing Jules's weekly manuscripts at the clandestine Paris printer and then deliver copies to the designated drop boxes in the city.

"You have enough to worry about," she told Nicole, "posing as a pregnant woman and carrying those heavy bags of vegetables strapped around your belly to safehouses all over the city. We haven't had any fliers brought to our door lately, so I need to help out. We'll take the same train from Fontainebleau, do our jobs, and then meet back at Gare de Lyon."

When Nicole and Jules both protested it was too dangerous for Brooke to show her face in Paris so often, she simply ignored them until they both gave up trying to dissuade her.

One early September day outside Gare de Lyon, the pair stood side-by-side with the bicycles they'd brought on the train. Brooke bid Nicole good luck in her pregnancy disguise. For her part, Brooke could only hope that her dark wig and nondescript dress topped by a moth-eaten sweater would look different enough from the blonde persona in the "Wanted" poster to avoid calling attention to herself at the series of checkpoints she'd have to pass delivering *La Libération*.

With a wave to her companion, she headed for the Second Arrondissement, a section of Paris famous for its red-light district, the old Stock Exchange, and an area similar to London's Fleet Street that once housed several of the city's now-shuttered daily and weekly newspapers.

Brooke felt her blood pressure rise at the sight of *Le Figaro*'s building that currently flew an enormous black, white, and red flag flouting a giant swastika, an offense repeated on other vacant buildings on that street. Not far away stood the empty Leblanc newspaper building with its temperamental printing press housed in the office's deserted, below-ground basement.

She walked down the now-familiar short flight of concrete steps and into the large room. Looming in the shadows was a black behemoth of a press with giant metal cylinders that had once produced editions of the centrist Leblanc publication.

"Hello again," she greeted Alphonse Moreau, the newspaper's former pressman who had overseen printing operations for decades.

Abundant gray hair and bushy eyebrows accentuated the old man's gaunt face, evidence that severe food rationing in Paris had taken its toll in recent months. Brooke was suddenly grateful for the plentiful crop of vegetables produced at the villa during the summer and offered Alphonse a bag of her carrots, onions and two precious potatoes.

"Thank you," he said, his face lighting up at the sight of her gift. He nodded over his shoulder in the direction of a small room with a large window overlooking the former press floor. "The gentleman you see back there is the son of my old boss. It's thanks to him *La Libération* has seen the light of day. I'll share some of this with him," he declared, pointing to the food she'd brought.

Brooke's gaze drifted to a table stacked high with Nazi posters warning the populace of the latest raft of strictures laid down by the occupiers.

"A member of the Leblanc family prints these? And you trust him?" she wondered, pointing to the broadsides she imagined were destined to be plastered next to her "Wanted" poster all over Paris.

"Monsieur Leblanc *is* our cover," Alphonse noted acerbically. "It's how we stay in business. To restart the press over there, he made a deal with the Krauts to print their garbage and the buffoons have no idea we roll out anti-Nazi propaganda alongside their orders every week."

Brooke knew that Christopher's cover story had him posing as an ink and paper salesman in northern France, so Jules's connection with Leblanc now made sense.

Alphonse pointed to the pile of Nazi posters. His sour expression told her he now regretted having given her the information about his boss.

"So you didn't see this Nazi crap, all right?" he warned.

"Right, I didn't," Brooke agreed.

The Leblanc family scion, a good-looking man of middle years with a touch of gray at his temples, remained in his office while Brooke waited for the copies of the contraband newspaper she was to distribute that day.

Alphonse, noting her inquiring gaze, reignited what was left of the cigarette he'd been smoking when she'd arrived and said pointedly, "You also understand that you don't see Leblanc and he doesn't see you, got that? It's safer that way."

"I understand," she assured him.

Within the hour she departed back up the stairs into the street, stashing her allotted copies of *La Libération* beneath a pile of smelly, oily rags in her bicycle basket. In the next hours, she went about her delivery rounds without incident.

By dusk, she caught sight of an exhausted-looking Nicole waiting outside Gare de Lyon. Her latest cold was gone, but it had left her still not quite feeling her normal, healthy self.

"Everything go all right?" Brooke asked.

"I made the deliveries," Nicole reported. She gave a surreptitious punch to the pillow that had replaced the bag of vegetables she'd had around her waist on the incoming journey. Leaning close to Brooke's ear she said, "I bring you greetings from Picasso, who is desperate for more canvas as well as food, he tells me. And Josephine Baker says to say hello."

How long ago it seemed she'd felt a jealous pang when it came to her imaginings of Victor's "friendship" with the flamboyant performer, famous for her provocative feather dance. Brooke sensed a sudden, strange kinship with the African-American who apparently had also joined the French Resistance.

"Well, next time you see her, tell her I say hello back."

"And your day?" Nicole asked as they entered the cavernous train station, wheeling their bikes by their sides.

"Mission accomplished," Brooke said with a shrug, a wave of fatigue that matched Nicole's sweeping over her. She pointed at the clock looking down at the row of trains clanging in and out of the station. "With any luck, our train to Fontainebleau is about to arrive to take us back. It'll be good to get home."

BROOKE'S standard poodle gave the first indication that the 22nd of September 1942, would be unlike any other.

It was early morning. Brooke was kneeling beside a raised bed of potatoes digging up her bounty before the sun became unbearably hot. At the sound of Ondie's persistent barking, she glanced over her shoulder to see her large dog backing up in her direction.

Brooke knew instantly that strangers had entered the villa compound. Quickly she shoved stray strands of her blonde hair under her straw gardening hat that covered her head. A border of lilac bushes prevented her from seeing who was approaching. To her surprise, the figure that first appeared on the path was Nicole, her face white and pinched with fear.

"Madame de Varney," she began, her voice strained as she addressed her employer in a formal manner.

Suddenly appearing behind her were two men, one a very large German soldier with pale hair, dressed in his gray-green uniform. Behind him was a much shorter Frenchman in ill-fitting civilian clothes. Around the German's neck hung the distinctive silver chain with its outsized brass medallion that Nazi guards favored, a feature that to Brooke made the man look like a very threatening wine steward.

The little fellow following in his footsteps was French. He struck Brooke as equally ridiculous-looking, swaggering toward her like a bantam rooster in contrast to his gigantic, blond companion.

Nicole said, "These men are from the Gestapo in Melun, and they say you have to report at once to the commandant there."

Brooke's heart pounded in alarm.

"Not Schiller?" she asked, rising to her feet while brushing off the dirt clotted on her knees.

This was the moment she had always dreaded, the moment

when the Germans might round up the woman wanted for "attacking the Fatherland" on French and international radio.

She looked at the Nazi. "And just why must I go to Melun?"

She was wearing grimy overalls, a pair of patched sandals, thankfully, her tattered straw hat completely covered her wig-free head, but she swiftly tucked any stray blonde hairs above the brim line. The Nazi guard clicked his heels while the Frenchman thrust out his hands in greeting.

"*Bonjour,* Madame," he said in French. "I serve as this officer's interpreter. He says that you must come to our Melun headquarters for an hour's questioning."

Brooke struggled to keep her tone even and her expression bland while her stomach was churning.

Sucking in a breath, she replied in as calm a voice as she could, "And can you explain to me why I can't speak to Commandant Schiller here in Barbizon?"

The French collaborator vehemently shook his head and the Nazi officer barked something angrily in German.

"We have orders to bring you to Melun," insisted the shrimpy visitor, a scowl darkening his expression. "Schiller has nothing to do with this matter."

In response, Brooke mustered a smile, saying to the French flunky, "As you're this man's interpreter, please tell your friend that I'm happy to come later on my bicycle. I've got to get these potatoes harvested." Forcing another smile, she added, "May I give you both a few for your supper?"

Fresh food, even among the Germans, had become scarce, but her offer was brushed aside.

"No!" the French collaborationist said harshly. "We have a car and our orders are to bring you at once."

Brooke realized that their request was no mere formality like her registering with Schiller at his local headquarters.

"Well, at least give me time to have a bath and clean up." She gestured to her dirty overalls and filthy hands and feet. "I can't go to Melun looking like this!" She needed a minimum of five minutes to put on better clothing, sturdier shoes, and gather a few important items, should this truly mean she was to be arrested.

"We haven't time for that," snapped the Frenchman, glancing at his glowering companion. "You must come with us *now!*"

Brooke put down her hand spade and began picking up the potatoes and storing them in a gunny sack beside her on the ground.

The Frenchman pointed to Nicole, saying impatiently, "She can do that! Come!"

The German behemoth gestured at Brooke who was putting one last potato in her sack and cried, "*Nein! Nein!*"

"Leave that!" yelled the Frenchman as if he feared the Nazi guard would strike them both.

Brooke shot a glance at Nicole, attempting to keep her voice level, and urged, "Well, come into the house and have a drink while I get my identification papers and handbag."

To her relief, the pair agreed to this delaying tactic. She and Nicole led them into the kitchen.

"We'll just get the cognac and glasses," she said over her shoulder, following Nicole into the pantry and whispering to her to warn Jules not to leave his farmhouse and then to serve the men drinks.

Emerging with two glasses that she set down on the table, Brooke announced, "I'll just be a moment while you enjoy your drinks," fleeing the room before they could call her back.

She could hear Nicole begin pouring them their cognac while she dashed toward her bedroom, her heart nearly bursting out of her chest. First gathering her identification papers and stowing them in her handbag, she then rummaged in her drawers and closet, panic beginning to seize her. For a moment, she thought she'd be sick to her stomach.

Taking deep breaths to steady her nerves, her hands trembling, she put on her brown pair of shoes with the medical letter from Dr. Jackson hidden under the lining of her left foot. Certain they would take from her the cash that was in her dresser drawer, she slipped the banknotes under the lining of her right shoe, the folded money's thickness filling the arch of her foot. Although it was a hot day, she grabbed a sweater and wrapped a skirt, blouse, and underwear in it and stuffed the bulk, along with her purse into her knapsack. For a moment, she gazed out her bedroom window, wishing she dared make a dash for it.

Had the German authorities finally figured out that she was the blonde woman on the "Wanted" posters in Paris? She ripped her straw gardening hat off her head and settled her brunette wig on top of her head, once again tucking all strands of her blonde hair out of sight. Quickly, she reached for a small pot of brown eyeshadow and lightly dabbed a bit under each eye to appear older and even more haggard than she already felt. Anything she could do to look less like her poster was the best defense she had. Her anxiety mounting by the minute, she was desperately afraid of what would happen to Nicole and Jules and Felix if they all were arrested. God only knew what the Nazis would do to her if only *she* were.

A sudden cramping in her abdomen was an unwelcome reminder that her period was due in a few days.

Merde, merde, merde!

Just in case the Nazis were actually going to jail her, she was about to run to the bathroom for sanitary supplies when she heard Ondie barking furiously outside the kitchen door.

Sprinting back to the kitchen, she saw the enormous blond Nazi officer pointing his luger at her dog. Without thinking, Brooke ran to the open back door, placing her body and knapsack squarely in front of the barrel of the guard's gun.

She screamed "*Nein! Nein! Nein!*" and then turned on the Frenchman who sat looking stunned, his glass of cognac halfway to his lips.

"You tell this oaf if he tries to hurt my dog he'll have to shoot me first!" she yelled, amazed by her excellent command of French.

Ruefully, she recognized that her words were hardly a threat to this Nazi goon whom she imagined had already performed his fair share of executions. The Frenchman said something to the guard who lowered his gun with a glare at Brooke. She steeled herself to speak as calmly as she could.

"Nicole, please take the dog to the potting shed and put her inside with a bowl of water."

She stepped out of the doorway to allow Nicole to go into the courtyard and fulfill her request.

"But—"

Brooke interrupted her, whispering rapidly in English "If I'm not back in a few hours, you know who to tell."

IN THE HOURS after Brooke had been abruptly ordered from the villa in Barbizon to appear for questioning, she was initially rigorously interrogated in Melun about the status of her "French husband, now presumed dead."

At every step of harsh questioning which consisted thus far of verbal browbeating and vocal assaults, she feared the moment the German authorities might make the connection that she was the infamous American movie actress who'd broadcast derogatory reports against the German Third Reich. By day two, she was breathing a small sigh of relief that her interrogators did not appear to realize "Madame B. de Varney" as written on her identity papers was actually "Brooke Bradley," the former film star whose image was plastered all over Paris. Brooke could only credit this to the authorities' bureaucratic disorganization, as well as her various disguises.

By noon into her second day of inquisitions conducted by several equally menacing Nazis at the Melun Gestapo headquarters, Brooke suddenly felt moisture oozing between her thighs after standing for several hours under a naked lightbulb in the interrogation room.

Soon she felt blood running down her legs and realized that the stress and anxiety of the situation had apparently prompted her menstrual cycle to arrive early!

Oh, my God! I never got sanitary supplies out of the bathroom!

At first, Brooke was mortified, but soon rejoiced when the German officers' distaste for such a development prompted them to speedily declare her just another American caught up in their recent dragnet of undesirables scheduled for internment as 'enemy aliens.'

"*Mein Gott!*" cried one of her questioners, pointing to red blotches on the concrete floor.

She quickly pleaded with the French translator to allow her to go to the bathroom and try to remedy her embarrassing situation. The "Bantam," as she'd mentally dubbed the pint-sized Frenchman who'd first come into her garden, in turn, explained her situation to the German interrogators, his face turning as scarlet a hue as the blood on the floor.

Within minutes, she was unceremoniously sent to the washroom where she stuffed some wadded-up newspaper doubling as toilet paper into her underwear. As soon as she emerged, a guard ushered her out of the Gestapo headquarters and put her on a train headed for Paris with the other Americans likewise arrested as enemy aliens. Weak with relief, Brooke thanked her lucky stars they hadn't arrested her for the 'crimes' she had committed when working for Radio Mondiale, merely for being an American among many stranded in France once the Germans occupied the country.

Sitting in the crowded carriage as it left the station in Melun and rolled toward Gare de Lyon, she worried that it might be only a matter of time before one of the enemy grew suspicious and pulled off her hair piece, detecting her subterfuge. When guards were looking elsewhere, she constantly checked the rims of her wig to make sure no stray blonde hairs were peeping out.

Brooke gazed around at a car filled with nearly a dozen arrested Americans who'd been living in the immediate area. She was relieved to see that her elderly landlady, Madame St. Claire was not among them, most probably because of her age and infirmities.

"Does any woman on board this train have a sanitary napkin to help me out?" she called out. The French gendarmes assigned to guard them stood at both ends of the carriage and swiftly looked down at their shoe tops, making no attempt to intervene. To Brooke's undying gratitude, several female passengers kindly handed over the needed supplies that mostly consisted of clean rags, due to the rationing of cotton used to dress wounds.

She smiled her thanks and fled to the filthy restroom at the end of the train car, wondering if ever in her life she would have regarded *rags* as a complete blessing?

She did, today.

25

The prisoners' stay in Paris turned out to be for only a few hours. Brooke and her fellow prisoners were swiftly pushed aboard a jam-packed third-class carriage at the Pantin station, some seven kilometers from central Paris on the Paris-Strasbourg railway.

"At least the goons haven't herded us into cattle cars," a passenger sitting next to Brooke mumbled.

"Surely the Germans wouldn't do that to American *women*?" someone else sitting behind her whispered under her breath.

Their next destination unknown, Brooke couldn't help but fear the worst— they were headed for some labor camp in Germany.

The train car she shared with her fellow U.S. citizens had not been cleaned since Nazi troops had recently occupied it. Under their feet and spread all over the floor were pieces of sausage and cheese and cigarette butts. The air was fetid this hot, muggy September day and there was a filthy toilet at the end of the car, but no drinking water.

When Brooke complained about the disgusting conditions to the German officer in charge, he retorted, "It's the fault of the French, Madame. We asked them for railroad cars to transport you American females and this is what they provide!"

"Nazi propaganda!" whispered Sarah Watson, one of six women in Brooke's car whom she'd known, slightly, in Paris.

For Brooke, herself, the most incredible part of it all was that the Nazis in Melun— who had questioned her roughly and confiscated her silver hairbrush —apparently still had no idea that not only had she worked for Radio Mondiale, but that she was the Madame de Varney married to France's celebrated film star, Victor de Varney, a man now being considered a 'traitor to France' for having joined the Free French military effort fighting French Vichy forces.

Not that Victor-the-Survivor has sent me any word as to where the hell he is!

Of course, Brooke also realized there was no way for her to know if he remained alive wherever he'd been sent after making it to London.

The train the American women had been loaded onto hours before hadn't moved an inch. Brooke leaned to whisper to her seatmate, Sylvia Beach of the Shakespeare and Company bookstore fame. She had felt a rush of pure relief when she spotted both Sylvia and Sarah Watson boarding her car, her spirits rising a notch to know someone who shared her plight. At least she wasn't so alone, she told herself, seeking some small shred of hope to cheer her.

"Sorry to see you're caught up in this," she murmured.

"Oh, my stars!" exclaimed Sylvia. "At first, I didn't recognize you with your dark hair and couldn't believe it when I saw you sitting in this car. I thought you were long gone back to Hollywood!"

Brooke lowered her voice and implored her in English not to mention who she was or the work she had done for Radio Mondiale. Sylvia nodded, pantomiming turning a key in a lock in front of her own lips. Seeing the hundreds of American women being put on a single train, Brooke could only assume the reason she'd been arrested was that a general order had gone out to lock up all American women residing in France as official enemy aliens. She could only pray none of the American women on board revealed her true identity by speaking her name out loud.

The bookstore owner pointed to her lapel which displayed the Legion of Honor rosette for her service to France in the Great War.

"The Nazis questioning me when they barged into the bookstore today had no idea what this little piece of ribbon even meant, the bastards!" Sylvia also lowered her voice and said, "I heard we're going to Vittel, that spa east of here where the British female enemy aliens are already locked up at that resort east of here."

"Really?" Brooke replied, happy to cling to this latest rumor. "I suppose it could be worse for us Americans. They could be sending us to somewhere dreadful in Germany."

That very fear had been plaguing her from the moment they were told they'd be put on the train at the Pantin station, notorious for shipping people to labor camps in Germany.

"Surely not us!" declared Noel Murphy, a tall, blonde, middle-aged woman who looked like a Viking. She had studied opera in Germany and sung in concerts in Paris.

"I wouldn't be so sure," mumbled a woman swathed in an ermine stole despite the warm September temperatures. "There's no guarantee we're going to Vittel. I've heard that there are terrible places— death camps, really —where they've sent their enemies and put people in ovens!"

"No! That's got to be just another wild rumor," hissed another woman, chic in a Coco Chanel suit and impressive jewelry. "Jews, maybe, but not people like us!"

Without warning, the train they were on lurched forward, slowly pulling out of the Pantin station while incoming train cars filled with Nazi troops passed on both sides of their track. Brooke stared out the window, mindless of the views of Pantin's backyards and empty streets streaming by. Her thoughts were filled with concern for Nicole, Felix, and Jules back in Barbizon. The memory of her beloved Ondie barking fiercely at the hulking Gestapo officer in her kitchen as he aimed his gun at the dog's head made her blood pound. How she missed that furry friend! She could only hope to God Nicole and the others in her Barbizon orbit were safe. Had anyone been able to get word to Luc so Christopher's deputy could pass on the news that she'd been arrested and could no longer serve as one of the Comet Line's escape crew?

Brooke fought a creeping sense of helplessness as the train headed east, leaving her beloved Paris behind. Maybe their being sent to the spa town *was* a lie? And even if it wasn't, once they were all behind barbed wire, how could they ever return home?

The train moved at a snail's pace, often halting on sidetracks to allow German troop trains to pass by. Gazing out the window at people standing on the platforms waiting for regular train service to resume, Brooke's thoughts drifted back to Union Station in Los Angeles. She saw in her mind's eye Estelle's grim expression as Errol squirmed in her embrace, his chubby arms extended toward the moving train as the car Brooke rode gathered speed, heading eastward down the tracks and out of his sight.

Regardless of who knew or would learn about her uncertain fate at the hands of the Gestapo, Brooke understood one thing for certain. The fact that she was being imprisoned as an enemy alien wouldn't absolve her from the requirement to pay penance for what had happened to her son. Her main goal now was to devise some way of escaping from a luxurious spa resort bound to be surrounded by armed guards who were as dangerous and vicious as the oaf who almost killed her dog.

If the airmen she had hidden had been able to make it back to Britain to fly for the Allies again, Brooke vowed she would somehow make a getaway from Vittel to fight the damned Krauts on another day— and soon.

THE SPA RESORT OF VITTEL, some 350 kilometers east of Paris, featured formerly elegant hotels, lush parks, a lake, and a gambling casino. Brooke was greatly relieved when her group exited the train, confirming that they weren't being sent to Germany. Despite this, she was appalled by how the town's distinctive architecture had been scarred by their captors who had installed endless lengths of metal fences and rolls of barbed wire throughout the former resort.

Brooke and her little band of five who had known each other in Paris— or had friends in common —kept together as the hundreds of American female detainees tramped from the train station into the center of the spa town. The resort's deluxe hotels had already taken on the air of tenements. Washing hung outside on lines stretched window-to-window. British women draped themselves over the sills of the same windows shouting a welcome and sticking their tongues out at the soldiers guarding the incoming group.

"Those Brits look excited to see us," Sylvia said, waving at their greeters.

"Just wait until they find out they have to share rooms and food with us," Noel Murphy answered in a cynical aside.

The new internees were led into the Casino next to the Grand Hotel where they were told they would be staying. Inside the casino's rotunda, the women lined up while the Nazis examined their papers and took their money, promising the women they could draw 600 francs a month, each.

Brooke was thankful that she still had some 3000 francs hidden under the lining of one shoe— along with her medical certificate issued by Dr. Jackson of the American Hospital concealed in the other. Although her silver hairbrush had been confiscated, Brooke's interrogators in Melun hadn't made her shed her footwear or noticed she was wearing a wig. When asked to empty her handbag by the authorities at Vittel, she assumed a sad face and declared she had only taken from home what now lay in a small pile in front of her examining officer.

Brooke's group, "The Paris Six" as they'd come to call themselves, proposed trying to get assigned a room together. Across from where Brooke had her handbag searched she spied a Nazi officer who'd displayed pleasant enough manners. Her friends trailed behind her when she approached him with a smile.

After introducing each of the women in turn, she made her appeal in French, only to have him answer in English.

"All six sharing one room? I think that could be arranged," he said to the shock and pleasure of the group. Then he laughed. "Yes, I speak your language. I worked in a sugar factory in Yonkers, New York, and I intend to go right back there when this war is over."

BROOKE AND HER "ROOMMATES" settled into the routine as political captives held at the once luxurious hotel in the currently down-at-the-heels resort where pre-war wealthy Europeans had come to "take the waters."

"I stayed here a few years back," Noel Murphy remarked as they entered their assigned hotel room with windows that afforded a lovely view of the park below. She looked up at the peeling wall-paper and a cracked and smokey mirror hanging above a fireplace and sniffed, "Not quite the place it was in better days."

Over the next weeks, the prisoners settled into their captivity inside the five-story building with its impressive stone, double stair-case that adorned the approach to a colonnaded entrance leading to an expansive lobby. The Belle Epoch-era establishment had once welcomed Hermes, Elizabeth Arden, and others luxury retailers that had once operated shops off the terrace.

In these small, former luxury stores the internees could buy espadrilles made with string saved from Red Cross boxes. Brooke was especially pleased to purchase a pair, since walking with a wad of French francs pushing against the instep of her brown shoes had grown exceedingly uncomfortable.

"And did you know that next to that 'boutique,'" she said with a stab at humor, "there's an English seamstress who makes over clothes at bargain prices."

Sylvia Beach chimed in, "And next to her, did you notice the Frenchwoman from the town selling buttons, thread, and other sewing notions— that is, of course, if we prisoners have the money to pay."

September rolled into October, and the neglected lavish inte-riors grew even shabbier and very cold with the lack of heat and absence of a cleaning staff.

And the inmates grew crankier.

The British and American women staked out opposite ends of a big room off the lobby. The large open area that once was a ball-room had a terrace overlooking the Vittel park. Outside was the valley of the Vosges which consisted of lush, rolling countryside that was often filled with fog, making the autumn weather even more miserable for the residents.

"Do you play tennis?" one of the friendlier Brits asked Brooke one morning before fall temperatures made batting a tennis ball back-and-forth decidedly unappealing. Brooke, recalling how she'd forgotten to pack sanitary napkins, could only wonder how someone being arrested by the Gestapo had the presence of mind to bring along sports equipment in her luggage!

Brooke smiled her thanks for the invitation, mentioning that she had noticed the tennis courts on the hotel property, along with a bowling green, and even a maypole, all vestiges of happier times for the well-to-do.

"I used to play clay court in the States" she declared, recalling sun-filled days on private courts in Beverly Hills. She shrugged, "But sorry, I didn't bring my racket with me."

Without further comment, the woman wandered off, looking for someone more suitable, leaving Brooke with the sense of how totally surreal everything in this "spa" prison camp was.

Fortunately, both groups of female enemy aliens were willing to share books and had created an ad hoc lending library. Classes in languages and bridge were also organized to help pass the time.

The second week of November, Sylvia took Brooke aside with a look of distress pinching her features.

"The Free Zone south of Vichy is no longer free!"

"What do you mean?" Brooke asked with a stab of alarm.

"I just heard when I was in one of the shops downstairs that on November 11th, German troops moved beyond the former Occupied Zone, all the way to the South of France!" She waved her hand. "Pffft! No more Free Zone!"

"You mean the Krauts have taken over entirely from the Vichy French administrators?"

She thought of old man Pétain mouthing his platitudes into the microphone that day in Bordeaux while he sold out the country to the Nazis. With total enemy occupation of France, the traitorous job was now complete.

"Yes, they rule everything, now!" complained Sylvia. "Apparently, the Germans have taken complete control and administration of the entire country! As of two days ago, all police departments and former French authorities now report to the Gestapo and the other German military leaders."

Just then, Noel Murphy arrived in their room, motioning for the other five to gather around her.

"Someone on the second floor who heard a BBC broadcast on their hidden radio claims U.S. forces began an invasion of North Africa November eighth!" Noel whispered.

"*That* must be why the Germans suddenly decided to take over all of France this week," Brooke said, a rush of hope lifting her spirits. "All this sounds like the Nazis are worried about Allied attacks coming through the Mediterranean to the South of France."

"When in God's name will the Allied invasion of France arrive *somewhere* in this country and end_this nightmare?" mourned Sylvia.

As the days grew even colder, Brooke and the other women huddled in their sweaters and jackets inside their frigid hotel room where the peeling wallpaper shredded like dandruff onto their six cots.

The weeks began to merge one into the other with no further news. Brooke mostly kept to herself at Vittel, except for the five women with whom she lived. Every single day she feared that someone of the larger group might recognize her as the "Wanted" actress Brooke Bradley and inform their guards. Her group, who had known her in Paris as Victor's wife, swore to keep her secret and at least in her room she felt safe to slip off her wig at night. Even so, the danger of discovery was ever present since it became very clear to her that a few of the women in the camp were actually pro-German, antisemitic, and definitely anti-American.

By early December, the winter weather had become genuinely harsh. Shivering in their room one morning, Brooke decided it was time to produce the medical certificate that Christopher had urged her to obtain from Dr. Jackson at the American Hospital. She determined to make the case for a release on "health grounds."

"Please, may I have an appointment to see a doctor?" she told the warden overseeing her group.

"I'll request an appointment for you at the town hospital," the officer said, amiably enough, adding, "but you'll have to get the approval of Dr. Von Weber who runs it now."

Later that day when she mentioned to Sylvia Beach that she

had entreated the authorities for a medical appointment, Sylvia said, "I found out from one of the women who was in there as a patient that there are four French and one Scottish doctor forced to work there. Let's hope you get one of those."

"Allied prisoners-of-war, I suspect," Brooke said, cheered by this news. "Don't you imagine that they've been pressed into service by the Nazis?"

Brooke could only hope they'd be more willing than the German physician Dr. Von Weber to accept the validity of a health certificate made by an American doctor.

From beneath the lining of her right shoe she removed the medical form attesting to a "severe condition of uterine cancer."

Curious, Sylvia peered over Brooke's shoulder and gasped.

"Oh, you poor dear! Uterine cancer? I had no idea! Surely they'll let you out of here when they see that diagnosis?"

Brooke felt a pang of guilt that her health ruse would bring stress and anxiety to Sylvia, who had become a good friend, and to Brooke's other close companions at the decaying Grand Hotel.

But there's no help for it, she thought, putting on a brave face to calm Sylvia's alarm. Wasn't it just another secret of the many that she'd had to keep? At least it was one that might allow her to get back to Barbizon to help Christopher's team save more downed fliers and fellow allies in danger of being captured by the damn Nazis!

Christopher...

Brooke was startled that merely thinking his name triggered feelings she had for so long refused to acknowledge. They were emotions that had no place in a war, but even so, she couldn't help wondering if he'd learned by now that she'd been arrested.

There was no denying their kissing in her kitchen had been a sort of "crossing the Rubicon" moment, as he'd said that morning, a line between them they could never erase. For the safety of both of them, however, she had to ignore it ever happened. One thing she couldn't repress was that her feelings for the man who'd given her a chance to be a radio news broadcaster were unlike anything she'd ever experienced before. Who could have ever imagined that she'd be more worried for *his* safety than for her own?

And isn't that the point, Brooke? Your job is to escape from here and get back to work helping him get those escapees out of France!

THE DAY after Sylvia had seen her medical letter, Brooke was informed that the hospital scheduler had arranged an appointment for her that afternoon.

She swiftly stashed the various documents in her handbag that she'd need to show at the hospital, realizing with a start, that she had one more thing in her favor as she prepared for her medical examination.

That very morning— as she had hoped and planned when she'd asked for an appointment —her monthly menstrual period had begun. And this time she was more than happy to welcome it for reasons she didn't dare share even with the few women she'd come to trust the most.

Lying prone on the hospital examining table, Brooke looked up at the tall Prussian with his finely chiseled features and shocks of pale hair that put Christopher's blond thatch to shame.

Just before Dr. Von Weber had entered the room, one of the French doctors wearing a yellow Star of David on his white coat whispered, "Von Weber is a bone man, a battlefield surgeon. I'm afraid I must warn you, he knows absolutely *nothing* about a woman's insides. Lucky for you, he has asked for my diagnosis, but he might well insist on examining you with a speculum."

Brooke's stomach clenched both at the thought of the Nazi touching her, to say nothing of the very real possibility that Von Weber would see through her fake condition if he probed her with the device. What if it gave him a clear look past her cervix into her uterus? And even if it didn't, he could also palpate her ovaries and find they were in perfect condition in contrast to what was laid out in Dr. Jackson's written "diagnosis."

The minute the German doctor reached Brooke's bedside, she asked, "Have you seen my medical certificate, Dr. Von Weber?" She could hear that her voice sounded weak with her own fear.

"Yah," Von Weber replied with a sneer, "but you can well

imagine how many are presented to me that are fake! I must examine you and draw my own conclusions."

The gruff doctor pulled away the sheet and reared back at the sight of her bloody bedclothes and bottom sheet that she had deliberately soiled while waiting for him to arrive.

"*Mein Gott!*" he exclaimed, his distaste for what he saw approaching horror and disgust. Turning to Dr. Levy, he began speaking in his guttural French. "Very bad, very bad!" Addressing the nursing nun standing near the door, he directed, "I want you, Sister, and Dr. Levy here to follow up on this case and give me your opinions, yah? I'll decide in a week."

With a surprisingly sympathetic smile directed at Brooke, he turned and swept out of the room, the nun following him like a duckling on his weekly rounds of the patients under his watch.

Once the door had closed, Dr. Levy glanced down at the bed and said, "Let's get you cleaned up. Do you think you can walk to the showers down the hall?"

Brooke stared at the six-pointed star sewn on his doctor's coat and took the chance of her life.

"Von Weber is right, Dr. Levy. My medical certificate *is* a fake. I have my period, is all, but I absolutely *must* get out of Vittel and get back to my Resistance work! Won't you please help me? Just tell Von Weber that you agree with the diagnosis detailed in my certificate."

Levy's face paled and he appeared to be in a state of panic having been told the truth about the document she'd presented to the German doctor.

"It's practically impossible for me to do anything for you," he protested, fear punctuating his words. "I'm barely avoiding deportation as it is. If I were caught having sworn to a fake medical diagnosis—"

"I realize that, but—"

The Jewish doctor continued as if he hadn't heard her.

"My father is locked up and half my family members have already been sent to forced labor camps in Germany."

"I totally understand," Brooke insisted, her sympathy sincere. "But if you could just confirm the diagnosis specified by Dr. Jackson in the medical certificate, I think Von Weber would be glad to be rid of me."

"But by next week when Von Weber does his rounds again, your menses will have ceased or drastically diminished. He'll know for sure that anything I've said is a lie!"

Brooke was silent, and inquired hopefully, "But isn't there some drug that could make me continue to bleed? What can I do to look genuinely ill when he comes next week?"

"Keep you hemorrhaging?" he asked, aghast. "But that would be dangerous."

"Staying in this internment camp is dangerous for me in ways I can't risk explaining to you," she declared desperately. "Just give me something to take until he comes back next week," she pleaded "All you have to do, really, is say you *agree* with the respected head of the American Hospital in Paris and his diagnosis of uterine cancer. Then point out that Dr. Jackson says in the medical certificate that I should be sent to Paris for X-ray treatments."

Brooke watched Dr. Levy inhale a deep breath. He slowly turned and opened the glass-fronted door to a medicine cabinet. After a brief search, he withdrew a dark, amber vial.

"You do understand, don't you? This is totally against my principles and the oath I took as a doctor to 'do no harm.'" He handed her the tincture. "Take a quarter of the stopper every four hours over the next twenty-four," he directed. "Don't take any more than that, or you could bleed to death. This is a very potent blood thinner."

AT THE CONCLUSION of the following week, Sylvia Beach's expression of alarm told Brooke everything she needed to know when her friend entered the medical ward where Brooke had remained.

"Oh, my God, Brooke! You're so *pale!* Are they feeding you? How bad are you feeling?"

The truth of the matter was that she was feeling ghastly. The blood-thinning medicine had rendered her as weak as one of her newborn rabbits. She constantly had to be helped cleaning herself and she wondered if she were truly bleeding to death.

"I'm not feeling great," she admitted, "but I'm hoping they'll release me from here to go to Paris for treatment, which they aren't equipped to do here."

Just then, the door swung open and in walked the nurse in her nun's robes, Dr. Levy with the yellow star on his white doctor's coat, and Dr. Von Weber, a giant of a man with a perpetually grim look on his face.

"All visitors must leave!" barked Von Weber. "I must talk to the patient."

Sylvia scurried out of the room, the nun firmly closing the door behind her.

The Prussian head of the hospital approached Brooke's bedside and peered down at her with another look of sympathy that put his patient off-balance.

"I concur with Dr. Levy's diagnosis and Sister's observations," he pronounced. "You are a very sick woman. In my professional opinion, you need an operation."

"Operation?" echoed Brooke, her heart racing wildly at this assertion.

"We will remove your female organs, yah?" He looked at Levy questioningly. "Tomorrow I will perform a... what is it, Levy?"

"A hysterectomy?" Levy said, his tone reflecting his own uncertainty and alarm.

Both shock and horror swept over Brooke. Von Weber wanted to rip her insides out, which was far worse than merely remaining at the Grand Hotel until she could think of some other way to escape.

26

The German doctor's proposal to surgically remove all of Brooke's female organs filled her with a kind of terror she'd never before experienced. She began to weep genuine tears. Von Weber's plan was to virtually mutilate her body! This *bone man* wanted to yank out the womb that had carried Errol to term.

"Oh, no, not surgery!" she wailed. "The doctors in Paris said my best hope was X-Ray treatments on their latest machines! Please, sir, just allow me to go to where they have the most modern equipment that might give me my best chance to live! If my husband ever comes back from this war, he'll want children, and—"

She began to cry hysterically, and not only out of fear of what Von Weber proposed to do to her, but at the thought the man didn't even know how to *pronounce* hysterectomy, let alone have any experience performing the surgery.

The weaker Levy's medicine had made her, the stronger the avalanche of fear and anger she felt. She had tried to keep her fury at bay since the day that the fatso Gestapo officer with the ridiculous chain and medallion had arrived at her potato patch to haul her in for questioning. But *this*! She was to have this idiot orthopedist perform his first hysterectomy by cutting out her insides?

Brooke couldn't seem to control the waves of emotion that clutched at her throat, her sobs filling the air. All her fear, anger, and the resentments she'd stifled for so long poured out and the sounds were practically deafening to her own ears.

I despise these Nazis so much! she cried silently, while another wave of loud sobs took hold of her.

Von Weber shouted over her cries of distress, "Oh, for God's sakes! I'm a busy man! I would be more than glad *not* to treat this ungrateful woman!" He waved a hand in dismissal. Yelling at Dr. Levy, he announced, "I'm done with this case!"

"Then shall you sign her release from Vittel?" Dr. Levy ventured with a boldness that shocked Brooke. "That way we can send her to the Paris X-ray specialists recommended in her medical certificate and they will deal with her."

"Yah, yah!" Weber said, again waving his hand at Brooke in disgust. "An excellent plan. Contact the French Red Cross and demand they remove her from my hospital as quickly as possible!"

Within seconds, Dr. Von Weber had stormed out of the room.

THE NEWS SPREAD RAPIDLY through the hospital and the Grand Hotel that Madame de Varney, late of Barbizon, was to be released December 10th, "in time for Christmas," noted Sylvia, adding, "although I can't imagine we'll have much to celebrate, no matter where any of us are."

As it turned out, Brooke, along with Sarah Watson, Noel Murphy, and another American with a Nazi officer for a boyfriend, were also to be put on yet another filthy, crowded train, but this one was heading back to Paris.

Sylvia explained, "A Hungarian clergyman interceded for Sarah, due to the fact that she'd taken care of German and Japanese students at her Foyer International student exchange before the war."

Brooke looked over at Noel Murphy, whose family was wealthy on both sides and who merely shrugged, saying "Some friends in Paris made the case for me and I'm to go on the same train as you."

Brooke wondered if Noel, as she'd heard rumored of Coco Chanel, had had friends among the Germans and French Nazi sympathizers currently housed in the Ritz Hotel. Both women had been known to frequent its lobby bar following the invasion.

The next morning, the doctors, several nuns, and the inmates with whom she'd shared a hotel room lined up to say goodbye in front of the ambulance parked at the foot of the Grand Hotel's sweeping double staircase. Brooke felt dreadful that she was leaving them with the impression she was most likely a dying woman. What if they learned her release was based on a fake medical diagnosis?

She felt even guiltier seeing that Sylvia Beach had tears in her eyes when she bent to give her friend a hug.

"I will see you in Paris," Brooke said, looking at her intently and hoping Sylvia saw something telling in her gaze.

Her book-loving companion squeezed her own eyes shut and stepped back, swiping the tears from her cheeks.

"I so very much hope to see you again," she answered, her voice full of emotion.

Once at the Vittel train station, Brooke was put into a compartment with Sarah and Noel, along with the woman bragging about her Nazi officer boyfriend. Swathed in her furs, apparently her lover had sent her a case of champagne— a large portion of which she had consumed prior to boarding the train. As the car began to move, she declared in a slurry voice, "The Germans aren't s-s-such a bad people after all, are they?"

Sarah and Brooke remained silent. Noel Murphy merely looked out the train window and then closed her eyes as if she planned to sleep for the entire journey ahead.

BROOKE, too, tried to sleep on the trip back to Paris, but at the train station in Nancy, an air-raid alarm sounded. The guards rushed their charges into the French Red Cross canteen and then left to dash down to the shelter. As Allied bombs fell nearby, Brooke and the other Americans could only pray there would be no direct hit on the railyards by their own countrymen.

Once the all-clear signal sounded, their connecting train soon pulled out of the station. Brooke began to worry about what would happen to her friends back in Vittel after the three long months they had already been interned there.

"So many people love Sylvia," she said to Noel. "Surely there are strings to pull to try to get her out of Vittel."

Noel nodded, replying, "I'll see what I can do," but did not elaborate.

Hours later, arriving at Gare de l'Est in the cold, rainy dawn of that mid-December day, some of Sarah Watson's students were there to greet her holding a large bunch of flowers. Three very chic-looking friends of their companion who'd drunk all the champagne earlier were also at the station and whisked her away in a large, black Citroën driven by a man in the tell-tale gray-green uniform of a Nazi officer. Noel hailed a rare taxi and was soon on her way.

To Brooke's amazement, two Red Cross personnel appeared on the platform to meet her. As they helped her toward their car, she almost fainted from dizziness and was grateful for their support as they held her on each side by her arms.

Once she was settled in the back seat, a blanket around her legs, the driver asked, "We think it best if you rest in Paris until you feel stronger before you begin your X-ray treatments. Where would it be best to take you, Madame de Varney?"

For a moment, the question confounded her.

If only I'd brought the keys that Christopher gave me to his flat!

Despite the official document of release signed by the Vittel authorities stowed in her handbag, Brooke longed to be sheltered in one of the safehouses she and Nicole had supplied with food for so many months. Yet, if she gave one of those addresses, she might compromise the brave souls offering protection to those trying to escape the Nazi grip. Did she dare risk simply returning to her own flat?

She glanced down at her handbag and the thought struck her, *at least I had the wits to keep the keys to my own apartment in my purse.*

"I... I think my old flat at seventeen, Rue Saint-Dominique hasn't been requisitioned, so please take me there and we'll see."

As much as Brooke relished being out of confinement and back in the city she had come to love, she wasn't sure she wanted to return to the place she'd shared with Victor. However, it was great good fortune she had somewhere to go in her weakened condition and made no protest as the car pulled away from the curb. Closing her eyes, she gave in to the exhaustion that swept over her. Twenty minutes later, the Red Cross attendant sitting beside her gently shook her shoulder.

"We are here, Madame," she said softly. "Let us help you upstairs."

The concierge was the first to greet her, smiling broadly as she summoned the 'birdcage' elevator so Brooke didn't have to mount the stairs to the second floor.

"Welcome back, Madame," she said, and then appeared to think better of saying anything more in front of Brooke's attendants. "Everyone will be so relieved to see you."

The French don't even trust the Red Cross workers not to be snitches, Brooke thought wearily.

Leaning heavily on the attendant as she crossed the familiar hallway, Brooke had barely inserted her key when the door swung open.

Jules Dumont's wife, Germaine, stood in the threshold with an astonished expression.

"Brooke! Oh my God! It's you!" She glanced at the Red Cross attendants and back at Brooke. "They let you go!"

The Red Cross worker who'd served as her driver said by way of explanation, "Madame's been ill and has been released from the internment camp on medical grounds."

"Yes, yes, of course," Germaine replied. "You poor dear. Come in! Come in!"

"We'll just leave you, then," said the other attendant who had helped Brooke from the car. "I'm happy to see you have someone to take care of you, Madame, while you recover your strength. We wish you success with your X-Ray treatments."

The driver handed over a Red Cross care package that Germaine accepted and set on the floor inside the door. The pair nodded farewell to Germaine and Brooke, and in a trice, descended the stairs to the ground floor.

To Brooke's astonishment, the minute the door was closed, Germaine enfolded her in her arms and began to weep.

When she finally released Brooke and wiped her cheek with the back of her hand, she said, her voice raw, "There is so much to tell you."

Brooke was dumbfounded to see that Germaine Dumont was in her flat and overwhelmed by the woman's warmth and kindness. Jules's wife had always seemed mildly jealous of Brooke's working relationship with her husband. Gazing at the older woman's tear-streaked face, Brooke could only murmur that, indeed, a lot had happened since last they'd seen each other.

She pointed to the Red Cross box deposited just inside the foyer.

"I suspect there's some real coffee in there," Brooke said, instructing Germaine to open the box. "We'll have a good, strong cup and then we two can figure out where we go from here."

From the shadowed hallway that led to the bedroom she'd shared with Victor a voice firmly declared, "*Au contraire,* Cub. We *three* will have to figure out what our next moves should be from here on out."

PART IV

27

DECEMBER 1942

Christopher was shocked to his core by the drained, unhealthy appearance of the person who had inhabited his dreams— and his nightmares —since he'd first learned Brooke had been arrested. Yes, as the deputy for MI9's escape line in northern France, it was his duty to make a damage assessment after the arrest of one of his "helpers," but this was personal. He almost grimaced, taking in Brooke's haggard expression as he sat across from her and Jules's wife, Germaine Dumont, at the kitchen table in the de Varney flat to which he'd recently used the housekey Brooke had given him so long ago.

"Jules got word to me through Luc that the Gestapo had come to Barbizon and taken you away," he related to Brooke, taking a stab at filling her in on the previous three months.

He did not reveal to her he'd made a secret visit to Barbizon in September in the wake of her arrest and had learned that Brooke had not been herself in the days leading up to the Gestapo's arrest.

Nicole had told him, "She wouldn't reveal anything about transporting that first downed flier to Paris, but I tell you, Christopher, she almost seemed like a different person after she came home."

Jules had also confirmed a similar impression during Christopher's last, unannounced visit to the farmstead.

"Brooke came back from that trip to Paris full of anger and a kind of sadness I'd never seen in her before." Jules reported.

Studying Brooke now, so pale, thin, and hollow-eyed and deprived of her usual energy, Christopher was tempted to think their assessment might merely have been prompted by the enormous stress she'd been under for months prior to her arrest.

He summoned a warm smile and offered her a sincere compliment.

"You were amazingly quick-thinking to have slipped that medical letter beneath the lining of your shoe."

"That's what you'd told me to do, so I'd kept it in that pair of shoes," she said without emotion.

"Well, hats off that you *remembered* to wear them when they dragged you out of the villa so quickly," he praised her. "Nicole said you barely had five minutes once the Gestapo showed up to take you to Melun."

"You've seen Nicole? And Felix?" Brooke said, her eyes wide with apprehension. "Are they all right? Did the Gestapo harass them after I left?"

"They're both fine," Christopher assured her quickly, seeing the fear that had sprung to her eyes. "Nicole would want you to know the rabbits and the vegetables are thriving."

Germaine chimed in, still tearful, "Everyone feared the Gestapo knew of your work ferrying groceries and downed fliers to Paris and distributing Jules's essays to the drop boxes."

Christopher added, quickly, "And of course we all knew what the consequences would be for *you* if they had connected you and those "Wanted" posters to your work as an anti-Nazi broadcaster."

The latter concern was what had kept Christopher up at night for months. He still couldn't quite believe Brooke was actually sitting across the kitchen table from him.

"Believe me," she said, "I assumed those very same things were at play until I realized that the Krauts' line of questioning only centered on whether Victor was alive or dead. If he was dead, they said, I lost any protection from internment as an enemy alien because I'd no longer be the wife of a French citizen, but rather the American widow of a traitorous soldier who'd deservedly died fighting Germans." She managed to give a rueful laugh. "No one was more surprised than I that they never connected dark-haired *me* with the blonde in their damn "Wanted" posters. In the end, the bastards simply locked me up as a garden-variety American enemy of the Third Reich."

With that, she swept off her dark wig, shaking out her own, shoulder length blonde curls. The mere action appeared to leave her looking even more exhausted, Christopher thought.

Startled by Brooke's frank mention of Victor, he pushed one of the cups of coffee Germaine had brewed closer to their recent arrival.

"So I take it from what I heard at the front doorway that the medical letter from Dr. Jackson persuaded the Nazis to let you out of interment at Vittel?" Christopher asked.

"The Jackson letter was important, but so was a brave Jewish doctor at the Vittel hospital who gave me a drug to make me bleed and then seconded my fake diagnosis."

Brooke recounted for them the series of harrowing events that led to her ultimate release to Paris for X-ray treatments.

Germaine gasped. "Good God, Brooke, no wonder you look so pale. You could have bled to death! Let's get you to bed so you can begin to recover from this horrid ordeal."

With a nod, Brooke rose unsteadily to her feet. Christopher was deeply shocked to learn how much she had risked in her attempt to escape internment.

"Here," he said, leaping up from his kitchen chair. "Take my arm. You must feel so weak after all this."

"The bleeding has finally stopped," she announced matter-of-factly, "but the train trip didn't help the rest of my aching body." She struggled to maintain her balance, saying "If nobody minds, I'd like to take a bath... and... I-I'd prefer to sleep on the leather chaise in the library, near the fireplace tonight."

"Not in your own, gorgeous bed?" Germaine asked with a puzzled expression.

"No."

Brooke's reply was abrupt and Christopher sensed a genuine revulsion in her words. Her vehement response only made him wonder how she would react to the latest news he had about her husband. But that would have to wait for later.

"I'll get some sheets and blankets," he offered while Germaine took hold of Brooke's other arm and guided her down the hallway toward the bathroom with its large, porcelain tub.

Within twenty minutes, Brooke was in and out of the bath. In an armoire, Germaine had found a night gown and robe for Brooke to put on. Jules's wife then slowly walked Brooke, clad in her pink, silk peignoir, into the library.

Christopher had closed the drapes and the two of them helped Brooke recline on the chaise that he had covered in a sheet and a pile of blankets.

"Thank you both so much," Brooke murmured, as Christopher put a pillow under her head and drew the covers up to her shoulders.

"Sleep, now," he urged "and just call out if you need anything."

"Wait!" Brooke cried, gazing at him and then at Germaine. "There's so much for us to catch up on! Sit for a while and tell me everything."

Christopher saw that Germaine's eyes were filling with tears once again.

"Later, when you've had a good rest," he temporized. "We'll be right here." His stomach in a knot, he added, "I'll have another good, strong cup of that delicious coffee waiting for you when you wake up and we can talk then."

By this time it was nearing five o'clock in the afternoon. Germaine had left the room, heading back to the kitchen. Christopher turned and asked Brooke a question he was unwilling to postpone any longer.

"Are you at all bruised? Were you beaten? Should I get a doctor to come here?"

Brooke rose onto one elbow, her blonde hair framing her thin face, her complexion drawn and drained of color.

"Amazingly, no torture and no beatings," she assured him. "Just no sleep. Nobody ever attacked me physically, but for three days after they arrested me, they kept me awake until dawn. They were trying to break my cover story as a hapless American caught in France with a missing husband— which somehow I managed to stick to."

She gave a weak laugh, and Christopher knew there was more to her tale than she had the energy to tell him.

"So they eventually believed you'd been given a cancer diagnosis?" he asked, knowing he should just let her sleep.

"Finally, yes, they believed it. But, truly, the hero in all this was that Jewish doctor named Levy who gave me the blood thinner. He knew how squeamish the German doctor Von Weber was about 'female conditions,'" she related with a wry expression. "Me turning into such a bloody mess, *literally*, was what convinced the German creep that my condition was terminal." She met Christopher's glance. "Von Weber wanted to operate. Take out all my female parts. I threw a fit— a real one —and I think just to get rid of me, he agreed to send me to Paris for X-ray treatments as specified in Jackson's letter."

"Jesus, Brooke! You could have killed yourself taking that drug!"

She raised her chin with a familiar look of defiance.

"Either that, or a 'bone man' who'd never performed a hysterectomy would have butchered me, so I chose to take the risk, just like you take risks all the time," she added pointedly.

Christopher shook his head, horrified that she might have lost any chance of motherhood.

"You know something?" he said, gazing down at her on the chaise. "You've certainly come a long way since you were the starlet who walked into my office that day. You do realize, don't you," he said with admiration he couldn't disguise, "not many men or women I know could have pulled off what you just did."

"You mean get themselves released from prison with a letter of safe conduct, signed by a Nazi doctor?" she said with some of her former humor and a good dose of pride.

All Christopher wanted to do at that moment was take her in his arms, but he merely smiled. "Yeah. That, too."

He turned off the wall light switch, plunging the shuttered library into sepulchral darkness.

In the gloom he heard Brooke murmur, "I can't believe you're actually here. Please don't disappear on me…"

"I'm not going anywhere tonight," he reassured her softly, his pulse quickening so that he felt the reverberations in his chest.

He had a sudden, unbidden vision of kissing her passionately in the kitchen at Barbizon before disappearing once again in his usual fashion. He wanted so to kiss her now. Tell her how the burden of feeling responsible for her arrest had been lifted a bit, knowing she'd escaped from the Nazis' grip. Yes, he wanted so much to kiss her senseless.

But I won't, will I?

He would first have to tell her the news it was now his duty to reveal and God only knew what her reaction would be. He walked back to the chaise, bent down, and barely brushed his lips against her forehead, her freshly washed blonde hair tickling his upper lip.

"Just sleep for a while," he whispered against her ear and tiptoed out of the library, shutting the door.

∾

IT WAS NEARLY midnight before Brooke awoke. Sitting in the desk chair in the library, Christopher had taken up watching over her for these last hours. A single, small lamp illuminated the book he'd pulled from a shelf to help him pass the time. On the floor under the desk was the secret radio that MI9 had issued him on his last clandestine trip flying to London. Luckily, it hadn't been damaged when he parachuted back into France the previous week.

He glanced down at it now, remembering how shocked he'd been by the last communication he'd been sent, part of a message he would have to deliver to Brooke when she felt stronger. He was suddenly aware that her eyes had fluttered open and she shifted her body under the covers.

"Well, hello, Sleeping Beauty," Christopher said. "How do you feel, now?"

"Disoriented," she replied, glancing around the darkened room. "You didn't leave."

"No, but Germaine did," he said. "Her father was expecting her attention this evening, but she'll be back if we need her."

"I'm starving," Brooke blurted, sitting up. "How about some of that coffee you promised. Did you find anything else decent to eat in the Red Cross care package?"

"It's the middle of the night. Shouldn't you sleep some more?"

"Feed me first," she demanded, swinging her legs to the side of the chaise.

Christopher rose from the desk, offering her both his hands to help steady her as she struggled to stand up. She swayed and leaned into his chest for support.

"Dizzy?"

Her body felt soft and so at home against his own.

"A bit," she whispered. "Just give me a minute and I'll be all right."

He gripped her more tightly, saying, "There's some nice cheese, a chunk of bread, and a bit of chocolate, even."

Brooke leaned back in his arms, a shade more color in her cheeks and vibrancy in her voice.

"Well, take me to it!" she demanded, her first faint smile on her lips.

Christopher was thankful that she sounded strong enough to hear what he had to say. While Brooke sat at the kitchen table sipping a cup of their precious coffee, Christopher toasted some bread on the stove, melted cheese on top, and sliced an apple he found at the bottom of the care package to crown his concoction. He handed it to Brooke, keeping a second portion for himself.

"Quite the inventive cook you are," she said admiringly. "I'm famished and after the food I was fed for three months at Vittel, this is like dining at the Ritz."

They ate in silence, Christopher's mind debating several ways to impart his news. Finally he decided to start with what had happened to Jules.

"While you were locked up, Jules left France."

Brooke dropped her bread on its plate, her eyes wide.

"What? He's left the country? *Why*? Where did he go?"

"You're asking all the right questions, Cub."

Brooke waved her hand in dismissal.

"Then answer them! No wonder Germaine had tears in her eyes all evening."

He could tell she was as stunned by this revelation of Dumont's departure as he had been when Germaine had been told by Luc that Jules had left Barbizon in a frantic hurry.

"Jules got word from Nicole that Schiller had been notified by 'higher authority' that there was a Frenchman now in Barbizon who'd been deputy-in-charge of the former Information Ministry before the Nazi takeover. This person— namely Jules —was now wanted for questioning in Paris. Since Jules had registered with the local mayor's office and the Commandant had met him once in your company," he explained to Brooke, "Schiller came around to your villa asking where Jules was."

"Nicole repeated what I had said to Schiller earlier when he'd asked about Jules reading Schiller's poetry, namely that Jules had gone to the South of France for his fragile health," Brooke replied. "Thank God we'd moved Jules from the villa out to the farmstead."

Christopher nodded. "Yes, Nicole told Schiller Jules had left the area, but as soon as the Nazi was out the door, she went to the farm-stead and repeated to Jules what the Commandant had said. Jules wisely felt he could no longer stay in the Barbizon area, nor did he dare go back to Paris."

"So where did he go?" Brooke asked.

"South to Marseilles. Once the Nazis invaded the Free Zone last November and took over all of France, Jules sent word through people on our escape line that he would head by ship for North Africa with some comrades to see if he could help the Free French fighting there."

"Even with that bad back of his?" Brooke protested.

"Apparently he thought he could be of use behind the lines with his writing skills."

"Well, that's not too far-fetched," she agreed. "But where is he now?"

Christopher inhaled a deep breath.

"There's been no word. We do know that a ship with several Resistance men aboard was sunk by a U-boat in the Mediterranean on its way to North Africa just about the time Jules said he was to depart."

Brooke's stricken look and cry, "Oh no! You think he *drowned*? And Germaine's heard nothing?" she asked, her voice choked. "The poor woman."

Christopher nodded. "No. Nothing. Jules's brother who lives near Marseilles confirmed he'd booked on a ship heading for North Africa. We think it's the one hit by the U-boat."

"Oh, Jules..." murmured Brooke.

"Well, at this juncture, Germaine and I can only presume he was one of those traveling on that vessel, but nothing's confirmed."

"Just like the *Lancastria* that the Germans sank with all those thousands of people on board. How horrible!"

Brooke sank back against her chair, her eyes wet. Christopher was stunned when her next move was to reach for his hand, her mood growing hopeful.

"Maybe it'll be like what happened with Victor. Isn't it possible that Jules either wasn't on that ship, or that he made it to shore somewhere and we just haven't gotten word?"

"Knowing Jules, by this time he would have found a way to let us know where he was, just as he did before he left for Marseilles." Christopher met her glance, adding, "And just the way he made sure I knew you'd been arrested last September and taken to Vittel."

"Oh, my God," Brooke whispered, her head sinking into her hands. "Jules, dead? Poor Germaine," she repeated.

"I know," Christopher agreed soberly. "Since I had your keys, I figured the safest way to tell her the latest news about the U-boat attack was to meet her here. Then, by some miracle, *you* were released and suddenly appeared here as well. I couldn't believe it when I heard your voice while you were speaking to Germaine at the front door."

"I was amazed that the apartment still had the U.S. Embassy seal on it, weren't you? You knew somehow it had never been requisitioned by the Germans.

"It must have been one of those bureaucratic flukes that some

German officer never claimed your flat, but thank goodness none have."

"You'd had this building regularly watched, am I right?"

He realized that she had figured out he'd had her shadowed on her first mission to take a downed flier to Gare Montparnasse for transfer to the Comet Line— and that afterward she'd come back to her flat that night.

"Yes, I knew because I had one of my men follow you on your first mission as an escape helper," he confessed with the candor he knew he owed her. "I wanted to be sure you'd be safe on your maiden trip delivering one of our 'packages.'" He paused. "I was told you did an exemplary job that night, although I wasn't happy to hear you hadn't followed strict orders to take the next train back to Barbizon." He glanced at their surroundings. "I can certainly understand how you might have longed to be in your own home and take a bath in your own bathtub," he added with a forgiving smile, noting how that was the first thing Brooke had wanted when she'd arrived earlier that day.

"And you've used this flat as a safehouse before?" she wondered aloud.

Christopher sensed how intently she was regarding him.

"Yes," he answered. "I'd stay here on occasion soon after you originally left for Barbizon. I hope that was all right with you."

"Good thing I gave you my keys, wasn't it?"

"It saved my life a few times, so thank you."

"But didn't the concierge wonder who you were, going in and out at all hours?"

"I told her I was your brother. I'd call at her door each time and she'd give me a thumb's up that it still hadn't been requisitioned by the Nazis."

Brooke reared back in her chair and regarded him with an unreadable expression. Finally she said, "So you *were* here. Inside the flat for more than a year, now?"

He nodded affirmatively. "On and off over those months."

"Well, I guess with your American accent and blond hair, we could pass for siblings. Do you think my concierge believed you?"

"I knew she wanted to," he said, suppressing a smile. "Every time she sees me, she merely waves her thumb and makes no further inquiries."

"Well that's a relief."

He wondered how many times Brooke may have tipped the woman or left chocolate and other delicacies at her door.

After a moment she asked, "Did you happen to notice any mail pushed under the door the times you stayed here? That's where the concierge usually puts it when I was away."

"I did see a few envelopes," he answered, hoping she didn't think he'd snoop in her post, "but I left them where they were. I didn't want there to be any sign someone had been staying here. Mail on the floor was a good cover," he added. "There's always the chance that the Germans might suddenly recall this place was no longer protected by the American Embassy seal and move in."

"I didn't see any mail when I got here today," she said, regarding him steadily.

"Germaine picked up a pile off the floor when we first came in today and put it in the desk drawer in the library."

"Ah."

Brooke stared into her cup of cooling coffee, then suddenly looked up as if the subject of her mail was apparently forgotten.

"I want to get back to Barbizon as soon as I feel a bit stronger," she announced, her tone resolute. "Can you fill me in about the latest regarding the escape routes? Has that bastard Harold Cole or anyone else collaborating with the Nazis blown up the entire Comet Line by now?"

"Funny you should mention Harold Cole," he said, amazed how focused Brooke was on returning to her Resistance work, given all she had suffered when she was arrested and interned.

He leaned toward her and filled her cup with the last drops in the pot Germaine had left them.

"As it happens, there are quite a few more things I need to tell you," he began.

Christopher pointed to the leather suitcase which he kept close to him at all times, now parked beneath Brooke's kitchen table. "Inside this case is a radio issued me by MI9. I assure you I have never risked receiving or transmitting from your flat here."

"The detection vans," she said, understanding his meaning. "Good to avoid attracting any attention to a safehouse."

"Exactly, and especially this one. But it has brought me news concerning Harold Cole. He's recently betrayed another escape organization to the Nazis. Dozens in other units have recently been arrested in and around Paris, which is why I started coming here to lay low for a while."

"Does Brit Intelligence in London know or care about Cole?" she demanded, her ire regarding the subject obvious. "Have they done *anything* about this guy? After he nearly had me arrested in Paris and I had to leave so quickly, I thought your people in London would take action. Cole was clearly in cahoots with the German goon in the black fedora when I went to have my bicycle repaired."

"And we've seen him whispering to the Nazi guards at the checkpoints leading in and out of the train stations," Christopher confirmed.

Brooke then briefly reminded Christopher of the day Cole posed as a member of British Intelligence, arriving at her door with the odious socialite, Gillian Wingate-Jones.

"Less than a week later, he followed Nicole and me to the bike shop and marketplace and then pointed us out to a German thug in the café! It was a miracle that we both managed to get away."

"Many of us in the field have done our damnedest to convince the bigwigs in London that Cole is a traitor, a menace, and a total fraud, so we'll see," he commented with a tired sigh.

"Well, it's certainly taking them long enough to figure out he's a damn turncoat!"

"No kidding," he agreed.

Christopher had radioed his contact at MI9 detailing the recent arrests of escape helpers in Paris and received little in response. Cole had always claimed he was working for Allied intelligence, but Christopher had long ago suspected the bastard might be a double agent. There were even indications that he could be a *triple* agent, run by the wily Claude Dansey, the deputy to the head of MI6. These were the ultimate tricksters in an intelligence game where it was often difficult to discern whose side anyone was on. Christopher could only wonder if this might account for his higher-ups not ordering the liquidation of the guy.

Christopher frowned. "The subject of Harold Cole brings me to something else I need to tell you," he said, "but first you need to tell *me* something. Did you ever reveal to anyone your work bringing rescued fliers to Paris?"

Brooke looked daggers at him.

"Who do you take me for, asking me that question"?

Christopher steeled himself to answer calmly. "Because I need to know the answer. I've been told there were women interned at Vittel who weren't particularly loyal to the Allied cause, be they Brits or Americans. I would totally understand if somehow, inadvertently, given the stress you must have been under, you might have mentioned—"

"I didn't— *ever* —let anyone know anything of the work I've done for the escape line."

"I didn't think so, but I had to ask."

There was no mistaking how offended she was by his query. She turned to leave the kitchen. "I think we should both get some more sleep."

With a resigned sigh, he rose from his chair. He'd wait until tomorrow to inform her of what he'd just learned himself.

"Yes, it's a good idea for both of us to get some rest, while we can," he said, keeping his tone deliberately casual. "I've requisitioned Nicole's bedroom off the kitchen."

Of course, he wanted nothing more than to have Brooke fall asleep in his arms this night.

Yet, given the other news he would tell her the next day, it probably wasn't the best idea to let her know how much he cared about her and how frantic he'd been for her safety these last months. The notion of suggesting they sleep in the same room definitely wasn't the right move at this moment.

He was startled, then, when Brooke accepted his hand in both of hers, apparently having forgiven him for asking if she'd inadvertently compromised the escape line.

"Will you stay with me in the library until I fall asleep?" she asked, an unexpected and gratifying request.

"Of course, but I don't promise not to doze in my chair."

Brooke confessed, "Now that I'm actually back in this flat, I find it gets a bit on my nerves".

He glanced down the hallway toward the library. She had made it clear when she'd first arrived that she didn't want to sleep in the master bedroom, a fact that made him wonder what her reaction was going to be when he told her his other news.

28

A night spent sitting upright in a chair in the library turned out to be a very poor way to awake refreshed. With weariness weighing heavily on body and soul, Christopher stood in Brooke's Paris kitchen the following morning pouring boiling water over the last of the Red Cross coffee grounds.

He was about to tip the remaining water into the powdered eggs he'd found at the bottom of the care package when Brooke appeared at the door, her color improved and looking more like her beautiful self.

"Ah, I see my personal chef is hard at work," she teased, advancing into the room, still clothed in her silk dressing gown. Seating herself at the wooden table, she held out both hands to receive the cup of coffee. She bent to inhale the steam coming off its surface before she took a sip. "Heavenly!" she pronounced.

"How are you feeling this morning?" he asked, dreading the next duty he must perform.

"Not quite heavenly like the coffee, but a thousand times better than yesterday," she replied, taking a second sip.

He left the egg concoction in its bowl and took his own cup in hand, settling in a chair across from her. His radio gear was safely in its leather case, but it's presence under the table prompted him to delay no further. He drew in a deep breath, searching for the best way to tell Brooke about the contents of the last message he'd received a day before she'd made a startling appearance at her own front door.

"In the same dispatch from London when I learned about Jules, I was sent other news," he began.

"And *Monsieur Mystérieux* is allowed to impart such secrets to little ol' *moi*?" she teased.

"It's my duty to," was his short reply.

Brooke's cup was midway to her lips, but she abruptly set it down.

"What? Who else have we lost?"

He could almost count the seconds before he made himself answer.

"Victor."

"*Victor*?" she repeated, her mouth slightly ajar. "Victor has died? For real, this time? Do we even know where he's been?"

He detected no tears, just shock at hearing this news.

"Yes. In North Africa. Syria and Algeria, to be exact."

"And...?" Brooke asked cautiously.

Christopher hesitated only a moment before he revealed, "Victor died of his wounds last November. This time, his death has been confirmed. They've buried him there. The paperwork made its way to London right after, but you were interned and apparently his death was then a closely-guarded secret."

He watched intently as she glanced down at her cup. The silence between them grew interminable and Christopher couldn't think what to say.

Looking up to meet his gaze, she demanded quietly, "Tell me what you know."

Christopher despised not having been given more details than the few he'd pieced together about the strange circumstances surrounding Victor's death. He'd *asked* more questions in response to the message he'd recently received over his radio, but was told he was only authorized to "tell the widow that Victor de Varney was killed and when. Nothing more."

Christopher related what he knew as gently as he could.

"He'd been sent to Algeria with the French Fourteenth Corps.

The Fourteenth had been fighting fierce battles with the Vichy French troops in North Africa last year and this one."

"Frenchmen against Frenchmen, which was everyone's worst fear," Brooke commented, shaking her head with resignation. Then she looked puzzled. "But I thought Victor was never slated for actual combat."

"He wasn't. At this time, de Gaulle himself remained in London wrangling with both British and American military and political leaders," Christopher elaborated, "campaigning for the full recognition as France's leader. Victor was assigned to somebody else in the unit and went to Africa with the main contingent."

"And in the meantime, de Gaulle's troops were risking their lives taking on the Vichy in North Africa," she said bitterly. "But Victor was a *translator*, for pity's sake, not a real soldier! You and everyone else said he'd be far behind enemy lines."

"He was," Christopher replied carefully, "until after de Gaulle's Free French troops won a big battle in early November."

"He was caught up in the battle?" she asked with astonishment.

"He apparently was involved in the... uh... aftermath," Christopher said and then wondered if he'd revealed too much.

"You mean Victor died once the battle was *over*?" she asked, incredulous at hearing this news.

"That was what I was told in the dispatch I received. He died November eighth in a field hospital."

Christopher had surmised there was far more to the story of Victor's demise than the cable stated but refrained from offering any speculation.

"How did he die? Why was he killed if the Vichy had surrendered?" she protested. "Did he die of some illness? His asthma?"

Christopher could see what a persevering journalist Brooke had become, but he'd been warned that the Secrets Act forbade his giving any more sensitive details about the fate of France's famous film star. He refrained from saying aloud the only assumption he could make.

Something had gone terribly wrong.

"The transmissions sent me about Jules and Victor were very

cryptic," he temporized. "I was authorized to disclose to both you and Germaine the information the War Office was willing to confirm. If more emerges, I'm sure I'll be informed." He covered Brooke's hands still wrapped around her coffee mug with his own. "I'm so very sorry to be the one to have to tell you this after all you've been through."

"So he's buried in Algiers?" she asked softly.

"That's what the transmission said."

She looked at him steadily. "And that's all you know? No more details than that?"

It was Christopher's turn to stare into his coffee cup.

"The dispatches over these secret radios are notoriously short to prevent being detected by those Nazi roving vans." He looked up. "When the war is over, I'm certain more details will be revealed about what happened."

He waited for her to begin to weep, but she merely looked sad and confused.

"I'd mourned and had accepted Victor's death on the *Lancastria*," she said, almost as if speaking to herself, "and felt myself his widow for all those months. And then when you brought the news he hadn't been on that ship and that he was alive, none of it seemed real to me anymore." She met his glance, her tone almost accusatory. "I had a hard time knowing what to believe, especially since I was never told specifically where he'd been sent after you'd both made it safely to London. Now, you tell me he's *actually* dead. It just seems to me as if death is everywhere. It's normal. It's to be expected. It isn't a shock anymore."

Death is everywhere...

Christopher studied Brooke's expression, seeing in it something he didn't understand. Something that didn't feel even related to the news about Victor.

"Perhaps it will take a while to sink in?" he suggested.

"Oh, the reality of my relationship with Victor sank in long ago." She traced her forefinger around the ring of her cup. "The truth is, I feel sadder for Germaine than I do for myself." She paused and then asked, "Do Monique de Varney and the rest of his family know Victor has been killed?"

"When I received the news from London, I sent one of my

couriers to Château de Varney. They deserved to be told in person, as I've told you."

"That was really kind of you," she murmured.

A pang of guilt skewered him. He'd done it to spare her having that chore and not out of any feeling for Victor's family.

And I wonder if any of them— Brooke included —will ever learn what truly happened to France's most famous movie star...

It had been Christopher's experience that the War Office only wanted to put the best spin on what might have been somebody's gigantic mistake on the battlefront in Algeria... which is why he was suspicious as to how few details had been given him in the dispatch from London this week.

Brooke rose and turned toward the door.

"I'm not very hungry," she announced softly. "I'm suddenly very tired again. If you don't mind, I think I'll go back to bed."

"Are you sure you're all right?" Christopher asked, shoving back the kitchen chair.

Brooke paused, as if carefully considering his question.

"Nobody's 'all right' these days, but I guess I'm grateful not to be behind barbed wire any longer." She offered him a small, sad smile. "And I'm glad to be with a friend I can trust."

Christopher fished in his pocket and pulled out the letter Victor had given him in what seemed a lifetime ago.

"Your husband entrusted me to give this to you only if it was confirmed he'd been killed."

Brooke's expression told him this news did truly shock her. She retraced her steps to the kitchen table and held out her hand. Christopher felt an odd sense of relief when the letter left his keeping.

"So, Victor gave you this that time when you were together in London?"

Christopher nodded, pushing away the memory of that miserable night.

"And you had it with you all this time?"

"I didn't give it to you before because I knew he had not gone down with the *Lancastria*. He'd instructed me to hand it to you only in case of his confirmed death, and that's what I'm doing."

Without further comment she disappeared down the hall, the crumpled envelope in hand.

Christopher stared at the empty threshold, her words echoing in his ears.

I'm glad to be with a friend I can trust.

But Christopher knew that she couldn't truly rely on him to tell her the complete circumstances surrounding Victor's death. Thanks to the Secrets Act, that would most likely continue to be an impossibility.

CHRISTOPHER PLACED the last coffee cup on the drainboard to dry when he heard Brooke's rapid footsteps in the hallway returning to the kitchen. He had barely turned from the sink when she appeared at the doorway waving Victor's letter in front of her like a dirty dishrag.

"Did Victor *show* this to you?" she demanded.

"Absolutely not," he assured her. "He wrote it, sealed it, and left it for me in the hotel room we shared in London."

"Well, let me be the first to say I don't believe one damn word he wrote in this letter! It's all a lie!" She gestured toward the hallway. "Come with me to the library. I need a drink!"

"Brooke!" he protested. "It's barely nine o'clock in the morning!"

She didn't respond, so he followed in her wake, listening as they walked down the hallway while she read a portion of the letter in the voice of an actor performing in a melodrama.

"'You are the *only* woman I ever loved or ever *will* love!'"

By this time, Christopher and she had crossed the foyer and entered the library. Brooke turned, nearly bumping into him, waving the letter in his face. "What a load of absolute crap!"

Storming toward the fireplace, she pointed. "Here's the very place Victor threw the letters from Olivia Eriksen, his costar in Norway that I told you about. He deliberately destroyed the pile he'd previously locked in that drawer," she raged, gesturing toward the desk, "tossing them right onto the flames so I couldn't read about their affair while they were making the movie!"

Christopher could only nod, remembering she'd told him about letters from the Norwegian actress that she'd found so soon after their marriage. He recalled how depressed it had made him when an inebriated Victor had recited with relish the details of his liaison with Eriksen, along with his many other female conquests on and off his movie sets.

"He lied then, and no doubt he lied about other women I never even knew about!" she cried. "And I'm supposed to mourn the great French war hero? He was only an *actor!*" she declared with a loathing so fierce, Christopher was shocked to realize how much anger she must have been suppressing— until now. "And don't start telling me that boys will be boys and that he loved me to the degree he was capable, blah, blah, blah!"

Christopher answered in a tone nearly as sharp as hers, "*Boys* behave like Victor. Men aren't supposed to."

"Well, let me enlighten you, this letter was just another one of Victor de Varney's grand gestures, like his getting down on one knee to propose to me within days of leaving Olivia Eriksen's bed in Norway. Or like volunteering for the army, despite having asthma, just so he could wear a captain's insignia on his posh uniform. Meanwhile, he left *me*, his bride who didn't speak French and had left her own country to be with him!"

At her last outburst, he was shocked to see that tears had begun to stream down her cheeks. She put ten fingers on Victor's letter of farewell and ripped it two, then four, then eight pieces.

"Maybe this sounds harsh," Christopher said quietly, "but, after all, it was your decision to follow Victor to Europe and leave America after knowing him only a few weeks. That might not have been enough time to really know a person."

Christopher could see his observation had found its mark.

"Trust me," she retorted, and he could hear the defensiveness in her tone, "consummate performer that he was, he put on a very convincing *act* that he'd finally found the woman he wanted to spend his life with!" She paused a moment and then added in a quieter tone, "And I was more than willing to overlook certain behaviors and believe his every word." Waving the letter fragments in both hands, she exclaimed, "And, guess what? Whatever caused the disaster starring Victor and me, these flowery words in this damn thing mean *nothing* to me now. He was a flatterer and a cheat. I doubt our marriage would have lasted a month after the war— even if we'd both managed to survive!"

With savage force, she tossed the pieces of Victor's handwritten missive onto the fireplace's cold grate. Her hands were trembling as she grabbed a wooden match out of a box nearby and struck it. She crouched before the hearth and with unsteady fingers, set a corner of the paper on fire. Christopher and she watched in silence as the pieces quickly ignited, curled, and turned to ash.

Brooke slowly rose to her feet and crossed the room. Christopher could only stare as she crumpled onto the library chaise amidst the scattered blankets and began to weep with gut-wrenching cries that brought tears to his own eyes.

Betrayal in love was like cancer, he thought. It ate through the heart as well as pierced the soul. He strode to her side, sank onto the chaise beside her, and carefully took her into his arms. He didn't speak but rocked her gently back and forth. He felt her sobs ricocheting through her body, penetrating his own, as if feelings she'd tamped down for a very long time were erupting from a bottomless pit.

When, finally, her crying subsided and she began to relax against him, he eased the two of them down beside each other, pulling up the blanket and putting a pillow beneath both their heads.

"Shh," he crooned. "Let's sleep awhile. Shh, now... Just rest... just rest."

"Don't go," she whimpered in a tone he'd never before heard her utter.

"I'm not going anywhere," he whispered, but a voice echoed in his head, *at least not right now...*

He carefully urged her to turn onto her side as he did the same so her body cradled against his from head to toe. Her back felt so thin and vulnerable against his chest, but her hair's fresh, clean scent was as he'd always imagined it might be.

He felt his own exhaustion from the last hours settle over him and before he knew it, they were both fast asleep as the day approached noon.

SOME TWO HOURS LATER, Christopher awoke alone on the chaise. As he walked toward the kitchen, he heard water running in the bath down the hall. There was no coffee left, so he added tap water to the powdered eggs from the Red Cross package and hoped for the best as something they could consider their late lunch. Neither he nor Brooke had eaten a real dinner the previous night and his stomach was grumbling.

He left half the scrambled concoction he made in the pan and sat down at the table with the other half on a plate, along with a piece of bread he'd toasted on the stove.

At the sound of Brooke's footsteps, he turned with a smile which soon faded when she barely acknowledged his presence.

"Good morning, or rather good afternoon," he greeted her.

"Is it?" she mumbled, scraping the eggs from the pan onto a plate and sitting at the table opposite him.

He wondered if her moodiness was actually embarrassment for her emotional outbursts earlier.

Brooke's fork toyed with eggs the color of dirty chalk.

Finally, she said, "I woke up thinking of all the things you knew and *I* didn't. But what does it matter in the end? Jules is dead. Victor is dead. Even—" She paused abruptly, not finishing her sentence, and bit her lip. "It almost feels as if even being alive is a betrayal of every soldier and civilian that's died because of this war."

Christopher reached across the table to cover her hand with his. Her depression was almost palpable.

"I realize that a lot happened while you were locked away at Vittel. It must be a blow to hear about the losses all at once."

"And now you'll be off and I'll go back to Barbizon, almost as if nothing happened."

She shook her head as if she realized instantly that's not how things were. Momentous things *had* happened to her, and Christopher guessed that he didn't know the half of it when it came to the events that followed her arrest.

She shrugged. "I suppose our only choice is just to keep going, doing what we can to end this hideous thing."

"Well, I hope you'll concentrate on just growing food for the safehouses for a while," he proposed gently. "You need a good rest. Time to recover from all the stress you've been under. Let Nicole take on escorting any escapees to the Paris collection point for a while."

He was startled when Brooke pounded the table once with her fist.

"She's already risked too much!" she cried, shocking Christopher with her vehemence. "Now that we won't be taking Jules's essays to the printers, it's *my* job to guide downed fliers and anyone else who needs help getting to the escape routes!"

Her amber eyes were shooting sparks at him and her entire manner had shifted from the broken, grieving woman of the previous evening to someone who seemed almost eager to take life-threatening risks. He knew from long experience that the dare-devils in the Resistance always came to a bad end and he couldn't stand for that to happen to Brooke.

He regarded her flushed face. His gut told him something else was at play other than not wanting Nicole to take the risks Brooke just said she was willing to assume all by herself.

"Brooke," he began, attempting to keep his tone calm, "I take my orders from MI9's Chief of the Escape and Evade division in London. In turn, I'm asking you to follow *my*... let's call them 'requests' that I'm making as MI9's deputy for central France. At least let Nicole shoulder some of the burden. She's proved herself, just as you have."

"Perhaps you prefer her work to mine," Brooke replied, looking away.

"I'm grateful to you both," he replied cautiously, "but when you return to Barbizon, promise me you'll lean on Nicole and Felix and Luc to get our packages to Paris as safely as possible."

Brooke merely nodded half-hearted assent. Christopher rose

from the kitchen table and reluctantly announced, "I must be on my way. Soon."

"Fine," she replied, meaning things were definitely not fine between them.

He grabbed his chair and sat down again at the table.

"For God's sake, Brooke! What's eating you? You were offended that I slept with you on the chaise? You now regret all the things you said about Victor? You're sorry you burned his farewell letter? *What* aren't you telling me?"

Refusing to answer, Brooke merely fiddled with her uneaten eggs.

Exasperated, he demanded, "Don't you realize that you deserved far better than a man like Victor de Varney?"

"The *late* Victor de Varney! Maybe he was braver than either you or I, have you thought of that?"

"Or maybe he wasn't so brave, just foolish," Christopher shot back. "Who knows what really happened? But yes, he's dead. And you're alive, but something else is happening here and you're not being straight with me about whatever it is."

"And just how 'straight' have you been with me since this war started, O Man of Mystery?" she retorted.

Christopher snapped his lips shut and rose again from his chair.

"I've got to go. Please take care of yourself," he pleaded. "Are you strong enough to take a train today to Fontainebleau? We shouldn't hang about in this flat any longer than we already have." He hesitated and then added, "And please follow my orders, lay low for a time and just grow vegetables."

"I'll grow the damn carrots and potatoes and feed the rabbits," she retorted, "but I'm paying for the villa and *I'll* be the one who rescues any unexpected visitors dropping out of the sky who arrive at my door and takes them to Paris! Luc will let Felix's brother, Gaspard, the trainman in Fontainebleau, know if the Comet Line should expect any new packages coming up from Rabbit Run, and that's the end of it!"

Christopher felt his own temper fraying.

"Well, I'll be sure to let you know if the Comet Line can even still operate," he replied, wondering at her strident tone.

Stone-faced, she stared at her plate. For people like Brooke and him, both on the Gestapo's wanted list, Paris was the worst possible place to be. He absolutely had to leave but he longed for them at least to part on good terms. Rising from the kitchen table to stand next to her, he rested his hand lightly on her shoulder.

"I'm glad you'll coordinate with Felix's brother," he said quietly by way of a peace offering. "And if you ever need to reach me, just know that Luc or Felix or his brother will find a way to get in touch with me... wherever I am."

Her eyes still averted, Brooke gave a brief nod to confirm she'd taken in what he said.

He seized hold of the handle of his leather suitcase with the all-important radio sequestered beneath its false bottom. Scores of tasks rose up in his mind like a memo pad devoid of checkmarks.

"*A bientôt*," he offered.

"Until we meet again?" she translated, leaving it a question between them. "One hopes, I suppose."

He wondered suddenly if Brooke's time at Vittel had been even worse than the nightmare she'd described. And she was right about his not being utterly candid about certain things. Hadn't he often needed to withhold information from her? Maybe there were crucial things she wasn't telling him? Could *that* account for her strange, about-face behavior after the previous night?

"I love you, Brooke," he said, surprising himself with this spoken admission. "Try to take care of yourself."

He didn't wait for an answer and let himself out through the foyer's front door without looking back.

29

Following the bleak winter, Brooke made a determined effort to ignore what Christopher had declared so abruptly at the very moment he was departing her flat— that he loved her. He wouldn't have said that if he truly *knew* her, would he? If he learned she'd never told him she'd been married *twice,* or that she'd borne a son whom she'd left in the care of her alcoholic mother. Of all people, Christopher would be sickened by her impulsive choices then, just as he'd remarked on her precipitous decision to come to Europe with Victor after knowing him such a short time.

She believed he'd meant the feelings he'd blurted out that last day together, but Brooke concluded the best thing for her sanity and the misery of worrying about his welfare as she had Victor's in the war's early days was to consign Christopher's wellbeing and whereabouts to the back of her mind.

In the months that followed their last parting, she had forced herself to make a conscious decision simply to settle back into her former routine in Barbizon. Despite this, she felt a growing uneasiness invading her life as one month succeeded another without any direct communication from MI9's deputy of northern France's escape-and-evade lines. He was either deliberately avoiding contact, or he'd returned to England to work for British Intelligence in London— or he'd been arrested.

But surely, Felix or Luc would have heard...

By June, she had begun to face the deadening sense of guilt for having hid her secrets from both her late husband and Christopher. As she weeded her vegetables or climbed on a train to transport a jittery downed airmen to Paris, a constant thought went around and around in her head.

Christopher is so scrupulously honest... but I'm not. If he knew my whole story—

Maybe it was better that she not have to face him. After all, if she were ever arrested by the Nazis and killed, the problem of confessing all to Christopher would be moot.

But then the other worry that kept her up at night began to haunt her relentlessly. Perhaps Christopher's silence was due to his being locked away somewhere in a Gestapo dungeon, or worse, even.... what if he'd been transported to internment in Germany? Or killed?

During the long spring and the advent of summer during this fourth year of the war, Nicole had been Brooke's rock. The younger woman made a concerted effort to cope with— and enhance where she could —life at the Villa du Lapin d'Or. The local shops had little to sell. Firewood was scarce, not to mention there were those among her fellow villagers who would sell their grandmothers for the fertilizer they needed for their crops or a chicken to roast, or a metal part required to fix a truck or a tractor. Nicole, bless her, always found a way to make the best of all their trying circumstances.

Brooke was gratified, too, that Felix had taken on more responsibility for trapping rabbits and caring for them in their hutch at the back of the property.

As they anticipated, Commandant Schiller had paid the villa a call and appeared distinctly disgruntled when Brooke showed him her letter of release from Dr. Von Weber.

"We are keeping a close watch on any remaining enemy aliens in our region," he harumphed officiously when departing with no invitation from Brooke to share a glass of calvados.

∽

THROUGHOUT JULY AND AUGUST, Allied bombing missions appeared to be stepping up their attacks dramatically, with a shocking number of planes being shot down by either tracer fire from the ground, or from the German *Luftwaffe* making a kill.

In the wake of Jules's mourned absence, Luc, the clean-shaven young man who had first come to her door with downed fliers for her to hide, now traveled back and forth to Paris as part of his Resistance work. Brooke had learned that his leg had been injured in an agricultural accident, a fate that had kept him from conscription. Presumably, Christopher had ordered that he move into Jules's former farmstead since plans were afoot in the coming months, Luc revealed, for "drops" of supplies, weapons, and ammunition onto the farm's nearby wheatfields.

"I've collected five downed fliers since Tuesday and have them in hiding with me," Luc announced one day, charging through the back gate to find Brooke weeding the carrots.

"*Five?*" Brooke gasped. "We'll have to make at least two separate trips to Paris, and how the hell can we disguise so many?"

Before Luc could answer, a thought struck her. Nicole had mentioned she'd stopped at the local schoolyard to watch some teenagers, too young to be sent to work in Germany, play *le football* on the field one afternoon.

"It almost seemed as if life were normal," Nicole told Brooke. "I stood and watched for fifteen minutes and felt almost as if there were no war."

"What if we got them *soccer* uniforms?" Brooke blurted, prompting a look of admiration from Luc. "And dress them as members of a team."

"Soccer? You mean football?" he corrected. He pantomimed holding a ball between the palms of his hands and then doing a drop kick.

"Right!" she said with a laugh. "You call American soccer European football, don't you? Do you think you could find some old uniforms somewhere?"

"I used to play on a local club team with some school chums," Luc replied. "Let me see what I can do."

Brooke clapped her hands, feeling a spark of pleasure that had been absent in her life since the moment she read the first line in her mother's letter declaring Errol had died.

"If we can find some matching uniforms, the men can pose as a group of regional champions, heading south for another tournament," she declared.

"I even have an old trophy one of them could carry," Luc proposed with a laugh.

Brooke sprang to her feet beside the carrot bed.

"You are absolutely brilliant!"

Luc gave a warning shake of his head. "Brilliance will be *you* getting this many men safely to Paris. We just don't have enough time for you to make two trips."

"You will come with me as their coach— in uniform!" she instructed Luc. "And I will be your doting wife."

"They're all Americans," Luc said worriedly. "And... how do you say? 'Wise guys' some of them. The hardest thing will be to keep them from talking and giving themselves away."

THE FOLLOWING DAY, Brooke instructed the group lined up in the potting shed to don the sports gear that Luc had procured from friends he trusted. She guessed that one of the men, tall, with jet black hair and a tanned complexion, was of Latino origin.

"By any chance, do you speak Spanish?" she asked.

"Si, Señora," he said, ogling her with a silly grin.

She pushed the silver loving cup trophy into his hand that Luc had shined to a gleam.

"Well, congratulations! You're the captain of this team."

He grinned and resumed speaking English. "I actually played soccer before I joined the U.S. Army's air force and I *was* the captain of my team in West Texas."

"Good! You're to speak *only* Spanish once we get to the train station," she ordered. Turning to the others she commanded, "And not a word out of any of *you* lot, except to say, '*Si, si!*' If you follow my instructions *exactly*, you have a fighting chance to get out of this country where every single German wants you dead."

ON THIS UNUSUAL TRIP, Felix passed the word to Brooke that she was to take the faux sports team to Gare Austerlitz.

"The route starting at the Montparnasse station has recently had a number of helpers apprehended by the Nazis," Felix reported that his brother, Gaspard, had told him.

"Anyone we know been arrested?" she asked, holding her breath until she heard the answer.

"Don't know, but the change was captain's orders," Felix disclosed. Nodding toward the men in their sports uniforms, he added, "Our group of five is being sent via Orléans where they'll change trains for Tours and on to Bordeaux to points south and the Spanish border."

Brooke shrugged, figuring one Paris train station posed as many dangers of being stopped by German guards as another. Even so, it gave her pause to hear that some of Christopher's helpers had been arrested. Was that double-agent Harold Cole involved, she wondered.

And what about Christopher himself? The entire summer had passed without him making an appearance in either Barbizon or Paris, even though Brooke guessed he must be aware of her many assignments, including her current one.

Pushing such thoughts to one side, she urged, "Come along, boys, stay together, and don't talk!"

The five aviators in their team uniforms, along with Luc in his, set off to walk to Fontainebleau. Once in Paris, the group emerged from the metro without being accosted by any official and trod the short distance to Gare Austerlitz, entering through a side door.

Brooke's spirits rose a notch when they were met by a woman named Virginia and her French husband, Philippe, who miraculously had gotten the word to dress as a team coach, traveling with his wife. Brooke loved that Virginia was a fellow American like her, fighting in the Resistance for her adopted country. Brooke, Philippe, and Luc walked with the group to the platform where the night train to Orléans was about to depart.

Out of the corner of her eye, Brooke caught sight of the person she most dreaded ever seeing again.

Harold Cole.

That little weasel! she fumed. *I can only guess what he's up to!*

Next to the thin Brit with the narrow mustache stood a strapping, blond, uniformed Nazi guarding the checkpoint where the majority of the crowds exited the station. She watched as Cole leaned to whisper something in the German soldier's ear, who then nodded and turned to another guard who reached out and grabbed the arm of a woman carrying a battered suitcase.

In seconds, the unlucky soul was hustled through the doors toward a black car that Brooke could just glimpse waiting at the curb outside the station.

Holy Jesus! Brooke thought, shocked she had witnessed Cole's treachery in plain sight. *I might easily have chosen that door to exit. That poor woman could have been me.*

The damn turncoat was clearly assisting the Nazis to identify escape helpers that the collaborator must have known when he pretended to be part of the Comet Line in the early days of the war!

She could only imagine how Cole would use the money the Nazis paid him to buy more booze, sex with women, and those stupid silk cravats she'd seen around his neck when he and Gillian Wingate-Jones appeared at her door.

To Brooke's compatriots standing at the entrance of the train platform she announced as calmly as she could, "I'm afraid we must bid you all farewell. Come, Luc. We must be off." She took hold of Virginia's hand. "Good luck and safe journey," she murmured, feeling certain this latest 'partner in crime' would become a friend if they saw each other again.

Warmly squeezing her hand in return, Virginia turned and handed each flier a ticket as they filed onto the train. Brooke suppressed a smile at the sight of the faux squad clad in their borrowed team uniforms, a few carrying sports equipment. A gendarme looked over at the gathering with mild curiosity but let them pass without stopping them.

With an enormous sigh of relief, Brooke watched with Luc by

her side as the locomotive gave a shriek and began to chug down the track.

"Listen, coach," she said, hoping she sounded relaxed, "I want you to leave by the exit over there."

She gestured to where Cole and the Nazi continued surveying the crowd as they left the station. Luc, in his team togs, would likely have the best chance of leaving the area without incident and hopefully distract Cole from spotting *her*.

Relieved she had on her dark wig and a felt hat with a wide brim, Brooke announced, "I'll go out the way we came in. Take the first train back to Fontainebleau and don't worry if you don't see me. Just head for the farmstead and I'll go back to the villa on my own. It's better that we travel separately, now." With a glance at Luc's uniform, she paused and then added with a forced smile, "Your story, if they stop you, is that you just saw your club team off to a regional match in Orléans."

Luc gave her a brief nod and headed off in the direction of Cole and his Nazi confederate. Holding her breath, she watched as Christopher's deputy passed through the checkpoint without either man giving him a glance.

Brooke forced herself to walk at a normal pace in the opposite direction. Her heart pounding as she finally made her way through the exit, she then headed, unimpeded, to the nearest metro station and boarded a train that would take her close to Rue Saint-Dominique. She was fairly certain that if she could just avoid ever running into Harold Cole again, the letter in her handbag, signed by Dr. Von Weber and guaranteeing her safe conduct to "X-ray treatments in Paris," should allow her to spend a night without harassment in her old flat. Sinking onto a seat on the metro, a bone-deep exhaustion pulled her head back against the car's filthy window.

After a day like today I deserve a nice, hot bath.

30

AUGUST 1943

Soon after finishing a supper of Nicole's "classic rabbit stew," and despite the heat of an August evening, Brooke retrieved a pair of sinister-looking restraint garments from their hiding place in a bin in the pantry. Holding them aloft, she commented to Nicole, "I think the two airmen out there in our potting shed deserve the old 'strait jacket treatment,' don't you?"

"At least that disagreeable American pilot certainly does," replied the usually placid Nicole, giving an emphatic nod. "On the other hand, the gunner is just a boy."

"I, for one, can't wait until they're off our hands. That pilot's arrogance is one for the books."

Brooke would never forget the moment the pilot's tail gunner, a kid from Pasadena, California of all places, recognized her as the ill-fated blonde heroine from her Charlie Chan films. The gunner wasn't a bad sort, but he and his misogynistic American pilot were a package deal, so into the restraints they both must go if the fliers had any chance of getting past the increasingly stringent Nazi checkpoints.

As far as Brooke was concerned, the last few missions to Paris had been beyond harrowing, with many close calls for her and the men in her charge. She hadn't seen Harold Cole lately, but even so, escape agents like Nicole and Brooke were being stopped and arrested with frightening frequency. Sometimes the helpers were caught with the escapees, but just as often they were arrested the moment they attempted to leave the train station.

"I am certain that Brit turncoat is the reason so many escape lines have been blown lately," Brooke fumed, "and *still* no one from MI9 has ordered Harold Cole eliminated!"

While Nicole did the dishes from their meal, along with the plates they'd supplied to the airmen hidden in the potting shed, Brooke donned her bogus nurse's uniform. She walked through the kitchen again and out to the back garden, handing the straitjackets to Captain Gallagher and his gunner.

"You expect me to wear this?" the American pilot blurted, anger flushing his Irish-American cheeks bright red. "I won't be able to move my arms an inch in this contraption. We'll be sitting ducks if this hare-brained scheme of yours goes wrong."

"You're sitting ducks as it is," she snapped, completely out of patience with this conceited Yank officer. "Both of you, put these on," she ordered, "and be quick about it. I'll strap you in. We've got to get going. It's getting late!"

To her relief, the three of them sailed past all the guarded checkpoints at the station at Fontainebleau and on the Paris metro with only curious, rather alarmed glances from both civilians and uniformed German military personnel alike.

Once at Gare Austerlitz, and safely past the startled sentries at the entrance, Brooke surreptitiously flicked open the buckles and ordered the fliers to go inside the nearby restroom to jettison the restraints. As directed, they swiftly exchanged the straitjackets for train workers' uniforms, once again donated by Felix's brother Gaspard at the Fontainebleau station. Also as instructed by Brooke, they stowed the despised restraints inside the woven canvas duffel bag she'd handed them that had contained the trainmen attire.

Without further conversation, Brooke handed over her bad-tempered charges to the appointed person standing near the waiting room kiosk with a German-published French newspaper under his arm. Now dressed in the uniforms of trainmen, the plan for the airmen was to board the mail car like any other shift workers, thanks to a partisan being on duty that night.

"Good riddance!" she mumbled under her breath when the

Comet Line escort she'd never worked with before ushered "Prick and Pasadena"— as Brooke had silently dubbed them —onto the train headed for the Spanish border beyond Biarritz.

Her satchel containing the two canvas jackets weighing heavily on her arm, Brooke sauntered toward the nearest exit. She looked forward to making her way to Gare de Lyon and catching the last train back to Barbizon.

"You!" called out a strapping young guard in guttural French. Brooke had nearly reached the brass-framed door leading to the street.

She turned slightly to see who was being singled out.

"Yes, *you!*" he barked, pointing directly at her. "Come over here."

Her heart racing, Brooke turned around, relieved to see there was no sign of Harold Cole anywhere.

"Open your bag," the Nazi guard ordered.

Brooke complied, setting the satchel on the ground while she scrambled to come up with a convincing cover story as to why she had two straitjackets in her possession.

"What are these?" he demanded, lifting one of the canvas arms with its dangling metal belt buckle.

"Restraints for patients suffering mental infirmities," she answered politely.

"And why do you have them?"

"I was escorting two men onto the train that just left the station under guard for Orléans." She leaned toward his ear, noting with distaste the thicket of blond fuzz growing inside. "There's an insane asylum there, you know."

The guard observed her closely.

"So, you are a nurse, I see," he said, giving her figure the once over. "You work here in Paris?"

She gave a brief nod.

"You have a flat here, yah?"

Oh, no you don't, buster! No roll-in-the-hay under my *roof!*

"No, sir. I have a room at a small hospital for the mentally disturbed." She glanced at others passing her by and exiting through the door. "Please, sir, may I go? It's been a long day and I'm expected back at the hospital."

Ignoring her plea, the uniformed guard smiled suddenly and said, "That must be difficult work. Surely you're in need of a little schnapps, yah?" She remained silent. He said, "I'm just going off duty. Let us go somewhere I can buy you a drink."

Her mind whirling, she quickly replied, "I'm afraid I must report back to my supervisor to... uh... let him know the patients were transferred safely. P-Perhaps I could meet you somewhere a little later?"

Fat chance of that, buddy! she told him silently.

She'd dealt with these situations many times in Hollywood.

The guard gazed at her for a long moment. "Let me escort you there to report in and then we can find a café."

Unable to think of an answer, Brooke felt her stomach clench as the young Nazi said something briefly in German to another guard nearby and seized her by the arm. As soon as they were out of the station and a few yards down the walkway, the soldier increased his iron grip on her elbow. When they reached the corner of the train station, without warning, he pushed her into an alley and pinned her roughly against the wall of the adjacent building.

"What are you *doing*?" she cried in English and realized she was in more danger than she'd ever been in her life.

"You are British woman? A pretty American?" he growled, reaching down to take hold of the hem of her nurse's uniform. He swiftly pushed the fabric up to her waist and seize the waistband of her underwear with his other hand, yanking it to her below her knees. Pressing her hard against the brick wall, he fumbled to release his rampant erection that Brooke could feel pressing against her midsection and his revolver, a presence on his thigh.

All during their struggle, she had managed to keep a grip on the satchel crammed with the pair of straitjackets. With all her might, she swung the heavy canvas luggage toward the side of the Nazi's knees, the weight causing his legs to buckle. Instantly, he loosened his grip on her body. The space between them was just enough to allow her to flatten her free hand against his chest and shove him a few inches away from her torso, making room for her to raise her right knee in a ferocious move. She aimed squarely for her attacker's groin. It was a sequence of defense moves she'd learned when she filmed a scene in one of her "women-in-jeopardy" films she hated so much.

She was rewarded with an "Ow-oo-oo!" when her kneecap connected squarely with the oaf's testicles.

The Nazi's subsequent high-pitched screams pierced her ears. He pitched to the ground, curled in a ball writhing in pain. For good measure, she swiftly gave him a stomp in the small of his back with the heel of her brogue and turned to run. She was suddenly aware of footsteps rounding the corner of the train station heading into the alley.

Oh, God. More guards must be coming!

Dropping the heavy satchel from her aching right arm, she yanked up her underwear and took off running, continuing down the alley and into the next street, racing for the nearest metro station and charging down the stairs.

Four stops and a half-hour later, she was still trembling when she hopped off the car she'd boarded in her deadly haste. She caught a train heading in the opposite direction and doubled back, finally exiting half an hour later at the station nearest Number 17 Rue Saint-Dominique. It was after curfew, but once again, her residential street was deserted. She waited in the shadows several long minutes until she was certain the coast was clear.

Her heart finally slowing to its normal rhythm, she dashed toward her building's front door, grateful she always carried her house keys whenever she came to Paris in case of just such an emergency.

Removing her thick-heeled shoes, she darted silently through the lobby and up the winding stairs in her stocking feet, once again bypassing the clanking elevator. Fumbling for the key to her flat, she was startled to hear the lock click on the other side.

She sucked in a breath as the door swung open. All she could see in the dim light was the gray nose of a pistol aimed directly at her chest.

"You must learn not to be so predictable," said a voice tinged with amusement, as the gun lowered.

"Good God, Christopher!" Brooke cried hoarsely. "You just took twenty years off my life!"

"I do apologize," was his reply, "but I've been waiting for you."

"What the hell are *you* doing here?" she demanded. "I thought you said we shouldn't use this flat as a safehouse anymore."

"Well, since *you* have, several times after I gave that order, I figured it was a good bet you'd end up here."

She regarded him for a long moment and then shook her head.

"So you were at Austerlitz," she said. "Spying on me?"

Ignoring her accusation he replied, "I arrived here ten minutes before you did. Won't you come in?" he asked with a wry twitch of his lips.

As soon as she'd stepped over the threshold and closed the door, he roughly pulled her against his chest. Brooke could feel him planting kisses on the top of her head, a shock, considering how they'd parted the last time they were together.

"You have no idea how relieved I am I guessed correctly that you'd come here after that goon—"

"So you *were* following me?" she mumbled into his shirt.

She felt him shrug, his arms still tight around her.

"Our agents are getting picked off practically every mission. I'm trying to get proof who's orchestrating it all— and how. I knew you were due to forward a package tonight. Call it serious research."

"So nothing special about your being there tonight, right?" she said, skeptically. "Just routine surveillance?"

"No," he corrected her. "My original intention tonight was to make up for leaving your kitchen so abruptly last time."

She looked up at him, amazed. "Really?"

"Really."

"You were put out with me that day," she said.

"You were irritated with me as well because I said you weren't being straight with me about whatever was bothering you," he replied.

Brooke didn't answer.

Christopher waited, then said, "But tonight, before I could get your attention at the station, that damn Kraut strong-armed you out the door and down the street."

Brooke leaned back in his arms.

"So it was *your* footsteps I heard running into the alleyway! Were you worried I couldn't take care of that rotten Nazi?"

"I'd be worried about any woman being corralled by a soldier twice her size with rape in mind," he retorted. "I came to the station tonight *especially* because I knew you were doing a handoff. I wanted to see you, but before we could connect—"

"Then, you saw what happened in the alley?"

"Yes, I saw," he said, his eyes flashing. "And I made damn sure that Nazi won't be assaulting any more women in this war."

Brooke stepped away from his arms entirely, absorbing the fact that Christopher Laurent, well-mannered former journalist, had apparently used the very gun on her assailant that he'd pointed at her minutes before when he opened the front door.

"You shot him in the alley?"

"Too noisy. I delivered the butt end of my weapon on the side of his head, just like they taught me to at Silent Killing School," he admitted, though he didn't look very happy about it.

"Well, thank you for making sure he couldn't chase me down that alley once I kneed his family jewels."

"Neither could I. Chase you, I mean. I tried to catch up with you but I tripped over that satchel you had been carrying." He turned and pointed to it sitting on the floor near the front door. "My sprawling, face down in the alley, gave you just enough time to get away from both of us. Fortunately for you, your assailant was still groggy from your stomping on his nuts before I made him terminally so."

"And then you guessed accurately I'd come here?" she said, amazed.

"Where else would you go? The last train to Fontainebleau would have left by the time you got back to Gare de Lyon and there was no other way to return to Barbizon at this hour." He seized both her hands. "Jesus, Marie, and Joseph, Brooke! You were amazing, but you also took years off *my* life when you fought that lout."

"I was taught to defend myself at a Hollywood karate school," she revealed. "And I guess we could say we're even because I've been worried about your safety for months, now."

Brushing her comment aside he asked, "Did you see Harold Cole?"

"Not tonight. Don't tell me that he *was* there at Austerlitz again?" she asked, shocked. How could she have missed spotting him?

"The swine was standing at one of the side doors, pointing out certain people passing through."

A shudder passed through her body. There were so many times when she could easily have chosen the exit where Cole was and would have been arrested for sure.

"Isn't it obvious to your London bosses by now that Cole's working for the enemy?" she seethed.

"It *is* to those of us on the ground who've seen how he picks out resisters he knows from the time when he claimed to be one of us."

"But how could your MI9 allow this to continue so long?" she demanded angrily.

Christopher offered a resigned shrug.

"I'll report about Cole again on my next radio transmission, but I've become convinced he's MI6's man and they're using him as a triple agent, despite how many of us working for MI9 get arrested or killed."

"Please tell me that *your* boss or Churchill would never sanction such a thing as employing a triple agent who causes the capture of so many on our side?"

"No, of course not, but the number two man at MI6 operates unto himself," Christopher replied. "One theory is that a triple agent reports back enough good stuff to his handlers to make the losses on our side appear worth it to the overall effort in terms of the enemy intelligence gained. Having a guy like Cole on the 'inside' might give them advanced warnings about what Hitler and his flunkies are planning next."

"In other words," Brooke said, devastated that someone in British Intelligence might be the cause of so much misery and death, "I suppose this MI6 fellow figures the tradeoff of scores of volunteer civilian *résistants* being tortured and killed is nothing compared to the thrill he gets moving around the toy soldiers and ships on that big map in the War Room."

"Scores now *have* been arrested. Too bad you're not in that room giving them a piece of your mind," Christopher replied with a weary smile.

"Well if what you are saying is true, how do you feel about this war, *now*?"

She was exhausted and fed up and she wondered if Christopher might be feeling the same.

"Like you, I want it all to be over," he replied, confirming her sentiments. "And, without leaking any State Secrets, I think it will be fairly soon, so I'm hanging on— barely."

"I've heard *that* before," she murmured. "I mean, that an invasion is coming soon."

"It has to be," he said, and she could see his deep fatigue etching new lines at the corners of his eyes.

She released an audible sigh. "I don't know how much more either of us can take of this crap. In case you aren't aware, some of those fliers whose lives we save are arrogant jerks, you know?"

He gave a slight nod. "Yes, I know. I figured these last two guys must have really gotten on your nerves since you put them in those straitjackets that you only trot out for special cases."

Brooke laughed in spite of how rattled her nerves still were. She drank in the sight of him, hardly able to believe that after so many months since they'd last seen each other, Christopher was actually standing a foot away from her.

"Sometimes I wonder what you and I are doing all this for?" she asked. "Risking everything, when there are tricksters higher up on the food chain whose actions and motivations we know nothing about and can't begin to understand. Yet, they're willing to see us killed, even though we're supposedly all on the same side."

"Haven't you caught on to them yet?" he chided. "Let's just call them self-seekers and profiteers. It's certainly not true of everyone in London but for them, the war is just the game of being cleverer than their competitors fighting for power, money, and prestige in the War Office."

"So *why* are we doing this?" she repeated.

"Because for us, this war isn't about them or the games they play. The war is about just wanting to live our lives in peace and freedom and wanting that for our neighbors."

"You make it sound so simple," Brooke sighed.

"It is, pretty much, if you're clear on what you believe. What you care about and are willing to fight for. And if you care, at least a little bit, about the welfare of others as well as yourself."

"Well, there's one thing I know," she said, amazed that the heavy burden of guilt about her son's death she'd been carrying these long months was diminished somewhat by the sheer joy of seeing Christopher again. "I care about *you*, Christopher. Even if you've been avoiding me for months."

Christopher put his arms around her once again.

"Last time I saw you, you were pretty tough on yourself as well as on *me*, don't you think? I left feeling accused of something I didn't understand very well."

She took a deep breath, troubled yet again by guilt for the part she'd played in Errol's death. She felt compelled to look away from him, her untold tale once again an instant barrier between them. She stiffened slightly when he leaned toward her and ran the back of two fingers down one side of her face. The gesture was so tender and his expression so loving, she felt tears welling in her eyes.

"Come here, will you?" he asked softly.

Brooke felt a knot in her stomach loosen slightly. She gazed at him for a long moment, and then, took a step nearer allowing him to envelop her in his arms a second time in as many minutes. "We two are such asses," he breathed into her ear. "Why have we wasted —" His sentence trailed off, and he pulled her even closer. "All I could think of when I rounded that alley and saw the bastard lifting the hem of your skirt," he said, his voice raw, "was that I'd gotten you in this mess when I swore I'd do my best to keep you safe."

"I *am* safe, thanks to both of us," she whispered back.

He kissed her again, this time long and hard before releasing her.

"You are one brave woman, you know that?" he declared. "A superior member of your species." He grinned at her. "In point of fact, I've never met a woman like you before: brainy *and* beautiful... courageous but *generally* not reckless," he chided gently. "You're a person that— when she doesn't know something —she's willing to learn."

His next kiss took time to explore her mouth with his lips and tongue while he cupped one breast in his hand. She felt him smile against her lips.

Lifting his head he said, "Given that goon tried to attack you tonight, this may not be the best moment to mention that you are one hell of a sexy lady."

She looked up at him, wanting him to kiss her again, but he stood back, staring at her, his dark, blue eyes reflecting a vulnerability she'd never seen before.

"I love you, dammit!" he said in a rush. "I should have merely knocked the Nazi bastard out, but when I saw him with his hands on you, knew he meant to rape you and likely kill you when he was done—" He shook his head. "I lost complete control. I'm pretty sure I left him for dead and that feels... personal... and not quite honorable."

"This is war!" Brooke exclaimed. "I would have done the same if it had been you!"

In that moment, she realized how much she loved this man in a way she'd never loved another human being in her entire life. Christopher seized her by the shoulders as if convincing them both they should stop pretending they weren't totally insane about each other.

"We're so alike," he said. "It absolutely kills me when I leave you each time, not knowing if either of us will survive until it's over..."

His sentence trailed off, but his eyes continued to bore into hers as he pulled her close again. A wave of naked desire invaded her own exhausted body.

"Well, even dead tired as we both are," she whispered, "let's keep kissing and see where that takes us."

She seized him by one hand, turned, and led him down the shadowed hallway into the master bedroom. Christopher halted mid-step, gazing up at the gilded wooden crown affixed high on the wall above the bed, yards of silk cascading on either side.

"Good God... you slept under that?" he exclaimed.

"You never came in here before when you hid out in the flat?" she asked skeptically.

"Not on your life," he retorted. "When I stayed here before, I wouldn't come near this room. It made me sick to my stomach every time I thought of you with—"

She grabbed his hand again, halting at the foot of the bed.

Pointing to the silk duvet and lace-trimmed pillows, she declared, "Trust me, with you in this place, the ghosts in this room are suddenly banished." She leaned forward, cupping his face in her hands. In this horrible time of treachery and death, she felt in her gut and her heart that this was the moment to let him love her and she him. It was time to put all else aside.

"It's going to be only you and me in this big, comfortable bed, Christopher, my love."

"At last," he whispered. "At long, long last."

31

When Christopher awoke the following morning, the bedroom with the carved, gilded wooden crown plastered on the wall above his head struck him as surreal. He was in the bed Victor had shared with his then-new bride, yet Victor was dead and Christopher was here beside her. There was war raging beyond the streets of Paris on this muggy August day, yet Brooke lay naked by his side.

He smiled at the thought of her clad in the tattered overalls she usually wore when wading into her wheatfields to guide a downed airman to safety. What a contrast to this moment, where her head lay against a lace-edged pillow, flaxen hair splayed like a fan above her lovely features, peaceful, for once, relaxed in sleep. Gazing at her beautiful face with its gently arching blonde eyebrows and porcelain complexion, a thousand questions swirled in his head.

Would this conflict ever end? Would either or both of them even survive this war, he wondered as his eyes drifted to the soft lips he had tasted just hours before.

With a glance at the bedside clock, he was jolted into the realization that they both should rise and be on their respective ways. Nicole and Felix would start to worry if Brooke didn't soon return to Barbizon. As for him, he thought, pushing himself upright in bed, he was due at a secret landing field outside Paris. With any luck, a one-engine Lysander would make a two-minute landing and then whisk him across the Channel for a crucial conference with Colonel Crockatt.

It was long past the time to insist to MI9 and the bosses at MI6 that the benefits of a triple agent like Cole— if that's what he was — didn't outweigh the havoc the rotter was causing in the ranks of the brave escape-and-evade volunteers risking their lives every single day. A sickening number of civilians had been arrested, deported and executed. Christopher was more than convinced Harold Cole was playing a central role in all of it and wanted Crockatt to do something about the travesty it was making of everything Brooke, Luc, and their team had tried to achieve.

Christopher's gloomy thoughts were abruptly halted when Brooke opened her eyes and smiled up at him in a way that confirmed she had reveled in their lovemaking as much as he had. Both lay on their sides, facing each other and he could feel a silly grin on his lips.

"Hello, beautiful," he whispered. "I see that you— finally —got some decent rest."

He gently seized a strand of her golden hair and twisted it around his forefinger.

"Hello to you, too, handsome," she whispered, teasing, "new in town?"

Christopher burst out laughing, sliding back under the covers to pull her close, luxuriating in the feel of her slender form against him, head-to-toe. Then he grew serious.

"You realize, don't you, that last night you and I crossed a Rubicon of sorts?"

She nodded, equally solemn. "You mean because we finally made love after fighting the inclination for years?"

"That, yes. And I want to make you a promise... that is, if you've finally forgiven me that time for leaving Radio Mondiale without telling you."

She tapped his nose playfully.

"You mean you swear that in the future, you will never do such a bad thing again and forthwith, behave better than the rest of your inferior species?"

He rested his forefinger beneath her chin.

"Even more than that. If we both somehow make it through this war, I want us to marry."

He wondered what her startled look actually meant but continued to speak.

"If you agree to do me the honor of becoming my wife, you can be certain I will never, *ever* betray you with another woman." He kissed her gently. "Once this war is over, I will tell you the truth on all subjects at every turn. I want you in my life— always."

Brooke's eyes cast him a stricken look. To his alarm, she held up her hand like a German guard at a check point and sat up against the tufted headboard.

"Wait! Please wait," she pleaded, her words laced with emotion. "I have to tell you something. Something I should have told you long ago. Something that might change your mind about marrying me. It might even change your mind about me altogether."

Christopher once again sat up in bed and angled his body so he could face her.

"Nothing you can say will change how I feel about you," he insisted. "I can't believe you don't know that by now!"

"*This* might." He watched her suck in a deep breath as if she were about to jump off a cliff. "I never told you that I gave birth to a son in May of 1937, near the end of a brief but dreadful marriage to a man I ultimately divorced before I'd met Victor," she began as if declaring the first of several unhappy revelations.

Christopher did his best to control his shocked reaction. Not so much that she might have been married before Victor, but that she'd never disclosed that fact, nor that she'd had a child in all the time they'd known each other.

Brooke was gazing past his shoulder, looking into space.

"My son's name was Errol. His father insisted he be named after the movie star, Errol Flynn. He'd worked with him as a stage-hand on a few pictures and figured it was some kind of employment insurance," she said, her tone harsh. "After I divorced Arnie, I'd left Errol, a thirteen-month-old, with my mother when I moved to New York to play on Broadway. Then I met Victor and followed him to Europe." Tears welled in from Brooke's eyes and down her cheeks. She averted her gaze, whispering, "My boy died two winters ago of influenza, just four-and-a-half years old, and—"

A quiet sob halted her mid-sentence.

Christopher sought her eyes. "Oh, darling, I am so sorry. Your baby died? And all this time you never told me?"

"Victor knew I'd been married briefly, but I've never told anyone, including him, that I *had* a son," she confessed. "That I'd left him behind when I moved to New York."

In truth, Christopher was shaken to learn Brooke had borne a child who had died. He was even more stunned that she'd never told Victor about her baby.

Even so, he had a few phases of his own life he wasn't particularly proud of that he hadn't disclosed to her. People whose innocent family members suffered as a result of revelations his reporting had laid bare. Girlfriends he had hurt by neglecting them cruelly to attend to the rigors of his job, and when they protested, ending the relationship. And then there was his father whom he deeply resented for reasons he'd done his best to forget. He could easily name a few other things, if he had the courage she'd just shown dredging it all up.

He reached for her hand and gave it a gentle squeeze.

"We all have things in our past that don't exactly show us in the best light."

"Well, I'm sure nothing as shameful as what I did," she responded, withdrawing her hand and grasping the edge of the silk sheet to swipe at the moisture dampening both her cheeks.

"Sweetheart, you are being so hard on yourself. I could tell how stricken you were to see those poor refugee children when we did the story at Gare Montparnasse. You couldn't help if your child got sick. Kids can—"

Almost shouting, Brooke cried, "Wait! Hear me out! I *abandoned* my child. I met the dashing Victor de Varney and only weeks later, flew with him to Europe on the brink of war."

Christopher had learned details of their brief courtship the night Victor had spent hours talking about his female conquests. But of course, he'd made no mention of a stepson living in California. Brooke shook her head slowly from side to side.

"I left my little boy who barely had learned to walk with my mother, a woman who's a *drunk* and was a terrible parent to *me.*"

As her description of her child's caregiver hung in the air, his own thoughts flew to images of his father coming home soused from assignments after shacking up with various ladies of his acquaintance.

"Darling... look, I—" he began, but she cut him off.

"And you should know that I left Errol because I wanted to be a *star,* like Victor was. *I* wanted to be famous and celebrated, just as Victor was striving to be." She shook a finger at him. "Don't you see? I am here to confess that I am a totally rotten mother and no less vain and shallow than you've judged *him* to be."

The silence crackled between them and was deafening in Christopher's ears. He searched for words to express how much he'd seen her change from the pampered starlet she'd probably been in Hollywood to an able, hardworking reporter, and now Resistance fighter in France. He had *seen* her willingness to work for the things she knew, now, were more important to her than the celebrity life she'd had in America.

Misinterpreting his silence, she declared, "Hearing what I've just told you, who in his right mind would want to marry someone who'd behaved like that toward an innocent *child*?"

She covered her face with her hands and began to cry with such ferocity her shoulders heaved and the strangled sounds brought tears to Christopher's own eyes.

He moved swiftly to gather her in his arms. At first, she struggled against him, but finally, she allowed him to hold her while her body was wracked with an avalanche of sorrow and regret that he guessed had been building for a very long time.

Christopher spoke slowly, willing her to hear his next words.

"We've all— myself included —done things we'll regret for the rest of our lives," he soothed. "But leaving a child in the care of someone who drank isn't anything you'd choose to do now." He used the corner of the bedsheet to dry the moisture on her cheeks. "Darling... I *love* you for the woman you are now and hearing this doesn't change that in any way."

His mind went to his viciously pistol-whipping the Nazi guard

— probably to death —the previous night in a rage because the soldier had accosted the woman Christopher claimed as his own. Then there was the day a few months past when he ambushed a young, nameless German foot soldier. How swiftly and efficiently he'd killed him with a garrote in order to save a Resistance fighter about to be arrested whose cover had been blown, thanks to Harold Cole.

Yes, it was war, but the kid looked so young and bewildered...

Pushing aside the memory, he declared, "You were a different woman than when you first walked into the press office. I've seen you risk your life to save these fliers. I saw how devastated you were to see that dead baby in the mother's arms at Gare Montparnasse. You would never behave like that toward a child of yours now. You care too much about the welfare of others to be a person who would make the decisions you did when you were younger. The war, for all its hideousness, has changed that for us."

He began kissing the top of her head between his reassurances that neither of them were perfect people. "God knows I've not led a saintly life, and neither have our parents for damn sure. But if we both make it through this nightmare, we can choose a new path together."

"I don't know..."

"Brooke, sweetheart! I want us to be reporters together. To chase the stories that matter." He could feel her relaxing against his chest. "I want us to live in a wonderful apartment—"

"Not this one," she interrupted.

"Absolutely not," he agreed with a laugh, glancing up at the gilded wooden crown looming above their heads. "And not my flat in Montmartre, either," he added, recalling the last screaming match he'd had with his journalist father for walking out on Christopher's long-suffering mother. An argument that preceded his father's fatal heart attack by two days.

Brooke cast him a puzzled look, but he sensed she was pulling out of her spiral of self-incrimination. Nuzzling her ear, he whispered, "Maybe we'll buy a wonderful river barge and paint the gunwales turquoise with a black hull below and dock it on the Seine across from the Eiffel Tower!"

"What a lovely idea..." she murmured, brushing the back of her hand against her cheek to wipe away her remaining tears.

"We can host small parties on the back deck. We can cook wonderful meals together in our galley kitchen on board. We can buy a barge big enough to house children of our own someday and—"

Christopher felt Brooke's body instantly stiffen and she drew away from him, her face suddenly ashen.

"Don't say that!" she exclaimed, jumping out of bed and grabbing her silk dressing gown, her fingers fumbling with its flimsy belt. "And if you mean it, you need to know that I don't want to have another child! I don't *deserve* to have another child! Don't you dare think for one second that I have the right to 'replace' a child I never really cared for... a little boy for whom I never felt that maternal rush women are *supposed* to feel."

Christopher remained mute amid Brooke's verbal onslaught, shocked and distressed by both what she was saying and the bitter vehemence in her voice.

"Don't you get it, Christopher? I'm not a natural mother. Can't you see that I'm not? I'm somehow *missing* that maternal gene. I never felt like a cherished child myself, so I don't have a clue what it *is* to cherish my own child. I would never risk foisting *me* on another baby ever again. *Never!*"

She stared at Christopher as she paced back and forth at the end of their rumpled bed. Suddenly, she took a step toward him, her hands on her hips in a stance so familiar to him when she was seriously upset.

"And since I'm laying it all out here, what kind of parent would *you* be if the world ever becomes sane again? Don't you imagine that you'd likely become like your own father, constantly traveling for work, an attractive male figure to the women you'd meet, always preoccupied with the next big interview, the next blockbuster story?"

How did this women intuit my father's exact behavior...?

Christopher watched Brooke become a person he hardly recognized, raging against him, against herself, against the idea that the two of them could forge a happy life together.

Where is the woman who showed such love last night? Such caring and tenderness?

Brooke continued to rail while fingering the silk tie around her waist.

"You *say* you'd want us to work together, but if I had our child, guess who'd be expected to take care of it?" When he didn't answer, she answered for him. "The little woman at home, that's who! The fact that I've always wanted to make something of myself in the working world would all be forgotten. I doubt you and I would be such a 'great team' as we have in the past when our baby got sick. No. *I'd* be the one responsible, and look what a terrible job I've done on *that* score. And anyway, don't you imagine you'd think it *was* my job? A woman's place is... well, you men know where it is, don't you?"

Christopher reared back against the headboard, stunned by her unrelenting assault.

Brooke pointed a finger at him, declaring, "I tried to be an actress and was mediocre, at best. You opened the world of journalism to me and I knew— finally —that I'd found the right path. I could 'perform' if you will, in front of a microphone or pounding a typewriter. I wanted to be as good a journalist as you are." She gave him a challenging look, declaring, "And I don't think I was half bad. I loved the work! It was important. It had meaning. But.... *me*, a mother again— and nothing else?" she cried.

"But it doesn't have to be an either-or," he countered. "With both of us working, we could afford to hire help. Isn't that what nannies are for?"

"I *hired* a nanny!" she shouted. "Errol's real grandmother was the 'nanny,' which showed what kind of judgment *I* have. For God's sake, Christopher, if people want to have kids, *they* should be the primary caretakers and not palm the duties off on someone else." Brooke leaned forward and pounded her fist against the mattress in frustration. "I simply shirked that duty in the name of my *ambition* and so would you!"

Christopher swung his feet to the side of the bed, pulling the sheet over his lap so he wouldn't feel so naked.

"So, you don't think I'm a man destined to be a good father?"

She shrugged her shoulders. "Well, *would* you be? Think about it. What kind of model did *you* have? Victor told me once your father had dropped dead at a fairly young age from overwork!" She took a step closer to where he sat on the side of the bed. "You have been totally consumed by journalism, and I don't blame you for that. But the answer isn't simply 'Hire a nanny!'"

She took a step closer, wagging her forefinger at him.

"One thing I *do* know is the woman that men of my experience seem to want— including you, most likely —is the female who cooks and cleans and cares for his children while he doesn't do much more than kiss the tykes on their little heads at bedtime. Then, he goes off into the wild, exciting world of men and their amazing accomplishments!"

"Don't you think it's a little harsh to apply that to every man alive?"

Part of him, though, was thinking her assessment of his being work-obsessed might be right on the money. Meanwhile, Brooke began pacing in front of the bed once again.

"Perhaps it's harsh to your ears, but I have to be tough on myself, as well, because I swear to you, Christopher Laurent: motherhood with a capital M is just not for me. I've proven that with Errol, and I'll say it again: I wouldn't inflict *me* as a mother on any child and neither should you! And if having children is one of your heart's desires, we'd immediately be at an impasse if I ever got pregnant."

Christopher sensed she was waiting for him to take issue with some of the things she'd said. He had the sense that her overwhelming guilt regarding the death of her son was driving her anger and judgment of herself as a parent, blotting out everything else. Meanwhile, what was revolving in his head were her accusations as to what kind of father he would make.

Any candid assessment would conclude that he was, indeed, a workaholic. Before the war, he had spent every waking hour sniffing out the next government scandal or investigating the latest egregious act of wrongdoing in high places. Had he ever fed a child? Diapered a baby? Stayed up all night with a fevered youngster? Had he any inclination to do so, either? What kind of a father *would* he make, given his own father had not proved such an admirable example?

The searing memory of his artistically-talented mother's inconsolable weeping over learning of his father's infidelities spun through his mind as he searched for the right words to express himself honestly. His mother had been forced to send him to his American grandparents every long summer in order to seek paying work while she was forced to abandon her career as a serious portrait painter. He'd hated her for banishing him to relatives he hardly knew and a language he didn't speak back then. He'd felt that way until he grew older and understood a bit better what it must have been like for her.

Before he could collect his disparate thoughts Brooke cried, "See? You and I *are* alike. We both would want to be chasing the next story, but you'd assume you should be the one to hit the road on assignment. Before long, you and the world around us would relegate me to hearth and home and when I protested or complained, you'd despise me for it. And besides," she said bitterly, "I've already shown I'm the worst possible candidate to play the role of wife and mother."

Silence filled the room. Christopher felt her slings and arrows penetrate his very core and couldn't seem to mount an adequate defense— for perhaps he had none.

With fresh tears flowing from the corners of her luminous amber eyes, Brooke said in a low voice, "I told you that if I leveled with you, it would change the way you feel about me. Truth can be very destructive, don't you see?"

"I agree," he said, quietly reviewing his own shortcomings in the silence that followed. "Some truths are very hard to take."

He slowly shook his head and glanced again at the bedside clock. He rose to stand beside the mattress, unmindful of the bed sheet falling away from his naked body. He reached for his clothes that were strewn in a pile on the floor, abandoned in his haste to make love to this woman who it turned out had found him so wanting.

"So off you go," Brooke said, and he heard fatalism laced with a kind of bone deep sorrow in her voice.

"Yes. I... I have to be somewhere miles from here by sundown today."

He quickly stepped into his underwear and trousers, glancing at her standing at the foot of the bed in her pink dressing gown. A sliver of her lovely long leg was revealed to his somber gaze because she hadn't securely tied her dressing gown's silk belt.

"I'm... glad you told me about your unhappy first marriage and about Errol," Christopher said quietly. "And I appreciate that you were honest about how you feel about having more children. I can see how hard confessing that had to be for you." He paused, struggling to keep any resentment out of his voice. "And I'm glad, in a strange way, that you let me know how you judge the kind of parent you think I'd be."

"And am I being unfair?" she challenged, her chin slightly raised. "If we got married and had children together, could you honestly say you wouldn't be missing-in-action most of the time?"

Christopher winced inwardly at her assessment, making an effort to adjust his post-war fantasies to the realities Brooke's tirade had made so crystal clear. Was the reason he'd never married nor thought much about having children because, as the cliché went, he was married to the job of journalism, or whatever worldly tasks MI9 confronted him with?

Or was it because he'd never been with a woman he'd want to create life with?

Christopher was simultaneously digesting their conversation while feeling the pressure that he needed to depart Paris very soon for an obligation he couldn't ignore.

"Yes, you're probably right about what kind of father I'd make," he agreed, fatigue suddenly invading his body despite having recently awakened. "And I doubt that you're surprised to learn that I absolutely must leave in the next few minutes— and, of course, I can't tell you why."

"I rest my case," she said, gazing at him as if she were sorry her words had proven so true. "Duty calls of one sort or the other, and it always will, war or no war."

He wanted to reach for her, but could only manage to say, "Promise me you'll go straight back to Barbizon, Brooke. The Nazi noose is tightening in Paris, more now than ever before." By this time, he'd donned his shirt, put on his shoes, and grabbed his coat, shrugging it on. "I want you to know," he continued, "that I respect you for having the courage to say what you have. Clearly, we all have our failings— and especially me." He paused and inhaled deeply. "What you've told me makes me sad on so many levels, but I'm glad you were honest. If those are your true sentiments about the two of us, and it feels to me as if they are, then..." He stared at her with the chasm of ten feet between them when, after last night, he'd thought they'd never feel separate again. "Well, then... I'll just let myself out," he completed his sentence quietly.

He turned away and strode down the hallway toward the kitchen's back door.

Focus, man! he lectured himself.

As the deputy in charge of northern France's escape-and-evade operations, Christopher knew full well that he faced a dangerous twelve hours ahead. He could only hope that sometime after midnight, the short-takeoff-and-landing Lysander would arrive safely in darkness in a farmer's field outside Paris and whisk him back to Britain. His goal: to tell MI9's Colonel Crockatt to his face that he'd better get the MI6 tricksters to do something about Harold Cole— and soon —or none of Christopher's Resistance teams would have a chance in hell of surviving the war.

And the worst part of this goddamned situation, he thought, dashing to the ground floor by the building's back stairs and then ducking down an alley at the end of Rue Saint-Dominique, was that the woman he loved— who wouldn't have him —could easily be among Cole's next victims.

PART V

32

NOVEMBER 1943

B rooke knocked softly on the door to the d'Albert-Lake flat on Rue Vaneau and held her breath until it opened a crack. She met the relieved expression on her compatriot Virginia's face with one of her own.

"You made it," Virginia murmured in hushed tones.

"Yes... somehow I did," Brooke whispered back.

Even during the German occupation, her American friend had been spared internment as an enemy alien, thanks to her husband, Philippe, a French citizen whose family had deep roots in the country. The couple had become stalwarts in the Paris branch of the Comet Line.

"Come in, come in!" Virginia urged, opening the door wider, allowing Brooke to quickly step inside. "Our fly boys are very hungry and I've completely run out of something to feed them."

It had been more than two months since either woman had seen or heard from Christopher, but Virginia had sent an urgent message through the courier, Luc, that she was in desperate need of more food for the "packages" that kept arriving at her door. Despite their leader advising Brooke to "lay low" behind the villa's walls in Barbizon, she had ignored the stricture and had continued bringing supplies to safehouses in Paris whenever she could, including the d'Albert-Lake's.

"Let me take off this damn thing," Brooke said, flinging her winter coat on a chair in the front room. She scooped up the hem of her dress to divest herself of the canvas sack full of vegetables that she'd strapped around her waist."

Virginia laughed softly.

"You looked as if you might deliver a baby in the next ten minutes!"

Brooke managed to chuckle, although Virginia's words summoned the memory of the day she gave birth to Errol. She recalled with shame her reaction to the pinched-faced, squalling infant put in her arms. It had been a difficult birth and all she felt afterward was her inadequacy as his caretaker. She hadn't a clue how to comfort him— or herself. She remembered so vividly her sense of dread that this dependent child was only going to hold her back as an actress.

A familiar wave of self-loathing swept over her as she massaged the base of her spine. It ached something fierce from carrying the load of carrots, potatoes, and a rabbit carcass in the sack around her mid-section.

Glad to be rid of the bag, she handed it over to her fellow *résistant*. On this latest journey, Brooke had been questioned by authorities at several points along the way, but somehow her masquerade had convinced the guards at the train stations she was, indeed, a very pregnant lady. By the time she'd knocked on Virginia's door, though, her nerves were shot.

Would this war never end, she wondered for the thousandth time. She struggled to quell the free-floating depression that often seemed to take hold whenever she allowed herself to recall the final, unhappy moments with Christopher at her flat. She couldn't banish her memory of the shock she saw reflected in his expression as she revealed the secrets about her past that she'd kept locked up for so long. She constantly told herself to put it all out of her mind, yet there was no way to ignore the fact that she hadn't seen or heard from him since that last day in August.

"I'm so relieved you made it here safely," Virginia said, gathering up the produce and leading the way into her kitchen. "Our agents are disappearing right and left and it's obvious someone on the inside is sabotaging our escape line."

"It's that bastard, Harold Cole," Brooke declared, following in her wake. "Christopher and I have both spotted him several times inside Gare Austerlitz pointing out people to the guards at the check points."

"Good God," Virginia exclaimed, "does Cole know who *you* are? Could he identify you to the SS?"

"Yes, but I know who *he* is, so I'm constantly on the lookout whenever I think he might be lurking around."

"Brooke, really," Virginia scolded. "You've done so much. You must promise me you'll let Nicole help more with the food distribution route, as well as escorting escapees to the train station."

Brooke ignored her plea, replying, "Whoever is in charge at the London War Office has done *nothing* about the son-of-a-bitch!"

"What if the rumors floating around that he's double agent are true?" Virginia said. "Wouldn't the higher ups in London do something then?"

"But what if the bigwigs are playing him as a triple?" Brooke said, darkly. "What's a few civilians taken down as long as London thinks it knows more than anyone is letting on."

"That's truly horrible," Virginia countered. "Please, God, don't let that be happening."

Virginia began unpacking the bag of vegetables, laying them in a row on her kitchen table.

"Well, one good bit of news," she said, admiring the batch of red beets and golden parsnips that Brooke had brought. "We're relieved that Christopher just returned safely from London. Maybe his superiors have listened to his raising his latest alarm that so many of us are being nabbed by the Gestapo."

Brooke's breath caught. "He's been in England?"

Virginia grimaced. "I suppose security protocol says I shouldn't tell you about his recent whereabouts, but yes. I learned by chance that he landed safely back in France two days ago."

"That's very good news to hear he made it back in one piece," she said softly.

Brooke stayed long enough at Virginia's to be given a cup of the vegetable soup that her escape colleague immediately put on the hob. While she sipped, she could hear the low murmur of male voices behind a closed door to Virginia's spare bedroom. Within the hour, Brooke was on the next train back to Fontainebleau and rode her bicycle parked there the few kilometers back to Barbizon.

In the following weeks, she felt even more on edge than usual, expecting, daily, that her supposed 'commander' would surface at the farmstead now that she knew he'd returned to France.

But Christopher didn't come to Barbizon.

As fall turned into early winter, Brooke continued to half-assume that the branch leader would travel south, if only to consult with Luc— but he failed to appear. She could only surmise that her honesty about dreading the idea of becoming a mother again, along with her accusation that he would be as absent a parent as she had been with Errol, had convinced him they were through and that, just as she'd predicted to herself, he wouldn't want to make a life with her, even if they both survived the war.

And you're surprised he couldn't accept the 'real' Brooke Bradley? she chided herself. *What man would?*

Brooke was moodily sitting at the kitchen table the Christmas morning of 1943 when Nicole appeared, intending to make a breakfast from two sausages a local farmer had traded her for an entire sack of potatoes.

"He also was kind enough to give us four eggs," she said.

Brooke could tell her housemate's cheery attitude was aimed at raising her flagging spirits.

"Lovely," breathed Brooke, but her mind was weighed down with nothing but thoughts of the deaths these last two years had brought. She ticked them off silently.

Victor, killed in a battle with his own countryman. Her little son, dead in a grave in California, and poor Jules, presumed drowned en route to North Africa. And then there were all those valiant people who accepted Christopher's call to provide escape routes out of France to perfect strangers. Thanks to Harold Cole and other traitors, what of them? Arrested. Tortured. Shot. Dead.

As WINTER MELDED into late spring, 1944. Brooke could no longer deny that a permanent breach existed between Christopher and her. With the perspective of time, she sorely regretted some of the things she had said to him in her visceral response about having another child.

Nicole, too, showed signs of increasing depression, often remarking how she longed to move back to Paris and dreaded to find out what had happened to her family in Alsace. Both women knew, of course, that as long as the Nazis held their grip on France, they didn't even dare leave Barbizon as their home base because the dangers had grown too great.

The only cheer in their lives was Ondie. The poodle whined to be let free to run along the side of the wheatfields and roll in muddy puddles after a spring rain. Her joy at lying in the sunshine or chasing a rabbit in the woods boosted their spirits a notch, but otherwise, the inhabitants of the villa could find little to be cheerful about.

In mid-May, Luc appeared at the villa's back gate, hailing Brooke who had just cleaned out the larger of two rabbit hutches.

"Madame de Varney," he began, and then his next words appeared to stick in his throat.

"What is it?" Brooke asked, steeling herself for what she could only guess was bad news.

"I was told to warn you that..."

He paused and Brooke could see he was fighting to control his emotions.

"What *is* it!" she demanded again.

"Last week, some of our agents have recently been arrested and many executed on the spot by the Nazis."

"Oh, God, *no*..." Brooke groaned.

She remembered all too well the news a year earlier that the 'Pat Line' named after its leader Patrick O'Leary had been entirely taken down in April of 1943 by a French turncoat named Roger Leveneu. What if Christopher had been caught in Cole's net this time?

"Has Rabbit Run's leader been arrested, too?" Brooke asked Luc, dreading his answer.

Luc's confused expression struck Brooke as odd.

"The captain? No. Not him. He just said to tell you not to leave these walls for any reason right now. Our entire escape operation is shut down until he gives us the word as to what we must do."

Brooke felt suddenly shocked.

Luc's message came directly from Christopher? Had he been to the farmstead? Where the hell was *the elusive son-of-a-gun?*

"But what if a plane is shot down and—"

Luc shrugged. "I guess you do what you think best, but just know the *Boches* sense something big is about to happen in this war and they are taking no prisoners alive... but just shooting them." He paused, adding ominously, "Even in Barbizon."

Before she could question him further, he slipped out the back gate and was gone.

～

AFTER SUNDOWN IN LATE MAY, Brooke was thoroughly fed up with hiding behind the walls of the villa during these many months. Abruptly, she decided she would venture after dark to the farmstead to check on a small field of alfalfa she'd had the farmer, Antoine Boucher, plant that would help feed her rabbits the following winter.

Once the sun set, she set out clad in her wig and dark clothing on the dirt road that led from behind the stone compound to Jules's former hideout, glad that only a sliver of a moon shone overhead. When she arrived at the edge of the field, she peered through the gloom past the nicely growing alfalfa, making out the roofline of the decrepit farmhouse. Nicole had mentioned that Luc was laying low at his own house in an attempt to appear that he was hard at work, repairing broken farm machinery, as he did before the war.

Puzzled to see a solitary candle glowing in the window, she trod stealthily toward the side of the building and had only reached the weed-strewn front yard when the door swung open. A tall, broad-shouldered, familiar figure stood silhouetted in the door frame, pistol drawn.

"Don't you dare shoot me!" she protested loudly. "And why in the world are you *here*?"

She was jolted to see Christopher in the flesh after all these months, and angry, too, that she would never have known he was there if she hadn't decided to check on the alfalfa.

He slowly secured the weapon in his belt and descended the porch steps.

"I came down here hoping to find a safehouse," he said, "but obviously I was misinformed." Waving his hand, he ordered, "Come inside before anyone sees us."

Brooke did as she was told. Before the awkward silence between them lasted too long she asked, "Are things as dicey in Paris as I've heard?"

"Worse. The stranglehold on our work is ratcheting up more than ever since the Germans know they're losing the war."

He gestured for her to sit down at the rough, wooden table where Jules and Brooke had shared many a meal prior to his departure on the ill-fated ship heading for North Africa.

"How long will you stay here?" she asked, willing her tone to sound neutral.

Christopher shrugged. "Hard to know. Virginia was the one who urged me to leave Paris. She told me about your repeatedly seeing Harold Cole conversing with Nazi authorities at the various train stations where we send the airmen on the escape routes."

"By now, that can't be surprising news," Brooke said, an edge to her voice. "I understand you were in London. While you were there, could you make the supposedly 'intelligent' bigwigs do anything about Cole?"

"No," he answered shortly. "Even though there have been scores of Allied secret agents and escape helpers swept up in a major Nazi dragnet. The silence from certain quarters on the subject is deafening."

He stared at her across the table, then said, "I also reported how you'd been sexually assaulted by a Nazi soldier at the train station and had managed to get away by thwacking him in the legs with your satchel crammed with straitjackets. It made for quite a tale."

There was the hint of his old humor in his last words.

With a shrug, she said, "I doubt Cole had much to do with that German creep trying to rape me. My feeling was it was just business as usual with those thugs in gray-green."

Christopher nodded agreement. "A good-looking nurse would always attract attention— Cole or no Cole."

Was that a compliment...?

Meanwhile, Brooke could hardly believe MI6 still wouldn't order Cole apprehended.

"Good God, Christopher, why won't those suits in London finally *do* something about the bastard? Even in Barbizon we've heard about various escape lines in the north being blown by the man's treason. Why aren't they ordering his—"

Christopher interrupted her curtly, "All I was told by the higher-ups is that 'they have their reasons' not to liquidate him, so they won't. End of discussion, please."

"Wonderful. So now what?" she demanded.

"We wait."

"For what?"

"Can't tell you."

"Wonderful," she repeated.

The two stared at each other for a long moment, Brooke not knowing what to say or do next. It was clear to her that Christopher did not appear in the slightest bit happy to see her.

She rose from her chair, turned to go, and then halted.

"What in the world motivates a guy like Harold Cole to act like such a shit?" she asked over her shoulder.

"As I've said before, money turns out to be his primary thing, but ultimately," Christopher predicted, his scowl deepening, "he's just a petty criminal they let in the army who's conning his way through a world war. One day, though, his lust for cash, booze, and accommodating women will prove extremely dangerous."

"But not before he can get a lot of us killed."

Abruptly changing the subject, he asked, "Want some coffee?"

"You're kidding. You have some?"

"Via air mail," he said dryly, apparently referring to his recent flight over the Channel. "It'll warm you up before you head back."

Clearly, Christopher's invitation of hospitality was a limited one. The night air had cooled considerably and she hadn't had a decent cup of anything tasting remotely like coffee in months, so she replied, "Hot coffee sounds great."

Without further comment, Christopher stirred the flames in the wooden stove to heat the water in a dented kettle on the hob. Silence reigned once more as he prepared two cups, poured hot water over some grounds, and handed her a share of the brew.

"Sorry, no cream the way I know you like it."

It was the first personal reference he had made and Brooke could tell that he regretted it instantly, for in the next breath he launched into an impersonal recital of instructions.

"If any downed fliers land in your region, hold them here at the farmstead until further notice."

"What?" she protested. "*Why*? Isn't doing that dangerous for them *and* for us?"

"Can't be helped. It'll be more dangerous trying to send them to the Spanish border than to keep them hidden."

"It will? Why is it any more dangerous to speed them on their way than to keep them here where Schiller might find them?"

Christopher sighed.

"Will you stop playing the inquiring reporter?" he snapped, his irritation obvious. "And stop asking questions you know I've taken an oath not to answer."

"Then let me take a wild guess what's going on," she flung back. "Some big Allied effort we've been promised for ages is finally underway, right? The reason to keep downed fliers where they land is that there's not enough time to get escapers to the south, over the mountains, and back to Britain before whatever is going to happen... happens."

Proving to her that he trusted her at least a little he replied, "Oh, hell! You might as well know, this since you may be part of it. There's a new plan to hide escapees in two different obscure locations for the duration."

"Huh? I don't get it. Two locations? *Where*?"

She saw him inhale a deep breath, as if deciding whether or not to say anything beyond what he had already.

"I've been asked to help two intelligence colleagues set up a system of escorting newly downed fliers arriving in our region to a large forested region, south of Barbizon, near Châteaudun."

"Isn't it terribly risky to gather that many Allied fliers in one place?"

"Two places," he reminded her. "The other is about ten kilometers away from the first location, also densely wooded. And at this point, it's the least risky of some *very* risky options."

"Why now?" she asked. Before he could answer, she stared at him with new comprehension. "Ah! So, the invasion *is* finally coming?"

Christopher gazed out the window at the late May sky.

"If I tell you anything more, I'll have to kill you."

It was their old joke but for once, neither of them found it humorous.

"I get the distinct feeling you might like to do just that," she retorted, rising to leave.

In the dim light of the kerosene lantern, Christopher appeared to her drawn and exhausted. She placed her hand lightly on his shoulder, but he swiftly stood up as if shaking off her touch.

Wounded by the abruptness of his action, she ducked her head and made for the door nearly at a run.

"Brooke..." he called after her, but she kept going until she fumbled for the handlebars of her bike and sped away.

Her throat tight, she longed to cry, but she had no tears left to shed.

33

Despite Luc's continued warnings to stay behind the villa's walls, Brooke stubbornly set out in early June with part of the rich bounty that had burst forth from their raised vegetable beds.

Her first stop was the d'Albert-Lakes once again. Virginia whispered the second she'd closed the door behind Brooke, "We have *six* airmen in our back bedroom and absolutely no idea how we can get them to..."

She hesitated to complete her sentence, so Brooke did it for her.

"To the 'secret forest,' right?"

"*Forêt de Fréteval*? Oh, so you know about Operation Marathon?" Virginia said, sounding relieved.

"Yes," replied Brooke, although Christopher had never mentioned the mission's official name nor the name of the Fréteval Forest.

Virginia voiced her own doubts. "How in the world can we get so many airmen there at once? It's too risky to keep half of them behind and make two trips."

Brooke thought for a minute and then laughed.

"I've got an idea! Or let's say, I have a *recycled* idea."

Just then, Virginia's French husband, Philippe, appeared in the foyer.

"What idea?" he asked.

Brooke swiftly recounted pulling off the French football team caper with the Americans and their Latino soccer captain from Texas.

"Why not a cycling team? You two did a great job posing as the coach and his wife of the other fake team. I just read that the Nazi-sponsored *faux* Tour de France— the Vichy approved 'Grand Prix Tour of France' —is to be held in the Führer's honor. It's apparently launching soon, despite the war," she explained. "If we can get cycling clothing from a Paris bicycle shop or someplace, we could dress the aviators as a team supposedly training in the sunny South of France to compete in the Tour. You two can go as their coach and his wife."

"That's brilliant!" cried Virginia, clapping her hands.

"It's the only chance we've got to get these chaps out of Paris," agreed Philippe.

"Well, it worked with the soccer— I mean football —team," Brooke chortled. "Why not with cyclists?"

～

BROOKE WOULD FOREVER REMEMBER the 6th day of June 1944. She arrived at the d'Albert flat dressed in pregnancy attire that disguised six colorful jerseys and matching cycling shorts, plus pairs of thin, leather cycling shoes, all rolled into a ball and stuffed inside the canvas bag strapped around her waist. She had enlisted Luc who had miraculously secured the cycling apparel for six competitors and their 'coach.'

"It's started!" Virginia whispered hoarsely the minute Brooke had shut the door. "Thousands of Allied troops are landing today somewhere along the beaches of Normandy!"

"Swear to me it's not a joke," Brooke exclaimed.

Philippe stood beside his wife, a huge grin lighting up his face.

"No it's true! We have a radio that's usually well hidden, but early this morning I tuned into the BBC news. The invasion is finally happening!"

"Oh, glory!" Brooke said excitedly. "That's wonderful!"

Their jubilation was interrupted by a sharp knock on the front door. The three exchanged startled glances and Philippe motioned for the women to stand back.

"Who is it?" he demanded.

"You will soon learn if you open up," came a voice Brooke recognized only too well.

She stepped behind Philippe who flung the door wide.

"Good," Christopher said, glancing at Brooke. "You're here, too."

Brooke found his brusque greeting unsettling. She had anticipated a dressing-down for having disobeyed his stern recommendation via Luc that she remain behind the walls of the villa in Barbizon. Christopher's next statements, however, explained the reason he was not giving her hell.

"We're going to need everyone for what comes next." He turned to Philippe. "I want all three of you to bring the airmen to Gare Austerlitz tonight at midnight. Thanks to Brooke, here, you will also arrive with bicycles that Luc managed to assemble and delivered to your basement downstairs before he was arrested today."

"Luc's been arrested?" Brooke repeated, her stomach turning over.

Brooke could hardly believe that an invasion had finally begun, perhaps at long last putting an end to the massive suffering of everyone in France. And now, to think that Luc might die just as the nightmare could be coming to a close?

"What happened to Luc?" she demanded.

"My guess is that an informant at the bike shop tipped off the Gestapo that Luc was in on some sort of Resistance operation," he answered. "Let's hope we get these men on their way before the SS torture Luc to find out exactly what we're up to."

Brooke was sickened by what the Nazi goons might do to the brave young man to extract information about their operation. And didn't his being nabbed today mean the mission they were about to undertake had little chance of succeeding? A feeling of pure dread crept over her, and she glanced at Virginia and Philippe who both appeared to be thinking similar thoughts.

Brooke spoke up quickly. "Look, this notion of faking a cycling team was my idea. Given Luc's arrest, do you think we dare attempt to get all these men on to a train at one time?"

"We don't have a choice," Christopher countered sharply. "This number of escapees can't remain in this small flat any longer with no food, and we have no other place to hide them. We will proceed as planned. I will join you at the station with train tickets and documents and will guide your group to the Fréteval woods."

Brooke put her hand lightly on his sleeve as he prepared to go.

"Well, what's my assignment? What am I supposed to *do*?"

"Pose as my wife," he replied evenly. "Like Philippe, I'm now assuming the role of a second cycling coach in this little masquerade. Take my word for it, *none* of us dare remain in Paris any longer. This is the only way to get us all the hell out of here."

Speechless at this turn of events, Brooke watched Christopher spin on his heel, and disappear out the door.

A FEW HOURS LATER, Brooke surveyed six men of all shapes and sizes dressed in cycling gear and lined up beside their bikes a block away from Gare Austerlitz. In the next moment, Christopher and Philippe, attired in casual clothing that might pass muster for cycling coaches, joined their group that also included not only Brooke, but Virginia.

"Have you ever seen a genuine Tour de France?" Brooke whispered to Virginia.

"Oh, many times on the final stage concluding the race that was always held in Paris before the war," she whispered back. "It was quite thrilling."

"Well, if we get grilled by the Nazis, you'll have to speak for me," Brooke warned. "I know nothing about the sport *or* the famous race."

Christopher assigned the airmen blessed with the slimmest physiques to lead the way.

"You three have the best chance to pass for men who can ride a bike," he said. Pointing to the others, he ordered, "You follow close behind them and we can hope you won't be noticed much." To them all he commanded, "And *all* of you, keep your mouths shut. If we're stopped by the authorities, let Philippe or me do the talking."

Brooke noticed that Virginia's husband gently seized his wife's hand reassuringly. His gaze was filled with the same tenderness Christopher and Brooke had briefly shared. When husband and wife embraced, Brooke stared down at her feet. A sadness suddenly swept over her that made her question whether any of those gathered on this mad mission could possibly make it through the next few hours.

Christopher cast a glance at both Brooke and Virginia, commenting, "Clearly, it won't be hard for Virginia to play a coach's wife." He pointed to the space beside him and gestured to Brooke to stand beside him. "Please try to do the same as my dutiful spouse until we get to the Fréteval Forest. "

"Got it, coach," Brooke said, sarcasm hiding her hurt that he'd barely given her a moment's notice.

Finally meeting her eyes, Christopher said quietly, "All right, everyone, let's go!"

To Brooke's amazement and relief, the group clad in their cycling gear wheeled their bikes brazenly past the entrance to the train station with the German guards only giving a cursory glance to the stack of fake identification papers Philippe presented.

"*Bonne Chance*," enthused a gendarme standing nearby as the fraudulent cycling team and their sham coaches proceeded down the lengthy platform to the train car to which the group had been assigned, along with their bicycles stacked next door in the baggage car.

A few minutes past twelve, the night train to Dourdan pulled out of Gare Austerlitz and Brooke could almost hear each member of their bizarre *équipe cycliste* issue a sigh of gratitude for having made it this far.

My idea of a cycling team worked! Brooke exalted silently *We actually pulled it off!* In the next moment, however, she corrected herself. *So far, that is...*

Brooke had taken note that no newspaper on sale at the station kiosk had a headline announcing an Allied invasion in Normandy was underway.

Philippe and Virginia sat beside each other, Virginia's head resting on her husband's shoulder while they talked softly with an intimacy that literally made Brooke's heart ache. The icy separation between Christopher and his pretend wife felt like a barrier that could never be breeched.

Turning in her seat next to him, she sought his glance for any sign of praise or approval for the scheme she had devised. His back half-angled toward her, he kept his eyes glued on the train window while the backyards of Paris flew by.

"THIS TRAIN WILL ONLY GO AS FAR as Dourdan, eighty-seven kilometers from Châteaudun, which is the closest town to the forest," Christopher said barely above a whisper. "I'll be met by six other escapees who've been driven down by car. Our original six—plus the d'Albert-Lakes and you —will have to ride the bikes."

"Two of the airmen told me they'd never learned to ride a two-wheeler," Brooke whispered back.

"Then, those two non-riders will swap out with two from the other group who *can* ride and we'll drive on ahead. At Châteaudun, we'll load all the airmen onto a big hay wagon and cover them with straw. Philippe will drive the tractor and I'll sit at the back and keep the men quiet."

"And Virginia and I?" Brooke asked.

"The flier who can best ride a bike will lead off our procession with Virginia. You will ride behind the hay cart as lookout, forward and aft."

"Got it," Brooke said with a nod. "And once we get to the forest?"

"Philippe and I will guide the men to the camp deep inside the woods. You and Virginia cycle back to Châteaudun and then to the safehouse in Dourdan and we'll meet you there."

Eighty kilometers, both there and back... she groaned inwardly. She could only imagine how her poor derriere would feel after such an intense marathon.

To her relief, Christopher's plan proceeded as he'd described. When they dismounted behind the safehouse in Dourdan, a particularly disgruntled rider remarked, "I can't believe those stupid Nazis didn't notice how rusted and half-broken our bikes were! Tour de France? My Aunt Fanny!"

At that very moment, a siren shattered the air. Brooke's heart lurched at the dreaded but familiar sound overhead that she'd first witnessed, closeup, when the Radio Mondiale crew drove out of Paris. That terrible day the Nazis took over the city, low-flying planes fired on fleeing civilians from the air.

She could see the airmen who'd traveled south with them had likely never been on the ground before when all hell broke loose in the skies above. Everyone in their group looked up and took in the sight of the aerial dogfights raining havoc from the skies. The erstwhile fliers paled and glanced wildly about, seeking cover. Christopher led the way as they all made a dash for the basement of the safehouse.

Huddled on the floor with the earsplitting sound of planes roaring overhead, he shouted, "The Germans know it's over— which makes the retreating *Boches* all the more dangerous."

A few minutes later, the sound of an explosion rent the air.

"Somebody's been shot down," one of the airmen observed unnecessarily.

"Let it be the bloody Krauts!" cursed another.

Finally, it was over. After a night's uneasy rest, the escapees emerged in small groups of twos and threes and began the long journey to a farmhouse near the entrance to the forest. Brooke heard several of the airmen complaining about "sore butts and bruised balls" during the three days it took the motley assembly to make its way to Châteaudun. From there, the group proceeded on foot to a nearby farm, except for the three on bicycles, including Brooke.

Standing in a yard strewn with rusted machinery and a chicken or two wandering nearby, Christopher ordered all the aviators, except for the solitary designated cyclist named Leon, to lie down on the wagon's flatbed like logs at a mill.

"Pile the hay on top of their bodies," Christopher directed

Philippe, Virginia, and Brooke. Sneezes and complaints filled the air until Christopher barked, "Shut up, all of you, or you'll be the last Allied military men to die in France!"

Brooke exchanged glances with Virginia. Both women understood all too well the strain that everyone— and especially Christopher —had been under from the moment they'd left the d'Albert-Lake's flat on Rue Vaneau. Was this war actually coming to its end? When it came to everyone's mental health, she thought morosely, it could never be too soon.

Once the escapees were loaded onto the truck bed and covered with straw, Brooke and Virginia stood to one side while Christopher went over last-minute instructions with Philippe, who was to drive the tractor pulling the rig.

Brooke whispered to Virginia, "Can you even imagine what life will be like when this is over?"

Virginia squeezed her hand. "You mean you and Christopher coming to our flat for a nice meal?"

Brooke wondered if that had a snowball's chance in hell of ever happening, but all she replied was, "Think how wonderful it will be to be able to buy *foie gras* again to serve the guests?"

"And champagne," Virginia whispered. "Don't forget the champagne! We will toast each other again and again, dear friend!"

Christopher, seeing their heads bent toward each other, pointed to the three bikes they had brought with them to the farm and spoke up.

"Brooke? Virginia... Leon... you ready?"

The two women and the designated airman nodded as Philippe climbed up on the metal tractor seat of an ancient farm machine, his hands on the corroded wheel. Virginia and the aviator, Leon from Minnesota, climbed onto their bikes and positioned themselves in front of the tractor.

Christopher strode to the rear of the flatbed and hopped onto the wooden platform, his dangling legs covered in a pair of well-worn overalls the farmer had provided. The farmer and his wife stood silently to one side, watching the preparations.

"You okay?" Christopher asked Brooke, the first kind words he'd directed to her the entire journey.

Before she answered, she shed her light blue cardigan and stowed it in her straw basket attached to the handlebars.

"It's gotten hot, but I'm fine."

The truth was, she was far from fine. She glanced at the flatbed strewn with hay and considered how the men buried beneath it still had to make it past a German outpost near the forest that Christopher had earlier warned them about. He'd commanded the men not to speak a word from now until they were told they were safely deep into the forest with scores of other escapees. Brooke could feel her anxiety about the final leg of this perilous journey intensifying and she began to inhale deep breaths to try to calm herself.

She said to Christopher, "Virginia mentioned that the encampment of Allied military men you told us about is less than *two miles* from the German garrison we have to pass. How in the world do we get our big group into the woods without someone seeing us?"

Christopher's worried expression telegraphed to her that this factor had also been concerning him.

"Well, at least it's been done a number of times before," he replied. "Already, there are hundreds of fliers living in the woods right under the Germans' noses."

"Let us pray we can do this hat trick one more time," Brooke murmured.

Without further comment, she mounted her bike while waiting for Virginia and Leon to lead off, followed by Philippe driving the tractor. Black smoke from its ancient engine billowed through and around Christopher's legs half-covered with straw.

Coughing, Brooke allowed their odd caravan to proceed two hundred meters ahead as they headed down a dirt lane. The rough tract eventually merged with a narrow road that looked like an untended tarmac at a small, country airfield.

The route they traveled was bumpy and complicated with many turns and crossroads. The June sun beat down steadily, sweat dampening Brooke's back. Soon, fatigue from the last days of stress and physical exertion began to plague her muscles and mind.

She pushed harder on the pedals, cycling ahead to within speaking distance of Christopher.

"How much farther?" she asked, struggling to keep the complaining tone out of her voice.

"We're close," he replied. "Maybe three kilometers."

"And where, exactly, is that German outpost?" she wondered aloud, her anxiety mounting.

He pointed to his left at the edge of a wooded area that had just come into view. Then he put his finger to his lips and pointed behind her, a signal to return to her post behind their group.

Brooke obediently dismounted her bike and waited for the tractor and the forward observers to pull ahead once again, resuming her position as the rear lookout.

She had just remounted her bicycle when she saw a large, black car come into view around the far bend. From that distance, Brooke had to squint to see the vehicle turn abruptly from the highway that paralleled the road they were on. It nosed into their narrow thoroughfare at a point that she guessed was about the length of an American football field away. Halting, the vehicle effectively blocked any forward progress of their caravan.

Brooke wondered what such a fancy vehicle was doing in such a desolate place? Was it heading for the German outpost? She frantically waved at Christopher and pointed with vehement gestures ahead of their group.

He turned around, took in the scene, and leaped off the back of the wagon, shading one hand over his eyes to peer ahead. In the next second, he ran forward to alert Philippe to stop the tractor, letting him know that there might be trouble ahead. Brooke stared at Virginia and Leon who were now only meters away from the car blockading them. Brooke recognized the vehicle as a dreaded Citroën, the model most prized by Nazi officers.

Three men emerged from the vehicle. They were dressed in the unmistakable uniforms of German police.

"Oh, God, no!" Brooke moaned under her breath. She watched in horror as the tallest of the trio held out his hand for Virginia and Leon to hand him their identity papers.

34

Despite the brutal sun beating down on the fields and forest nearby, Brooke felt as if her muscles had frozen. She stared in horror as she saw one of the German policemen slap Virginia's cohort, Leon, across the face and slam him against the side of the Citroën.

Christopher hissed hoarsely to the airmen, "Get off the wagon and move to the *rear* of the platform. NOW!"

In a state of shock, Brooke watched as the eleven on the tractor's flatbed fought their way out of the blanket of straw that had been concealing them. Stricken with fear at the sight of the German officers down the road, they looked to Christopher for what to do next.

He turned toward Brooke and directed tersely, "Take your bike and ride back to the farm. Tell them what happened and then leave immediately for the safehouse in Dourdan. Wait for me there."

"But—"

Ignoring her, he rushed back to Philippe's side. Virginia's husband was watching with a look of terror on his face as she and Leon were being forced into the big, black car. Philippe reached for a pistol stuffed into the back of his trousers.

"No!" Christopher whispered harshly, "Don't, or we're all done for!"

Philippe's hand checked on his weapon, a look of searing pain and indecision held him in its grip.

"But my *wife!*" he protested, his voice mirroring his agony watching Virginia disappear into the back seat of the Citroën.

"There's nothing you can do now," Christopher exclaimed harshly, although Brooke glimpsed the anguish in their leader's eyes. Taking full command, he motioned for Philippe to jump down from the tractor seat. "Come on! We've got to save these men, at least."

"But I can't just let—"

"You *must*, Philippe. Get down from there! That's an order!"

And before Brooke could utter a word of dissent, the eleven fleeing aviators, along with Christopher and Philippe took off at a dead run, heading for a stand of thick trees some fifty meters to their left. Brooke could only pray they were not going to find themselves in the middle of the German outpost Christopher had pointed to moments before.

We're all a bunch of jackrabbits, running from the poacher's trap!

She glanced to her right just as the Citroën with Virginia and Leon in the backseat turned onto the main highway once again— the Germans apparently oblivious to the mad scramble occurring a hundred meters behind them.

Oh, dear God... poor Virginia! Brooke moaned inwardly. *Philippe must be beside himself.*

In a fog of fear, she turned her bike around and swiftly retraced her route to the farm that had provided the hay wagon. With tears streaming down her face, she related to the farmer and his wife the capture of Virginia and one of the airmen.

Wiping the perspiration off her face with her cardigan, she bemoaned, "I can't believe that they were nabbed by those swine four damn days after the Allies landed in Normandy!"

"And the others?" the farmer asked gravely. "What of the airmen?"

"I don't know," Brooke replied, distraught. "They ran toward the forest and I was ordered to come here to tell you and then return to Châteaudun."

"Well, your captain will get them to safety," declared the farmer's wife with remarkable confidence. She bid Brooke sit and rest at her kitchen table. With a look at her husband, who plainly served as a linchpin for Operation Marathon, she poured Brooke a tall glass of water. "Now you drink this down, dear, and have a bit of a rest before you head back."

Brooke was in awe of this heroic couple who had taken on the mission to assist getting as many stranded airmen as possible into the secret forest.

But what did it matter if friends and loved ones don't live to see?

Her friend, Virginia, arrested? Christopher and the others perhaps already dead, shot by German sharpshooters? As far as Brooke could tell, the enemy base looked practically adjacent to the extremely vulnerable hiding place designated for hundreds of escapees.

Brooke's entire body was still trembling. She knew that if she started crying again, she might never stop.

What will happen to those poor fliers who survived bailing out of their planes and now—

Catastrophic possible scenarios reverberated like scattershot in her brain.

"*Ma chérie*," said the farmer's wife gently to Brooke, "let me get you something to eat."

Brooke knew she should take some nourishment. And while she had nothing but gratitude for the woman's kindness, the thought of food turned her stomach. All she could think of was what must be happening to Virginia in the clutches of the brutal men who'd arrested her, or what they would do to poor Leon, whom they'd smashed against their car.

And then there was Luc. Brooke dreaded to consider his fate at that very moment now that he was in the clutches of the SS in Paris.

Plus, of course, the destiny of Christopher and Philippe was too horrible to even contemplate. She fought off the memory of the Nazi soldier slamming her against the alley wall behind the train station and ripping her undergarments down to her knees. Anyone caught by Nazi thugs could expect no mercy, especially leaders of the Resistance like one Captain Christopher Laurent.

"Here," said the farmer's wife, handing her a second, small

glass. "Drink this brandy. I imagine you need it. Once darkness falls, you can ride back to Châteaudun and on to Dourdan. Right now, there may be patrols— or even ordinary German foot soldiers beginning to flee east since hearing about the invasion on the coast."

~

THE JOURNEY back eighty-seven kilometers to the safehouse in Dourdan became a blur of pedaling fast and keeping a lookout for Germans who might be abroad in the night. Arriving D-Day-plus-seven at the very spot where Brooke had begun this dreadful escapade, she knocked the code on the basement door, gained entry, and collapsed on a pile of bedding heaped in the corner.

The first night back, she slept like the dead. When she awoke, she found herself alone in the basement. She spent the day cooped up, her nerves still a-jangle, wondering if Christopher and the rest had been caught and were never coming back.

She ate an apple the farmer's wife had given her and slept fitfully the second night, her mind whirling with dismal thoughts about Virginia's capture and fears of what the Germans would do to her friend and to the rest of their group.

And that poor soldier, Leon. If the SS realized he's an American airman, they probably already shot him on the spot!

The odds were a thousand-to-one that Christopher, Philippe, and the eleven airmen could have made it safely into the secret forest. What if those terrifying moments on that rutted road were the last she'd ever see Christopher? What if Virginia was never heard from again? And would she ever be able to erase from her memory the look of horror on Philippe's face as he watched his wife disappear into that car and could do nothing to save her?

Before long, Brooke's troubled musings drifted to thoughts of Nicole and Felix back in Barbizon and the *résistants* there. She shuddered every time she imagined what might be happening to Luc by now. Had lighted cigarettes been pressed into his eyes? Had the Nazi goons beaten him to a bloody pulp or zapped him with an electric prod?

Was he dead?

Stop! You'll drive yourself crazy imagining the worst.

But Brooke knew that the very worst was quite likely when it came to treating Allied prisoners apprehended by the German intelligence and security branches.

She burrowed her head under the cardigan she'd used as a pillow and finally drifted off in fitful slumber.

BROOKE HEARD the basement door open, startling her out of a light sleep.

"Brooke? Are you here?"

"Christopher?" she whispered, jumping to her stockinged feet, and hurtling herself into his arms.

"Oh my God! My God! My God! They didn't *kill* you!"

He held her for a long moment, then stood back.

"No. I'm quite alive. Get dressed," he ordered.

"Just look at me," Brooke said, imagining what a fright she must present. "I slept in my clothes for two days."

"Collect your things. There's an early train leaving for Paris in fifteen minutes. I'll take you to it."

"I thought we didn't dare show our faces in Paris?"

"There's no help for it. We can't stay here. Come quickly."

Her mind brimmed with questions when she met him outside just as dawn was breaking in the east. Walking to the train station, Christopher set a fast pace, allowing no time to talk. In his silence, Brooke felt her annoyance at his all-business behavior beginning to turn to anger and despair.

I was so glad to see him and he doesn't seem to give a damn!

She scrambled to match his stride, touching his sleeve to get his attention.

"So, *Monsieur* State Secrets, at least tell me what happened after I left you streaking into the forest," she gasped between labored breaths. "What about poor Virginia and the luckless Leon?" she demanded. "And how is Philippe holding up— although he must just be devastated," she amended, answering her own question.

"Philippe and all the men made it to the camp without any Germans tailing us," Christopher said, his words obviously chosen carefully.

"How in the world did you manage that?" Brooke said.

"Very carefully. Plus, pure luck. When we made that dash, it happened to be the Kraut's lunchtime."

Christopher didn't elaborate further and kept up his fast pace, his no-details demeanor signaling to Brooke that her assumptions were correct. He wasn't of a mind to share much unless she pressed him hard.

"And Virginia?"

"She and Leon were taken somewhere out of the area. Probably to the prison at Dancy."

"Oh, no... that's horrible. Poor Philippe."

A block from the Dourdan station, Christopher halted, drawing her into the shadows of a nearby building.

"As you'd expect, he's in agony that she got arrested and he didn't," he revealed. "He'll be on the same train as you, so if you see him, make no contact. He's got to clear out any evidence of his activities from their apartment on Rue Vaneau before the Gestapo get there." Christopher cast her a stern look. "Speak to no one. Once you get to Paris, just get yourself over to Gare de Lyon and go directly back to Barbizon."

"And do exactly what?" she shot back.

"Stay in the compound. The Germans are going to get crazy before they head east out of France. It may take a while for that to happen, though."

Brooke paused, allowing his words to sink in.

"So, you really think this war is finally going to be over?"

"There's a long road ahead, but yes. All reports are that the invading troops are battling beyond the coast of Normandy and are heading for Paris."

"When?"

"It'll be weeks."

"How did you find out all this?"

"In the forest. They have a shortwave radio."

"And what will *you* be doing in the meantime?"

"Can't tell you," Christopher answered shortly. "Come on. We've got to keep going."

Within minutes, they had entered the small station a hundred and forty kilometers from Paris. With his flawless French accent, Christopher purchased a ticket "for my wife," as he told the train worker, and handed it to her.

"Platform Two," he said, pointing. "The train's here, so you'd better get going."

He abruptly turned to leave.

"Christopher?" she said sharply.

He swiveled in place. "Yes?"

"You do know, don't you, that you're acting like a—"

He cut her off.

"No. I'm acting like your superior officer. Goodbye, Brooke." He paused and then said softly, "Good work, by the way. You helped me save some lives two days ago."

She responded coolly, "No congratulations are due either one of us. Yes, the men in the hay cart made it into the forest, but my friends Virginia and Luc got arrested and could have been executed by now. I suppose in the world of the MI6 games that you and Harold Cole play, you figure that's still a pretty good overall score."

She knew instantly she'd landed a blow, and a highly unfair one. Christopher had led all but one man among their contingent of escapees to safety.

Why do I strike out like that? Christopher despises Harold Cole. What devil makes me say such things as if I'm flinging well-crafted exit lines in a play?

So he wouldn't see the tears that filled her eyes, she whirled in place and literally ran to board her train.

Once inside the car, she found a seat near the window and collapsed against it, her shoulder bumping against the glass as the locomotive pulled out of the station. While the world flashed by the dirty window, Brooke's thoughts were equally dark and disheartened.

Yes, the war would probably be over before long, but whatever

might have existed between Christopher and her before their
heated conversation about marriage and children and her penchant
for slinging hurtful words to salve her own wounds, it was all, now,
clearly at an end.

35

JUNE 13, 1944

Brooke emerged from the echoing Austerlitz train station nearly dead on her feet and deeply depressed. She found that she was barely able to walk across the bridge to nearby Gare de Lyon to head south again to Barbizon. When the local train arrived at Fontainebleau, she literally fell into the arms of Felix's brother, Gaspard, the ticket master who was just coming off duty.

"You look as if you could use about a week's sleep," he commented with a worried frown. "Come home with me and rest before you return to Barbizon. My wife has made a decent soup from the bones of the rabbit you brought us last week."

Too exhausted to protest, she allowed him to guide her to his small house a block away that was provided by the railroad company. She drank some of his wife's broth seasoned with garden herbs and a few legumes and soon fell fast asleep in a chair by the hearth.

"Shall we let her rest here for the night?" Gaspard asked his wife.

"Yes, let her sleep if she can. I'll just get a blanket to put over her, poor dear."

By the time Brooke awoke, it was just coming on daylight. Embarrassed to find herself still in the chair near the fireplace, she scribbled a note of thanks to her hosts and mounted her bicycle that she'd left at the station in what felt like years before. Her muscles stiff, and still overcome by exhaustion, she rode the ten kilometers to Barbizon as the rising sun painted the fields of sprouting wheat gold on both sides of the narrow road.

All was quiet when she reached the villa's gate. She clicked the latch and walked her bicycle into the courtyard, leaning it against the inside stone wall.

She was startled by the sound of the kitchen door opening. Ondie came bounding out, running straight for her, barking with excitement. Before she could reach down to pet her, she saw the last person she expected standing at her kitchen threshold. Her breath caught, but she was determined to remain calm. She knelt and put her arms around her dog, inhaling her canine scent and taking strength from the animal's warm body.

Looking up at Christopher she said, "*You* again?"

The crushing feeling of fatigue seized her once more, squeezing her chest. Christopher's actions these last days made it perfectly clear that it was over between them.

So, why did he come here... to the villa?

His face drawn and unshaven, he appeared nearly as exhausted as she felt.

"I've been here a couple of hours, waiting for you. After I saw you to your train, I also got on board in a different car."

"You left for Paris the same time as I did?"

"I took a different local to Fontainebleau."

"That was so you wouldn't have to speak to me, I suppose," she snapped. She was totally out of patience with the tense dialogues they'd been exchanging every time they were together. "Just tell me why the hell are you here and be done with all this... this punishment you're dealing out."

He didn't respond to her charge and instead replied to her question.

"Once in Paris, I escorted some fliers to your farmstead who'd become stranded at a safehouse in the city. They're to remain with Luc until they can be escorted to the secret forest."

"Remain with Luc?" she exclaimed. "But you said he'd been arrested!"

Christopher offered a tired smile.

"That wily *garçon* managed to give his captors the slip when they pulled up in front of Gestapo headquarters on Avenue Foch."

Open-mouthed, she rose to stand beside Ondie.

"He got away from those goons on *Avenue Foch*?" she repeated in amazement. Avenue Foch, the Paris headquarters for the SS, of all places. "Good Lord! *How*?"

"As soon as the car halted at the curb of number 64, he bolted from the backseat and zig-zagged his way down the street."

"I can't believe he got away! Didn't the Germans just pull out their Mausers and start shooting?"

Another slight smile creased Christopher's lips.

"The SS has standing orders on Avenue Foch not to shoot in such a posh, residential neighborhood. Luc, the former footballer darting back and forth on his gimpy leg, managed to disappear into a nearby café where a barman swiftly cut the ropes around his wrists and shoved him out the back door."

Relief flooded Brooke's mind so forcefully, she actually felt lightheaded. Even so, she was desperate to learn if Christopher had word about Virginia's fate as well.

Remaining in the courtyard a safe ten feet from him, she asked, "Do we know if those SS thugs took Virginia to the prison at Dancy? Do you suppose there is any way we could—"

Christopher cut her off, his expression now grim.

"My sources learned in Paris that she and other Allied prisoners have already been sent on a train with German troops heading east."

"Out of the country?" Heartsick to hear this, Brooke was also astounded by what he'd just confirmed. "The Germans are definitely *retreating*?"

"Yes, some of the units assigned to Paris apparently want to avoid the coming onslaught of our men pushing toward the city from Normandy. It'll take a while, but the end is in sight."

"Hallelujah," Brooke murmured.

However, she could take no true joy in what Christopher was saying. Her friend was headed for God-only-knew-where with other unfortunate captives caught during these apparent final days of the conflict.

"So, Virginia is to be a prisoner of the Nazis in Germany just as the war is winding *down*?" she groaned.

Brooke speculated that her fellow American was being sent to an internment camp in enemy territory bound to be far worse than what she had endured at Vittel. She met Christopher's gaze.

"Luc could have told me all this, so why did you come to the villa, here?"

"I followed you because I want to tell you about something that I couldn't disclose until now." He inhaled a deep breath and continued. "I'm finally authorized to explain details that you're entitled to know."

"Explain? About what? I was with you *after* Virginia was arrested. Why didn't you tell me whatever it was then?"

"It's not about Virginia. I had communication with London when I got to Paris yesterday," he said.

"Ah... that magic leather suitcase of yours. What brilliance did the Almighty MI9 impart?"

"MI6 this time."

"Ah... the *big* bigwigs finally acknowledge Harold Cole is a turncoat bastard just as the war might be ending?" she said sarcastically. "They're a little late, wouldn't you say?"

Christopher took a long pause, then said, "No, not that, either. Come inside. Nicole has taken food to the escapees at the farm and left you some eggs."

Brooke realized he must be as exhausted as she, so she followed him inside the kitchen.

"Look, we're both literally dead on our feet. Would you be all right if you just say what you have to tell me *after* I've had a bath? You can rest in the sitting room with a glass of calvados. Once you've given me your news direct from your London handlers, I'm sure Luc will make room for you at the farmstead if you need to stay longer." She commanded her dog, "Come in the house, Ondie."

She marched past Christopher, lightly brushing his shoulder with her own as she walked toward her bedroom upstairs.

Ondie hesitated, wagging her tail at their visitor, and then obediently followed her mistress upstairs.

BROOKE EMERGED from her bath to the sound of cars and motorcycles roaring past the villa's one window that faced the street. Rushing into the sitting room wrapped in a towel, she practically collided with Christopher who was peering around the heavy velvet drapes to look out at the unexpected parade. Stretching before them both was the amazing sight of Barbizon's Commandant Schiller and his company of men leaving the town in a frantic hurry. Beside motorcycles with their green sidecars, the ominous black Citroëns so favored by the Nazis were at long last heading east.

As the sounds of their engines faded into the distance, Christopher turned and said, "I want you to keep the five airmen hidden at the farmstead until further notice."

"We need to discuss that," she declared. "I think that's a bad idea. I'll go get dressed."

Minutes later, she reentered the sitting room. She was clad in a pair of pleated slacks and the one silk shirt she had left. Her damp hair was wrapped, turban style, in a towel. Christopher sat in a chair, his eyes closed, his head resting on its leather back. Hearing her footsteps, he roused himself to slowly stand up.

"Unfortunately, the latest word I heard in Paris is that the Allied invasion has suddenly bogged down," revealed Christopher, "with roads clogged by debris from the fighting and German snipers making a last stand."

Our troops are bogged down?

At the mere thought of such a setback, Brooke felt her spirits plunging to a new low.

"Any more news about Virginia and the airman captured with her?"

"No, and," Christopher warned, "it's not safe to move the men who are billeted with Luc because we're told retreating soldiers could virtually be on any road around here. Our orders are to keep the fliers here for the duration."

"And how long do you imagine that will be?" Brooke asked,

wondering how she would feed them and her own household with food running so low. "I hope those guys like carrots."

"I've managed to supply Luc with his own secret radio. He'll tune in to the BBC every day this week and let you know if or when it's safe to move them."

Discouraged, Brooke said, "If Eisenhower's forces aren't making good progress toward Paris, it's hard to believe it all might be over any time soon."

"Oh, it will be over, but you're right. As I said before, it's probably going to take a while. Maybe even next year."

"And meanwhile, the rest of us wait and starve?"

Echoing the tenor of her reply, he said, "Waiting it out in a small town like Barbizon, prepare yourself for local citizens to start accusing one another of being collaborators with the Nazis to save their own hides."

Christopher's tone sounded as sour and defeated as hers.

Brooke gazed out the window at the street now empty of all traffic except for an old woman walking beside her emaciated dog.

Almost to herself she murmured, "After everything all of us have been through, if only Jules and Victor and the others would be alive to see the day when France is finally set free." Her voice tight, she added, "And Virginia..."

Searching Christopher's stone-faced expression, Brooke wondered if this would be her last chance to bridge the chasm that had grown so wide between them.

She said softly, "I doubt it matters much to you anymore, but if I'm ever to live with a man again, I want partnering in my life to be like Philippe and Virginia... someone who is as respectful of my feelings and talents as I am of his. Someone willing to remain true to our bond. I just can't believe she's been taken to Germany..." Brooke said, choking on her words.

"Well, it was fairly evident to most people who knew your late husband that the kind of a relationship you've just described wasn't *ever* his strong suit." Christopher paused as if carefully considering his next words, then added, "What I've never understood is why you didn't see that upon first acquaintance."

"Well, I may have been blinded by infatuation back then, but why even bring up Victor now?"

"As it happens," Christopher began, "that's why I've waited here all day until you had your bath. I only learned the specifics about Victor's last days when I was recently told the contents of an after-action report that reached London but has been closely held—until now."

"*After*-Action?" she echoed. "How long has that report been at the War Office?" she demanded.

Christopher shifted uncomfortably in the chair "It's been there for months, but the circumstances surrounding Victor's death were forbidden by London Intelligence to be disclosed to anyone outside MI6."

"Not even MI9? Not even to his widow?" she replied, aghast that such information would be withheld from her. "I realize there are national security issues about things I obviously don't understand, so, why are you here to tell me about the specifics of how Victor died at the front *now*?"

"When they called me back to London and the higher-ups wouldn't disavow Harold Cole," he continued. "It sat poorly with me, to say the least. I petitioned my MI9 boss to permit me to tell you what happened to your husband when he died. To clean our slates."

"Our slates," she repeated. "Oh. So that's what you call this two-step dance you and I have been doing?"

Brooke suddenly didn't know what to think. In all this time, the London War office, as well as Christopher, hadn't told her *or* Victor's family what had actually happened to him in the end.

With glacial precision she said, "I suppose de Gaulle didn't want word of the demise of France's famous movie star to tarnish the brigadier's image!" Jumping to her feet, she pointed her forefinger into Christopher's chest. "And you think *my* keeping a secret about the existence of my abbreviated first marriage or my doubts about my being a decent mother are terrible, inexcusable sins, and yet, you—"

"I *don't* feel that way about you!" he shouted with an anger he'd never shown her before, "and I didn't want to keep silent about Victor, but MI6 wouldn't—"

Brooke ignored his defense. "Screw MI6! The liars in the British Intelligence services and that blowhard, Charles de Gaulle, have no problems keeping it secret how my husband *died*! They have no problems keeping a double-dealing rotter like Harold Cole on Britain's secret agent roster so the men at their desks in the War Office can play their 3-D chess games! Why are you even a part of this?"

Christopher's expression darkened and Brooke wondered if her accusations would end it between them, once and for all.

Rising from his chair he replied, his voice steely, "It's *not* my chess game. I proved to them Cole is a traitor! I told them I think it stinks that you weren't being told what happened just so de Gaulle and his staff wouldn't be blamed for sending a famous— but amateur —soldier to take the Vichy surrender that day."

She stared at him, flabbergasted to hear such a thing. "He *physically* received the actual surrender documents from the Vichy troops?"

"Yes. He was sent there to garner good publicity," Christopher flung back, "but why won't you understand that I can't tell you all the details— ever —because I signed the Secrets Act—"

"Well, I *didn't* sign such a thing," she said, cutting him off, "and I've risked my life and Nicole's for the Allied cause. I had a right to know what actually happened to my husband and *why* I never heard a word from him from the moment I first saw him off at the train!"

"I hope you can hear me, Brooke," he said, his gaze boring into hers. "I *agree* with you. For months, I've kept pestering them, asking to be shown an after-action report rumored to exist about what happened to Victor. Finally my boss at MI9 cabled me yesterday with the go-ahead to tell you... most of the truth."

"Most," Brooke echoed. "How kind."

"But are you really sure you want to hear what I *can* tell you?"

For a split second, she wondered if she did. Finally, she said, "Yes, I want to know what happened, or as much as you can tell me."

The two of them silently took the measure of each other's willingness to reveal— or hear —something clearly disquieting.

At length Christopher said, "All right, but if you disclose what I say to you today, I—"

"I won't tell," Brooke interrupted, exasperated, "and I believe you actually would kill me if I did."

He shot her a disgusted look and then began to relate information he was only, the previous day, authorized to pass on to her.

"In the after-action report that MI6 allowed my boss in MI9 to see... and the same one my boss described to *me*," Christopher began, "Victor's commanding officer sent your husband, along with a Lieutenant Jacques Renault and a few British soldiers on their motorcycles, to receive the official paperwork of a surrender after an early battle fought in North Africa. They were to rendezvous at an isolated spot in order to meet, Frenchman-to-Frenchman."

"Think about that for a moment," Brooke murmured. "Frenchmen fighting *each other* in this wretched war..."

"The victorious Free French wanted to impress upon the turncoat Vichy faction that the country's most famous actor had sided with de Gaulle's Free French Allied forces, so they took Victor with them."

"To stage a public relations stunt?" Brooke confirmed, aghast. "Photographs were taken, I imagine."

To her surprise, Christopher nodded affirmatively.

"You're exactly right. I haven't seen them, but I imagine they exist in some secret file at Whitehall. This was shortly after the Allied 'Operation Torch' launched in North Africa November 8, 1942."

"That's nearly two *years* ago!" Brooke protested.

With a shrug of agreement, Christopher continued. "It was one of the few, early victories for our side. Jacques Renault, the Free French soldier who signed the after-action report, described how the assembled Vichy troops had been required to throw their weapons in a pile as their leader signed the surrender documents."

"That must have made quite a picture with Victor in the mix," Brooke noted blandly. "Pure Hollywood."

Ignoring her, Christopher continued, "Then, witnesses interviewed in the report said Renault handed over the surrender papers and Victor put them into his saddle bag and climbed onto his motorcycle. According to Renault, Victor paused, looked over his shoulder, and made a jaunty, triumphant, 'up yours' sort of salute to the Vichy commander."

"Oh, Jeez..."

Christopher abruptly suspended his narrative as if considering carefully how to frame his next words. With a resigned sigh, he continued, "In the lieutenant's opinion, it appeared that Victor's flippant gesture gave the impression of his rubbing the Vichy's noses in their swift defeat."

"Oh glory. *Then* what?" Brooke's hands were clasped and she sank onto the worn, sitting room sofa.

"Just as Victor turned to start up his motorcycle, an angry Vichy soldier in the group that was surrounding their defeated leader grabbed a rifle from the pile of surrendered weapons."

Christopher paused and inhaled deeply. Then he said, "Renault reported that the enraged soldier took aim, fired the gun, and shot Victor in the back."

36

Brooke's hands flew to her face as she absorbed Christopher's account of how Victor had died.

"Oh, my God! The silly, self-important fool! Virtually taking a victory *bow* in front of a line of defeated countrymen?"

"Apparently, that's the way it looked to the infuriated Vichy marksman who shot him."

"Victor just *had* to take that last, final curtain call," Brooke despaired. "It's all just so damn pointless!"

Christopher turned to gaze out the villa's sitting room window. Without looking at Brooke he said, "Victor didn't actually die there, though."

Brooke's head rose and she stared at him. "What? He didn't *die* when they shot him, point blank, in the back?"

"Renault ordered the military photographer who had come with him to help pick up Victor's body off the ground and stretch it across the lieutenant's lap sitting on his motorcycle."

Brooke could imagine all too clearly the sight of the lieutenant, with one hand on the cycle's handlebars and the other on Victor's back, driving the few miles to their camp with the wounded man he'd been charged to protect.

Christopher continued, "The report emphasized that the army doctors took all the heroic measures at their disposal, but Victor died inside the hospital tent a few hours later."

Brooke shook her head in disbelief. "His family would be devastated, but not surprised, I imagine, if they ever learn of the way this happened."

"They won't learn. That is, if neither of us ever tells anyone else. Another secret kept, agreed?" Christopher asked pointedly.

"They'll be given the sanitized 'he was such a hero' version?"

"Yes, and you'll certainly keep the true version to yourself, okay?" Christopher pressed.

Brooke nodded, but countered, "Well, you certainly kept the truth from *me* a very long time. After you first told me he died in battle in North Africa, I felt so guilty for being angry that he'd never contacted me from the moment he left Paris on that troop train. I said to myself back then, 'You bitch, Brooke. The poor man arrived there and was in the thick of all that fighting and wouldn't have had a moment to write.'" Brooke shook her finger at her informant. "The truth nobody deigned to tell me was that very early on in this blasted war he was already *dead*! Killed because he'd acted like an ass." Almost to herself she said, "The bald truth is... he *never* wrote me once from Norway, England, France, *or* North Africa. His being a stinking correspondent had nothing to do with his being in the army. It had everything to do with his being monumentally self-centered and incredibly mindless of others."

"And *you* felt guilty for being angry?" Christopher asked, incredulous. "The ugly truth was, as you say, he hadn't *bothered* to write you, except that one letter he gave to me when he was about to ship out to Africa."

"Another one of his Grand Gestures." Brooke gave a harsh laugh. "I'll bet he didn't even write back to Olivia Eriksen, despite all the letters she wrote him."

Christopher gazed at her for a long moment. Then he said quietly, "Is Oliva Eriksen the woman you once told me that you'd suspected he'd had an affair with? His Norwegian co-star?"

"Yes, though he hotly denied it," Brooke murmured, taking in Christopher's somber expression as a signal he dreaded revealing something else.

"And I'll just bet he accused you of acting like a jealous spouse."

"He did."

"Well, no more blaming yourself."

Brooke looked at Christopher in surprise.

"He talked to you about making the film in Norway with his co-star?"

Christopher nodded. "That night I was with him in London, he'd had a few whiskeys and—"

"Let me guess," Brooke interrupted. "He proudly let you know how crazy Olivia was about him." Christopher merely offered a shrug. Brooke continued, "When I found the pile of letters from her within a month of our marriage, he mocked me for being suspicious, saying he found my jealousy as a new bride 'quite charming.'"

Christopher grimaced faintly. "Well, in a rambling soliloquy that night, he spoke about a dalliance he had with a woman on the film shooting in Norway in the days just prior to the Germans invading the country."

"And, incidentally, just prior to going down on one knee in my London dressing room asking me to *marry* him," she disclosed, her throat aching from unshed tears.

Christopher's face clouded. "Look, the man was falling-down-drunk when he confessed all this garbage to me, but you should know, Brooke, that he kept repeating that the liaison with that Olivia person meant nothing to him."

Brooke began pacing back and forth in front of the sitting room fireplace.

"So what? Victor lied to my face about sleeping with her, implying that I was being over-dramatic. A little bit off my rocker! Then he burned Olivia's letters right in front of me, destroying the very proof of how he'd behaved in Norway!"

From Christopher's pained expression, she could tell that he clearly wished to conclude the entire conversation.

She watched him take another deep breath.

"I'll just say one more thing and then I'm done," Christopher declared. "As much as I grew to dislike your late husband, you have a right to know that even dead drunk, he said he felt terrible for betraying you like he did with that actress. For 'betraying your *trust*' was how he put it, especially since you'd given up so much to come with him to Europe and had written him every day when he was on location in Scandinavia."

"His claiming to feel 'terrible' never stopped him from taking Olivia to bed, though, did it?" Brooke retorted. "Or any of the others, I just bet."

She closed her eyes, seeing the letters from Olivia Eriksen stacked on top of his desk. She felt sick to her stomach, but also vindicated by what Christopher had revealed. She *hadn't* been crazy or a jealous fool— but Victor encouraged her to feel as if she were.

In the next moment, she forced herself to acknowledge that she'd kept the secret of Errol's existence from everyone, which was its own terrible lie. Who is she to criticize Victor— *or* Christopher, for that matter.

Brooke opened her eyes and said softly, "Every decision Victor de Varney made was always about *him* and what he needed and wanted. It's what we actors do."

"It would seem so," Christopher agreed, and Brooke could tell he'd had his fill of the subject, and probably of *her* as well.

He made a move for the door. "And now I've told you the entire story. I wanted to make a clean breast of it all. I know nothing more. Let's just say this entire conversation today has put a period at the end of the sentence."

"At the end of *our* sentence, you mean," she replied, fighting the well of emotion that threatened to strangle her.

She longed to tell him how much she'd missed him. How much she hated the estrangement that had grown between them. But in the silence that followed, Christopher reached for a canvas rucksack he'd left near the door. Brooke could only stare into space, trying to absorb the impact of everything she'd just learned.

Victor was shot in the back by a fellow Frenchman... and he's buried in the sand thousands of miles away...

Christopher's next words were spoken softly, which made them all the more powerful.

"The truth is that I understood why Victor fell in love with you, Brooke. Because I did the same. Years ago."

"*Years* ago?"

He nodded.

"Well, then, why didn't you just *tell* me how you felt back then?" she demanded, her words strangled.

"It was... complicated. When I learned that Victor had been killed in North Africa, I hadn't been informed of the contents of the MI6 report. I didn't know then he'd died so early in the fighting in North Africa, nor that he'd made that stupid, dramatic... *gesture* after he took the surrender, instead of staying close to Lieutenant Renault, who was assigned as his bodyguard. Given the paltry facts I'd been told at that point, I didn't want to dishonor his memory in your eyes by reporting the dreary details of the last night I spent with him in London or, as you said before, 'denigrate a man buried in some sand pit in North Africa.'"

He made a grab for Brooke's right hand and gripped it tightly.

"Go ahead. Think what you want about me. About all men! But one thing I don't do is steal other men's wives. And after we both learned Victor was killed and when you and I made love that night, I felt sure you wanted it too! You knew, then, that the news that Victor had died was true that time. I thought that you'd gotten past the initial sting of such a terrible loss and that you could love me, too. That you might, someday, want to have a life with me. Before all that, Victor was just a colleague type of friend, an acquaintance, but..."

He looked at her with the regret of someone who had seen too much betrayal in this war.

"But *what*?" Brooke demanded.

Christopher gazed off into space once more. "With every day perhaps our last, I wanted you like I have never wanted another woman in my entire life. But I stupidly held off."

His words shattered every defense she had built up against him to protect herself.

That was exactly how I felt about you... and I didn't tell you, either... she acknowledged silently.

Christopher sought her gaze and admitted, "That first night when we merely slept side-by-side on the chaise, and the second time when we made love in your bedroom, I... I could no longer keep myself from showing you how I felt about you. How all I wanted was for us to be together someday... have a life together. Even have kids someday..."

"*Kids!* You say that, after what I told you the last time we were together?" Brooke protested, snatching her hand away from his, her heart the weight of a rock in her chest.

Even the mere mention of having more children seemed to trigger a visceral, emotional response she couldn't seem to control. She couldn't really blame Christopher, but his raising the subject again felt as if he was ripping the scab off the unhealed wound of her son's death.

"Why don't you just admit it, Christopher?" she said, her defenses returning full force. "If we were together and I didn't want to have children, you'd hate me for it." Thinking back to heated arguments with Arnie, she said in a low voice, "It's been my experience that what most men want, ultimately, is just a brood mare for the offspring whom they'll hardly ever see because they'll be off on their own adventures in Hollywood, or on some battlefield or... or... in *Journalism* Land."

Christopher grabbed her arm, forcing her to face him.

"What I felt about you and what I wanted to have *with* you wasn't a Hollywood fantasy, it was what I truly desired in my life after the war." Releasing her arm, he lowered his voice, his gaze steady. "I had started imagining a life with you if we both could somehow manage to make it through this nightmare, fighting together for what we believed. But, if that's what you truly think of me... that I'm only looking for a 'brood mare?' If that's the low opinion you have, and that I wouldn't consider your wishes on the subject of having children, then there's not much more to be said, is there?"

He turned to go.

Stricken by the reality that he was about to walk out the door, Brooke whispered hoarsely, "Christopher, please... can't we just—"

His eyes flashing, he turned back.

"I can't deal with this push-pull anymore, Brooke. I tell you the absolute truth of what I deeply believe, and no matter what I say from my heart that is absolutely *true* about me, you still write the script your way to play the martyr when it comes to men. You *actors* are the ones who live in fantasy." His anger unleashed, he shouted, "You think you can now 'play' the journalist when you don't bother to be sure of your facts! When you don't dig deeper, but just *assume* you know everything there is to know about the male of the species." He glared at her, spitting out his words. "Well, clearly, you don't know *me*. I was very wrong to think you did. So, be my guest, Brooke Bradley. Play this your way. Remain the star in your own movie!"

His words felt as if an ice pick had just penetrated her chest. The sense of worry and apprehension she'd experienced during Victor's long silences came back in a rush. Hadn't Christopher also disappeared for months after she'd told him about Errol and her fears of being a mother once again? He'd stayed away that time, just as he'd abruptly left Radio Mondiale the night they were to evacuate from Paris before the Nazis stormed in. He hadn't signed the Secrets Act *yet*— even so, he left without telling her he was going or saying goodbye.

A voice in the back of her head rose up, blasting her with precisely what she didn't want to hear.

For once in your life, Brooke... don't you realize the last five years weren't all about you? *Like he said, it was complicated...*

But the breach between them now felt like a bridge blown up from both sides of the river. The damage seemed too extensive even to attempt repairs. In what almost felt like a reflex action, Brooke summoned a snappy salute with her right hand to her eyebrow.

"Well, you've done your duty. Completed your assigned task." Holding her fist in front of her lips like a pretend microphone, she intoned, "International News flash: *Miss Brooke Bradley no longer needs looking after*." Dropping both hands rigidly by her side she said, "So, both of us can now assume that the war will officially end soon. As of today, you can stand down. It's over."

Her voice rising in her own ears, she ticked the fingers of one hand in succession.

"Victor's dead. Jules is dead. My son is dead. Virginia is *probably* dead, but it looks as if *I'm* going to make it through alive." She raised her chin defiantly. "So, if you think I'm such an on-again, off-again, bad sort, you're free to go, Captain Laurent. I survived, thanks to you. Mission accomplished."

Christopher held her unwavering gaze for a long moment and then took a firm hold of his rucksack and strode angrily out of the room. Ondie gave a mournful bark when the back door slammed shut.

After several seconds, she heard the gate click and he was gone.

His final words reverberated in a loop in her head...

"... no matter what I tell you is true about me, you still write the script your way to play the martyr when it comes to men..."

PART VI

37

AUTUMN 1944

F rom the day Christopher stormed out of the villa in Barbizon until Paris was finally liberated on August 24 of the momentous year of 1944, Brooke did as she had been advised: laid low behind her stone walls. She and Nicole hibernated in the villa with the rabbits in their hutches at the back of the property and Ondie by their sides. She tried to silence Christopher's last words to her and only succeeded when she tended the garden each morning and made up her own version of 'care packages' with Nicole delivering them to neighbors who had helped her in various ways during the war.

On "Paris Liberation Day," Luc, along with the five airmen still billeted at the farmstead, as well as Felix, his brother Gaspard and his wife, and farmers Antoine Boucher and Raymond Pouillet— who'd both been so helpful to Brooke's rabbit-raising project — gathered in the flagstone courtyard of the Villa du Lapin d'Or for a meager celebration. All of Brooke's guests brought food to contribute and the party drank every drop of wine remaining in their collective cellars.

War still raged in the east and in Germany, but by September, it was safe to return to Paris. Brooke and Nicole packed their few belongings, bequeathed the remaining domesticated rabbits to Felix and Luc, and bid farewell to Barbizon, retaking possession of the de Varney flat on Rue Saint-Dominique, while the fliers made their way to gathering points for Allied military.

One of the first calls Brooke made on her newly-resurrected telephone line was to the American Hospital to find out what had happened to Viv, her friend, classmate at Mademoiselle Arquette's French class, and fearless ambulance driver. She was put through to Nurse Comte, who confirmed Viv had made it through the war and was off to New York to see her family.

"Please give her this number if she ever returns and checks in with you," Brooke petitioned. "And thank you and everyone who helped me at the hospital. Those straitjackets saved the lives of four Allied aviators."

Brooke had only just learned that Dr. and Mrs. Jackson had both been deported to Germany for their "crimes against the Third Reich," with no word yet as to their fate. The same was true of Virginia d'Albert-Lake who had vanished on a prisoner train headed east.

In Paris, no one felt much like celebrating the reopening of a city rife with continuing food shortages and the violent reprisals against anyone suspected of collaborating with the Germans.

"Isn't it remarkable," Nicole said with disgust one morning in early October, "how so many Parisians are now claiming to have been part of the Resistance?"

Brooke nodded her agreement as she stirred a brew containing more chicory than coffee grounds in her cup.

"Yet, some known collaborators like Coco Chanel who lived at the Ritz with a German intelligence officer the entire war have managed to wriggle free and flee to Switzerland."

"Oh, she'll be back and all will be forgiven," predicted Nicole. "Too many Parisians wear her Number 5 perfume and love those little black dresses she designs."

IN THE WEEKS that followed their return to the city, both women remained at home except to search for groceries to buy and to walk Ondie. Neither Brooke nor Nicole had the energy or heart to socialize while the war still continued in eastern France and across Germany. They followed the BBC news reporting of Allied troops storming into enemy territory, liberating the "death camps" as the newspaper headlines screamed daily.

Brooke felt lead in the pit of her stomach every time she thought of Virginia d'Albert-Lake. After that recollection, her memory of Christopher's angry outburst the last day they were together usually followed.

"You think you can now 'play' the journalist when you don't bother to be sure of your facts! When you don't dig deeper, but just assume you know everything there is to know about the male of the species."

She had thought the evidence was clear: Christopher disappeared at crucial moments just like other men she'd thought she'd loved...

But had he?

Brooke had accepted the likelihood that he wouldn't contact her after their bitter farewell— and he hadn't. His words had dealt such a blow, she dreaded encountering any of the people she'd known at Radio Mondiale, including Victor's agent, Denise Louette, and Jules Dumont's wife, Germaine.

But what of all the people she'd worked with in Rabbit Run and the Comet Line? Other than Luc and Felix, who had no phones, Christopher was the only contact she had to learn how many of them had survived.

"I can't bear to think what's happened to Virginia, or how Philippe is coping," Brooke despaired, flipping off the radio program she and Nicole had been listening to describing an especially graphic report of Soviet troops advancing through the gates of a camp called Majdanek in Poland. She'd called Philippe once and confirmed that he'd eventually returned to Paris, but like Brooke, he hadn't the heart or energy to arrange a get-together.

Nicole had become as morose as Brooke during the uncertain days in Paris during the post-Normandy winter of 1944 when their lives seemed as unfocused and grim as before the Allied invasion of France.

When spring of 1945 finally arrived, the purple wisteria and pink blossoms on the trees along the Seine near the Eiffel Tower burst into bloom. Brooke remained glued to the radio, thrilled when she heard the report that American forces liberated Buchenwald concentration camp on April 11. Four days later, the BBC's staid news presenter couldn't keep the joy from his voice when confirming that British troops had stormed the gates of Bergen-Belsen. Her delight, though, turned into despair as reports confirmed that the liberators found some sixty thousand prisoners more dead than alive. The photographs of their skeletal bodies shocked her to her core. The number of Jews the Germans had exterminated remained unknown, but estimates were staggeringly large.

With the improvement in the weather, she was cheered by the news the Nazis were being beaten back on nearly every front. She began asking herself what sort of life she would likely have if she remained in Paris.

One stunningly sunny day she announced to Nicole, "We can't stay barricaded in this flat forever. It's time we did something about our self-imposed exile."

That same morning, May 7, 1945, the BBC had announced the unconditional surrender of all German forces to the Allies. Then, the next day, victory in Europe was officially declared and bells tolled all over Paris to announce the longed-for news.

With the sounds ringing in their ears, Nicole burst into Brooke's study, waving a bottle of champagne.

"I found one last bottle of bubbly behind a bin in the pantry! Shall we drink it?"

"Of *course,* we should," cried Brooke, jumping up from her desk where she had been going over a financial statement she'd requested from her bank. "Let's get some glasses and start guzzling it down!"

The two women repaired to the kitchen and raised their drinks in toasts to each other and even put a splash of champagne in Ondie's water bowl.

Nicole blurted out, "You're so right, Brooke. We can't just sit here moping about. We've got to start making plans for the future."

But *what* would the future hold, Brooke wondered, feeling an all too familiar wave of emotional paralysis taking hold once more.

Later that day, sitting at her dressing table, she peered critically into the mirror, noting the beginnings of crow's feet around her eyes. At 37, she was an ingenue no longer. Who would hire a thin, depressed, world-weary actress, she asked herself? And besides, everything in Hollywood had undoubtedly changed since the war. Who was there in California who even remembered her work in a bunch of B movies? And besides, the thought of competing for acting jobs in the dog-eat-dog world of the film industry filled her with dread.

Even worse, the notion of her mother still living in her rental south of Wilshire Boulevard plunged Brooke deeper into gloom. The last thing in the world she could handle emotionally was reconnecting with her alcoholic parent any time soon. Worse even than that was facing the reality that little Errol didn't even have his own gravestone to mark where he'd been buried somewhere in the San Fernando Valley.

I'll see to that... eventually...

Her resolution about that plunged her into even more gloom.

As for working on Broadway again? Brooke leaned closer to the mirror and ran her fingers through her hair, searching for the first appearance of gray roots. Was there anyone in New York she could contact in the vast world of the legitimate theater?

"I did exactly *one* play there, plus, I hated that life," she admitted to Nicole the next day when they'd cautiously returned to the subject of trying to make future plans. "An actress like me can go years before getting cast again in a show."

"What about working in broadcasting again here in France?" Nicole suggested. "Your French is practically perfect, now," she said with a smile.

Once again, Christopher's final condemnation reverberated in Brooke's head. Her thoughts went immediately to the memory of him sitting at his cluttered desk in Radio Mondiale. Her heart literally ached remembering the sight of his rumpled sports coat, tousled blond hair, and the staccato sound of his typewriter pounding out a story. She felt an almost physical longing for the excitement the two of them had shared when they'd worked together on a broadcast like the one they did about refugee children marooned in Paris's train stations.

But his final words came rushing back.

"I can't deal with this push-pull anymore, Brooke. I tell you the absolute truth of what I deeply believe, but you still write the script your way."

Is that what she'd done? What she'd always done? Written the script of her life to please herself? To advance her career? To make herself the worthy heroine? To shirk responsibility for what *she* might have contributed to a problem? Hadn't she always endeavored to get what she wanted and protect herself from being hurt or betrayed again? Her automatic defense system meant she built barriers all around herself, barriers that even people who loved her couldn't breach.

Even more damning, didn't Christopher essentially point out that she had a habit of making others wrong so she could feel justified in what *she* was saying or doing? She'd made him 'wrong' over the issue of having children when his last words belied that very statement.

If that's the low opinion you have... that I wouldn't consider your wishes on the subject of having children, then there's not much more to be said, is there?

Pushing such crushing recollections aside, Brooke shook her head with discouragement. She'd never told Nicole about Christopher's damning words, yet his absence in their lives and the reasons for it were subjects carefully avoided by an unwritten but mutual consent.

Brooke sought to answer Nicole's suggestion of becoming an on-air reporter again with a reasonable excuse.

"I'm certain there's an entirely new crew in the broadcasting business in Paris these days. I doubt I could even get a job interview there."

The truth was, now that the war was over, she wouldn't take the chance she might run into Christopher Laurent.

A FEW DAYS LATER, Nicole came into the kitchen where Brooke was chopping vegetables for a soup.

She sat down at the kitchen table, clasped her hands on its surface and blurted, "Brooke... I've been doing a lot of thinking since we talked. I've gone over my options and it makes the most sense for me to return to Alsace. I want to see my family. That is, if anyone is left."

Nicole leaving Paris for good?

Somehow, the suggestion felt like a blow to her solar plexus. Yet one more abandonment. Even so, the second that Nicole voiced her proposal, it did seem like the right solution for the woman who had gone from Brooke's housekeeper to an amazingly resilient Resistance operative who'd fought to save her homeland, and a best friend.

Summoning the will not to feel like a deserted child, Brooke stood up and embraced the younger woman who had loyally remained by her side more than four years.

"Yes," Brooke agreed reluctantly, resuming chopping the vegetables. "You need to go home and see if that's the place for you." Setting down the vegetable knife, she shook her index finger at Nicole with mock severity. "But if it isn't what you want, just know you'll always have a home with me."

"Will you be here?" Nicole asked, her brow furrowed with concern. "In Paris, I mean?"

Brooke shrugged, forcing a smile.

"Who knows? But I promise to always stay in touch so you can find me wherever I finally land."

FOR THE FIRST time in her life, Brooke had absolutely no idea what she should do next. As Victor's widow, she'd been contacted by his brother and told she would have a share in the family's Calvados enterprise. Thanks to that surprising news, she determined that she would have enough funds to get by for a few years even without gainful employment. She'd avoided accepting their invitation to visit Château de Varney, not wanting to challenge the family's belief in the heroism of her late husband.

The question was, what should she spend her days *doing,* she wondered, as a wave of utter dejection came over her. Then a new thought popped in her head.

Maybe I should write about the war?

She wouldn't act as a journalist, but merely chronicle her experiences in a memoir, she thought with a glimmer of hope.

In the next instant, she realized that most of the stories she wanted to tell would involve clandestine subjects and material that undoubtedly were still classified "top secret." She had never signed the government agreement that Christopher had, but she was under no illusions that higher ups in the intelligence services would probably cause her legal problems if she tried to publish tales that told the unvarnished truth so soon after the war.

What would happen if I ever told what I believe to be the true story of that triple turncoat, Harold Cole?

~

In early June of 1945, a month after victory in Europe had been declared, Brooke's phone rang on the desk in the library. She hurried into the room toward the very spot on the desk where she'd found the stack of letters from Olivia Eriksen.

"This entire apartment is full of ghosts," she declared out loud, glancing at the chaise where Christopher and she had once spent the night. Not for the first time she began to think she would put the flat up for sale.

Seizing the receiver she said in French, *"Allo? C'est Brooke Bradley qui parle."*

"Brooke?" answered a querulous voice in English. "Oh, it's really you! It's Virginia. Virginia d'Albert-Lake, here!"

Stunned, Brooke sank onto the chair behind the desk.

"Oh, my God, *Virginia!* I can't believe it!"

"It *is* pretty miraculous," she agreed. "I was released from Ravensbrück a few weeks ago and finally made it home. You're one of the first people I wanted to call."

To Brooke's shock, she found herself bursting into tears.

"Oh, God! You were sent to Ravensbrück? I've read such awful things..."

"And they were all true," Virginia replied, her voice choking, "but *I survived*, Brooke! I'm back in Paris. And so did Toquette Jackson. We were on the same train sent east and we managed to keep contact nearly the entire time." There was a pause and then Virginia added sadly, "But Dr. Jackson was killed... just days before it was all over."

Brooke clutched the phone. Dr. Jackson's letter was one of the reasons she was still alive.

Why is it some of us live... and some don't make it?

In Brooke's opinion, Dr. Jackson should be known as one of the saints of his time.

"Brooke? Brooke, are you still on the line?"

Attempting to recover her composure, Brooke replied, "You bet I am. You can't know how happy I am to hear your voice. So, you're in Paris? Philippe is with you? You're all right?"

"I weigh seventy-six pounds and look like a cadaver, and I'll probably never be the same. But yes. I'm all right because I'm *alive*! And because Philippe never gave up trying to find me."

"Oh, d-darling..." Brooke stuttered, knowing she was blubbering like a child. "If it will make you feel any better, I look a fright, too. I think I've been in a fog ever since that day those damn goons pushed you and that airman into the backseat of that Citroën!"

There was sudden silence on the other end of the phone.

Now Virginia was the one outright crying, her words rasping in Brooke's ear.

"That poor Leon. The SS took him away the first day. I don't know what happened to him, but I imagine he's dead."

"But you're *alive*, thank God!" Brooke countered quickly.

"Only twenty-five of the two hundred fifty in our group sent east survived," Virginia whispered, and Brooke heard her muffled sobs, her hand probably covering the phone.

"Oh, Virginia... I am so sorry. But knowing you're safe and in Paris, now, has given me such a lift."

"I look so... *ugly*, Brooke!" Virginia said, blowing her nose on a handkerchief Philippe had probably handed his wife. "I can't see how Philippe can love me, but he does."

Brooke heard the smile creep into her friend's voice and was certain Philippe *was* standing right beside her as she spoke into the phone.

"Of course, he does!" Brooke assured her. "I love you, too!"

She could hear Virginia sniffling in response to her declaration. Suddenly, the former captive's voice brightened.

"And what of the man I always knew *you* loved, Brooke? What of you and Christopher? Do you still..."

Brooke felt tears threaten once more.

"Maybe you already know," Brooke began, "Christopher made it through somehow, like we have. I heard that confirmed from our friend Luc, in Barbizon, who told me that before I came back to Paris."

"That's why I asked about you two," Virginia said softly. "Philippe also learned, apparently, that remarkable man survived the last months of the war operating on the *front lines*, mind you! I thought, perhaps, you two were still—"

"No," Brooke quickly intervened, "we... we parted company just as the war in northern France was ending. We haven't seen each other since Paris was liberated last summer."

Virginia's voice held genuine regret. "I'm so sorry it didn't work out between you both. I truly thought you—"

"I thought so too," Brooke interrupted, "but no." Unsure what else to say, she added feebly, "It was... complicated."

Brooke steeled herself not to give way to her emotions again and quickly changed the subject.

"When you feel up to company, Virginia, please let me know. I'd so love to see you and Philippe again."

"Me too, you," Virginia replied. "That's why I called. It will be a while before I can bear for anyone to see me, I'm afraid, but I promise I will get in touch."

38

SUMMER 1945

After hearing from Virginia, Brooke's life seemed to be on a proverbial roller coaster. She sporadically dropped notes to her recovering friend hoping they could meet, only to learn she was, miraculously enough, pregnant. Her doctors had urged mostly bed rest and to stay close to home, given the still-fragile state of her health.

As the summer days grew warmer and Nicole set a date certain to return to Alsace by the end of August, a dread of the unknown took a firm hold of Brooke's emotions.

By early August, Paris had grown muggy and hot.

"I've got to get out of this stuffy flat," Brooke declared to Nicole. "Want to go with me and take Ondie on a walk?"

"No, you go," Nicole said. "I still have some things to pack and send on to Alsace before I leave."

Brooke could hardly imagine her life without Nicole by her side, but they both had recognized it was far past time when the two of them should begin creating paths of their own.

At least the air felt much fresher, Brooke thought, as she walked with Ondie along the Seine. She paused at one of the bookstalls that had reappeared beside the river. With the poodle sitting obediently next to her, she perused the meager offerings laid out on a collapsible wooden table. A few minutes later, she felt a tap on her shoulder.

"Too bad there's no more Shakespeare and Company or you might have found a better selection."

Brooke whirled in place and burst out laughing for the first time in months.

"Sylvia Beach!" she exclaimed. "Oh, my goodness! How wonderful to see you!"

Then she felt stricken by guilt, only too aware of the stress her pretense of having cancer at Vittel must have caused Sylvia, her closest companion at the internment camp.

"Oh, God, Sylvia! I've meant to get in touch to tell you of the sham medical diagnosis I used to get out of Vittel, but—"

"I heard ages ago that you hadn't died, you clever girl!"

"You're not mad at me?"

Sylvia shrugged. "Not anymore, but I felt terrible *for* you that day when I saw you leave our bizarre prison at that damned resort. I figured then that I might not ever see you again if your treatments in Paris didn't work." A scowl furrowed Sylvia's brow. "Why haven't you 'fessed up about your cancer ruse and made amends before *now* for scaring me to death?" she scolded.

For her part, Brooke completely understood why her friend was cross with her.

"It's no excuse, but perhaps here's an explanation," Brooke ventured, seizing both of Sylvia's hands. "I think I've just been in a permanent funk since the war wound down."

Sylvia offered her own sad smile.

"Actually, so have I. Hemingway symbolically liberated my bookshop last year, but I decided it's just too hard to run a business at this point."

"Oh, Sylvia, the shop is truly no more?"

Brooke couldn't think of anything comforting to say. Sylvia offered a shrug.

"I'll probably write a memoir about it all someday, but for now — guess what I'm doing this week? I'm giving a dinner party on Saturday. Will you come?"

Brooke hesitated. Nicole was due to leave soon and she certainly didn't feel in a festive mood. And what if Christopher were invited?

You're bound to run into him at some point. Pull your socks up, girl! she commanded herself.

She took in the sight of the woman who had been a stalwart supporter of the local *literati*, even as the Nazis rolled into Paris. It was a shot in the arm to see that Sylvia had made it through the war and was still willing to be her friend.

And besides, she owed her an apology.

"I've been an awful hermit," Brooke confessed. "Please forgive me for not trying to get in touch much sooner. I might not be a very good dinner party companion, but yes. I'll come." Impulsively, she gave Sylvia a hug. "And thank you for inviting me. I need a very swift kick in the pants."

"Happy to oblige," Sylvia replied cheerfully. "See you Saturday at eight and bring a bottle of wine, if you can scrounge one up."

BROOKE FELT a sharp pang of guilt for donning her one Chanel "little black dress" she'd bought before the war, but it was the only decent thing hanging in her closet suitable to wear to Sylvia's dinner party. She'd purchased it when she first came to Paris and before the designer had moved into the Ritz with her German lover.

A quick glance around Sylvia's front room revealed Christopher was not among the guests. Mixed emotions sat in the pit of Brooke's stomach. But, the gathering included a few familiar faces like the writer Colette and, much to Brooke's discomfort, Josephine Baker, one of the women with whom she suspected Victor had had an affair. The exotic musical performer was quick to express her condolences about Victor's death, sympathy that Brooke was surprised to perceive as completely sincere.

At this point, it's all just blood under the bridge Brooke decided silently.

Sylvia had previously described the brave deeds the singer had undertaken for the Free French underground, including passing crucial information written to the Allies in invisible ink on the entertainer's sheet music.

After drinks in the sitting room, their hostess clapped her

hands, saying gaily, "Dinner, everyone! Look for your place cards and be prepared to eat beans. It's all we could find."

"Cassoulet?" declared one guest, referring to a French peasant dish made of cannellini legumes, chicken broth, pork parts, and salt.

"How wonderful!" they all chorused.

In the dining room, a tall, dark-haired young man gallantly pulled out a straight-backed chair for Brooke. She glanced down at his place card next to hers and stifled a gasp.

Lt. Jacques Renault

"How do you do?" she said politely. She tried to keep her voice steady as she gazed into the eyes of the former soldier who Christopher had revealed was present at the Vichy surrender, along with Victor. "I'm... Brooke Bradley. Lovely to meet you."

She prayed he wouldn't make the connection between her and Victor de Varney. But this wasn't going to be Brooke's lucky night.

"I don't know if Sylvia told you," he said softly as he settled in his chair beside her, "but I knew your husband. We both served in North Africa. Sylvia happened to mention you were coming tonight and I asked to sit next to you."

Struggling for composure, Brooke took a deep draught of wine from a glass waiting on their table and turned to Renault.

"And I know who *you* are," she managed to say.

Clearly startled to hear this, he stuttered, "I-I wanted merely to convey my condolences to you." Adding obliquely, "In person."

Brooke decided to get the worst part over with as quickly as possible.

"You were there when Victor was shot. In the back. After taking the surrender, weren't you?" she confirmed quietly. "You were sent as his bodyguard, I understand."

Renault reared back with a shocked expression.

"You know all that? May I ask how?"

"I'm afraid I can't tell you how I was informed of what happened, but I want to thank you for trying to save his life. You were not the cause of his getting killed."

"But I failed," Lieutenant Renault said, looking miserable. "Your husband was brave to volunteer for the mission, but—"

"But he wasn't properly trained for it, am I right?" she said pointedly.

"No, he wasn't," Jacques Renault allowed. "He hadn't the combat experience to know to stay close to me and get on the motorcycle without... fanfare."

Brooke felt genuine sorrow for the poor man, and placed her hand lightly on his sleeve.

"Your superior officers should never have sent Victor to an actual battlefield." She paused. "He was just an actor, not a real soldier."

"But it was my job to protect him and I didn't do that. I wrongly assumed he would stick to the plan to ride out ahead of me as we left. He wasn't someone trained to cope with situations as unstable as confronting a defeated enemy."

"Victor was *trained* to take a bow when he finished his work," Brooke said bluntly. "Like so many actors, he felt he was the star of his own show. He'd never actually fought in combat, but still, he was given centerstage by sycophants in the War Office."

Renault confessed, "I felt I had to resign my commission."

"That's terrible," she murmured. "I'm so sorry."

Brooke could almost see the scene as if it were a movie: Victor, standing tall, proud to be the one to whom they handed the proof of surrender.

How cruel you are to judge him so, she scolded herself. Another voice in her head declared: *But look how Victor's impulsiveness had ruined Renault's military career!*

How well she understood her former tribe. Weren't all thespians trying to make up for the love they didn't get enough of when they were younger? she mused, thinking of her own life story while staring into her wine glass.

This need for the spotlight was all so foreign to her now. Her overarching desire during the last four years had been merely to survive— and to help a few shot-down fliers do the same.

Her attention was drawn back to Jacques who was pulling a small box from his inside jacket pocket.

"I didn't know how to find you after peace in Europe was declared." He raised the box eye level. "I've kept this with me since the day Victor and I both were given the Croix de Guerre in North Africa for loyalty to France. He, posthumously, of course," Renault added quickly. "I thought one day you and I might encounter each other, given we know people in common. When Sylvia told me you'd be here tonight, I brought this to give you."

He placed the box in her hand. The small, velvet case felt like a rock in her palm. While the lieutenant watched, she pried open the lid. Inside was a square, silver, beribboned cross.

A medal for Victor's loyalty? she questioned silently.

She quickly closed it, and found herself considering how Christopher— who had taken so seriously his perceived duty to look after her if her husband died in the war —had been the loyal one. *He* had been the person who did the hard, grinding work of running his section of the Comet Line. He had always kept her best interests in his sights. He was the person who'd saved her from harm countless times when they worked together as part of Barbizon's Rabbit Run escape line.

And Victor? From the start, his affection had been ephemeral. A will-o'-the-wisp, depending on his mood or his needs. In contrast, Christopher's care for her had endured for the entirety of this ghastly, bloody war.

And what had *she* done?

Brooke swallowed the last of her wine in one gulp.

I pushed him away, she admitted with brutal honesty.

She'd spurned the truth of every word Christopher had tried to tell her. That he'd fallen in love with her, despite his best intentions. That he'd kept his distance until word of Victor's death was confirmed. That he wanted a life with her, with or without having children together. Certainly, he'd expressed his desire for a family, but hadn't he let her know by his *actions* that he loved her either way?

But it's too late for all that.

His last words clearly conveyed that he couldn't stomach her *own* will-o'-the-wisp behavior any longer. The 'push-pull,' as he'd described her actions. And he'd meant what he'd said. He'd never reached out to her again, even after peace had been officially declared.

Brooke focused her gaze once again on Jacques, speaking softly so the others wouldn't hear.

"I will say it again, Lieutenant Renault, so I hope you'll hear me more clearly this time. Please know that in *no way* do I hold you responsible for what happened to my husband. You must, for both our sakes, accept that truth."

Renault's eyes misted over and he offered her a brief nod. The scent of the fragrant white beans and salty bacon wafting pleasantly to Brooke's nostrils, she bid those sitting nearest her, "*Bon Appétit.*" The lieutenant and she spooned the delicious flavors into their mouths, saying little to each other after that.

As dessert was being served, someone at the end of the table loudly tapped a knife against a wine glass and offered a toast to France "and to the end of this wretched war!"

Voices rose loudly in the room, Brooke's among them.

"*Liberté, Egalité, Fraternité.*"

At the conclusion of the meal, Jacques pushed back his chair as the other guests repaired to the sitting room for after-dinner coffee. Victor's former bodyguard politely held Brooke's chair as she rose from the table.

As if he were inquiring about the weather, Renault asked, "Do you imagine you'll return to Hollywood now, Madame de Varney?"

She halted mid-step as the two were making their way toward Sylvia's front room and turned to face her questioner.

"Hollywood?" she repeated. She slowly shook her head and answered, "No, not now. Not ever."

39

AUTUMN 1945

At the end of August, Nicole decided to postpone leaving for Alsace for another few months.

"But, why?" asked Brooke, feeling as if she'd had a reprieve from a Nazi firing squad.

"My cousin writes that the territory is in the process of being restored as a part of France again, but everything is still in flux."

"Which means worse than ever food shortages and living conditions there?" Brooke queried. "Well, you know you're welcome to stay here as long as you like. Forever, in fact."

Nicole smiled her thanks.

"At least things are slowly improving in Paris," Brooke remarked. "And, don't you imagine life will settle down in Alsace after the New Year?"

Nicole heaved a shrug. "Let us hope."

THE AUTUMN of 1945 deepened into shorter days and soon, colder temperatures began blowing off the Seine. One afternoon in late November, Brooke and Ondie set off on their daily walk along the *quai*. Each time she ventured out of her flat, life around Paris took on the appearance of near-normality, whatever that was, Brooke mused. It seemed so strange for her that she still felt the echoes of the war everywhere and she wondered as she took in the sight of children playing in the parks if she would ever get past the sense of danger she'd lived under for so long, unknown perils that might be lurking around every corner.

Crossing the street to have a coffee at an outdoor café, she stopped short and stared at a poster affixed to a wall. Blinking several times, she could hardly believe what she was seeing.

Much like the wartime "Wanted" billboards sporting *her* photo that the Nazis had once plastered all over Paris, she stared into the black-and-white eyes of an all-too-familiar face.

"*Harold Cole!*" she exclaimed aloud. "Why, you son-of-a-bitch!"

She peered at the words printed under the picture of a thin-faced man in a fedora and sporting a trim mustache. Now that the war was finally over in Europe, apparently there was a massive manhunt underway for "Britain's most notorious traitor."

At this late date they're going to arrest him? Brooke thought with disgust, recollecting all the lives of volunteer escape helpers lost due to his double-dealing with the Nazis. She wondered if none of the high-ups at MI6 wanted to be known as the Intelligence genius that had turned Cole into a triple agent?

She hurried to the nearest kiosk and bought a copy of the *British Daily Mail,* along with a recently resurrected newspaper sold in France and printed in English.

When she arrived back at the flat, Nicole was in the kitchen preparing their evening meal. Pointing at the headlines, Brooke exclaimed, "Can you believe this? They apparently had the bastard in *custody* and he just blithely walked out November eighteenth, wearing an American sergeant's overcoat, can you imagine?"

"No wonder his poster is all over Paris," Nicole said, gesturing to Cole's headshot in the newspaper. She pointed to a paragraph halfway down the page. "Oh! And listen to this," she said, reading further in the printed account. "'The traitor was arrested for multiple wartime activities before he boldly left the barracks where he'd been detained.'"

"'Boldly left?' He probably conned his captors just like he

outfoxed everybody in British Intelligence!" Brooke retorted. How could she ever forget the day Nicole and she had spotted him conferring with an SS agent when they'd taken their bicycles to a shop for repair— and that very same night, had to flee with Jules Dumont in tow to Barbizon to escape arrest.

"Well, I hope they catch him soon," Nicole said with a shiver. "A man like him must be pretty desperate, now that all his German comrades are gone."

To say nothing of no longer having the protection of some devious Brits who covered for him in MI6, Brooke thought resentfully.

CHRISTMAS, 1945, passed with a quiet celebration with the d'Albert-Lakes in their flat on Rue Vaneau. Virginia was still frightfully underweight, except for the bump in her midsection that was expanding every week.

"The doctors could hardly fathom I'd become pregnant!" she announced Christmas Eve to her guests. "Can you believe that the baby's due around the one-year anniversary of my arrival back in Paris from Ravensbrück?"

Brooke leaped up from her chair and embraced the expectant mother and Philippe as well. She silently considered how different Virginia's joy was from the dread she'd experienced learning she was going to have Arnold Warmsby's child. Despite the happiness she felt for her two friends, Brooke struggled with the sense of how perilous it was to bring a child into such a world as she'd lived through during the war. Merely four months earlier, the United States had dropped two bombs on Japan with devastation that humanity had never before witnessed. What kind of universe was that for a child to grow up in?

Pushing away such gloomy thoughts, she forced a smile to her lips, raised her champagne glass, and toasted her hosts.

SHORTLY AFTER THE NEW YEAR, Brooke was in the library stretched out on the chaise reading Hemingway's *For Whom the Bell Tolls*. It had been published in 1940, but she'd never found the time to read the copy Sylvia had given her as a Christmas gift, until now. The bell to her flat rang a few sharp trills, startling her from her absorption of the author's description of life during a war that preceded the one she'd lived through.

Brooke listened for the sound of Nicole's footsteps in the foyer heading to answer the front door. Ondie had been sent for the first time in years to the dog groomer that morning and Brooke surmised the poodle was about to be returned with a stylish trim befitting her fancy pedigree.

The bell rang again, this time more insistently. Concluding Nicole was in the back bedroom, packing the last of her things before her departure the next day, Brooke set aside the novel, exited the library into the foyer, and opened the door.

"Well, hello, Madame de Varney," said a slender young man with a pencil-thin mustache lining his upper lip. "Or should I say Mademoiselle Bradley?"

He smiled faintly, his slight body swallowed up by the U.S. Army overcoat he had on, its sergeant's insignia embroidered on his shoulders.

Brooke's heart began to pound in her chest at the sight of Harold Cole standing on her threshold.

"Yes?" she said, fighting to keep her voice steady while holding tight to the brass knob, preparing to slam the door in his face. He might think she hadn't remembered him on the day he'd come to the flat with the British socialite, Gillian Wingate-Jones— so Brooke pretended ignorance.

Holding his gaze, her heart sped up so much, blood throbbed in her head. Just when she had started to feel her surroundings were safe again, the Nazis gone from Paris, and life returning to normal, here was her worst nightmare standing at her door.

"It's smashing to see you again!" Cole greeted her with astounding bonhomie. "I wasn't sure you were back in Paris, but I'd hoped you were so I could congratulate you on all you did to help our RAF boys get back home."

Brooke was flabbergasted by the man's gall, but also his cunning. The newspaper accounts she'd been reading about the manhunt warned that he was likely to attempt to "masquerade as a British or American officer," and that "Cole will not hesitate, if he is armed, to fire."

Her thoughts spinning in all directions, she heard familiar footsteps coming down the hallway behind her.

Oh, God! Nicole!

She put one hand behind her back and waved a warning for Nicole to stay back. The sound of the steps ceased and Brooke prayed her housemate tiptoed back to the kitchen.

Cole took a step forward, as if he expected to be welcomed inside. He looked beyond Brooke's shoulder, but apparently didn't see anything other than the empty foyer. He smiled as if they were old friends and oozed cordiality in his phony posh British accent.

"I so enjoyed visiting here with my dear friend Gillian when I was working as an intelligence officer." He sighed. "That seems so long ago, doesn't it? I'm currently waiting for my discharge papers from the London War Office and wondered if I might impose upon you for a back bedroom or something until the documents come through in two days' time?"

The guy who would have had the SS arrest me to make a few francs wants to be my houseguest?

How dumb did he think this blonde was, she thought with a rush of pure hatred for the man. Brooke made no answer to his pleasantries, stunned by his request to seek refuge under her roof.

Meanwhile, Cole stuffed his hands in the pockets of his coat as if feeling a draft—or fingering a weapon.

With boyish but unconvincing sheepishness he ventured, "The November chill is brutal at our barracks, so I thought, perhaps... as a fellow warrior, now standing down, you might be so kind as to...?"

He left his sentence dangling and braced one hand on the front door itself.

Brooke felt both fear and rage igniting within her. How dare this traitor come to her door playing her for a fool! He was obviously on the run, with his first, desperate requirement being shelter and food since winter was hard upon Paris this early January day in the New Year.

"I'm awfully sorry," Brooke said, keeping her voice pleasant, "but I'm afraid I can't help you." Her mind desperately searched for a reason to keep him out. Miraculously, a thought surfaced that she hoped might save the situation. "The irony is, I've just sold this flat. And as it happens, the buyers are due any minute to take measurements for their furniture and—"

Before she could complete her sentence, Cole shoved his shoulder against the door and burst across the threshold, pulling a pistol out of his pocket.

He pointed his German Luger directly at Brooke's chest and snarled, "Well, since you're expecting company, I'll just have to bar the door and not let them in. Meanwhile, I suggest *you* leave by the back door so I may lock it behind you and declare this my new safehouse."

He gave her shoulder a brutal shove.

"Turn around," he ordered, "and walk down that hall. *Now!*"

Brooke immediately obeyed his command, certain as she entered the hall leading to the kitchen, that Cole would never allow her simply to leave by the back door. Both of them were well aware that she'd most likely head straight for the Prefecture of Police. Approaching the kitchen door, Brooke frantically tried to think what to do next.

Had Nicole, from the shadowed hall, recognized the traitor Brooke had railed against all these years? As housekeeper, Nicole had served Gillian Wingate-Jones and Harold Cole tea on that day the pair had paid an unwelcome call to this flat when Nazis lurked everywhere in the early days of the Paris occupation. Brooke could only pray that when she'd waved her warning signal, Nicole had retreated to the kitchen and gone for help.

Her stomach turning over on itself, she opened the door and saw to her relief the kitchen was empty. She had barely taken two steps forward before she felt a brush of wind and saw from the corner of her eye, Nicole bringing down a heavy, copper skillet onto Cole's wrist, knocking the gun from his hand. The world froze as the pistol skittered under a cabinet to Cole's right.

"Owww!" he cried, turning to curse his attacker who then swung the flat end of her weapon, full force, into his chest. Falling to his knees, the wind knocked out of him, Cole continued to howl in pain, cradling his shattered wrist in his other hand against ribs that had also taken Nicole's mighty blow.

Brooke dashed toward a kitchen cabinet, stooped down, and reached to grab ahold of the gun. At the same moment, Nicole stood over her wild-eyed victim, waving a large butcher knife in her other hand while he struggled to his feet. Blood pounding in Brooke's ear, she turned and pointed the Luger in Cole's direction.

The bastard has been responsible for so many deaths... he deserves to die!

Before she could fit her shaking finger into the trigger hole and take proper aim, Cole took one look at the barrel of his own gun and bolted toward the back door, pausing only seconds before he opened it with his uninjured hand, and disappeared.

Brooke and Nicole stared at each other for several long seconds. In the next instant, Brooke dashed to the half-opened backdoor that led to the flat's rear stairway, now empty except for a trash can standing against a wall. Relieved to see Cole was gone, she slammed the door shut and flipped the dead bolt.

Still trembling from the rush of adrenalin coursing through her veins, Brooke tore through the kitchen past Nicole, sprinted down the hallway and through the foyer to secure the lock on the front door as well.

Gasping for breath, she reentered the kitchen, exclaiming, "Nicole, you were absolutely brilliant!"

"Oh, I recognized him right away. I-I thought, at first... you were going to convince him to go away," Nicole replied, as winded as Brooke, "but then I heard him ask to stay here and I knew you were in trouble. When I heard you two coming toward the kitchen, I grabbed the frying pan and the knife and hid behind the door."

"Well, your choice of weapons, timing, and aim were impeccable!" Brooke declared, adding hurriedly, "just let me make a quick call." She sprinted down the hall toward the library a second time, shouting to Nicole over her shoulder, "I heard most of the old staff at the U.S. Embassy has returned. Let's hope that the very nice attaché I knew still works there and will answer his phone."

Both women well remembered the American authority who had issued Brooke an official seal to affix on the front door just before the Nazis invaded Paris. It had miraculously kept local German authorities from requisitioning the property for their private use when they first invaded Paris.

Dialing the Embassy's telephone number with fingers that still shook, Brooke could only hope that her latest 'intelligence' about the despicable Harold Cole would be forwarded to the Brits and local French authorities.

Whether they could catch him and would hand him over to the Allied High Command for trial was anybody's guess, she thought cynically. As far as she was concerned, he should be hung for treason.

After the call, Brooke sank back against the desk chair. Shen then summoned the energy to place the Luger she'd carried with her from the kitchen into the top drawer.

At least it might be useful if Cole ever decided to show his face again on Rue Saint-Dominique, she thought. She carefully pointed the barrel to the back of the library desk— but within easy reach.

Startling her as she shut the drawer, her front doorbell rang suddenly. She couldn't believe Harold Cole would have the gall to call again, but she dashed into the foyer and said loudly through the door, "Who is it?"

"*Bonjour, Madame de Varney. Je viens du 'Poodle Palace.' Voyez Ondie avec une coupe de caniche parfaite!*"

Brooke flung open the door, fell to her knees, and threw her arms around her dog, inhaling the sweet scent of her dearest companion's first day at a dog spa. Ondie looked stunning, indeed, with a head adorned by a fluffy pom-pom of curly, chocolate-colored hair. The rest of her furry coat had been trimmed to Parisi-enne perfection.

∾

LESS THAN A WEEK LATER, the headlines on the January 8, 1946, front page of the newly resurrected *Paris Herald Tribune* displayed in bold letters:

TRAITOR SHOT ABOVE PARIS BAR.

Notorious British turncoat Harold Cole on the run from authorities for months, was cornered above Billy's Bar on Rue de Grenelle in the 6th Arrondissment and shot in the heart by one of two French police officers when he tried to escape.

He was wanted as one of the most infamous double agents (some allege he was a triple agent) Britain had ever had the misfortune – or "stupidity" several sources say —to employ during the war.

BROOKE HAD SPREAD the English-language newspaper onto the broad kitchen table, reading the story several times with amazement and relief.

Except for Ondie's reassuring presence, the Rue Saint-Dominique flat seemed eerily empty now that Nicole had finally taken the train to Alsace. Gazing into space as Brooke turned over in her mind the startling recent events regarding Cole, she fought a renewed sense of gloom that she didn't have Nicole with her to share this amazing news.

She flipped the paper to the second page where her eyes fell on the *Tribune's* masthead. In a neat box above the advertising and subscription rates were listed the names of the newspaper's owner, publisher, editors, and reporters. One name printed below that of the *Trib's* editor-in-chief leapt out at her like a lightning strike.

Brooke slowly skimmed her finger over the print. Then, she jumped up from her seat, bumping her chair leg against Ondie's flank.

"Oh! Sorry, sweetheart," she apologized, rubbing the dog's rear quarters with the flat of her hand. Ondie looked up at her reproachfully. Patting her dog's recently fluffed-up head and then giving her a scratch behind her ear, Brooke said, "I promise we'll walk later, but now I've got to go!"

Racing into the foyer, she grabbed her newly purchased heavy winter coat from the front hall closet and dashed out the door, taking the stairs two at a time past the birdcage elevator.

40

B rooke ignored the receptionist in the outer office of the *Paris Herald Tribune* and walked into a newsroom full of men pounding away at typewriters. With a sweeping gaze above their heads, she spotted the person she had come to see sitting at a desk inside his glass-fronted office. He was on the phone.

Yanking open the door marked **Executive Editor**, she marched inside and shut it with a bang.

At the interruption, Christopher Laurent looked up with a scowl on his face. In the next moment, his expression changed to one of amazement and then to something Brooke couldn't quite decipher.

In one swift motion, she seized the receiver from his hand and swiftly returned it to its cradle.

Christopher commented mildly, "You just hung up on the newly-appointed Minister of Agriculture." He gestured to a nearby chair and said, "May I offer you a seat?"

"Yes, thank you," she replied. She flung her coat onto a small sofa nearby and plopped down in a chair opposite his cluttered desk.

Without preamble she asked, "You said you'd promised Victor to look after me, correct?"

"Correct," Christopher nodded, his expression opaque, "but I seem to remember the last words you said to me were that you no longer needed my services."

"Well, I was mistaken. I *do*. Need your services, I mean."

Christopher looked at her with a sideways glance.

"Well, that's rather intriguing. What kind? Of services, I mean?"

"You can give me a job. Here. At the paper."

"So, you think you're qualified to play the role of reporter again?"

Not quite what I hoped to hear, but fair enough, Brooke thought.

"No," she replied calmly. "Not nearly ready." He raised an eyebrow but allowed her to continue uninterrupted. "I'll type copy for the real reporters," she said in a rush, "or I'll make coffee... or I'll scrub floors at night to prove to you what a dunce I've been."

Christopher stood up behind his desk, staring across the narrow space separating them.

Swallowing hard, Brooke began to wonder if she was totally embarrassing herself in front of a room full of Christopher's colleagues whom she could sense were staring at them through the glass wall.

She leaned both hands on his cluttered desk, one palm resting on a ledger and the other on a pile of typescript.

Inhaling a deep, steadying breath she declared quietly, "I'll do virtually *anything* you require to show you that I can learn to dig deeper and never assume I know all there is to know about a subject— even when it comes to the male of the species. That is, until at least three separate, *reliable* sources tell me I've got it right."

Christopher cracked his first smile, commenting dryly, "Well, that's a start, Cub."

"And I'll also do virtually *anything* to convince you that you are the only man in the world whom I trust to understand what we've both been through. The only one whom I can't bear to go through life without... and who I think is the sexiest man alive, despite that permanently wrinkled jacket you've got on."

Christopher walked around his desk with an amazed look on his face.

"Did tangling with Harold Cole convince you that I'm not such a bad fellow?"

It was Brooke's turn to look amazed.

"How the hell do you know about *that*?"

"I interviewed all the principals involved in the story we just ran about Cole getting what he so roundly deserved above the Billy's Bar two days ago."

"You did?" Brooke murmured.

"Yup."

She shrugged. "Of course, you did."

"Your friend at the U.S. Embassy allowed me to see his notes about the way you and Nicole dispatched Cole with a broken wrist and cracked ribs to show for his troubling you."

"And why in the world am I surprised to hear you know all this?" she asked rhetorically.

Christopher strode over to the window and abruptly pulled down the shade, blocking his gawking colleagues' view of their animated conversation. He turned and crossed to stand next to her chair.

"You both could have been killed, you know," he said sternly, laying one hand on her shoulder. "So, when it comes to double—possibly triple agents —do you admit you could use a *little* looking after?"

Brooke swiveled in her chair to gaze up at him.

"You knew from the Embassy guy that I was still in Paris, yet you never..."

Her throat tight, she couldn't finish her sentence. She looked away and made a show of studying an apparently new map of France pasted to his wall. The truth was, Christopher had made no move to reach out to her in the wake of what happened with Cole. Clearly, she'd been in the wrong on so many things and had never owned up to it. Was it too late to make amends?

Christopher gently pulled her to her feet. He brought his forefinger under her chin, slightly tilting it up so she had to stare him squarely in the eye.

Reading her mind, as he had so often over the years, he said, "I didn't try to contact you because the only way it would work for us is if you decided what you really wanted— and if that was... me.

The real me." He leaned forward and touched her nose with his. "I think I was pretty clear to you what *I* wanted."

"Yes, you were," she whispered, tears hovering at the edge of her eyes. "And it was *you* I wanted almost from the day the two of us wrote that story together about the refugees in the train station."

Brooke covered her face with both hands and leaned against his chest.

"Oh, Christopher, I am so *truly* sorry it took me so long to sort it all out... and to get past how rotten it felt when you walked out of the villa in Barbizon." She looked up at him, adding, "You probably know by now, I'm a person who doesn't like to get *left*."

He looked down at her steadily.

"I finally got that straight about you. You and I had exchanged some pretty heated words before I walked out of your sitting room at the villa. I'd just forced you to see that Victor, for sure, was no saint— just like all the other men you'd thought you'd loved —and I couldn't make you see that *I* was no Victor."

Brooke nodded, inhaling a deep breath. "He was just an actor and so was I, but thanks to the damn war, I learned that you *are* the real deal. The guy who stands and delivers."

"Thanks for that, but I can't totally agree with you."

"What?"

Brooke leaned back in his arms and searched his face. Christopher let go of her and began pacing in front of the shuttered window facing the newspaper's bullpen full of reporters.

"You're not the only one who's had time to think and reflect since our last meeting," Christopher said soberly. "I've had these last months to consider what you said, questioning what kind of father I'd be, given the profession I'm in. It turns out, you weren't far wrong when it comes to my obsession with the news business. I realized much later why your judgment of me felt like such a kick in the gut. I didn't want to face that I might well turn into my father. Putting my job ahead of any family I might have. So when it came to keeping my distance from you all this time, I'm pretty sure that I mixed up some facts with pure pride."

"Well, here I am,' Brooke said. "I'm in your office, practically on my knees. I've come to you. Now it's your move."

He laughed softly. "Well, I've already pledged I'm a one woman man, so that subject is decided. Then, there's the subject of making babies with you."

"Yes?" she said, holding her breath.

"For sure, I love being around kids— up to a point."

"And...?"

"And... a cousin of mine just had an adorable daughter." He smiled sheepishly at Brooke. "I was totally enamored with her for about a half hour, and then I got antsy. I began to fret that perhaps something had come over the news wire that I needed to see."

"Did she need her diaper changed?" Brooke asked, keeping a straight face.

"She did, indeed. Her mother took her from my arms while my cousin and I went downstairs to a nearby café to have a glass of wine."

"Ah... and this gave you a moment of clarity?"

"My first thought was that I wished you were with me. Then, I had a sharp recollection of what you had said during our Battle of the Titans."

"Which was?" Brooke asked quietly.

Christopher seized one hand, his thumb drawing small circles on her palm.

"My thought that day drinking in the café with my cousin was that you and I can be the best aunt and uncle in the world— that is, between our assignments."

Brooke's heart began to beat wildly. It wasn't just she who had messed up their relationship. From Christopher's last statement, it appeared that they *both* were willing to examine what they'd each brought to the table that had pushed them apart.

"You know, Christopher, we might just have a chance to test out that uncle-aunt thing. Do you know that Virginia d'Albert-Lake's baby is due in June? She asked me to be the child's godmother and wondered if I'd be upset because Philippe hoped you'd be the godfather."

"So I'd heard."

"You *did*? She settled her hands on her hips in her customary way of showing she was peeved. "Why do you always know stuff before I do?" she demanded, but she couldn't keep a smile off her face.

Had Virginia and Philippe been scheming to bring about something Brooke and Christopher had just done for themselves—finding their way back to each other?

"Of *course,* I knew Virginia was having a baby," he teased, "and I've already accepted the honor of being a godparent."

"So have I," Brooke acknowledged.

Christopher's smile faded and Brooke braced herself.

"What you flung at me that day had some truth in it, Brooke. Working journalists are a different breed of cat from regular folk, but that's all right, I've decided. It takes all kinds, to make the world work."

"And journalists are an important part of making the world work for *everyone,*" Brooke declared. "At least good journalists are."

Christopher nodded. "And to be a good journalist, it takes most of a human's time and energy. After I saw how much time and effort goes into taking care of my cousin's baby, I thought, 'why can't there be devoted couples who choose honorable, totally demanding careers and *still* like to hang around other people's children? Friends *and* family have the time to give them what they need... consistent love and full-time attention? The whole kit-and-kaboodle."

"You know 'kit-and-kaboodle?'"

"Michigan," he explained shortly.

"Well, exactly!" Brooke exclaimed. "Childless folks like us can be the icing on the kids' birthday cake. We'll be listed in Virginia and Philippe's will as 'backups' if anything ever happens to them."

"And we'll make it a priority to appear for their children's name days, graduations, and weddings, yes?"

"That's precisely how I'd like it," she whispered. "But if you'd come to such a sensible realization," she asked, "why didn't you seek me out?"

"Because, as I said, it would only work for us if you truly knew what you wanted and if you sought *me* out because you trusted me to have your best interests at heart... the way I trust you."

She clasped both his hands and held his glance. "Well, that's easy. I've come to you today to tell you I want you and I trust you absolutely. And if we change our minds about having kids at some point down the road, so be it."

Christopher's broad grin lit up his face. He pulled her against his chest and held her close. "Yes, if we change our minds, so be it," he echoed, adding. "It always will be a joint decision and... only perfect nannies need apply. Meanwhile, Ondie is already our kid. She loves you madly, and so do I."

"She loves *you* madly, and so do I." Brooke smiled into his chest, her lips brushing against his tweed jacket, her nostrils inhaling his scent. Then, she determined to clear up one, last outstanding issue between them.

"Not only did I come here to tell you... to *beg* you to be my fella," she said, "but I truly want to learn to be an honest-to-God journalist. To never assume a damn thing until I have solid facts to confirm my intuition is correct. I want to write about the war," she said to him earnestly. "Write about the amazing, *ordinary* people like Luc and Felix and Nicole, Philippe and Virginia who did such brave, selfless acts of courage to help end the war. The story of that couple on the farm near the secret forest should be told... my concierge, who never ratted on us. Even if it's years before the powers-that-be let me publish anything, I want to get everything down while my memory is fresh. And I want to learn to tell stories of what has happened since peace was declared."

"You know, Brooke," Christopher insisted, smiling down at her, "you're not the novice you think you are. Instead of making coffee for the boys out there, I think you should dedicate your talents and that heart-throb voice of yours to the broadcast news unit I want to launch. Tell those stories about the *real* war heroes and heroines out loud."

Brooke felt herself beaming ear-to-ear.

"Christopher, you mean it? The paper's going to get into broadcasting? That would be a perfect fit for me! I loved working at Radio Mondiale."

He encircled her in his arms.

"Everything about you is a good fit," he said, his voice husky.

Suddenly, doubts crept into Brooke's near euphoria. "Will the higher ups here really let you give me a job?"

Christopher threw his head back and laughed.

"Hey! What you see before you is a man one step below the paper's Editor-in-Chief! Why wouldn't my boss agree to give a broadcasting contract to the Resistance heroine and former film star— the famous Brooke Bradley —whose "Wanted" posters were the talk of Paris during the occupation? Give that fabulous woman a slot as a commentator to launch the *Trib*'s latest media enterprise?" he declared stoutly. "Trust me, you're a shoo-in."

Brooke dismissed his last statements with a wave of her hand, asking in a deadly serious tone, "But will you help me to learn to be the fearless journalist I only playacted, but desperately wished I were?"

In her heart of hearts, she wondered if she could ever live up to Christopher's rock-solid judgment and exacting professional standards.

"C'mon here, you," he said, pulling her hard against his chest once more. "Get rid of any notion that you were pretending to be fearless," he said in a low voice. "You *are* the bravest, most steadfast, inventive woman I've ever known. I have no doubt that you'll bring that same moxie to broadcasting."

"Moxie?"

"Michigan."

He framed her face between his hands, his eyes full of the love she'd seen in those few, perfect moments they'd shared that solitary night in her bedroom on Rue Saint-Dominique.

"Who else but you, Miss Actress, would dress as a nurse, truss downed fliers in strait jackets, and escort them onto a train to safety?" He gently shook her shoulders, forcing her to look directly at him. "You are not only the cleverest escape-and-evade agent I ever worked with and the best budding broadcaster I know... but you're also the sexiest."

He kissed her with a fierceness she knew was just as pent up as the emotions she was feeling course throughout her entire body.

When they finally pulled apart, Brooke bit her lip.

"So we match up on that last thing, at least," she joked weakly, wishing they were lying on the chaise in her library instead of standing in an office constructed like a fishbowl. She gave him a sly grin and asked innocently, "By the way, Mr. Executive Editor, do you ever go home for lunch? Before Nicole left for Alsace, she taught me the art of making a perfect cheese soufflé."

In a lightning move, Christopher grabbed his overcoat off the back of his chair and tossed her the coat she'd thrown on his office sofa.

"As it happens," he said solemnly, "I'm free for lunch, today. And dinner. And... if you'll have me, I'll be joining you and Ondie for breakfast. Let's get out of here."

Brooke held up her hand to halt his progress and gazed at him steadily, the old devil doubt creeping into her consciousness.

"Is it just lunch?" she asked, only half in jest. "Or are you suggesting a tomorrow-and-always deal, here?"

Christopher shook his head with a mild expression of frustration.

"Just a lunch deal?" he chided her. "Oh, no, no, *no*, my darling Brooke. What I'm proposing— as the War Office used to say —is a Mr.-and-Mrs. Deal, which means dining together every single day for the *duration*."

Brooke smiled, swiftly donned her coat, and put her arm through his as they headed for his office door.

"Did anyone ever tell you, Monsieur Laurent, that you certainly do have a way with words?"

AUTHOR'S NOTE

Just so there is no confusion about *The Safety of Strangers*, the wartime saga of Brooke Bradley and Christopher Laurent is a work *fiction*. However, as with Book 1, *Landing by Moonlight* and Book 2, *A Spy Above the Clouds* in my American Spy Sisters series, Book 3 is inspired by a deep commitment to research, travel to key locations, and contemporary records of a number of true-life heroines and heroes whose amazing deeds helping the Allies win WW II have finally come to light during the last twenty-five years.

Just as with the previous two books in the series, I was required to grapple with the age-old issue of fact-versus-fiction in this imagined account whose origins are rooted in the true-life records of women (a few who were Americans) who joined in the clandestine effort to offer safe harbor to escaping Allied personnel and to join "relay teams" that guided the downed aviators, POWs on the run, and other at-risk individuals on a journey out of Nazi-occupied France, back to England, to hopefully fight or fly on another day. When interlacing historical figures with fictional characters, certain dates or timing may have been slightly altered, none of which, I trust, distorts the basic facts of the story being told.

After many government archives were finally opened to scholars and writers in 1995 on the 50th anniversary of the end of WW II, the outpouring of nonfiction and fiction works has been truly remarkable and marvelously enlightening. Previously untold stories by nonfiction writers inspired novelists aplenty to weave gripping tales of life, death, and daring-do that have captivated readers ever since. I will never forget the three-straight days I hardly ate or slept reading my friend Kristen Hannah's magnificent novel *The Nightingale*, published in 2015.

Because I majored in history in college and spent my career as a multi-published historical novelist asking the question: "What were the *women* doing during a particular era?" I naturally felt compelled to examine the clandestine warfare in WW II with the same thought in mind: What were the *American* women doing?

As I have mentioned in my two earlier WWII novels, what first inspired the Spy Sisters trilogy was being taken by my French friend, Claire Majola, to tour a tiny chalet/museum on the Resistance in the French Alps near where our 'Francophile' family had been visiting almost every year for several decades. Tacked onto the museum's green felt displays was an array of artifacts, ephemera, and photos of local Resistance members, many of whom, I saw, were female.

My curiosity piqued, I followed research "breadcrumbs" from there into the world of British, Belgian, American, and French women who were members of Britain's Special Operations Executive (SOE). This secret organization operating from London parachuted men and women agents into France to sabotage whatever they could of the German war machine that was bent on conquering and forever dominating most of Europe.

Most of us, thanks to Ian Fleming's James Bond character in his series of spy thrillers, have heard of the British intelligence agencies MI5 (domestic security service) and MI6 (national security and foreign intelligence service). In Book 3 in this series, I found myself burrowing down the rabbit hole of MI9— where Fleming was connected as head of the section overseeing German prisoners of war within that department. MI9 was the far lesser known intelligence authority in charge of the escape-and-evasion missions of Allied personnel from German occupied countries in WW II.

I immediately began to look for any American women who served in France as operatives for in-country MI9 activities. To my amazement, it mostly turned out that they were ordinary citizens who helped some 26,000 downed airmen and stranded soldiers evacuate from the active war zone, along with an estimated 23,000 escaped prisoners-of-war who made it back to Allied territory prior to the war's end.

My heroine, Brooke Bradley, and hero, Christopher Laurent, are *composite* characters inspired by the lives of several of these "escape helpers" whose heroism was little known to the general public until a few of them wrote their memoirs after the war. Even then, some of their experiences could not be revealed for "national security" reasons. In other words, Brooke and Christopher are fictional figures based on several actual Resistance escape agents who took on "escort missions" at great personal risk, serving their countries and the Allies behind enemy lines.

For instance, many of Brooke's and Christopher's harrowing adventures spiriting downed fliers out of France on slow-moving night trains were based on the successful missions of known escape line civilian volunteers who invented many disguises to get their "packages" past the watchful eyes of Nazi guards whose job it was to halt the escape and return of Allied soldiers.

Since the expense of training each pilot was £15,000 per man, the goal of secretly evacuating shot-down aviators back to Britain became the core MI9 mission of France's own "underground railroad." One American "escape helper" heroine I tracked down who — remarkably enough — had been an actress in B movies in Hollywood, was responsible for saving more than forty fliers in her area alone and guiding them on the first leg of their journey back to Britain. It has been estimated that for every *one* airman saved, *two* escaper helpers were arrested, many sent to brutal prison camps in Germany with only a small percentage making it back after the war concluded.

American Virginia d'Albert-Lake was one of the lucky ones and she did, indeed, have a baby exactly one year after her miraculous release from Ravensbrück, a hideous death camp where some 50,000 women died, including some 2,200 in gas chambers.

In recent years, additional, in-depth scholarship about the shadowy role of MI9, along with fresh information about the Comet Line and other escape routes, have revealed many new aspects of this slice of WW II cloak-and-dagger activities. Weaving this more recent information and the real-life participants' actual experiences into a compelling story made it a joy to write *The Safety of Strangers.*

A book with the aim of describing the five-year course of WW II itself, combined with stories of individuals moving upon this large world stage, certainly included moments that were both heart-wrenching, and comical.

I am happy to report that the French poodle, Odile (later-- "shortwave" Ondie), really existed and made it through the entire war. Another rather strange moment occurred for this author during the research when I discovered that a vintage villa in Barbizon that I chose as the prototype for invented La Villa du Lapin d'Or is now available to rent on Airbnb! Thanks to the "Google Machine," I was able to see photos of the entire layout of the property , its surrounding stone walls, and the interiors, albeit majorly updated since 1945.

I hope those of you interested in learning more about the real-life escape helpers for this novel will peruse my Selective Bibliography and click on the link to my photo collection at the end of this book— and perhaps dig deeper.

I don't think you will be disappointed.

AUTHOR ACKNOWLEDGEMENTS

The next time you scan a shelf full of books, I can say without hesitation, not one of those volumes would have ever made it between covers (or onto your electronic reader) without the "village" of talented colleagues and friends that is always required to create a work of fiction.

The Safety of Strangers is, of course, no exception.

First of all, I cannot express enough my appreciation for publisher Tanya Anne Crosby of Oliver-Heber Books selecting this latest addition to my thrillers in the American Spy Sisters series to make its debut in 2023, but also for proposing to reissue handsome new editions my body of work under the OHB imprint.

Her team has been superb: Editorial Director, Alaina Crosby, Senior Editor Katherine Ward, and the stalwart editor of this and many other of my novels under the OHB imprint, Kimberly Cates. They and unseen members of that crew have my deepest gratitude for their devotion to the AI-free written word.

Regarding the research undertaken to produce *The Safety of Strangers*, I can't thank David Kimball Anderson enough for graciously accepting my "cold call" when I used my reporter/sleuthing skills to track down the grandson of one of the few American women living in wartime France dedicated to saving downed Allied aviators. He not only loaned me his *only* copy of film starlet Drue Leyton Tartière's limited edition *The House Near Paris,* a vivid account of the life of an "escape helper" (I had tried everything to purchase my own copy and failed), but David spent several conversations helping me understand the complicated background of a fledgling actress who abandoned her young child to marry a Frenchman and travel to Europe just as war threatened. I needed to understand how a woman in these circumstances ultimately became a risk-taking, remarkably selfless heroine committing her very life to spiriting Allied personnel caught behind enemy lines onto slow-moving night trains toward freedom in Spain and then back to Britain. Her profile as a young, Hollywood actress was my jumping off spot, but I hasten to state the obvious: in contrast to *my* plot, Drue's young son (and David's father) did *not* die as a youngster! David's willingness and generosity pointing me to the Tartiére family papers helped me fathom something of his "complicated" grandmother's motivation and character as I put together a composite heroine equally based on several other examples of American women operating as "helpers" in the escape lines established (and betrayed by turncoats) during this period.

The nonfiction authors to whom I owe the most thanks are listed in the bibliography, but foremost among them is, of course, Drue (Leyton) Tartière's reflections of the war years and rescuing downed airmen; Virginia d'Albert-Lake's diary and memoir: *An American Heroine in the French Resistance,* edited with an introduction by Judy Barrett Litoff; 22 year old American Polly Peabody, who worked with British and French prisoners of war in Paris during the German occupation, and at that young age in 1941 as war was raging, wrote *Occupied Territory*; and the biography, *Little Cyclone,* by MI9's Airey Neave, a book that chronicles the story of Andrée de Jongh, the Belgian who established the Comet escape line. This young woman's wartime organization is credited with saving the lives of more than 800 airmen and soldiers stranded behind enemy lines.

There simply is no substitute for digging through family papers to read the actual words written by the figures themselves whose lives a novelist tries to bring to life in a work of fiction.

Here at home, the writing of Book 3 in this thriller trilogy bobbed along during the first year and throughout the second year of the Covid pandemic, a factor that made it much easier to get through that plague in better psychological shape than one might have assumed. Having something compelling to grapple with at my computer each morning helped a lot, as did the invention of Zoom which my critique group, "The Plotholes," employed regularly as we traded manuscript chapters back and forth over the internet and chatted face-to-face in our pajamas more than once.

So to dear friends and sister writers, Cynthia Wright and Kimberly Cates, more than mere thanks. Your observations and 'suggestions' made it both possible and inspirational to get to The End of this demanding story.

I also want to thank the 'real' chocolate brown standard poodle in my life, Marly, whose hair cut (huge, fuzzy "Afro" pom-pom head with an evenly fluffed-up body coat) has become "The Marly," a recognized doggie-style in our community. Named for the magnificent Estate of Marly, 7 kilometers north-west of Versailles, I imbued Brooke's Ondie with Marly's same perfect deportment, kind and empathetic amber eyes, and fervently loyal nature. So, thank you, pet parents Dr. Roger and Marian Taylor, our dear friends, for 'loaning' her to me for this novel.

Other 'civilian' friends, writer colleagues, and family members who had a look at earlier drafts of the manuscript include: Francophiles Sandraline Cederwall and Steve Barrager (thanks, Steve, for letting me borrow your name); the Honorable Judge Harry Dorfman (who has a far better command of French than I do and a wicked red pen); bookstore owner Cheryl Popp who, to my immense relief, declared the draft she read a "page turner"; multi-published cookbook author, Diane Rossen Worthington, who lived in Paris for several years and knows her *soupes de légumes, pain de compagne*, and *cassoulets*; novelist Diana Dempsey, also with a stellar command of the French language, who offered some incisive and key observations (and one incredible plot 'save:' "Where's the *dog* when Harold Cole bursts into the flat?") And then my dear friends and "regular" readers, Maria Paterno and Naomi Fliflet rounded out our merry band of booklovers.

All these "beta readers" made comments and corrections that I trust improved the final version published here. To these trusted "helpers," my sincerest thanks for their time and scrupulous attention to detail. Any remaining errors are clearly my own, happily corrected in subsequent editions.

And finally, as I have testified more than a few times during our four-and-a half decade marriage, I owe eternal gratitude to Tony

Cook, my partner in everything I do. We met as "cub" reporters back in the day of "real journalism," – me as a green TV reporter and he, as a newly-hired, fledgling print journalist for *Forbes Magazine*. In subsequent years, we have each adapted the skills we acquired in twenty years 'on the beat' to a variety of professions, including book writing, publishing, internet marketing and business consulting.

Tony is the reason I went to France so often in the first place. His service as a trustee of the MacJannet Foundation, a Franco-American educational non-profit based in Talloires in the French Alps, required board meeting attendance each year, and also afforded us a chance to visit various hotbeds of WW II Resistance. Together, we actually retraced the very footsteps of many *résistants* described in these pages.

This time around, however, my husband not only provided handholding, cheerleading, perceptive editorial advice, but also seriously-needed nursemaid skills to get me through an awful lung infection right before the finish line.

Basically, darling, I might as well 'fess up: you and your years as a rock'em-sock'em investigative financial journalist were the model for "my hero," Christopher Laurent.

SELECTIVE BIBLIOGRAPHY &
RESEARCH PHOTO LINK

What follows is *not* a list of every book I read during the research phase of this effort, but rather a compilation of the volumes that informed the particular subject of MI9 and the escape-and-evade activities during WW II upon which this thriller was focused.

Bodson, Herman, *Downed Allied Airmen and Evasion of Capture: The Role of Local Resistance Networks in World War* II. McFarland & Company. 2005

D'Albert-Lake, Virginia, *An American Heroine in the French Resistance – The Diary and Memoir of Virginia d'Albert-Lake.* Edited, with an introduction by Judy Barret Litoff. Fordham University Press. 2006.

Dear, Ian, *Escape and Evasion: Prisoner of War Breakouts and the Routes to Safety in World War Two.* Arms and Armour. 1997

Devereaux Rochester, *Full Moon to France.* Harper & Row. 1977

Eisner, Peter, *The Freedom Line: The Brave Men and Women who Rescued Allied Airmen from the Nazis During World War II* Harper Collins/Perennial. 2004

Fry, Helen, *MI9, A History of the Secret Service for Escape and Evasion in World War Two.* Yale University Press. 2020

Glass, Charles , *Americans in Paris: Life and Death Under Nazi Occupation.* Penguin. 2010

Heil, Jr., Alan L. *Voice of America – A History.* Columbia University Press, 2003

Hore, Peter, *Lindell's List – Saving British and American Women at Ravensbrück.* The History Press. 2016.

Kershaw, Alex, *Avenue of Spies – A True Story of Terror, Espionage, and one American Family's Heroic Resistance in Nazi-Occupied Paris.* Crown. 2015

Lyman, Robert, *Under a Darkening Sky – The American Experience in Nazi Europe 1939-1941.* Pegasus. 2018

Murphy, Brendan, *Turncoat- The Strange Case of British Sergeant Harold Cole, "The Worst Traitor of the War."* Harcourt Brace Jovanovich Publishers. 1987

Neave, Airey, *Little Cyclone*. Bite Back Publishing. 1954

Neave, Airey, *Saturday at M.I.9 – The Class Account of the WW II Allied Escape Organization*. Pen & Sword Military Publishing. 1969. Reprinted 2004

Ottis, Sherri Greene, *Silent Heroes - Downed Airmen and the French Underground*. The University of Kentucky Press. 2001

Peabody, Polly, *Occupied Territory*. The Cresset Press, London, 1941

Sebba, Anne. *Les Parisiennes – Resistance, Collaboration, and the Women of Paris Under Nazi Occupation*. St. Martin's Press, 2016

Tartière [Leyton], Drue, and M.R. Werner, *The House Near Paris*. Simon & Schuster. 1946

Vaughan, Hal, *Doctor to the Resistance–The Heroic True Story of An American Surgeon and His Family in Occupied France*. Brassey's Inc. 2004

Watt, George, *The Comet Connection – Escape from Hitler's Europe*. The University Press of Kentucky. 1990

Worrall, Raymond, *Escape from France – The True Story of the Second World War and The Secret Forest of Fréteval*. Silver Quill Publications. 2004

Research photos for Ware's American Spy Sisters series of novels can be found at Pinerest: www.pinterest.com/cijiware/

ABOUT CIJI WARE

Ciji Ware is the *New York Times* and *USA Today* bestselling author of thirteen historical and contemporary novels, a novella, and two nonfiction works. She is the daughter, niece, and descendant of writers, so writing fiction is just part of the "family business." She has been honored with the Dorothy Parker Award of Excellence and a *Romantic Times* Award for Best Fictionalized Biography for *Island of the Swans,* and in 2012, was shortlisted in the prestigious WILLA (Cather) Literary Award for *A Race to Splendor*.

An Emmy-award winning television producer, former radio and TV on-air broadcaster for ABC in Los Angeles for eighteen years, as well as print and online journalist, Ware received a BA in History from Harvard University and has the distinction of being the first woman graduate of Harvard College to serve as the President of the Harvard Alumni Association, Worldwide. As a result of Ware's first novel, *Island of the Swans,* she was made a Fellow of the Society of

Antiquaries of Scotland (FSA Scot), and in 2015 was named to the "Martha's Vineyard Writers-in-Residence" program—both honors she treasures. Ware lives in the San Francisco Bay Area with her husband, Tony Cook , and a boisterous "Covid Puppy," a Cavalier King Charles Spaniel named Dash. In recent years, the author has returned to taking ballet barre online from the San Francisco School of Ballet and participates in amateur theatricals whenever she is cast in a play.

Website: http://www.cijiware.com

Facebook: www.facebook.com/cijiwarenovelist

Join Ciji Ware's Readers Roundtable at https://www.facebook.com/groups/1755047761490960

MORE SPELLBINDING WORLD WAR II ADVENTURE AND INTRIGUE IN THE AMERICAN SPY SISTERS SERIES

Book 1: *Landing by Moonlight*

Book 2: *A Spy Above the Clouds*

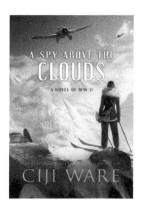

Don't miss any of Ciji Ware's WWII romantic thrillers!

Books 1, 2, and 3 in the series are inspired by the exceptional women who volunteered as secret agents and 'in-country' operatives for Allied

Intelligence to fight the Nazi invasion of France, some joining even *before* the United States entered the war after the attack on Pearl Harbor.

Landing by Moonlight's **CATHERINE THORNTON** in Book 1, a Washington D.C. debutante, is flung in her parachute through the moonlit sky back into France from a low-flying British Halifax after sneaking into an enemy's embassy and stealing the naval operations codes for the Mediterranean fleet. Once recruited as a secret agent and inserted into the French Riviera, Madam "Colette Durand" is definitely not prepared for the trial-by-fire to come.

A Spy Above the Clouds' **CONSTANCE "VIV" VIVIER-CLARKE** is a poor-little-rich girl from New York whose stepfather sells ball bearings to Hitler's war machine, leaving Viv to her own devices. These include failing out of her Swiss boarding school, being fired by her celebrated Olympic ski coach for lack of discipline, and defying her socialite mother to become an ambulance driver in Paris. Her next outrageous move is enlisting as an Allied secret agent and courier-on-skis, ferrying messages and weapons to the Resistance in the enemy-infested French Alps.

As readers learn from the exploits of **BROOKE BRADLEY de VARNY** in *The Safety of Strangers*, war changes those who participate in it, regardless of which side they may be on...and "therein lies the tale..."

"*New York Times & USA Today* bestselling author and Emmy Award-winning former broadcast journalist **Ciji Ware** once again displays her extraordinary talent for weaving historical fact into compelling historical fiction..."

ALSO BY CIJI WARE

Historical Novels

Island of the Swans

Wicked Company

A Race to Splendor

"Time-Slip" Historical Novels

A Cottage by the Sea

Midnight on Julia Street

A Light on the Veranda

Contemporary Novels

That Summer in Cornwall

That Autumn in Edinburgh

That Winter in Venice

That Spring in Paris

Contemporary Novellas

Ring of Truth: "The Ring of Kerry Hannigan"

Nonfiction

Rightsizing Your Life

Joint Custody After Divorce